Capital Kill

MARC RAINER

ISBN: 1468180215
ISBN-13: 9781468180213
Library of Congress Control Number: 2012900578
CreateSpace, North Charleston, SC

To the men and women of law enforcement,
from the first responders to those who remain
until the verdicts are read in a court of law.

Preface

In the 1980s, the violence that was the hallmark of elections in the island nation of Jamaica rose to the point where elections were decided as much by bullets as they were by ballots. Criminal street gangs calling themselves "posses" (after groups of armed men in American Westerns) rose out of the various neighborhoods of Kingston, the capital city, and allied themselves with the two major political parties. Financed by the drug trade, initially in marijuana and later in cocaine, the posses armed themselves with automatic weapons and conducted open warfare in the streets. Operating with impunity, they fired on rival posses, the residents of the communities controlled by those rival posses, and even on the police.

There was a much larger customer base for cocaine outside Jamaica, and so the posses followed the money—to the United States. By the mid-1980s, the two largest posses—the Shower Posse and their archenemies, the Spangler Posse—had formed cells in every major American city on the eastern seaboard and were selling crack cocaine from Miami to New England. They then spread their operations westward to cities like Kansas City and Dallas. As in Kingston, when a Shower soldier saw that a Spangler had moved into his territory, warfare erupted. Hundreds of murders were committed before federal, state, and local authorities realized the extent of the problem and the forces behind it.

This is a work of fiction, and the characters are fictional as well. Certain events from real investigations and trials have, however, been incorporated into the story.

Prologue

The unmistakable smell told him they were in the right place.

Trask wiped his eyes dry and moved around behind the CSI techs to the other side of the pit, hoping to gain some small relief from the stench of decaying flesh. It wasn't any better upwind of the dig, so he circled back, trying to get a better view.

The crime scene specialists worked somberly, methodically, speaking only when necessary. Trask watched closely, grateful for their care and precision as they brushed away the clay and dirt from the two corpses. He knew that every speck of evidence had to be preserved, every clue maintained, all to confirm what they already knew.

The bodies were visible now. The feet were tied together, the hands taped behind their backs, with skeletal digits showing where the flesh had fallen away from the fingers. The dig team was working around the heads, buried at the deeper end of the shallow trench.

One of the CSIs took a brush and gently flicked the dirt from one partially buried head—a head that had been wrapped from neck to crown in gray duct tape.

Trask turned and walked into the trees to retch.

Chapter One

It was just before 7:00 p.m. in Anacostia, and James P. "Junebug" Wilson's crack pipe was empty. Wilson was pushing forty, but he looked sixty. His weathered black face was encased in a dirty beard, his eyes dull and desperate. Wilson's four-year love affair with cocaine base—"crack" on the street—had made him smaller, dropping his weight from 165 to under 130. He was no longer employable and spent his days searching for something to steal—a car radio here, an unguarded bicycle there—anything he could fence for money to support his habit. His wife and daughter had left him two years ago, and he had been evicted from his apartment after the rent money burned up in his pipe. Now he moved from one condemned building to another, sleeping wherever he could find a roof that required no payment. He'd spent the last few days in an unoccupied apartment in one of the projects off Wheeler Road and kept quiet enough that none of the neighbors ratted him out to the management.

Wilson looked at the singed glass tube he had been puffing on for thirty minutes, trying to will the small beige rock back into existence. The piece of Chore-Boy scrubbing pad he had crammed into one end to hold the crack in place now held only flecks of charred residue. Wilson forced himself up from the floor, leaning against the wall he had been using as a chair back. He reached into his pants pocket and pulled out a dirty, crumpled twenty, his reward for a welfare check he'd been able to pry out of one of the mailboxes inside the building door. His fence was good at identification fraud and would have sufficient documentation to cash the check by the next morning. It was only when his stomach screamed in pain or he felt dizzy and weak that Junebug diverted some portion of his crack fund to the purchase of food. The two doughnuts he'd had the night before were sufficient, so he set off once again to find his only remaining priority.

———

After their shift meeting, detectives Dixon Carter and Juan Ramirez of the Seventh District, Metropolitan Police Department left the 7D station at 2455 Alabama, SE, driving un unmarked unit that was astonishingly functional. Over two hundred cars were awaiting repairs at the departmental garage at Montana and West Virginia Avenues, NE, and the cops knew the brass in any district simply by the vehicles they drove. Thanks to budget shortfalls and other priorities, patrol units and unmarked vehicles alike sat at the garage for months, while marked units that were still operable roamed city streets with crumpled fenders and broken lights. Watch commanders knew that turning a working car in for repairs meant losing the unit without hope of a replacement, so they kept driving the eyesores. Patrol officers even did their own minor repairs, maintenance, or part switch-outs when they could find replacements for eight- and ten-year-old Crown Victorias at a junkyard or parts store.

Carter, an eighteen-year veteran of the force, had worked narcotics for the majority of the ten years he'd carried a detective's shield. His fellow officers called him either Dix or DC. He preferred the latter nickname, taking real pride in the city of his birth. He wore a well-tailored blue suit over his ample, six-foot-three, 230-pound frame.

His partner, by contrast, was about five-foot-six and dressed in a worn leather jacket and jeans. Ramirez wore a bushy mustache and a hairstyle that would pass for a "mullet" were it an inch longer in the back. He had fifteen years on the force, and had been Carter's partner for the last eight. Due to their complete dissimilarity in appearance, dress, demeanor, and temperament, they were referred to in the District's law enforcement circles as The Twins.

Ramirez turned the green Buick onto Wheeler from Alabama, and flowed with traffic. It was a rare night, schedule-wise, since The Twins had just wrapped up testimony in federal district court on a heroin conspiracy trial. Now they were back on the street, looking to identify their next target. There was never a shortage of dope work in 7D; it was just a matter of sorting out the major targets from the run-of-the-mill crack monsters and penny-ante pushers who served up dime bags of weed.

Carter watched the right sidewalk while Ramirez drove, noting a young tough who was speaking to an older man as the car passed. The youth gave them the traditional "gangsta glower," letting them know that he'd made them as police, then pulled up the hood on his sweatshirt with his left hand. Carter recognized the slight figure walking rapidly away from the kid.

"Looks like Junebug's in search of some smoking matter," Carter said, being careful not to look directly at Wilson as they passed him. The Twins had used the addict as a paid informant in the past, but speaking to him on the street would mark him as a snitch.

"We can pick him up later on a back block when it's not so crowded," Ramirez said. "Looks like he's headed for a hookup, though—might be really buzzed next time we see him."

"A risk that we will have to take, given the gentleman's proclivities," Carter said, well aware that his major in English at the University of Maryland was a subject of irritation to his partner.

"Proclivities." Ramirez snorted. "Dude's got to smoke five times a day now just to keep from goin' batshit. Any info we get from him might not even be worth a damn."

"As in the past," Carter replied, "Mr. Wilson might still be counted on to give up one of his suppliers in return for a small amount of police currency. He might then take the money to yet another provider of controlled substances, an individual about whom we could inquire at a later date. A method that continues to ensure job security for public servants such as ourselves."

"Your fat, black, bald head is stuffed about as full as that suit tonight."

"Information is ammunition." Carter chuckled, turning to check his side mirror. Wilson had not made them, and had taken a right turn up the sidewalk toward the Miller Gardens project complex. "Take the next right and come back around, please."

As Carter and Ramirez drove by, the teen in the hoodie pulled his right hand out of the shirt's kangaroo pocket and brought it up to his face, being careful not to reveal its contents to the unmarked unit. Ronald Fellows was already well known to the Family Court Division of the Superior Court of the District of Columbia as "R.F., a Juvenile Male," due to his lengthy arrest record.

That record remained sealed, of course, in hopes that the lack of unfavorable publicity and the efforts of the court and its social workers could persuade Ronald to mend his criminal ways before he reached the age of majority, when—God forbid—he would have to be incarcerated with adult criminals, many of whom had not committed crimes half as severe as "R.F." had at the tender age of seventeen. Fellows had already burglarized houses, stolen cars, and sold a lot of crack. Today, he was continuing the time-honored tradition of working for a major drug trafficker in the capacity of a juvenile lookout, one over whom the police had precious little leverage and who could be trusted to work and keep quiet in exchange for a fee without any real fear of being locked up.

Fellows' right hand held a fairly new Motorola Talkabout radio. He pressed the call button, and a voice in a heavy Jamaican patois responded.

"Yah, mon?"

"Five-O. Green Buick. Just passed Junebug, and he's headed your way."

"Ah see 'em, mon. Nice work." There was a pause, and the voice spoke more softly and deliberately. "Take the rest of the day off, mon."

"Sure—see ya tomorrow." Fellows shrugged.

He was careful not to address the other party by name over the public airways. He did not question why he and his employer were terminating their commercial operations at so early an hour on a business day. He knew better.

From a second-floor window in an end apartment in the Miller Gardens projects, a middle-aged man peered from behind a cheap drape as he pocketed the mate to Fellows' Talkabout. Demetrius Reid was not especially tall, but he was massive, with a bone structure that easily supported his 250 pounds. His wrists were larger than many men's knees.

He took another glance through the window at Wilson and quickly calculated that he had ample time to prepare for the task ahead. Care and preparation had, after all, kept him out of Lorton, the DC jail, and the Federal Bureau of Prisons while many of his more careless posse brothers had been convicted and were still "inside." He had long since abandoned the dreadlocks he'd worn off the boat into Miami and kept the flash factor down on the streets. While there was some risk in the matter at hand, the risk was acceptable.

He had heard from his people on the street that Junebug, though on the pipe himself, was working for two detectives they called The Twins. If true, this was both a problem and an opportunity. The risk was that Junebug might be contacting Fellows and others in an attempt to help the police climb the ladder to their employer. Now, however, there was an opportunity to eliminate that problem, with the bonus of reminding rats such as Wilson of the high cost of such folly. To that end, Fellows had been instructed that if Junebug came inquiring, he was to be directed *not* to apartment 21—a single-bedroom apartment currently occupied by another trusted underling who was selling the twenty-dollar rocks that day—but to apartment 25, a two-bedroom flat at the end of the hall.

This apartment had been meticulously chosen, partly for its near 360 degrees of available views. One bedroom window faced Wheeler Avenue, overlooking the roof of an abandoned gas station. The door to this bedroom opened into a small living area, modestly furnished to give the impression that someone actually resided there. Across the hall a window in an identically configured bedroom opened onto the quadrangle behind the building.

Reid had checked this view after seeing the events on the street, and had noted that everything appeared normal. Three other project buildings were arranged as sides of a square with the rear facades facing the grassy quad. That area was filled with the usual cacophony of unruly kids playing while their mothers argued with their boyfriends of the moment and circles of young wannabe gangster rappers gathered, their boom boxes or bass-heavy car stereos blaring the latest hip-hop. Nothing even smelled of police or surveillance. Not that any officer attempting to quietly enter the building from this side would have been successful; the entire neighborhood could be expected to greet even a plain-clothes cop with loud, sarcastic shouts of "Why, hello officer!" or "How are things at Seven-D today, Five-O?"

The kitchen of the apartment directly to the rear of the living room completed the perimeter, with windows providing a view of an alleyway running between the project complex and a fenced-off parking lot serving the Johnson & Sons commercial laundry service building. Directly beneath the kitchen window stood a huge dumpster, the refuse collection depot for the complex. The top had been pried off some years before by someone looking to make a buck off some scrap metal, and it remained open, stinking up the alleyway and guaranteeing a minimum of foot traffic.

The stench was also the reason that the end apartments in the next building were used only for storage. No one would be looking out of those windows. The sanitation worker who emptied the dumpster would drive by later that evening, but the dumpster couldn't be seen from the street.

Reid opened a small closet in the hallway between one of the bedrooms and the kitchen and retrieved a pair of black leather gloves from a shelf. Also on the shelf sat a box of forty-gallon trashcan liners and a new, plastic-sealed roll of duct tape. He put on the gloves and, with a handkerchief, re-wiped both the box and roll of tape clean so that no prints could be lifted from either surface. He was about to close the closet door when he looked down and noticed a small, blue, corrugated block on the floor of the closet. He smiled, thinking *how appropriate,* picked up the block, and turned toward the door just as Junebug Wilson knocked. He crossed the living room, checked through the security peephole to make sure Wilson was alone, and opened the door.

"C'mon in, mon!" he said as the smaller man crossed the threshold.

"Just lookin' for a little rock, and I got a twenty…" Junebug's eyes darted around the room to see where his host might be keeping the stash.

He brought his gaze back around just in time to see the huge gloved fist before it smashed into the side of his head.

The big man looked at the unconscious lump on the floor. Any blood from the blow would be subdural. He checked Wilson for a wire, though he didn't expect to find one. The cops didn't normally wire a snitch on his first foray into new territory; the new targets were far too likely to check for one. A body recorder would come later, after the snitch gained the trust of those under investigation. As expected, there was no wire.

He ripped the plastic covering off the roll of duct tape, throwing the wrapper and the small blue block into the bottom of one of the trash bags. He rolled Wilson onto his stomach, pulled both his arms to the rear, and bound his hands together with the first turns of the tape, which he then brought down around the feet. Once he had hog-tied his victim, he wrapped a second length of tape around Wilson's face, carefully covering his mouth. He pulled up one of the two cheaply cushioned chairs in the room, sat down, and waited.

It took nearly ten minutes for Junebug's eyes to flutter open. As he moaned and gradually regained consciousness, he became aware of the big man leaning over him.

"Well now, Mistah Snitch. Did ya really think that ol' D-Mon was going to let ya just walk in and set up his peoples for the po-lice? I saw ya walkin' away from da Twins' car and I know what ya were up to! I don't think I can have that goin' on here, mon."

Wilson tried to speak, but his voice was muffled by the duct tape. He shook his head from side to side, the only protestation he could manage.

"No use denyin' it now, mon," his captor continued, as he first stuffed Wilson's bound feet, and then his legs, into the trash bag that contained the duct tape wrapper. "I saw ya doin' it, and ah know ya've done it before. Just so ya know what I'm doin' here now, it's very common for a dyin' man to lose control of himself—ya know, to shit and piss all over da place—and I don't want ya messin' up my carpet." He bent down and smiled widely, noting with satisfaction the terror in his victim's eyes.

"Bye-bye now."

He grabbed the roll of duct tape, first covering the nose, pausing again to smile and gaze into the terrified eyes as Wilson strained desperately for air that would not come. When the body finally stopped twitching, he wrapped the tape even higher, covering the eyes and forehead up to the scalp line. He took a second trash bag and pulled it over the corpse's head and shoulders until it overlapped the other bag. He sealed the seam between the two bags and left the remainder of the roll of tape connected to his new package.

Reid crossed the floor into the kitchen, opened the window, and looked out to each side. Seeing no one, he returned to the corpse, picked it up, and carried it to the window. After checking once more, he dropped the body into the dumpster below. He then put the remainder of the trash bags and the gloves into a paper sack and left the apartment.

It was approaching 8:00 p.m., and he was hungry. He got into the 1998 Chevy Cavalier and headed for the McDonald's a few blocks down on Wheeler. As he pulled into the drive-thru and placed his order, he deposited the paper sack with the gloves and box of trash bags into a plastic-capped trashcan by the driveway.

———

At 10:27 p.m., a Morrison Waste Disposal garbage truck turned off Wheeler Road by the abandoned gas station into the alley between the Miller Gardens apartments and the Johnson & Sons Laundry. While single residences, duplexes, and triplexes received the benefit of trash collection from the District's Department of Public Works, larger complexes like Miller Gardens required larger trucks to empty their dumpsters, and contracted private firms—like Morrison Waste—to take out their trash. The operator of the Morrison truck this evening was Leonard Davis, and it was his first night on the route.

Davis made it a habit to check the contents of the dumpsters he was to empty, in order to avoid damage to his company's vehicles. There had been that time when some damn fool in Northeast had filled a bin with the remnants of a broken sidewalk, and the near ton of concrete rubble had wrecked the machinery that raised the forks to lift the dumpsters. The incident had nearly cost him his job, so he always checked before engaging the hydraulics. Checking the bins also had a collateral benefit; Davis could fix almost any appliance, and had returned many a broken lamp, television, and kitchen item to working condition, realizing small profits when he sold his rescued and refurbished wares.

When Davis reached the Miller Gardens dumpster he maneuvered the truck's forks into position, but stopped before inserting them into the slots on the bin. He jumped out of the cab and climbed up on the front fender to look into the bin, noting the usual odor of rotting meat and chicken bones, vegetable remains, and other mixed refuse. He was about to climb down when he spotted a large object wrapped in trash bags and sealed with duct tape, resting below the front lip of the dumpster. He paused for a moment, thinking that it might be a roll of carpet. Then he wondered why anyone discarding carpet would bother to waste two perfectly good trash bags and a role of tape on a bad rug.

He reached into his jeans, pulled out a pocketknife, and cut a slit just above the seal made by the duct tape. He then unhooked the small Maglite he wore on his belt and reached into the trash bag, the flashlight's beam focused on the slit.

At first, it looked like there were only clothes inside, but when Davis attempted to pull the shirt through the hole in the bag, two lifeless hands, bound with duct tape, came with it. Davis recoiled from the lip of the dumpster, bouncing off the grill of the truck and falling to the pavement below.

"SHIT!" he screamed, shivering involuntarily. "SHIT! SHIT! SHIT!"

He scrambled under the fork on the driver's side and grabbed the company cell phone from the cab, dialing 911 as he screamed again.

"SHIT!"

Chapter Two

The alarm clock rang at five-thirty, as it did every morning. Trask started a pot of coffee, gulped down a large glass of orange juice, then headed for the shower. He set the water at just the safe side of scalding and stood under the jet, pre-set at the intensity of a fire hose. Once the heat and water massage had completely awakened him, he dried and threw a towel around his waist.

He looked in the mirror, taking inventory. Overall, he was still comfortable with what he saw. Appearance was critical in his business; a good first impression was one of the keys to a successful courtroom presentation. He was thirty-four, and his front hairline was starting to retreat a little, while his waistline was starting to advance. He couldn't do anything about the former, but he resolved to add another set of crunches when he got home that night, and to lay off the fries at lunch. There were the first hints of graying around his temples, but that didn't concern him; it might even add some credibility points with a juror here or there.

In the walk-in closet he studied his three new suits, looking for something suitable for his first day in the new division. He was finally going back to trial work after two years in the appellate cloisters. Pulling out a single-breasted charcoal number, the ever-appropriate white oxford shirt and a subdued maroon tie, he chuckled. Fashion dilemmas were new. For the past seventeen years, counting his time at the Academy, he'd worn nothing but Air Force blue. The appellate division hadn't required anything but slacks and a blazer, except for the occasional oral arguments; his one navy-blue pinstripe had been adequate. Trials required several suits for several days, however, so he had spent the weekend shopping in the local malls, hunting for acceptable matching separates. Even the so-called "athletic cut" suits didn't come in 46 chest and 34 waist sizes.

He headed back toward the kitchen, smelling that the coffee was ready. The apartment was a modest one-bedroom, the furnishings Spartan. He had a bed, a dresser, and an armoire in the bedroom. The living room contained a large-screen TV, a huge stereo, a cabinet for all the discs and tapes, one recliner, and a homemade coffee table he had thrown together with some two-by-fours and lag bolts. There wasn't much room for anything else, since the Bowflex exercise machine took up half the room.

Typical bachelor pad. He'd heard that from every female who had ventured past his doorway.

There were a couple of nice watercolors on the wall, created by his father in the course of a lifelong career as an art professor. He had also put up a fairly impressive "I Love Me" section, including the citations for several Meritorious Service Medals, law school awards, and athletic trophies. In the center was the Air Force Academy diploma. The display's primary purpose had been to take up space on the bare walls. Its secondary purpose was to catch the eye of any female who might enter the room.

So far, there had been very few. He wondered if his standards were too high, or if he was starting to lose it. Maybe he had just been too damned busy.

Leaving the apartment at 6:15, Trask headed out of Waldorf toward the capitol. He pulled the Jeep onto Highway 5 and groaned when he saw the traffic. For a sleepy bedroom suburb in "historic southern Maryland," the place was getting crowded. Trask cursed himself for not shelling out a few hundred more a month for something close to a Metro access. On a typical morning, it could take him ninety minutes to drive the twenty-five miles to the office. On a bad morning, when the traffic system of the nation's seat of government snarled, it could take more than two hours. Some genius had decided years ago that it would be a good idea to merge I-95, the eastern seaboard's main north-south artery, with the Capitol Beltway, which had become Washington's Main Street. Now all it took was one semi-trailer jackknife to turn his commute into an obscene crawl.

At the first opportunity, Trask detoured south on a farm road he'd discovered and wound his way down to the Indian Head Highway. He flowed north with the traffic past Bolling Air Force Base, crossed the Anacostia River on the Douglass Bridge, and headed up South Capitol Street. Looking up at the Capitol building as he crossed the eastern edge of the Mall, he felt a little awe at his new station in life. He glanced down at his credentials on the seat beside him. *United States Department of Justice* was embossed in gold on the black, wallet-style cover. The leather was still crisp and new.

An attendant motioned him toward one of the unoccupied gaps on the unpaved, vacant lot that served as the parking lot for 555 Fourth Street, Northwest. Trask reminded himself to lock the car this time, so that the denizens from the homeless shelter a block away wouldn't use the vehicle as a bedroom, or worse. He'd had to fumigate the Jeep the last time.

He parked and crossed F Street, entering the building through the front doors on the west side. In the foyer, he glanced at the glass-encased directory. *Office of the United States Attorney for the District of Columbia.* Noting the room number for the Misdemeanor Trial Section, he opened the heavy glass inner door to the lobby and flashed his credentials. The guard nodded, and Trask crossed the lobby toward his new duty assignment.

Most of the dozen chairs in the room had already been taken, but Trask found one toward the rear of the large conference table next to Tim Wisniewski, another refugee from appellate. Like Trask, Wisniewski had considerable trial experience, having been an assistant district attorney in New Mexico before joining the office.

"Morning, Jeff. How ya doin'?" The smile was too cheery for the hour.

"I'll have to get back to you on that."

Trask shook hands as he sat down. A year in appeals with this big, friendly Polack from Santa Fe had shown that Tim Wisniewski was a talented attorney, and interested in the substance of the work, not self-promotion. As they spoke, Trask looked around the table, noting that their obvious friendship had been noticed by the newbies in the room, several of whom were in their first day on the job.

More introductions were in order, but before they could be made, a middle-aged, haggard-looking woman entered the room, followed by two men in suits. Trask recognized the trio as Maura Loxley, the chief of the misdemeanor trial section, Robert Lassiter, the chief of the office's criminal division, and his deputy, William Patrick.

"Good morning, ladies and gentlemen." Despite more than twenty years in the office, Loxley was obviously uncomfortable addressing a group.

"I am Maura Loxley, chief of the misdemeanor trial section, and your direct supervisor for the next few months. As some of you may be aware, it is the practice of our criminal division chief, Mr. Lassiter, to address each incoming group of attorneys, and so it is my pleasure to introduce to you Mr. Lassiter and the deputy chief of the criminal division, Bill Patrick. Bob, the floor is yours."

"Thank you, Maura."

Lassiter stood at the front of the table, his hands folded behind him. He was an impressive sight, even though he stood barely five-nine. At forty-five, his coal-black hair, cut close, was showing flecks of silver. He had the build of an athlete, having been a varsity wrestler at West Point. He was impeccably dressed in a dark-gray suit, white shirt with oxford collar, and a red tie. Trask smiled to himself, feeling appropriately attired.

"On behalf of the United States Attorney, I'd like to welcome you to your nation's capital, and to the Department of Justice. Each of you is now an Assistant United States Attorney for the District of Columbia, a federal prosecutor, and a member of this office's litigation team.

"There are nearly five hundred attorneys carrying the same credentials in this district. Some of you are here straight from law school. Some of you come from the real world of working adults. Some of you have never tried a case; some of you have had extensive trial experience. You come from all parts of the country. Some of you are here to pad your résumés and move on to the world of big-money law firms; you simply wish to be able to say that you have some litigation experience. Some of you are government attorneys here on detail from other agencies, again, for litigation experience. Some of you actually wish to be career federal prosecutors; others will jump to the other side of the courtroom at the first call of a better financial opportunity.

"Some of you come from the so-called best law schools; some of you come from others. Some of you already come from the *best* school for litigation; by that I mean quality training and experience. In time, we hope to give you all some of that here."

Trask suppressed a chuckle. This was pure Lassiter.

"There's more than enough work to be done in our fair city. While in the criminal division, you must realize that you are the last line of defense within our criminal justice system for the citizens of this city. To tourists, Washington, DC, is the seat of government, the Capitol Mall, and some monuments and museums, a town full of family photo ops. To the residents who live and work here, it is both home and one of the murder capitals of the country, with a broken school system and drug lords conducting turf wars in their backyards. Those who perpetrate these crimes are the vermin who prey on the helpless. We, in turn, hunt those predators. We expect you to prosecute these criminals fairly but firmly, and with integrity.

"As a prosecutor, you must serve the public and the courts. The truth, the law, and the rules of court must be your guiding lights. You are not here to put notches on your gun, but to *always* do the right thing."

Lassiter glanced around the room, recording the reactions of his new charges.

"Most of you can expect to spend about six months in this section. Misdemeanor trial will be your first exposure to the superior court of the District of Columbia. As federal prosecutors in this city, you will have the opportunity to try local offenses—'street crimes'—because this entire city is a federal enclave, and we have no local, county, or state prosecutors to handle such matters. If you successfully progress, you will advance to the grand jury section, and then to the felony trial section. Those who perform well in our local court system can expect to advance to the federal court side and to practice in the United States District Court.

"I encourage each of you to get to know the system, the office, the police officers, and the agents of the various investigative agencies as soon as you can. Get to know each other. You'll be working as teams here and throughout the sections in the criminal division. You will, as the cops say, have each other's backs from time to time."

"You can expect to spend some long hours in this job, hours which will put a strain on your personal and family lives. You will be asked to perform a nearly impossible balancing act in that regard: to spend whatever time is necessary to prepare and try your cases, while trying not to add to the country's divorce rate. If you find that the strains of this job become too much for you, if you are unable to fulfill your duties, please let me know immediately. The job is too important, too critical, to be done in a slipshod or half-hearted fashion. There *are* others waiting to take your places.

"I look forward to working with all of you."

Lassiter nodded toward Loxley and left the room, followed by Patrick.

For the next three hours, Maura Loxley presented a mundane review of the administrivia required of each new assistant US attorney in the misdemeanor trial section, with each form being described by the section chief as "critical," "extremely important," and essential to the operation of American jurisprudence.

Nothing was mentioned about trial work.

At eleven-thirty, Loxley dismissed them for lunch. Once she had left the room, Trask and Wisniewski wasted no time in heading for the exits.

"After all that inspiration, what ya feel like eating, Jeffrey?"

Trask laughed. "Something that bled when they killed it."

They crossed Fourth Street, walked past a Metro exit and through the National Law Enforcement Officers Memorial, a monument to all those slain in the line of duty. Trask had been a frequent contributor to the monument, and glanced at the statues of lions guarding the etched names of the fallen officers and agents, deputies and patrolmen.

There was a Roy Rogers franchise about a block away.

Wisniewski ordered a bacon-and-cheddar half-pound monster of a cheeseburger with large fries and a chocolate milkshake. Trask felt very pleased with his own restraint as he ordered the same sandwich with a diet coke, skipping the fries.

"Nothing like a cholesterol torpedo to make you forget the months to come," Trask said, recalling the onslaught of paperwork and section rules distributed by "Maura the Horror." It had taken Wisniewski all of five seconds after the declaration of the lunch break to rename their new supervisor.

When they returned to the office, they found her waiting for them in the hallway, looking anything but pleased.

"Are we late?" Trask tried to be appropriately deferential.

"No, not at all." Loxley attempted to force a smile. "Mr. Lassiter would like to see you both in his office as soon as possible. Fifth floor. Please hurry back when you're done."

As they stepped into the elevator, Wisniewski noticed the concerned look on Trask's face.

"Cheer up, you pessimist. We haven't had a chance to screw anything up yet."

"I've always thought that a pessimist was just a well-informed optimist."

The door to Lassiter's office was open, and he motioned Trask and Wisniewski in when he saw them in the hallway. It was a corner office—larger than the others on the floor—one of the perks afforded the division chief. As Trask entered, he saw Bill Patrick sitting in an overstuffed leather chair on the right side of Lassiter's desk. Patrick was a huge man, nearly six six and approaching three hundred well-distributed pounds. He sported an Old West style handlebar mustache, and was as gregarious as Lassiter was measured and reserved. He rose with Lassiter as Trask and Wisniewski entered the room, and beamed a wide smile as he reached out his hand to them.

"Welcome, gentleman! I hope the boss here didn't scare you fellas off with his pep talk this morning!"

"Oh, shut up, Bill." Lassiter was smiling, too. He motioned to two chairs, and walked around the desk before sitting on the front of it, facing them.

"I'll get straight to it, gentlemen." Lassiter was back on point. "We're starting a new, fast-track approach to bring some new attorneys to the federal side of the office to help with our criminal work. You two are our guinea pigs. I've gone over your files and trial records, and you have what it takes it terms of experience and ability. What this means, in summary, is that—assuming you give us no reason to change our minds in the meantime—you can both expect to be in federal court in about six months."

Trask shot a look at Tim, who gave him an I-told-you-so wink. They both had expected to spend at least a couple of years in the superior court sweatshops before advancing to the federal side of the office.

"You'll still need some time in the usual superior court rotation blocks. misdemeanors, superior court felony trial. You'll need to know how those sections of this office function, how we interact with the police and other investigative agencies at that level, but we need you up here as soon as possible. I trust you have no objections to this as a general proposal?"

Lassiter saw the happy responses he had expected. "Good. I didn't think so." He handed each of them a business card. "This has my direct office number on the front, and my cell number is written on the back. If there's anything I can do for you in the meantime—questions, advice, whatever—or *anything you can do for us,* call. Don't labor over the decision, just call. Thanks for coming up. We'll let you return to Maura and her forms, now."

Lassiter gave them a knowing smile as he held the door, shaking their hands as they left.

"You sure about this Bob?" Patrick asked.

"I *am* sure about it. For good career prosecutors like those two, the absolute worst thing we could do for them and for this office would be to sentence them to the bowels of our so-called superior court for the balance of their three-year commitments here. We'd probably chase them out of the department before they got a real taste of federal prosecution."

Patrick chuckled. "Always a fan of our fine local court system, aren't you?"

"It's a goddamn abortion, and you know it, Bill. The guys on the felony trial teams are each carrying more than *a hundred and seventy cases* in their individual assignment load at one time. They have trial docket calls three times a week, with five cases set for trial on each one of those days. Fifteen set for trial each week. They have no idea which case will actually go to trial. They walk into that damned auditorium of a witness room, yell out witness names for all five cases, and if enough witnesses actually show up for any particular case, they walk into the courtroom and lie to the judge by saying they're ready to try that one.

"They've never had a chance to speak to any witness before trial, no chance to visit a crime scene. They work from files drawn up only by cops, some of whom *might* know how to write a report in literate English. They fly by the seats of their pants in front of a hostile jury who views them as members of an enemy army of occupation, and if they manage a fifty-percent conviction rate, they're stars. In the process, they start to believe that this is the way you really prepare and prosecute a case. They develop every bad litigation habit you can think of, and when they finally get up here, we have to break 'em down and start the training process all over again. The only ones getting anything out of that system are the perps!"

"We both went through it."

"It wasn't such a disaster then, and you and I also had a lot in common with those two that just left: We knew how to do the job before we got here."

Lassiter had been an Army Judge Advocate General—or *JAG Corps*—attorney, trying scores of cases as both a prosecutor and defense counsel before accepting his appointment in the district. Patrick had been a very successful trial lawyer in a personal-injury firm before he tired of the games and overhead expenses of private practice.

"Are you convinced those pups know the job?" Patrick asked.

Lassiter opened the first of two manila file folders on his desk.

"Jeff Trask…" Lassiter looked over the top of the folder at his deputy before continuing. "Air Force Academy…"

"I should have known. Another ring-knocker."

"My class and I shall ignore that remark, sir." Lassiter glanced down at the large gold United States Military Academy ring wrapped around the fourth finger of his left hand. "May I continue?"

"Please, Captain."

"Air Force Academy. Highest ratings possible as a staff officer and squadron commander of some ground units after he graduated. It seems his knees kept him out of the cockpit. The Air Force picked him for their funded legal education program, one of only twenty-five selected that year. They sent him to law school on a full scholarship; top quarter of his class; got the Am Jur award for criminal law."

Patrick nodded. The American Jurisprudence Award was given to the top student in a course.

"He was part of their public defender intern program, trying real federal cases under the supervision of the law prof running the show. Lost the only one he was allowed to try, but he authored a brief in the case on appeal, alleging fatal instructional errors by the trial court. He was the first law student allowed to argue an appeal before the Fifth Circuit under their intern program. He won a reversal, and got an acquittal on the retrial.

"When he got back to the flyboys, they made him a circuit prosecutor within a year, handed him a quarter of the country—twenty-five bases—and turned him loose. I called Steve Wilson, one of the Air Force guys I met teaching at the Attorney General's Advocacy Institute. He's chief of the Air Force's prosecutors now, and Jeff's last boss. I asked him for a scouting report. He said their two-star almost cried when Trask handed in his papers. They had him doing their toughest cases. Murders, rapes, insanity defense rebuttals, dope conspiracies, sabotage trials, you name it."

"Why'd he leave?"

"Steve figured the road time burned him out. He had five years of three hundred plus days of travel in a row. More than 150 trials. Incredible professional experience, miserable on a personal life. He couldn't stay in the courtroom unless he was willing to stay on the road. Earned him a divorce."

"They should just issue us one in this business," Patrick grunted. Both he and Lassiter had been through the process. Patrick had since happily remarried. Lassiter had not.

"He did a year of appellate work before the Air Force cut him loose, so when he signed on, we stuck him in our appeals shop for the first year," Lassiter continued. "Handled the most complex drug conspiracy appeal you've ever seen. You remember it, the *Tarantola* case?"

"Yeah. Extradited Colombians, dirty mob lawyers, multiple conspiracy issues and every evidentiary claim of error you could think of."

"Right, and 26,000 pages of trial transcripts. The kid got the brief done solo, won every issue, and got all the counts affirmed. I read the brief myself. One of the best I've ever seen."

"Okay, sold. What about Wisniewski?"

"Former street cop in Santa Fe, went to night school for his shingle, worked in the county homicide bureau as an assistant district attorney. Great conviction rate, never reversed on appeal. He did a great job in our appellate section, too. Should be fine."

Patrick nodded. "Have you completely sold the boss on this?"

Lassiter paused, his enthusiasm for his new disciples momentarily diluted.

"For the most part. We'll have to monitor their progress through misdemeanors and felony trial. As usual, with the Honorable Ross Eastman, there's a catch."

For a political appointee, Lassiter actually liked the current United States Attorney. Eastman had actually been a DC AUSA himself early in his legal career before working into a congressional committee position and then being appointed as the United States Attorney for the District of Columbia. He had mastered the art of the favor: If someone asked something of him, he never forgot to secure consideration in return.

"And the imperial *quid pro quo* here is...?" Patrick asked.

"We get the fast track for Trask and Wisniewski if we provide a similarly greased path for one of his pet Ivy Leaguers."

"Of course."

Eastman had been Harvard Law, and was firmly convinced that those graduating from less-esteemed institutions were generally doomed to carry the briefcases of their betters.

"Which egghead are we getting?"

"Master Benjamin Prescott." Lassiter uttered the name as if he were a British butler, announcing the arrival of a guest to a formal ball. "Yale undergrad and law, scion and heir-apparent to a prominent Philadelphia plaintiff's firm partner—a partner who made sizeable contributions to the president's election campaign. After a brief interview, my impression of him is that of a young man who is firmly convinced of his own superiority and genius. He's currently down at felony-trial, batting about .250."

Patrick chuckled. "At least he's above the Mendoza line."

"At any rate, I've got to figure out what to do with him once he comes up next week." He smiled. "Perhaps, William, you'd like a second-chair to help you with the Wright case?"

"*No*."

As Trask and Wisniewski returned to the first floor and misdemeanors, they were met in the hallway by Maura Loxley.

"Mr. Trask, could I see you for a moment?" she asked.

"Sure."

Trask followed Loxley to her office as Tim turned into the trial team room. She sat down behind her desk, a small executive job. Trask continued to stand, and Loxley did not ask him to sit.

"I want you to know that I am aware of Mr. Lassiter's plans for you and Mr. Wiesniewski, and that—while I am naturally obligated to support the program—I think it is a mistake."

Trask put on his best poker face. He had expected to hear this speech—just not so soon.

"It is a break in an established office tradition," Loxley continued, "and one which I am not sure will give you the best background for long-term success in this office."

"I didn't ask for any special consideration."

"I appreciate that, but you are, nevertheless, receiving it." Loxley turned in her chair and sighed heavily.

"Anyway, the decision has been made. The real reason that I asked to speak with you is that—because you *are* more experienced than most of the other new attorneys in the section—I need you to work late tonight."

"Of course." Trask fought back the temptation to object to a sixteen-hour first day in the unit, but had no plans for the evening, and it was not the time to appear to be anything other than a dutiful team player.

"It's night papering. Drafting charges on the arrests made after hours. One of the felony assistants came down sick, and I was asked to send someone over to help out. There will be a felony assistant there to show you the forms and procedures and to help if you have questions."

"Happy to help."

"I thought you might be. Thank you."

A weak smile dismissed Trask, and he turned and left Loxley's office.

At five o'clock, Jeffrey Trask said goodnight to Wisniewski and the other members of his fledgling misdemeanor trial team and headed for the superior court.

Chapter Three

Trask looked up from the desk in the small room at the rear of the Superior Court lobby. The other AUSA in the papering office was on break, and Trask saw two more officers lined up behind the one already seated in front of him, waiting to present another story of a miscreant who had been apprehended that evening. Night papering, as it was known in the office, was where the cops brought their reports for arrests occurring after the close of regular court business hours. It was the responsibility of the assistants on duty to review the reports, and—in a kind of legal *triage*—to make a preliminary decision on what to charge, if anything, and where to send the case: misdemeanor or felony trial, or for federal prosecution.

"I'll be right with you, guys." Trask saw that the two detectives were a real pair. One was a large, athletically built black man, the other a small, wiry Hispanic. The taller of the two recognized the detective in the chair facing Trask's desk—a short, square black officer with a three-day growth of stubble.

"How are things in Vice this evening, Hammer?" Dixon Carter asked. "Working girls keeping you in trouble?"

Detective Gordon Hamilton turned when addressed, saw Carter and Ramirez, and grinned. "There is no drug-trafficking in 7D tonight, ladies and gentlemen," Hamilton announced. "The Twins are on the job!"

Seeing the puzzled look on Trask's face, Hamilton made the introductions, careful to point out to his fellow officers that the papering AUSA was brand-spanking new. This cued them to spoon-feed the rookie prosecutor, if necessary, in outlining the story of their arrest.

"Twins?" Trask couldn't help himself.

"Fraternal, of course," replied Carter, "I'm surprised, Counselor, that you missed the close family resemblance."

"Now that you mention it, there is a great deal of similarity," Trask smiled, shaking hands with both. "Let me get through with Romeo here, and you're next. Feel free to suggest anything I might miss."

Trask turned his attention back to Hamilton.

"OK, detective—you were alone in your vehicle near Fourteenth and K, the suspect came over to your open car window and asked if you wanted a date. Let's cut to the chase. What was the bargain that you reached?"

"Straight sex for cash." Hamilton seemed a bit hesitant to provide details with Carter and Ramirez leaning in the doorway behind him.

"Straight sex," Trask repeated, filling out a form on the desk, "for *how much* cash?"

"Six dollars," Hamilton said, wincing as Carter and Ramirez doubled over with laughter in the doorway behind him. "And two of that was supposed to be for the room."

After regaining some breath and wiping the tears from his eyes, Ramirez was able to speak.

"Christ, Hammer, how stoned *was* this ho? Or was she giving you a discount for your equipment?"

"Pretty messed up," Hamilton said, ignoring the second question. "She thought I was a regular—I actually locked her up last week—and she was too high to remember I busted her. I am proud to announce, however, that after arresting and turning Ms. Prentice over to the surveillance team, I moved on down the block and engaged the higher-priced spread."

Trask managed to get the rest of the required details from Hamilton, papering the offense as "felony soliciting," based upon the numerous prior, similar violations committed in recent years by "Tiffany," the working street alias for Chandra Prentice. Hamilton left after shaking hands with The Twins.

Carter then took the chair, while Ramirez, still grinning, stood leaning against the doorjamb.

"I present to you, Mr. Trask, the sad and sordid tale of one Scottie Masters, a career crack dealer infecting our fair city, who was seen by Detective

Ramirez and myself this evening continuing to ply his trade at the intersection of Wheeler and Mississippi Avenue, Southeast."

Ramirez rolled his eyes. "He was doin' hand-to-hands from the curb to passing cars; we saw him before he made us, and I jumped out and chased his fat ass down before he made it to his wheels."

"That is correct," continued Carter. "During the course of the foot chase initiated by my partner, I witnessed Mr. Masters attempt to discard a paper sack by throwing it behind a parked vehicle. I recovered the evidence while Detective Ramirez was recovering the suspect. I field-tested and weighed what appeared to me to be several rocks of cocaine base, and my digital scales indicated a total weight of about eight grams. The field-test was positive for cocaine."

"Got his rap sheet with you?" asked Trask.

"Of course," said Carter, handing over five sheets of computer printouts.

Trask looked over the summary provided by the National Crime Information Center, known to those in Law Enforcement as the NCIC.

"Give me a minute here, guys," he said, reaching into his shirt pocket for a business card while picking up the telephone. "It might be time to deal with Mr. Masters outside the auspices of the Superior Court."

Trask dialed the handwritten cell phone number.

"Mr. Lassiter? Jeff Trask. Sorry to disturb you at this hour but I have two detectives here who just grabbed a three-time loser for more than five grams of crack—about eight grams to be exact. He's got two priors for dealing, both crack-related, plus a felony for attempted auto theft."

"No trouble at all, Jeff," Lassiter answered. "That's what I get paid for. Didn't take long for you to hit papering, I take it."

"One of the felony guys got sick, and Ms. Loxley thought she'd give me a chance to excel."

"Or screw up on day one, thanks to me," chuckled Lassiter. "You did the right thing by calling. It normally wouldn't be a case we'd take federally with that low an amount, but with his priors he's..."

"Looking at a section 851 repeat offender enhancement and a ten-year mandatory?"

"Precisely. Write it up for the federal side and note on the jacket that I approved it. Thanks again for calling, Jeff."

"Yes, sir. Have a good night."

"Bob Lassiter?" Carter asked, one eyebrow cocked. This new AUSA was well connected for a papering virgin.

"Yes. He agrees that it's time for your Mr. Masters to become acquainted with the true federal court system. Please see to it that he's transferred to the Marshals' custody in the morning, and take your reports to the district court AUSAs so they can draft the complaint. You'll probably be doing the first appearance tomorrow afternoon."

"We know the drill," Carter responded. "Just didn't know that you did."

Trask gave the thirty-second version of his legal career, including the blue-suit time and his year in the appellate section.

"Pretty impressive." Carter shot a glance at his partner, then returned his look to Trask. "Had dinner yet?"

"No, and I'm starved." Trask checked his watch and saw that it was after 11:30 p.m.

"What's open now?"

"You may follow us to your friendly, neighborhood FOP, if you wish," Carter invited. "It's our lunch break."

Trask checked with the senior AUSA next door, who excused him for the remainder of the evening, and followed Carter and Ramirez half a block northward up Fifth Street. The Fraternal Order of Police Hall was located in an aging, three-story storefront on the west side of the street, facing Judiciary Square. Trask hesitated at the door, noting a sign that said Members Only.

"Don't sweat it," Ramirez said. You're our guest." He held the door open and motioned Trask in behind Carter.

The street-level floor of the aging building was long and narrow, with a mirrored bar along the left wall that ran almost the full length of the room. Even at the late hour, the bar stools were full and the place was humming with the chatter and raucous humor of police officers, some in uniform, many in civilian attire, some off-duty, other detectives and officers on their own lunch hours. The clang of cooking pans indicated that the main kitchen was straight back and to the rear, through two swinging doors. The bar and its stools took up at least half the floor, so that there was barely enough space along the opposite wall for a few small tables in a single row, each with four wooden chairs, few matching in style or condition. As The Twins and Trask passed the occupied tables, they saw a figure sitting alone at another.

"Have a seat, gentlemen, I've been expecting you." Lassiter motioned to the empty seats, nodding to Trask. "You pick your friends well, Jeff. Hooked up with my favorite police officers on your first night in papering."

The two detectives took seats on one side of the table, letting Trask have the chair next to his mentor.

Lassiter saw the question on Trask's face.

"I have the honor—as I'm sure you will soon—of having been sponsored by a regular FOP member, allowing me to become an associate member of this fine establishment. No better place in the District to measure the pulse of the local law enforcement scene."

Trask nodded his understanding as the barmaid emerged with menus, winking at Carter as she passed them out.

"How 'ya doin' DC?"

"Wonderful, Trish. How's your Dad?"

"Workin' days at a desk in 4D. Hates it, but otherwise he's fine."

"Good. Give him our best, please."

"Sure will. What'll it be?"

Lassiter had already eaten, and just wanted more coffee. Sandwiches were the choice of the evening for the others, who also requested caffeine. Trask's eyes followed their server as she headed back to the bar to call in the order.

"Pretty girl," observed Ramirez. "Jeff, you'd save my partner here from a painful divorce if you'd keep her from flirtin' with him." Then to Carter. "Mel would have your ass if she saw how you encourage that child."

"Mrs. Melody Carter," explained Lassiter. "Detective Carter's other partner in life, who is very jealous of her husband's continuing affair with Detective Ramirez."

"I don't encourage either of those rivals for my attention," Carter said, giving his shaven head a posed tilt. "They just can't help themselves. One desires this finely tuned temple of a body; the other covets my wisdom and keen investigative instincts."

"I just want a body that's bigger than mine to duck behind when the lead flies," Ramirez snorted. "You can finely tune the damn thing, or let it get fatter and wider for all I care. Your 'investigative instincts' are nuthin' compared to this homeboy's, so I'll have plenty of time to duck while you're still worryin' about which suit you'll be messin' up by hittin' the pavement."

"See what I mean?" Lassiter chuckled to Trask. "Just like an old married couple, aren't they?"

Trask noticed that his boss was more relaxed here than at the office. Like himself, Lassiter was more comfortable around cops than he was around the other barons of the bar. No posturing, no politicking to do, just the natural rhythm of the street and the real players in the field. The cops did the dirty work. The prosecutors might help plan, organize, write, and talk about an investigation or prosecution, but these were the guys in the trenches. The cops, in turn, respected those prosecutors who stuck with them, who made their efforts count in court, who gave up the lure of the big money in order to help them serve and protect.

Just as their food arrived at the table, Carter's cell phone rang. He checked the number of the incoming call before answering.

"Yes Cap'n. At FOP—we were just... WHAT? HOW? DAMN! Where is he now? Who's the crime scene tech? That's good, at least. Yeah, we'll see you at the morgue in about thirty." He spoke deliberately when he folded the phone shut.

"One of our sources got whacked tonight." Carter looked at his partner. "It's Junebug. Somebody mummified his head in duct tape, wrapped him up in trash bags, and threw him in a dumpster behind Miller Gardens. Cap'n Willie pulled his string, and they're starting the autopsy now." He looked up at Lassiter. "Frank Wilkes did the crime scene, thinks it's a retaliation hit."

"No wonder we couldn't find him." Ramirez shook his head. "We looked for him for damn near an hour. Lost him right in front of that project. Looked like he was tryin' to hook up a rock with some punk on the street."

Lassiter nodded. "Mind if we follow you out?"

"Of course not. You're always welcome. You know that."

They gulped down the coffee, wrapping the remains of the sandwiches in paper napkins to go. The green Buick was parked at the curb in front of the FOP. Lassiter's Toyota Camry was parked behind it. He motioned Trask to ride with him.

"I'll bring you back to your car when we're done," Lassiter said as they got in. "This could be one for our superior court homicide guys, or even a federal, witness-retaliation case." Lassiter pulled out behind The Twins and headed southeast.

"At any rate, you really did manage to pal up with the best street cops in the department."

"No problem riding with them on something like this?" Trask asked.

"I encourage it," Lassiter said, "Especially when you're going out with guys like DC and Juan. Any prosecutor worth his salt should learn his city—his turf. I can't imagine not visiting the crime scene of a case I'm about to try. You get a real feel for things looking at a room, a field, the front of a building, an alley. Scenes talk to you if you listen to them, and you get more than you ever could from reading some report…"

"Assuming it was accurately written."

"Exactly—a lot of them aren't. The police officers respect you for it, and when you have that respect, you get more information from them. They don't imitate monosyllabic, pull-string dolls when you're trying to get the rest of the story. You also make the other connections—like Captain Sivella and Frank Wilkes.

" The Metropolitan Police Department suffered for years as the result of Marion Barry's local-hire policy which *Hizzoner* the mayor instituted before losing his job as a result of that little cocaine episode back in the late eighties. The idea was well intentioned. Get your officers from the neighborhoods in your city; they'll already know the town and you solve some of your diversity issues. The problem is that the policy forced the department to hire new cops from homes where the kids looked up to the crack dealer on the block as their most prominent role model.

"Thank God for the exceptions like Carter and Ramirez," Lassiter continued. "For a while we had less than five percent of the force making over eighty percent of the arrests."

"What were the rest doing?"

"Collecting their checks, and doing every other sort of police work that didn't require them to arrest their own homeboys. Traffic and parking enforcement. Jailor duties. Administration. And then there've been the *real* problem officers."

"I know about some of them. I did some of the appeals where we had to concede error and dismiss because of the corruption issues."

"Right again. Dirty cops on the drug squad shaking down the dealers they arrested for their dope and profits, then putting them back on the streets. We used to get office bulletins fairly regularly instructing us to dismiss each case in which officer John Smith was an essential witness, because Officer Smith had been found to be on the wrong side of the law himself. Sometimes we'd have to kick more than a hundred pending cases at a time. You guys in appeals only saw the ones where we'd wasted the people's money going through what we thought was a clean and successful prosecution."

"I never knew the numbers were so high."

"Probably well over a thousand in the past twenty years or so."

"Is local hire still the policy?"

"It's now a preference, for all the difference that makes, but if you apply and are accepted, you still have to live inside the District lines for the first five years, pay through the nose for housing, and assume one of the highest tax burdens of any community in the nation. A new cop can't afford that much, which means he's not going to be residing in a town home on Capitol Hill or in Georgetown. Suffice it to say that we have a hard time attracting the best. That's why—guys like The Twins—you respect them even more."

"Who's this Captain Willie?"

Lassiter laughed out loud at the mention of the name of the 7D commanding officer. "William J. Sivella is actually a major now, in charge of the seventh district. Hell of a good cop, and one of the true characters on the force, which is why he was a captain forever and almost never made major. He's done some things truly outside the box, which have made him a local legend. Ever hear of the Arlington Hooker March?"

"Not that I recall."

"Willy was a sergeant in 2D at the time, working vice."

"I got some of that this evening in papering."

"Sergeant Sivella got tired of the revolving doors. You know—undercover ops, arrest, no time, hooker back on the street and arrested again the next night at the same parking meter. He had enough one night, got his squad together, rounded all the working girls up and took 'em on a forced march across the bridge into Arlington. The ruling fathers of Virginia seemed almost as unhappy about it as the streetwalkers.

"It took him a while to make his collar brass after that. He got to be a watch commander in 5D, where they had a problem with an open-air drug market on one of the residential boulevards. The pushers would stash their dope in paper bags behind the wheels of cars parked on the street. They'd hire juvenile runners to take the orders from customers, get the rocks or weed from the bags, give the dope to the buyers, then bring the cash to the pusher, who would be watching from the comfort of a lawn chair a few feet away.

"Willie got sick of trying to get info from the juvies, so he 'borrowed' a street sweeper from public works, put a bunch of uniformed guys on the block to keep the dealers from going to grab their paper sacks, and then Willie himself drove the sweeper down the street, laying down about eight inches of water against the curb and washing a million dollars of contraband into the city sewage system, while several grown men in their lawn chairs bawled like babies."

Trask laughed. "There's more?"

"Yes, when the department's hierarchy suggested the use of more conventional police work to address the 'bag' problem, Willie came up with Charlie the dope-sniffing chicken."

"A chicken?"

"Yep. Willie went out and bought a gauntlet glove—just like the one you junior birdmen use to handle your falcons at football games—"

"A symbol much swifter and nobler than a mule or a goat." Trask retorted, invoking the mascots of West Point and the Naval Academy.

"I'll grant you the speed issue only. At any rate, tied to Willie's wrist was not a falcon, but a rooster called Charlie. Willie, accompanied by other uniformed officers, approached several dealers in the same block that had been the scene of his prior initiative. He squeezed Charlie's feet, and when the rooster squawked, Willie informed the suspect that his drug-detection chicken had alerted. He would then ask the suspect for permission to search his person. The dealer, knowing that his stash was safely under a car or with a juvenile runner, often consented, resulting in a pat down which—although yielding no dope—on several occasions resulted in the seizure of enormous wads of cash."

"Who's this Wilkes?"

"One of the best crime scene guys in the PD," Lassiter replied. "A real forensics geek, but damned good at all of it. He's certified in fingerprints, ballistics, DNA, serology, hair and fiber analysis, footprint and tire impressions, and probably some other black arts that I can't remember at the moment. He doesn't miss much. We're almost here."

Lassiter followed The Twins' Buick as it pulled by the facades of several massive buildings, most of which appeared to be deserted.

"You are entering 1910 Massachusetts Avenue, Southeast, the 68-acre grounds of what was formerly known as DC General Hospital," Lassiter explained. "Now, there are only a few clinics staffed privately during the daytime, and of course, the morgue's still here."

They parked in a lot directly across from building number 27 in the old hospital complex, which bore a sign proclaiming it to be the Office of the Medical Examiner for the District of Columbia.

"I seem to have read where this place has had its own problems," Trask said.

"Both budget and professional problems," Lassiter nodded. "For a while there were bodies stacking up waiting for autopsies. We're lucky in this case to have Cap'n Willie's connection. He's dating one of the assistant MEs."

They reached the main door to the morgue offices on the heels of The Twins, and were met by two other men coming from the autopsy area. One was wearing a police uniform; the other wore dark blue cargo pants and a matching sweatshirt with *CST* in white letters across both the back and front. The CST was carrying several plastic bags, each labeled with a number.

"Major Sivella, Frank, this is Jeff Trask, one of our new AUSAs." Carter handled the introductions. "Jeff, Frank Wilkes here is our top crime scene guy."

It was obvious that everyone already knew Lassiter. Trask shook hands with Wilkes, then turned toward the major.

"Call me Willie. Everybody else does."

Sivella, looking rather rumpled in his uniform, was obviously still not dressing for departmental success. The shirt and pants had never been starched, and the shoes he wore might have seen polish only in a prior calendar year. Major Sivella was of average height, a gaunt-looking figure with a large, narrow face from which a beak of a nose protruded. His hairline was grey and receding, and Trask might have been singularly unimpressed had it not been for the firm handshake and bright, blue-gray eyes that flashed back at him. This was still a working cop, not a desk jockey satisfied after having made rank.

"It's a pleasure," Trask replied. "I heard quite a bit about you on the way over."

Sivella laughed, shooting Lassiter a mock warning glance and a waving finger.

"You only listen to Bob about legal matters. Come to me or my guys here for the truth on the street."

He motioned them all to chairs around one of the tables in the lobby.

"Kathy did me the favor of running Junebug's exam tonight. I now owe her about two million favors. She's doing the internal stuff now to confirm, but preliminary results didn't require any genius. Death by suffocation. Homicide. Poor fool's head was wrapped jaw to scalp in duct tape and he was hog-tied with the stuff. Somebody'd given him a hell of a shot to the side of the head before that, but nothing fatal, probably just put him out for the tape job. Frank's got the tape, and some other stuff for you."

"I'll take the tape back to the lab and 'scope it for fibers, hair, etcetera," Wilkes said, taking the cue. He was a tall, thin sort who spoke in the soft, thoughtful voice of a philosophy professor.

"There's nothing obviously significant on the tape itself, although I cleaned off what looked to be a couple of carpet fibers from the adhesive around the victim's head. No fingerprints evident anywhere at this point. When I got to the scene, the victim was bound with the tape and wrapped inside two trash bags, lying in a dumpster. No civilian footprints or tire tracks around the dumpster except for those of the trash truck and its driver, who called this in. He was evidently shaken, and the homicide detectives on the scene cleared him. The entire roll of duct tape was still attached to the trash bags. It's a new roll, and the killer put the wrapping from the roll into the trash bags with the body."

"What the hell is that about?" Ramirez asked.

"That's part one of a two-part message, in my opinion," Wilkes explained. "Our target is telling us that he knows that if he cut the tape and kept part of it, we could try and match the cut end with the rest of the roll—if we ever found it—or try and identify the cutting tool with adhesive residue."

"Why not just throw the rest of the tape away?" Carter inquired.

"Precisely why this is a message," Wilkes continued. "Had he done that, there would not be any communication going on here. I also found this inside one of the trash bags with your friend's body."

Wilkes pulled a small, clear plastic evidence bag from one of the larger, opaque bags. Inside the clear bag was a small, blue, corrugated cylinder.

"My turn to ask," sighed Lassiter.

"Bromadiolone," Wilkes said.

"Jesus. English please, Frank," Ramirez complained.

"Part two of the message. A pest control agent used in the control of rodents," Wilkes explained. "Rat poison."

Chapter Four

Trask's body clock woke him just before five thirty, even though he'd only slept for four hours. Lassiter had ordered him to take the day off as comp time and said he would make it right with Maura Loxley, though Trask doubted that was possible. He reset the alarm clock and grabbed another two hours of sleep before heading for the shower. While drying, he picked up the phone and dialed a number from memory.

"Appellate Government. Mrs. Mitchell."

"Hi, Sandy. Jeff Trask."

"Well, hello, Major! How's the big bad civilian world treating you these days?"

"Little fish in a very big pond. Is the boss around?"

"He is. Hold on, I'll transfer you. We miss you around here, you know."

"I miss you, too. I was thinking about putting the suit back on and coming in to pull a reserve tour or two today."

Trask was required to perform two half-day periods per month as a reserve officer. He usually did them in the appellate shop at Bolling Air Force Base on Tuesday evenings with other members of the JAG reserve's so-called Tuesday Knights club, but his day off gave him the chance to free up a couple of evenings without burning precious leave time.

"Great. Here's the colonel."

"Thanks, Sandy."

"Jeffrey! Just can't stay away, can you?" Colonel Steve Wilson, the chief government appellate counsel for the Air Force, supervisor of the service's traveling prosecutors, was his usual, cheerful self.

"No, sir. Thought I might come in today while the suit still fits; that is, if you have something for me to do."

"Always, but the circuit guys are here this week for their conference. You know some of them, and a lot of the new troops would love the chance to bounce some stuff off a living legend like yourself. We're supposed to tour the OSI headquarters over at Andrews today, so why don't you meet us over there?"

"You're too kind, boss. When does the bus pull up at OSI?"

"O-nine-hundred. Nine o'clock for you civilian types. Uniform of the day is the short-sleeve blue, so you don't even have to find your BDUs."

"I'll see you there." Trask laughed to himself and wondered if he could even locate the Battle Dress Uniform he'd boxed up after his resignation.

He buttoned the short-sleeve, light-blue shirt, pulled on his Major's epaulets, and stepped into the dark-blue trousers. The black, low-quarter shoes were next, and he instinctively retrieved the matching blue flight cap from his upper dresser drawer. It was a routine he'd performed hundreds of time before, and he missed the comfortable simplicity of a career in which he'd already excelled. *Living legend,* he said to himself, shaking his head. He was genuinely pleased to hear such a compliment from his former supervisor. Steve Wilson was the rare officer who trusted his people to do the right thing.

He drove west on Highway 5 from Waldorf toward Camp Springs, Maryland. Heading into the main gate for Andrews Air Force Base, he returned the guard's salute as the enlisted man recognized the officer's decal in the lower left corner of the windshield. He turned onto Command Drive, saw the headquarters building for the Air Force Office of Special Investigations, and pulled into the parking lot. As he walked toward the entrance, he heard a bus making the corner behind him. He saw the Bolling AFB logo on the side of the vehicle, so he stopped and waited at the curb. Colonel Wilson was the first off the bus, and after returning Trask's salute, offered his hand for a firm handshake.

"Great to see you, Jeff. I don't get around the Tuesday night reserve sessions too often. You'll have to pull some more daylight tours so we can catch up."

Trask smiled. "I'd love to, boss, but the feds only give me six hours of leave per pay period right now, and if I burned 'em all doing my tours, I'd never get any time off."

"I know. Just the same, we love to get the good ones back when we can. Sure I can't get you back on active duty?"

"My demands remain the same, sir. Match the DOJ offer. Double my pay, let me stay at home and in the courtroom, and I'll be back in blue tomorrow."

The older man laughed. "Would that I could, then we'd never lose anybody."

"I know, boss. Don't tell me you don't miss trial work yourself."

The colonel looked suddenly older and tired. "I do sometimes. Then I remember the hours and the stress. I'm starting to think that being a trial dog is a younger man's game. Man's and woman's, I should say. Half our circuit riders are female now, as you can see."

Twenty-one captains and majors, along with a couple of enlisted paralegals, had now finished spilling off the bus, and began heading toward the entrance of the building.

The tour of the OSI Headquarters went according to the usual military formula. The group was ushered into the commander's conference room, where they took seats around a huge mahogany conference table. Trask sat next to Colonel Wilson near the center. The AFOSI commander, a brigadier general, entered shortly thereafter, and someone called the room to attention. The general welcomed them, gave a brief history of the "FBI of the Air Force," explaining his organization's mission. He used a drop screen behind his lectern to run through the past three years' investigation and case statistics, then turned the briefings over to members of his staff and left the room.

Colonel Wilson noticed that Trask did not seem particularly impressed with the introduction. "Not a fan, Jeff?"

"No, sir," Trask whispered. "I knew him in the field. More interested in keeping down his travel budget than getting witnesses to trial. I had to pull strings just to get chain-of-custody witnesses to court." He glanced at the speaker then back at the colonel. Looks like he managed enough budget numbers to earn a star."

The colonel chuckled. "I thought all you academy types were military automatons." He turned his head politely to the front of the table, setting an example for the younger officers as an OSI lieutenant colonel explained the new intelligence role of his agency in the global war on terror.

"You know better, boss." Trask whispered. "It's another reason I left. Even in JAG, it seemed like who you knew was more important than what you'd done, especially when it came to promotions at the upper level. When I saw who was making some of the last sets of stars, I..."

Trask's voice tailed off in mid-sentence as he noticed the next OSI speaker enter the room and take a position to the rear of the lieutenant colonel. She was dressed in a conservative civilian business suit, with a skirt that topped a very shapely pair of legs.

"Friend of yours?" Colonel Wilson noticed that the lady and Trask had made eye contact, and were smiling at each other.

"Best undercover agent in OSI," Trask replied. "She was the narc who blew the lid off that dirty hospital at Shaw. I had thirty general courts-martial—all drug cases—come out of that operation, and we got convictions and near-max sentences in all of 'em."

"Our next speaker," concluded the lieutenant colonel, wrapping up his own presentation, "is Special Agent Lynn Preston, who is the new special agent in charge of OSI's undercover source program."

Although he continued to look intently at the face of Lynn Preston, Trask never heard her lecture. He remembered sitting at a desk in the Shaw Air Force Base legal office five years earlier, reading the case files from the operation when Lynn walked in for their first trial-prep meeting. An emergency room medical technician before being recruited by OSI, Lynn had been the ideal choice to assign to the hospital staff and identify the dozens of airmen who were dissatisfied enough with their military salaries to take up commerce in the drug trade. For months, she had posed as the younger sister of a major drug dealer in Chicago, using the ruse that she was buying the cheaper Southern cocaine and marijuana to send to her brother. The dope pushers who sold their stock to her had soon found themselves before courts-martial, and Trask's trial presentations—with Special Agent Preston as his star witness—had sent them to the military prison at Leavenworth.

Trask had still been married at the time, although the marriage was by then one in name only, but he had secretly wished that he had met Lynn Preston in another time and place. He had noticed that while she was all woman, there was nothing about her that was dainty or for show. She could hold her own with the criminal element on the street, playing the highest-stakes games of bluff poker when challenged by drug dealers trying to determine if she was a cop. She had been a bulletproof trial witness, and handed several highly paid civilian defense counsel their heads when they made the mistake of challenging her in court. The word got around, and after the first two or three trials, the rest of the Shaw drug ring had simply pleaded guilty, rather than take on the team of Preston and Trask.

There was something more that interested Trask about Lynn Preston. When he looked into her dark brown eyes *there was actually somebody home.* She was more than attractive, but Trask also respected her and her work, and he felt ten feet tall when Lynn gave him an affectionate peck on the cheek as he left Shaw. He had always watched the docket at the circuit office, hoping to return for another trial there, but his schedule had pulled him away to other bases and other cases.

"So in conclusion…"

Trask returned his attention to the presentation, and to the present.

"…if you need any assistance in identifying an undercover agent or a cooperating source for an operation, or in securing the necessary documents to provide them with a cover identity for your operation, then please call me at the numbers shown on the screen. They are also in your handouts."

To his dismay, Special Agent Preston left the conference room. Another speaker followed before the meeting broke for fifteen minutes. Trask followed Colonel Wilson and the rest of the group to a lounge area, where refreshments waited on linen-covered folding tables. He greeted several of the circuit counsel, some of whom he had taught as a guest lecturer at the JAG School at Maxwell Air Force Base in Alabama. There was the expected small talk about his new job as an AUSA, and how he'd gotten his foot in the door with the Department of Justice. There were inquiries about how he'd approach certain tactical trial situations, and which rules of evidence might be employed to the government's advantage in conspiracy cases.

He was talking to a young captain named Manders about the tension between the hearsay rule and the admissibility of co-conspirators' statements, when a familiar voice interrupted them.

"I thought I'd heard that Major Jeffrey Trask had left us for the world of big-time federal prosecutions. Have you returned to us for good?"

Trask turned and saw those brown eyes looking up at him. Manders saw the looks being passed between the two, and excused himself for a more promising mingle.

"Just a part-time gig for the day, Ms. Preston," Trask replied. "I'm flattered that you kept track of me."

"And I'm upset that you didn't keep track of *me*—especially since it looks like there's been a change in your social status." She took his left hand and examined the heavy academy class ring on his ring finger. "I seem to remember something else that you used to wear behind this hunk of metal."

"The divorce was final about eighteen months ago."

"I'm supposed to say 'I'm sorry' here, but I won't. What I will say is that you can pick me up at seven for dinner."

Trask laughed. "You were never one for games, Lynn. Seven it is, assuming you are willing to give me an address within a hundred miles or so."

"I'm in an apartment in LaPlata, right off the highway." She wrote a phone number and address on the back of a business card. "You can't miss it." She paused for a moment. "I have missed you."

"I'll see you tonight," Trask replied.

After an afternoon of the longest and most boring series of briefings in human history, concluding at the usual military closing hour of 4:15 p.m., Trask returned home, re-showered and re-shaved, and spent an inordinate amount of time selecting something potentially flattering from his still-limited selection of civilian casual wear. When he finally got dressed and looked at his watch for the twentieth time, he was mortified to see that it was still only five-thirty. La Plata, Maryland, was only a ten-minute drive from Waldorf. He cursed, then decided to burn the next hour or so at the local mall where he could pick up some flowers. After parking the Jeep, he walked by every store in the shopping center three times, finally decided on a date destination for the evening, and picked up a small but attractive bouquet of carnations from a florist near the exit.

He arrived at her apartment door at 6:55, and rang the doorbell.

"You're early," she said as she opened the door, "but I've been ready for five years."

As Trask stepped inside, she took the flowers and placed them on a lamp table, then turned back to him, and kissed him long, hard, and close. When they came up for air, she smiled, picked up the bouquet, and headed for the kitchen to find a vase.

"Where are we dining tonight?"

"Do you know Legends in Waldorf?" Trask asked.

"I've been by it a hundred times."

"Wish I'd known. It's about two blocks from my place. Nothing too fancy, but I think you'll like it."

"I'm starved, and I know I'll like the company."

Trask had selected the restaurant for two reasons. He liked the food and the atmosphere, but the place also had a dance floor and a DJ who played lots of slow stuff mixed in with some classic rock standards. They each had a steak, talked for two hours about cases past and present, and danced for another hour before returning to the Jeep.

He walked her to her door, having decided on the drive back that he would not risk it all by pressing his luck on the first date. He kissed her and held her close in the doorway, then held her face in his hands.

"I've missed you, too, Lynn, more than I could ever tell you. I want to do this again very soon—and very often."

He kissed her again and held the door for her after she unlocked it.

Trask drove home and opened the door to his own apartment, mentally kicking himself for playing it safe. He grabbed the remote and turned on the television as he started to unbutton his shirt. He was watching the late news when the telephone rang.

"Do you have cable?" she asked.

"Yes. Why?"

"Turn to channel twenty-one, hotshot."

Trask entered the channel on the remote, and the screen changed to a Cinemax soft-porn flick.

"What is this, some form of torture?" he asked, laughing.

"Just an honest question," she said. "How do those boobs compare to mine?"

"Why, how forward of you, Ms. Preston. I'm sure that I don't have a basis for comparison."

"If you hadn't run off like a timid schoolboy, you could have had one. Can you be back here in ten minutes?"

Trask made it in six, violating most of the traffic laws of the Commonwealth of Maryland in the process.

Chapter Five

The green, gold, and black flag of Jamaica hung on the wall behind the desk in the office in the rear of The Caribe restaurant on Fourteenth Street, NE, in the nation's capital. Displayed underneath the flag was a green-bordered campaign poster from 1980 bearing the likeness of Edward Seaga, the longtime leader of the Jamaica Labor Party, or JLP, as it was known in Kingston.

Demetrius Reid sat at a desk under the flag. He had been born in 1965 in a squalid apartment in a squalid section of southwest Kingston called the Tivoli Gardens, one of the political garrison communities loyal to Seaga and the JLP. Sectors like Tivoli, Denham and Spanish Town were called garrisons because they voted at strictly enforced 100 percent rates for their party, both at the ballot box and in the street wars. It had long been the misfortune of the Tivoli constituents and other JLP supporters that their rival party—the People's National Party, or PNP—held the loyalty of more than twice as many garrison neighborhoods. In a country where elections were settled by bullets as well as ballots, the numbers of both had weighed heavily against the JLP for years. The result had been long periods of governmental neglect for residents of the JLP garrisons while the PNP held power.

The restaurant owner's father, a dockworker at Port Royal, had been an outspoken supporter of Seaga in Tivoli, until his voice was silenced in 1976 by a police bullet. Following the death of her husband, his mother had worked double shifts in the kitchen of a Kingston restaurant to pay the rent for the flat and to feed and clothe him and his younger brother, Desmond. She was close to both her boys but more so to her eldest, who at an early age began to help her cook in the apartment's kitchen. As soon as he was able to shoulder this burden alone, she allowed him to do so, since she was sick of cooking by the time she returned home in the evening. Besides, the boy showed a real talent for it, and she constantly praised him for being a better chef than the ones who paid her meager wages. When she walked up the stairs to the apartment, she could smell the jerk chicken, pork, or goat, and knew that her own meal had been expertly prepared and was waiting on the table for her. After dinner she would smile and heap well-deserved praise upon the cook, who always beamed with pride.

She told him that once he learned some other dishes, he could earn a good wage as a chef at one of the resort cities on the north coast—Montego Bay or Ocho Rios—and spoke of moving the family north after she saved some money. She had good reason for wanting to make the move, as she knew that even in election years the tourist havens were spared the violence that had claimed her husband. The island's government depended too heavily on the tourism dollars to let the gunplay infect these sanitized pockets of nirvana, where the clear waters of the Caribbean met the perfect beaches in the harbors where the cruise ships anchored. Unfortunately, the bills left no money to save for the move.

By the time he turned fourteen, he had developed other interests besides cooking. He was large and tremendously strong for his age, and in the concrete chaos that was the Tivoli Gardens, these characteristics did not go unnoticed. He was recruited by the Shower Posse, the paramilitary arm of the JLP in Tivoli. Reminding him of his father's death, his mother begged him not to become too involved with the Posse "brothers," but she realized that her son's refusal to join might prove to be fatal. He began leaving the apartment every evening after dinner for training sessions in which he learned to fire the TEC-9 automatic pistols and other firearms in the Posse's arsenal. The Shower Posse was named for the hail of bullets it often unleashed upon its enemies, and the posses were gearing up for another national election.

By late 1979, he had already earned a name for himself in the raids the Shower troops conducted against the PNP strongholds in other areas of Kingston. At first, emptying a magazine into a Spangler Posse rival meant revenge for his father's murder. Then came the evening he was called upon by older brothers to execute a captured Spangler lieutenant. He had chosen to decapitate the man with a machete, and cleanly severed the head with one powerful stroke. He had never felt such power, and the cheers of the older Tivoli troops reinforced the rush. He was the talk of the street, and the talk spread outside Tivoli to the nearby Arnett Gardens neighborhood, where the orange colors of the Spanglers were displayed and the PNP ruled. He had become a marked man while only a boy.

The elections of 1980 were a national disaster for Jamaica and its capital. In the street warfare between the posses, more than eight hundred were gunned down, and the fires set by the raiding bands left more than twenty thousand homeless. He kissed his mother after dinner one evening, collected his gun, and headed east in the bed of a pickup truck, followed by two other vehicles filled with his heavily armed Shower brethren. The Shower raid into Arnett was particularly successful on this occasion, as they completely surprised a PNP precinct hall, which had been left more lightly guarded than usual. The Shower brothers flashed their victory signs over the bodies of eight hapless Spanglers, and smoked the ganja from the hall's pantry as they piled into their vehicles for the drive back into friendly territory, firing along the way at any Arnett residents who were foolish enough to venture outside their homes.

As the laughing Tivoli troops turned south onto Bustamente Highway, they suddenly took fire from other vehicles heading north—vehicles whose occupants were wearing Spangler orange. The celebratory mood sobered immediately, as they realized that the paltry defense at Arnett had been the product of a simultaneous raid by the Spanglers into Tivoli. Each side had drained its defensive forces in order to attack the other.

He bolted from the truck and ran toward the gray tenement building that had been his home, breaking into a sprint when he saw the flames in almost every window of the structure. He raced up the stairs and through the door to the apartment, noticing in horror that the lock had been blown off. He found his mother's body draped backward over the dining table, her legs dangling lifelessly above the floor. Her head was gone above the lower jaw, the result of a twelve-gauge shotgun blast through the mouth. At her feet was Desmond. His younger brother still held the kitchen knife he had grabbed for his mother's defense. There were two gunshot wounds to the torso. The head—cleanly severed by a machete—gazed wide-eyed at him from the floor under the table.

In the continuing election warfare that followed, many more Spanglers—or their allies in the Jungle or Tel Aviv posses—fell victim to the cold rage that now consumed him. His Shower brothers cheered him on, for he was an unstoppable force. He was the first through an enemy doorway, impervious to any danger, killing with guns, the machete, and often his bare hands.

When the Shower Posse carried the JLP to victory in the elections and the killing slowed, the posse command decided that their young warrior needed to be rewarded. A Tivoli elder who had known his mother gave him the bus ticket for Ocho Rios, and thanked him for his service to the cause. A position in a resort kitchen had been secured for him.

———

A knock on the office door made him look up. "Yah, mon. C'mon in."

The well-dressed and immaculately groomed personage of Spencer Goode, Esquire, attorney at law and rising star among the District of Columbia's criminal defense bar, entered the office.

"Same as the last trip, mon." The Jamaican wasted no time with pleasantries. He slid a metal briefcase across the desk toward Goode. "Two hundred t'ousand for twelve, pure. I'll see you tomorrow night, then. Take no chances."

Goode nodded, picked up the briefcase by the handle, and turned for the door.

Chapter Six

Trask entered the Misdemeanor Section workroom a full hour early to make up for his absence on the previous day. Despite little sleep, thanks to Lynn and the energies they'd released, he knew not to expect any slack from Maura Loxley. He had not, however, expected to see Tim Wisniewski already hard at work upon his arrival.

"Hey there, Tom Sawyer! Aunt Polly wasn't very happy that you played hooky yesterday. Hope it was worth it."

"More than you can imagine," Trask said. "Besides, she's the one that started the whole mess with that first-day overtime shift in papering. I ended up running into Lassiter and getting diverted into a homicide investigation and a ride-along to the morgue. Got home about two-thirty in the morning, and he told me to take the day off yesterday—said he'd clear it with Loxley."

"Well, here's the result of all that high-level influence."

Tim grabbed a foot-high stack of case jackets from the worktable in the center of the room and dropped it into the chair beside Trask's desk.

"What the hell...?"

"Five trials, all set for today in front of Judge Pike. Loxley came in late yesterday and said that since you and I had 'all that experience,' she knew we could handle first-chair duties on two calendars this morning. I get to meet Judge Stevens. I was supposed to have a new hire sit in with me, but he called in sick. Your second chair's Sheila Flynn."

"The gal from Postal?" Trask recalled their introductions from two days before. Sheila Flynn was a temporary from the Postal Service, sent by her agency to the United States Attorney's Office in order to gain what would almost certainly be the only trial experience she would ever see in her governmental career.

She had impressed him as a shrinking violet who probably should never think of entering a courtroom.

"Yep. Why don't you just give her one of those files and tell her to wing it? Should be good for a laugh or two, especially in front of Pike."

Trask shot back a look of mock anger. The Honorable Benton Ross Pike had been the most tyrannical and feared judge in the felony section of superior court until he'd been rotated to the misdemeanor bench for his health—and, thought Trask—for the health of the felony attorneys who appeared before him.

"I don't think it would be good for my reputation here to have my trial assistant die from fright in my first effort," Trask replied. "By the way, did you pick Pike for me or did Loxley?"

Wisniewski laughed. "You may again thank our learned superior for that pleasure. She made it quite clear to me that you, being the 'most experienced new trial attorney in the office,' would be the most capable of holding your own in Judge Pike's courtroom."

"And she gave me the least experienced second for help," Trask noted. "Wonderful."

The warning look on Tim's face caused Trask to shut up. He turned to the door just in time, relieved to see that it was Sheila Flynn, and not Loxley, entering the room.

"Good morning," she said.

"Morning." Trask told himself that Sheila Flynn's high-pitched, soft voice, emanating from a timid and mousy bespectacled face, was sure to inspire fear in the criminal element of the District. "Looks like we're a trial team today."

"Yes, I looked at the files for some time yesterday while you were out..."

"Sorry about that; couldn't be helped," Trask offered. "So what do we have here?" He motioned to the stack of papers still lying in his chair.

"Five cases. Three shoplifting incidents, one embezzlement of apartment rent proceeds, and an assault."

Trask nodded. At least Ms. Flynn could read files at this stage of her legal career. "Are any of the shoplifting complainants Asian?"

"No, I don't think so, at least their names..." A completely confused look came over the face of Sheila Flynn. "Why would that make any—?"

"Because they're the only store owners likely to show up and testify," explained Trask. "Politically correct or not, it's a fact of life that ninety percent of the residential population in this city is black. The Asian storeowners don't get along with many of their customers. The black storeowners—and many others—will call the cops to arrest a shoplifter, but they know that if they actually take the stand at trial, bad things happen. They may have to close the store for the day and lose money. The arrest is all the deterrence they're interested in. A conviction and jail sentence for the thief usually means reprisals from the perp and his buddies in the neighborhood. So the shop owners sign the complaints and promise the cops they'll be here, but they never are. If these were white Georgetown merchants, we probably wouldn't be trying misdemeanors, but felonies. They have more expensive stuff to steal."

Trask looked past Flynn toward Wisniewski, who was shaking with silent laughter behind Sheila's back. "At any rate, we probably won't be trying any shoplifters today."

"Well, I don't think we should just assume—"

"We're not assuming, just speaking probabilities so we can concentrate our efforts on where they're most needed. We'll have to see if anyone showed up on those cases anyway, so when we get to the witness room, you can take these and see if I'm wrong." Trask thumbed through the case jackets, giving Flynn the files for the shoplifting cases. "I'll do the other two and we'll try to get our trial identified—if we have one."

The walk through Judiciary Square to the Superior Court took about five minutes. The witness room on the main floor was the usual zoo. Forty-two assistant United States attorneys were barking out the names of witnesses to offenses, some petty, many serious, and some that would have been capital in other cities. The attorneys called the names of those subpoenaed. Those citizens who had actually shown up were sitting in rows of metal folding chairs, raising their hands or coming forward to meet the prosecutor assigned to their case. Many of the names called were met only with silence, indicating that those witnesses simply had better things to do that day. They had little fear of the judges of the superior court, who used their contempt powers sparingly, if ever.

Trask succeeded in finding both the complainant in the embezzlement matter and the victim and another witness in the assault case. From the case file and a five-minute interview, he quickly sized up the first case as a loser in its current form. The apartment complex owner had trusted the collection of rent payments to his manager—the defendant set for trial on this docket—who had come up some thirty percent short on the expected deposits for the last five months. Even though the amount lost to the theft was well over a thousand dollars, a felony-amount loss, the case had been charged down as a misdemeanor because of the crowded felony dockets. The owner had dutifully interviewed some tenants who had been listed by the manager as non-payers, but who had produced receipts allegedly signed by the manager. These witnesses had been subpoenaed, but had not shown up for court. Their testimony could not be introduced through the owner without blowing the hell out of the hearsay rule. If Trask announced "not ready," he would get a lecture from Judge Pike, the case would be dismissed, and all the work previously done to get the case into court would be wasted.

Trask saw that the defense counsel in the matter was William Autry, a cordial—if not energetic—gentleman of the bar whom he had opposed in three earlier appeals. He also saw that the same Mr. Autry was trundling by the entrance to the witness room. Trask walked briskly through the door and caught up to Autry in the hallway.

"Bill, I see that you're my opposition in the Forster case today. Looking forward to a trial today in front of old Bent Pike?"

"Hello, Jeff. Of course not." Autry was a portly, middle-aged caricature of a lawyer with a very bad comb-over. "Did you have an escape route in mind?"

"I think I might. It seems to me that your client's alleged signature on these rent receipts should have been submitted for handwriting analysis before we got to this stage. Would you oppose a delay for that to be accomplished? Your client has a prior felony hit for theft. If the lab report points to your guy, I think he's dead, but if it's not his writing, we'll dismiss."

"A reasonable proposal, and one that my client will agree to," Autry replied in his most official tone. "With that in mind, I'll go consult with him in the coffee shop."

"Great. I'll see in you in court, and send my witnesses home," said Trask. He returned to the witness room, having successfully avoided the topic of how many witnesses he actually had present and ready to take the stand. His use of the plural "witnesses" had not been a complete fabrication, as he was reasonably sure that the detective assigned to the case was somewhere in the courthouse. He was scanning the room to relocate the assault witnesses when he felt a tug on his left sleeve. Turning, he saw Sheila Flynn.

"As you predicted, we seem to have no shoplifting complainants," she sighed.

Trask wondered for a moment if a witness might actually have shown up, but had been unable to hear the dog-whistle frequencies at which his co-counsel spoke.

"That's OK. I think we've identified our battle for the day. It's the assault case."

He motioned in the direction of two women standing against a wall on the right side of the room. "Let me talk to these ladies for a bit. You know where the police waiting room is? Second floor."

"I can find it."

"Good. Our witness is an Officer Gentry. Have him wake up and come down here."

"Wake up?"

"The file says he's on dogwatch—he works the graveyard shift. He probably worked his shift last night, in which case he'll be stretched out up there on one of the couches."

"Right..." Sheila Flynn headed for the escalator.

Trask checked his watch. It was 8:35 a.m., twenty minutes before he needed to be seated and awaiting the grand entry of the Honorable Judge Pike.

"Sorry, Mrs. Nguyen, Mrs. Keating. We're ready to concentrate on your case now. Why don't we move over here for a bit?"

Trask led the women to a small circular table in the corner and away from the center of the room, where the din was actually growing louder.

"Mrs. Nguyen, I see from the file that your husband is the defendant here, and that he's also a dentist. You worked with him at the time of the assault as a dental assistant, and he was actually working on Mrs. Keating here at the time he struck you, is that correct?"

"Yes, sir." The small Vietnamese woman sitting in front of Trask spoke in measured but very good English. "I came to this country as a girl in 1975 after the fall of Saigon. I met my husband when I went to work for him years ago. There have always been times when he would hit me when he was not satisfied with things at home, but this is the first time he humiliated me so in public—in front of a patient." Tears began to show in the woman's eyes. "He said I had not correctly prepared the anesthetic."

"Thass right." Mrs. Keating, a matronly black woman, nodded affirmatively.

Trask glanced down at the police incident report. "It says here that he struck you with a closed fist, knocked you down, and then got on top of you and continued to strike you. Is that correct also?"

"Every word of it, Counselor."

The voice came not from the women in front of him, but from a deep bass behind him. Trask turned to see Sheila Flynn standing beside a very large police officer with the nametag "Gentry" displayed over his right chest pocket. The officer was rubbing the sleep out of tired brown eyes. Trask introduced himself and shook hands.

"Thought you might like to see these."

Gentry dropped three eight-by-ten photographs on the table. Each displayed the right side of Mrs. Doan Nguyen's face after her husband's rage had transformed it into a swollen, bleeding mass.

"When were these taken?" Trask directed the question to Gentry.

"About three hours after I got the call to go to Dr. Nguyen's office. Mrs. Keating there had jumped out of the chair and called it in—she had a filling about half done and was in some pain herself. Apparently the good doc didn't shoot her with enough Novocain, and when she complained he blamed the wife there for it. I showed up and he ran into another room and locked the door. I had to knock it down to take him into custody."

"Thass right." Mrs. Keating was nodding again.

Trask paused for a moment. Since the photographs had not been in the office file, he wondered if his obligation to present them to opposing counsel had been satisfied. Otherwise, the pictures might not be admissible in evidence. "Were these ever given to…?"

"I gave copies of the photos to the good doctor himself." Gentry anticipated the question. "Made sure he signed for 'em when he bonded out."

Trask nodded and turned his attention back to Mrs. Nguyen. "Am I correct—I see the injuries were to the right side of your face—in assuming that your husband is left-handed?"

"Yes, sir."

"And am I correct in saying that by now you've had enough, your marriage is over, you've left him, and there is no possibility of reconciliation?"

"Yes, but why do you ask?"

"Mrs. Nguyen, we're about to ask a judge and twelve jurors to sit through a trial. If there's any chance that you'll change your mind in the middle of this thing, want to go back to your husband, forgive him and deny that this ever happened, or say that you slipped on a gauze pad and hit your face on the floor, I simply need to know that now."

"Mr. Trask," the smaller woman leaned forward so that her face was inches away from Trask's.

"I *have* had enough. I cannot take any more. I have left him for good. I live with my son and his family now. My children and I have been victims of this man's temper and rage for years. It is time for him to be punished. Maybe then he will stop hurting people."

"We'll do what we can, then. Officer Gentry will stay here with you until we call for you to come to the courtroom."

Trask nodded to Sheila Flynn, and they left the witness room and walked toward the escalator in the center of the courthouse atrium. They got off on the second floor. He held the door to the courtroom for his co-counsel, and saw from her awe-struck reaction that this was Sheila Flynn's first time inside a real court of law.

"Just another office to work in," he said, attempting some reassurance. While his first impression of her God-given trial abilities had not been a positive one, he had been wrong on some first impressions before, and did not want to prematurely discard any possibility that Ms. Flynn might ultimately prove to be a trial wolf in sheep's clothing. She nodded, petrified.

They moved past the wooden pews reserved for observers—usually a disinterested reporter or two and the families of the accused—and through the swinging wooden gate that separated the peanut gallery from the well of the court. Trask dropped the case files on the left of two large counsel tables facing the elevated judge's bench. He nodded pleasantly at a row of attorneys seated inside the bar but behind the second table. There were five defense lawyers waiting for the clerk to call their cases on the docket.

"ALL RISE. The Superior Court for the District of Columbia is now in session, the Honorable Benton R. Pike presiding."

The bailiff's announcement had come precisely at 9:00 a.m., and Trask was glad that he had been in place on time. He and Flynn stood with the others as a short, thin, bald troll of a figure in a black robe stepped through a door behind the judge's bench and seated himself on his throne.

"Be seated." The Hon. Benton Pike spoke in a voice resembling a hoarse parrot. The screech cut through the air like a rusty knife. "The clerk will call the first case."

"*People v. Dugan,*" announced a woman sitting in the clerk's box, below the judge's bench and to the left.

"May it please the Court, Antoine Turner for Mr. Dugan, who appears in person, Your Honor."

A tall and well-dressed attorney stepped forward, motioning for his client to join him. Jerome Dugan was a typical young tough from the 'hood, displaying his respect for the court and the rule of law by arriving for his trial dressed in a dark-grey hooded sweatshirt and oversized jeans, which hung almost at thigh level, revealing that he preferred Hanes tighty-whities as a foundational garment. He stepped through the gate and stood at the defense table beside his counsel, sneering at Trask.

"Jeffrey Trask and Sheila Flynn for the government, Your Honor."

"Very well, Mr. Trask," Judge Pike croaked. "Is the prosecution prepared to proceed in this matter?"

"We are not, Your Honor."

Pike leaned forward, then suddenly screeched, "AND WHY THE HELL NOT?"

Trask had been prepared for irrational outbursts, having dealt with several of Judge Pike's cases on appeal, but the unprovoked challenge caught him flat footed for a moment. He paused, staring calmly but firmly back at the robed figure sitting above him, not so long as to be regarded as a challenge, but long enough for Pike to know that he was not willing to be bullied.

"We would be perfectly prepared to proceed, Your Honor," Trask spoke in a measured but firm voice, "but the complaining witness—despite having been lawfully served with a subpoena directing that he appear today—has apparently chosen not to comply with the Court's directive to do so. I might add that the next two cases on the docket, the Williams and Duke matters, also suffer from the same problem, and we are therefore unable to proceed on those cases as well."

"Then, counsel, because the United States Attorney's Office is unprepared to proceed, I am ordering those cases dismissed!" Pike smiled sardonically, and nodded toward the defense table. "Those defendants and their attorneys are free to go, and I will apologize on behalf of the federal prosecutors for the inconvenience imposed on you here today. Any objection, Mr. Trask?"

"Not to the dismissal of those matters, as such is required by law," Trask responded. "I do, however, object to the apology offered to these defendants by the court on behalf of my office, which—as I previously indicated—was actually prepared to go forward had the complainants in these matters complied with the court's subpoenas."

Trask glanced toward Sheila Flynn, and saw that the confrontation appeared to have her in the initial stages of a nervous breakdown.

"I'LL ISSUE THAT APOLOGY WHEN I GODDAMN WELL FEEL LIKE IT AND WHEN I THINK IT'S APPROPRIATE!" Pike was now so red faced that his complexion matched the stripes on the flag standing behind him. He looked down and bellowed at the clerk. "WHAT'S THE NEXT GODDAMN CASE?"

"*People v. Forster,* Your Honor."

The clerk had apparently been through the drill before, and was working calmly through the tirade.

"William Autry for Mr. Forster, who appears in person, Your Honor."

Autry and his client approached the defense table and remained standing.

"IS THE GOVERNMENT READY ON THIS CASE?" Pike demanded.

"Mr. Autry and I met before court this morning and agreed upon a continuance—subject, of course, to the court's approval—because—"

"I DO NOT APPROVE, MR. TRASK!"

"If the court would indulge my explanation, I was about to explain that both parties to the case have come to the realization that if certain evidence not yet pursued—"

"WHAT KIND OF GODDAMN EVIDENCE?"

Pike's face now looked like a boiler on the verge of explosion.

"As I was about to explain, respectfully," Trask seized the opportunity to correct Pike's manners, a move calculated either to calm the situation or to elevate it to a conflict just short of a contempt citation. He felt Flynn tugging on the tail of his suit coat, and looking down, saw that she was completely ashen faced. "May I have a brief moment with co-counsel, Your Honor?"

"HURRY THE HELL UP!" Pike's forehead was now bathed in beads of sweat.

"What in God's name are you doing?" Sheila Flynn whispered as Trask bent down to her.

"Just helping this old bastard finish the stroke he's trying to have," whispered Trask in return.

Flynn sank back in her seat with a blank look on her face, certain that she would be joining the madman next to her in jail for at least a night.

"As I was saying, Your Honor," Trask continued, "Mr. Autry and I had agreed that if certain evidence—"

"AND I HAD ASKED WHAT KIND OF EVIDENCE, DAMMIT!" Pike shrieked. He was now spending so much energy on his bellows that the minimal tonal quality that remained in his voice was disappearing with each scream.

"As I was trying to explain, *respectfully*," Trask continued, "there are handwriting analyses to be performed on documents in the case that would conclusively establish either the guilt or innocence of the defendant."

"AND WHY HAVEN'T THESE TESTS BEEN CONDUCTED BEFORE NOW?"

"I'm sure I don't know, your honor, having just seen the file for the first time this morning," Trask said, "but I'm sure the court would not wish to deprive the *defendant* of a chance to exonerate himself from these charges, and I would note again that this is a joint motion of the parties for a first continuance."

"Why couldn't I just exonerate him by dismissing the damn case with prejudice?" Pike's voice was now completely shot, and his rasp was like crumpled cellophane over the courtroom microphone.

"We would appeal that order, respectfully, as a dispositive order entered in an abuse of discretion, Judge, and if we prevailed on that appeal, we could re-file this matter, or even indict it as a felony charge—something the defense here is very reasonably trying to avoid."

Autry nodded affirmatively at the defense table. A prosecutor had just called him reasonable.

Pike paused, staring angrily at Trask. Among all the sitting judges in the superior court, he had been reversed most often for rulings characterized by the court of appeals as abuses of discretion, and he recalled the name of Jeffrey Trask as the government attorney on some of those appeals. His bluff had been called.

"I'll continue this matter for thirty days," Pike squawked. "If the tests haven't been done by then, I'll dismiss the matter."

"Thank you, Your Honor!"

Autry rushed his client through the door of the bar before Pike could change his mind.

"What's the next case?" Pike asked, impatiently.

"*People v. Nguyen,*" the clerk called.

"Is the government ready on this matter?" Pike hissed.

"We are prepared to proceed on this case," Trask responded as matter-of-factly as he could, correctly figuring that this would irritate Pike even more.

"Anne Braun for Doctor Nguyen, Your Honor."

Trask looked to his right to see an Asian man in a suit and a grossly overweight, pony-tailed woman in her early fifties entering the well of the court from the spectator gallery. Anne Braun's pale, puffy jowls protruded above the collar of the most hideous sack of a dress Trask had ever seen. He wondered why the woman had chosen to wear garments that appeared to have been fashioned out of bad upholstery fabric.

"I think we may have the advantage of a favorable first impression with the jury," Trask whispered, bending down to Sheila Flynn. His co-counsel remained stone-faced, staring straight ahead.

"And are you ready, Ms. Braun?" Pike asked weakly.

"We are, Your Honor."

"Call for the panel." Pike nodded to the clerk. "We'll take a fifteen-minute recess before we begin jury selection." He banged his gavel weakly, stood, and shuffled slowly from the courtroom as the bailiff again shouted, "ALL RISE!"

"I think that went well, don't you?" Trask asked Flynn.

"God!" she exclaimed, shaking as she bolted for the door.

Fifteen minutes later, court resumed with two parties notably absent. Sheila Flynn had not returned. The other officer of the court missing in action was the Honorable Benton Ross Pike. In his place was Judge Linda Worthington. She explained that Judge Pike was not feeling well and had been forced to go home for the day. She would be sitting in for him the balance of the day, and possibly longer.

Trask felt a very brief pang of regret, wondering if he had, in fact, sent Pike over the edge to cardiac arrest, but he concluded that the old coot had simply not wanted a trial with counsel he could not manipulate.

There were also eighty additional persons in the spectator pews. The assembled panel of prospective jurors squirmed nervously as the clerk called the roll of their names.

"We might as well get the tough one out of the way first," announced Judge Worthington.

Trask knew that this meant the required, three-part inquiry. The judge had decided to thin the herd before proceeding to other questions.

"How many of you in the panel, within the last five years, have been accused of, convicted of, or a victim of a serious criminal offense; by that I mean something other than a traffic ticket or a municipal ordinance violation like letting your dog run loose?"

Trask turned and was astonished to see that all eighty members of the panel had risen.

"Would counsel approach the bench, please?" Judge Worthington's invitation was a welcome contrast to Pike's manner that morning. Trask and Anne Braun walked forward. The judge leaned forward and spoke in a voice just above a whisper.

"As I'm sure you are both aware, we have to take these answers individually at the bench. We are, therefore, going to be here awhile."

Chapter Seven

Spencer Goode, Esquire, turned his Acura MDX northeastward on Interstate 95, glancing down momentarily to turn on a small citizens band radio plugged into one of the vehicle's auxiliary power sockets. He normally listened to a classic R&B channel through his XM radio, but on these trips to New York it was critical for him to avoid the scrutiny of the various state police who might wish to inspect his car, and the idiot cracker truckers that plied the roads between the nation's commercial and governmental capitals were simply the best source of real-time information regarding speed traps and other road problems. The downside was, of course, that in lieu of Marvin Gaye, he was forced to listen to the inane conversations of individuals using handles like Starvin' Marvin or Peterbilt Peter.

He had chosen the MDX for a number of reasons. The Acura brand advertised his success as a rising trial attorney and member of the defense bar without being gauche. He would have actually liked something a bit larger—like a Cadillac Escalade—but that vehicle had become the ride of choice for the crack dealers of the nation, and it was Goode's intention to avoid, not attract, the attention of law enforcement whenever possible, especially on these trips made for the Jamaican. A similar decision-making process had gone into his choice of license plates for the vehicle. He had been tempted to emulate other members of the defense bar by opting for a personalized plate that would advertise his profession—something like NOTGLTY, or DEFENSE—but most of the obvious choices had already been taken, and such a plate would also be likely to attract the most aggressive cops. Some police officers just loved to jack with defense attorneys, and Goode had decided that the wisest course was not to give them a reason. Accordingly, his DC plates were the usual innocuous collection of letters and numbers.

If, despite all his precautions, Goode were to be stopped on this occasion by any member of the law enforcement community, he would be prepared to use his status as an attorney in a respectful but firm manner. His DC Bar membership card and his business card were purposefully shown above and below his driver's license in plastic windows in a tri-fold wallet chosen for its ability to accommodate this display. He was dressed in a distinguished three-piece suit, with the coat neatly hung behind the driver's seat on a valet-styled wooden hanger attached to the headrest. He gave his adversaries no excuse to stop him, and—if stopped anyway—no excuse to even ask for his permission to search the vehicle. As a final precautionary measure, the locked metal briefcase provided to him by the Jamaican was concealed inside an even larger, leather attaché case, which bore a large tag proclaiming the contents to be "confidential legal papers."

He smiled to himself, feeling very superior. He had nothing but contempt for the addicts who ruined their lives by pumping themselves full of whatever artificial additives they could find. Whether it was weed to get mellow, or crack to get high, he had no use for such things. It would mean that something else would be controlling him. He had simply worked too hard, through college, law school, and the side jobs, to throw it all away by diving into a pipe.

On the other hand, if fools wished to throw themselves into such folly, he saw absolutely nothing wrong with profiting from such stupidity. It was, after all, the American way. Simple entrepreneurship. If someone else were dumb enough to throw their money at you, whether for booze, a circus, a bad movie, or some other frivolous entertainment, what was the difference? He was only doing something that many of the white barons of industry had done during Prohibition. When Congress came to their senses and legalized dope, any and all of his undiscovered sins would be washed away.

In the interim, he chose to profit both by running a few errands for the Jamaican, and by representing those who—unlike himself—were stupid enough to get caught. Unlike most of the defense attorneys who had respect for the rules of society and behaved accordingly, Goode had weighed the nation's drug laws and found them to be wanting—so severely wanting that he felt justified in ignoring them.

Goode heard truckers on the CB squawking about an overturned tanker on the road ahead, and turned up the volume to make sure he got all of the details. He turned the radio off, picked up his cell phone, and informed the Jamaican that he would be forced to find an alternate route due to I-95 being closed south of Philadelphia. He was in no hurry, and reasoned that he could take the coastal Garden State Parkway into New York. He turned southeast on U.S. 40 toward Atlantic City.

William Patrick strode briskly across the floor of Lassiter's office, performed a perfect British double-stomp, rendered a British, palm-forward salute, and staring straight ahead, shouted, "Scouting party reporting as ordered, suh!"

"Well Sergeant-Major, what do you have to report?" Lassiter laughed as he finished typing a sentence on his desktop terminal, and swiveled his chair to face the very large and very absurd looking figure before him.

"May I sit, suh?"

"Yes, please, before you have a stroke from standing there too hard."

Patrick lowered his immense frame into one of the side chairs.

"Which do you want first, the good news or the bad?"

"Let's start with something pleasant, if we might. I already have an idea of what the bad news may be."

"Very well. Master Wisniewski completed his trial of a purse-snatcher in front of the Honorable Robert Stevens, and secured a conviction from a jury of the perp's peers, despite the fact that the victim had made a career of professionally providing sexual favors on the streets of our nation's capital city. His closing argument was simple, to the point, and persuasive."

"Not an easy win, with that kind of victim," Lassiter said. "What was the gender composition of the jury?" Knowing the contempt that most women had for hookers, he wondered what the odds had been going into deliberation.

"Eight women, four men."

"Even more impressive. I'll send him a note congratulating him on his first win."

"Which will also let him know that we're continuing to monitor his progress," Patrick noted.

"So jovial in appearance, so cynical in reality," Lassiter replied.

"I *am* a man of mystery, after all."

"Yeah, Bill. You're about as opaque as a fish bowl. What's the other news?"

"The other *good* news is that your man Trask went head-to-head with old Benton Pike, stood his ground, and may have actually chased him off the bench for a day or two. The *bad* news is..."

"That some ingénue from postal went running to Maura Loxley and told her that Jeff was trying to give the judge a stroke?"

"You heard?"

"Yeah, Maura called me the day it happened."

"Well, you may inform her that I was a witness to the exchange, that I felt that Pike was out of line, as usual, and that Mr. Trask conducted himself with restraint and decorum, regardless of his motives."

"I already told her that. I'm glad I wasn't lying at the time."

"Oh? And if she had asked me about it before now..."

"You would have backed me up anyway, regardless of what you'd actually observed."

"You're right. I am a fish bowl." Patrick hung his head in mock despair.

"What about the balance of the trial?"

"You don't already know?" Patrick was going to play coy, but Lassiter gave him "the look," and so he resumed his narrative.

"As I'm sure Your Lordship is aware..." Again, the look. Patrick reached into his jacket's inside pocket, and pulled out a small notebook.

"After Pike left the bench, proceedings resumed before Judge Worthington. It took two days to seat the jury for this misdemeanor trial, since it seems that the prospective jurors all had some sort of prior contact with our city's criminal justice system. The accused was ably, though not persuasively, represented by Anne Braun, who appeared to be wearing an old chair of some sort. Once they got a jury picked—ten women, two men—the prosecution's opening statement portrayed the defendant dentist as a bullying, abusive cad. That was proved beyond a reasonable doubt, according to the verdict. The jury was only out about an hour, and I'd bet half of that time was spent picking a foreperson."

Patrick looked up from his notes. "Trask was damned good, Bob. All the bleeding and bellyaching objections by Ms. Braun bounced off him like the spitballs they were. Judge Worthington would just smile and agree with your boy's responses. After a while, Braun just kept her ample ass in her chair and shut up."

"Portraying a petulant brat, no doubt."

"Of course. To the detriment of her client, and to the benefit of the United States. The defendant got stepped back after the jury said, 'Guilty.'"

"Worthington denied him bail on a misdemeanor?"

"Yep. She said he was a danger to the community and to the complaining witness. Gave him a hell of a lecture on what would happen if his ex-wife-to-be got so much as a hangnail in the future."

"Move 'em both up to felony trial, Bill."

"This soon?"

"You know we're wasting 'em down there. We need some new trial team horses on the fourth floor—just had two resignations. I also want to keep Maura Loxley from torpedoing these guys, or them from killing her first."

"Suh!" Patrick rose, and repeated his stomp and salute. He executed the worst about-face Lassiter had ever seen, and headed for the door.

Trask pulled the Jeep into his assigned parking spot in the apartment complex. The vehicle's clock read 7:30 p.m. He smiled seeing that the lights were on inside his apartment. He'd called Lynn shortly after the verdict had been returned, and suggested that they go out to celebrate. Even though it had been just a misdemeanor case, it had taken almost all week to try the thing, and a win was a win. She suggested meeting at his place to save time, and he told her where to find his emergency key—in her purse, where he'd dropped it the night before.

She didn't meet him at the door, but the aroma did. The table was set with full place settings, wine glasses, and candles, none of it his own.

"What's all this? And what's in that?" He pointed to a pressure cooker sizzling on the stove.

She smiled and turned to kiss him. She was wearing jeans and a T-shirt, both of which did nothing to hide the figure underneath them. They'd be spending the evening in the apartment.

"Just something I threw together."

"Feel free to come over and throw it together whenever you feel the urge. It smells delicious. I had planned to take you out, you know."

"I know. Just change your clothes and sit down over there." She pointed to his little dining table, barely large enough for all the dishes and silverware awaiting the feast.

"You lugged all this over here?"

"You know I did…on my second trip, after I found out that you had nothing. You're lucky I live close to you. I can't believe you've been getting by on two plates and two bowls, and *no cookware whatsoever!*"

"Lost it all in the settlement. Stouffer's and Campbell's do the cooking for me, and I don't have to do their dishes."

"Just go change and sit down," she repeated.

He did as instructed, losing the suit. He returned to the table and sat facing his chef. She had poured the wine and brought out two plates heaped with steamed rice and chunks of meat and vegetables in the best-smelling sauce he'd ever encountered.

"It's just beef stew and rice, but I spice it up a little."

"If the aroma's any indication—and I know it will be—it won't be here long. I had to work through lunch, and I'm starved." He dug in, and the first bite made him look up at her with a startled look on his face.

"What's wrong? Don't you like it?"

"I love it," he said. "It may be the best thing I've ever tasted. I was confused because you told me that you didn't cook. This is wonderful."

"I never said I couldn't cook; I said I didn't *like* to cook, so don't get the impression that this is an every night thing."

"Damn. I knew you couldn't be as perfect as you seemed."

She sailed a cloth napkin past his ear as he ducked.

"How much of this did you make?"

"Enough for seconds, if you really like it."

He held up a plate that was already empty.

"Please, ma'am, is there more?"

She giggled, retreated back to the pressure cooker on the stove and reloaded his plate. She brought it back to the table, placed it in front of him, sat on his lap and kissed him again.

"When I finish this, what's for dessert?"

"Me," she whispered, kissing him again. "And if you take your time, there's seconds on that, too."

It was almost eleven when he woke up. Her head was resting on his shoulder, and she purred when he kissed her on the forehead.

"Are you staying here tonight?" he asked.

"I'd planned to. Are you throwing me out?" She raised her head and brushed the hair out her face.

"Of course not." He kissed her lips slowly. "I have some unholy plans to repeat this debauchery in the morning."

"Fine with me." She smiled and put her head back on his shoulder.

"I would suggest then," he cautioned, "that we change the sheets, because I seem to be lying in some kind of pool."

She sat up, and saw the borders of the sweat stains.

"Where do you keep them?" She asked, laughing.

"The narrow little closet in the hall by the AC."

He started pulling the current coverings from the mattress. She returned, and stood in the doorway, still gorgeously naked.

"What the hell is this?" She was holding a perfectly folded flat sheet in one hand, and a crumpled mound of fitted sheet in the other.

"Looks like a clean set of sheets to me."

"You know what I mean, smart-ass. Why is this one folded and the other just tossed in the closet? Were you interrupted by some legal emergency in the middle of your laundry?"

"No," he chuckled. "I have a handicap which prevents me from being able to fold those fitted things."

"A handicap?"

"Yeah. A Y chromosome."

She laughed and jumped into his arms again, knocking him backwards onto the sheet-less bed.

"I believe," she said, "that if we wait a few minutes, they'll still be clean when we're *really* ready to put them on the bed."

Ronald Fellows was celebrating his eighteenth birthday making some extra money by transferring a one-ounce bottle labeled "vanilla extract," but actually containing the hallucinogenic liquid PCP, to a young white man. The purchaser had ventured into the Anacostia section of the District from the Baltimore suburb of Dundalk for the express purpose of scoring some "wet." Because faces such as his own were demographically rare in 7D, the police working the area referred to such customers as "seal pups," since they stood out like baby harp seals on the ice flows of Canada, and were easy targets for arrest teams.

As he neared the age of emancipation in the District of Columbia, Fellows had been forced to seek alternate forms of employment, as his lookout duties for the Jamaican had suddenly been terminated without explanation. Ronald had spent the morning working his way through a prime dime bag of weed, a birthday present to himself from himself. Still mellow and sluggish from the herb, he ambled down Wheeler, in front of the Miller Gardens projects, looking to make enough to start another session of his chosen escape therapy. He was so mellow that he failed to notice the green Buick that quickly pulled to a stop behind him along the curb.

As Fellows started to exchange the bottle for the cash being offered by his customer, he looked down to make sure the white hand coming toward him contained cash and not a weapon of some type. Instead, he was astonished to see a *light brown* hand reach around from behind him, containing an open handcuff that then swiftly closed around his right wrist. He tried to pull free and to follow the white youth who was fleeing down the sidewalk, but the wiry Hispanic man nearly jerked his arm out of its socket. Fellows clinched his left hand into a fist, and was preparing to swing when a larger black fist enveloped his own, and he was spun, face first, down to the sidewalk.

"Not a good idea, my man." Dixon Carter said, pulling Fellows' left hand behind his back and clicking the open cuff shut around his left wrist. "Attempted distribution of PCP, attempted assault on a law enforcement officer, and hmmmm, let's see here..." Carter retrieved an object causing a noticeable bulge in the rear of Fellows' sweat pants. "Possession of a firearm during and in furtherance of a drug-trafficking offense. That, my young sir, is a federal violation. You've made the big time."

Fellows felt himself being lifted to his feet. His head was then forced down by the same large black hand as he was ushered skillfully into the backseat of the Buick.

———

Spencer Goode, Esquire, put another twenty into the video poker machine as he sipped a complimentary Crown and water. His previous trips to Harrah's had been entertaining, if not entirely profitable, and he'd been reading up on the finer points of video poker, which seemed to him to be superior to the slot machine experience. He had looked around for a higher pay table, but this 9-6 machine—paying nine times the amount bet for a full house, and six for a flush—was apparently the house's best-paying maximum for a quarter machine, yielding about a 98 percent return overall.

Goode felt superior to most of the other patrons, the AARP members scattered about wasting their social security checks on high-risk, almost no-reward slots, and the loud, drunken goombahs from New York and Jersey making a racket at a nearby craps table. He had set a fixed limit of a hundred dollars for the evening's entertainment, and reasoned that he would have spent that much if not more on another hotel's room and dinner, whereas the room here had been comped based upon his play on prior trips. He also had a coupon for the casino buffet and figured this was the only way he could get a decent room, a meal, and actually stand to win a buck or two in the process. At any rate, he had to wait out the thunderstorm that had transformed the highways to New York into parking lots. He also enjoyed being waited on by the cocktail waitresses, whom he tipped generously, and who seemed happy to serve him and spend a moment chatting with someone other than a grumpy seventy-something who reeked of cigarettes or cheap cigars.

He hit the Max Play button again, drawing five cards on the screen with a wager of five quarters. He looked at his hand—two of clubs, king of hearts, jack of hearts, eight of spades and three of diamonds—held the hearts, and saw the three other kings pop up on the draw, paying him $62.50 for his $1.25 wager. Five hands later he held an ace, king, queen, and ten of diamonds, and saw the jack fill the hand on the draw for a royal flush, which paid him the progressive jackpot of $1,158.49, much to the envy and disgust of a cranky crone two seats away who cashed out and stomped off in a huff. He took his ticket, cashed it in at one of the automatic cashier machines nearby, and headed for the buffet, feeling very satisfied.

Chapter Eight

"Got a moment, boss?"

Major William Sivella looked up to see the large figure of Detective Dixon Carter in his doorway.

"Sure, Dix. Have a seat. Where's your partner?" The shadow of Juan Ramirez was missing.

"He's printing a kid we just brought in for selling an ounce of wet to a pup on Wheeler. The kid resisted, and had a loaded Glock nine on him when we took him down. I think I recognized him."

"From where?"

"I can't be absolutely positive, but I'm pretty sure I saw him talking to Junebug Wilson a little while before the trash guy found him in the dumpster outside Miller Gardens. That's where we just arrested the kid, too. I was thinking that if we..."

"Called Lassiter he might be willing to put a 924c on the kid to give us some leverage?"

Sivella referred to Title 18 of the United States Code, Section 924c, which mandated a consecutive, five-year sentence for using or carrying a firearm in a drug-trafficking offense. The sentencing judge—assuming the charge was prosecuted in federal district court—would have no choice but to impose this congressionally mandated penalty. Five years in a real federal pen spoke much more loudly to a potential cooperator than a two-year stint in Lorton, which would actually mean serving less than a year.

"Yeah. I told the kid when we popped him that he was looking at a federal case."

"Dammit, Dix, one of these days you're gonna make a promise to somebody that I can't keep for you." Sivella spun sideways in his chair, shaking his head, then turned back to face Carter. "What if Bob decides he ain't gonna burn his federal assistants' time over a single ounce of wet?"

"We have complete confidence in you, Cap. Might be a murder case inside that ounce bottle."

"What if the kid is the one who whacked your snitch?"

"He's no criminal mastermind. He didn't duct tape Junebug and leave messages for us in the wrapping. If this little punk ever did take somebody out, it would be with the nine that he had in his waistband, or with whatever other piece he could find on the street. He weighs 145 pounds soaking wet, and even Junebug, coming down off a smoke, would be able to keep him from taping his face up. Odds are this kid was a runner-lookout, and told June where to get his next rock. We find the seller, we've probably got the killer."

Sivella nodded and shrugged his shoulders. He'd never been reluctant to go for long shots in his own cases, and he'd never been burned by trusting the judgment of his best detective team. He picked up the phone on his desk and dialed the number from memory. When he heard an answer, he pressed the speakerphone button and put the handset down.

"Bob? Willie. The Twins just brought in some kid for selling an ounce of wet in front of the Miller Gardens project. Had a loaded handgun in his pants. Dix thinks he may know something about the Wilson murder, and wants to go federal with it for leverage. Can you help us out?"

"A one-time, one-ounce deal, Willie? I can just hear one of our imperial jurists squawking about the tail wagging the dog when your perp gets probation for the PCP and five years for the gun." Lassiter had heard from the district court far too often about having to process cases that the judges did not consider to be worth their precious time and effort. "What kind of record does he have?"

"Juvenile stuff only, I'm afraid," Carter answered, responding to the inquiring look from his commander. "He just turned eighteen." He repeated his suspicions about Fellows' connection to the demise of Junebug Wilson.

Lassiter paused. "Okay, but only for my favorite detectives. Get me a complaint affidavit as soon as possible. And Dix?"

"Yes sir?" Carter was already smiling at Sivella.

"I'm sticking it out for you on this one, so do *me* a favor, please."

"Of course. Name it."

"Find your connection to that murder and make it stick. We're going to look pretty silly, otherwise."

Ramirez knew from the look on Carter's face when he entered the interrogation room that the game was on. He sat on one side of the gray, metal table, occupying one of two chairs facing Ronald Fellows, who sat with one of his hands cuffed to a chair arm. Fellows glared at Carter as the detective took the vacant seat, thinking there was no way this oversized cop was going to have any effect on his daily routine except for a couple of pain-in-the-ass court hearings. He'd get his first-offender suspended sentence and have to piss in a cup a couple of times a month.

"Uncle Tom mutherfucker," Fellows muttered.

"I assure you, my stupid young friend," Carter began in a measured deep baritone, fixing his eyes firmly on Fellows, "that I have never had intimate relations with my own mother. I am also an only child, as is my wife, so it logically follows that I can be nobody's uncle, and my first name is not Tom. To you, from this point on, it is either Officer or Detective.

"I can now further advise you that the prosecuting authorities in the District of Columbia have—as I told you they would—decided to prosecute your young and foolish behind in the United States District Court for the District of Columbia. That is our *federal* court, you see. The charges that will be filed against you include distribution of PCP and the carrying of a firearm in furtherance of that crime.

"*When* convicted of these charges…" Carter intentionally avoided the use of the word *if*.

"You will not be joining your homies in Lorton. You will instead be sentenced to a term of no less than five years in a federal penitentiary to be chosen by the Federal Bureau of Prisons. The judge will have no choice but to give you such a sentence, for that is the statutory minimum. To put that into ninth-grade terms, which I believe is the extent of your current education, it's the law and a done deal. The only way out from under that very sizeable rock is cooperation in an investigation currently underway…"

"I want a lawyer." Fellows' lips were curling up into a sneer again.

"And I very much want you to have one, especially in this case," Carter responded calmly, not missing a beat in the tempo of the exchange. A look of confusion appeared on Fellows' face. "I didn't even *want* to try and question you now, because we haven't given you your Miranda warnings yet. More importantly, you're not going to believe anything I tell you *until* you talk to a lawyer. Once you do talk to your *appointed* attorney—you see, I know he'll be appointed because you, as an unemployed street punk with no education, can't afford one—he will tell you exactly what I have already told you. Then, and only then, the rays of light will filter into your mind, yielding brief glimmers of clarity as your brain and body begin to purge the effects of the weed you've been smoking for the past two days. Then you'll realize that ol' Uncle Tom here was telling you the truth. You'll face a road with not two, but three forks in it. The first road has you doing five the hard way. The second has your dead little ass lying on a slab in the Medical Examiner's Office—just like Junebug—while we try to figure out who wanted to keep your mouth shut. The third road has you cooperating, and somebody else doing the hard time.

"So for now, and the balance of the weekend, considering that this is Friday and the courts aren't open tomorrow, you'll be locked up. I encourage you to get a taste of what the next five years may be like for you. You'll get your three hots and a cot, and Monday you can talk to your *appointed* attorney. After that, when you're ready, we'll listen to your story." Carter turned and tapped on the door to the room, at which point a uniformed officer appeared.

"Please take Mr. Fellows to lockup, Officer. He'll be going to federal court on a criminal complaint on Monday morning."

"He lawyered up…" Ramirez explained, "Even after Dark-tor Phil here gave him the old Three Roads speech and a free sociology lesson."

"Only after *you'd* had an entire hour with him through processing and printing," countered Carter. "I correctly deduced that he wasn't going to tell us anything if he hadn't already surrendered to your legendary powers of Latin persuasion."

"Easy, ladies, before I refer you both to remedial race-relations training. I'm almost done with this thing." Lassiter tapped a few more times on the keyboard in front of him, took a final glance at the monitor, and then hit Print. "Here's your complaint and affidavit. I'm afraid you drew Chief Magistrate Judge Noble today."

"Wonderful," gasped Ramirez, rolling his eyes skyward. "We've got about a 1 percent chance of detention now." Any officer who ever worked federal cases knew of the chief magistrate's reluctance to keep an offender incarcerated prior to trial. Ramirez shot another look at his partner. "Are you sure you saw that kid talkin' to Junebug?"

"The more I think about it, the more certain I am, Bob." Carter intentionally directed his remarks to Lassiter.

"I hope so. Otherwise this is probably a waste of time." Lassiter looked at a duty schedule on his computer calendar. "A new AUSA in the federal drug unit will be handling the complaint process and the detention hearing; he just moved up from felony trial..."

"Jeff Trask?" Ramirez asked hopefully.

"No, not quite yet, although it shouldn't take him long to get here now." Lassiter suppressed a smile. It was never a bad sign when the better cops on the street agreed with his assessment of a prosecutor's potential.

"The new guy's name is Ben Prescott. Just got here. He's politically connected, but he did OK in felony trial in superior court." Lassiter fudged the evaluation upward a bit, reasoning that even the U.S. attorney's political pet deserved an honest chance to succeed. He looked up at Carter. "Let me know how he does with your hearing."

"Thanks again for the help," Carter nodded to Lassiter, accepting the paperwork as he rose from the chair. "We'll work it hard."

"Not a problem, guys, you always do."

They left Lassiter's office, waved to Bill Patrick as they passed his open door, and turned into the office of Benjamin G. Prescott, Assistant United States Attorney, whose name and title were now prominently displayed on plastic inserts in the two-by-eight-inch metal slots on the hallway wall by his door. Carter knocked, and the bearded figure behind the desk looked up.

"Yes?"

"Mr. Prescott, my name is Dixon Carter and this is my partner, Juan Ramirez. We're both detectives from 7D. Mr. Lassiter told us to see you about getting this complaint filed. We know it's a bit of a long shot, but we were also hoping to get the defendant detained. He's currently in custody."

Prescott rose and shook hands, without mentioning his own name. It was, after all, on the door, and he assumed that these police officers could at least read. Carter noted that the handshake he was offered was limp—the fingers of Prescott's hand long, thin, and weak. The attorney took the affidavit and complaint and began scrutinizing them, silently motioning the officers to sit as he sat down into a leather swivel chair. Carter and Ramirez shot looks at each other with raised eyebrows, both recognizing that the furniture in the office was not standard Government Issue. It had obviously been personally selected and purchased by the new occupant of the room.

Prescott was tall and thin, with a long neck and narrow shoulders. Carter figured that the beard had been intended to achieve some appearance of an additional degree of masculinity. The hair above the beard was thin and the same mousey-brown in color, parted high on the head. The suit Prescott was wearing was a navy, high-quality, tailored job, which had to have set him back a thousand bucks or more. The shirt was not the usual cotton-blend oxford seen on most of the prosecutors in the office, but a pinpoint, also very expensive. The tie was a traditional pattern, diagonal stripe, mostly hidden by a cashmere cardigan sweater. Although the shoes were concealed behind the substantial mahogany desk, Carter placed a bet with himself that they were expensive and banker-toed. He stood up, ostensibly to read the large, oak-framed law school diploma on the wall to the left of the desk.

"Yale Law. Very impressive." Carter turned toward the desk, and was able to see that his guess regarding the footwear had been correct. He also saw that Ramirez was suppressing his gag reflex at the obvious suck up.

"Yes. Thank you. Third generation, actually." The tone in Prescott's voice was more genuine than it had been previously. "Detective…"

"Carter."

"Yes. This affidavit mentions only a single ounce of PCP."

"And a loaded handgun, and resisting arrest." Ramirez added.

"That may be the case," Prescott frowned, "but I see from the case number that the complaint has been drawn by Judge Noble…"

"We know it's a long shot, Counselor." Carter responded. "We have reason to believe that the defendant knows something about the murder of one of our informants."

"Can you prove that?"

"Not yet. We were hoping that with some detention time, we could persuade him to cooperate."

"I see." Prescott's tone was dismissive. He was dealing with local police officers on a street-level case, a nuisance to be suffered for the time being. He reasoned that it was a time-filler assigned to him by Lassiter until management could find the right project for him—one with real federal agents, a large number of defendants, and the potential for media publicity. "Well, we have an appointment with Judge Noble in twenty minutes. I'll see you there, and we'll ask for detention."

Carter and Ramirez nodded, rose, and left the office.

"Nice of him to offer to walk with us, wasn't it?" Ramirez asked, as they headed southward on a Fourth Street sidewalk toward the federal courthouse about three blocks away.

Carter chuckled. "When we get our summer homes in the Hamptons, I'm sure Mister Prescott and his friends will welcome us with open arms."

"Yeah. I'll be welcome to cut his shrubs and you can be his butler. Look at that." Ramirez pointed to a Mercedes passing them, driven by none other than Benjamin G. Prescott, who was speaking on a cell phone. "Where the hell is he going to park?"

"I have no idea. No one from the U.S. Attorney's Office has a space down there. Maybe we can see where he *thinks* he can park after he's driven a whole hundred yards."

They quickened their pace and reached the concrete wall overlooking the parking lot in the back of the courthouse just as Prescott's Mercedes completed the three-block drive, turning into the east gate of the lot. The spaces facing the rear wall of the courthouse were marked with Reserved signs, each showing the three initials of one of the federal district judges or magistrates assigned to the United States District Court for the District of Columbia, or one of the appellate judges of the Court of Appeals for the District of Columbia Circuit. Prescott's Mercedes proceeded slowly along the row, until a figure in a navy blazer emerged and motioned for the car to take a vacant space. Prescott left the vehicle, handed the man what appeared to be a bill of United States currency, then followed him into the rear door of the court house.

"I didn't know the courtroom security guys were offering valet service, did you?" Ramirez asked sarcastically.

"Judge Owens is out of town this week." Carter pulled out a small memo pad from his suit coat, and made note of the date and time. "At some point, I think he may be interested to know that someone was subletting his parking space in his absence."

They met Prescott at the hallway door leading to the chambers of Chief Magistrate Judge Thomas Noble. Carter pushed the intercom button before Prescott could do the same, letting the attorney know that he—the mere police officer—had done this before. The law clerk inside knew The Twins' faces when she saw them on the security monitor, and buzzed them in. Carter and Ramirez immediately made themselves at home by taking seats on a sofa in the outer room, while Prescott stood awkwardly in front of the clerk's desk, offering the complaint and affidavit to her in a halting motion.

"Oh, the judge will take that when he's ready for you," she said. "Have a seat by the detectives there, and I'll let you know when to go in."

"Of course." Prescott nodded officially, then sat in an armchair across from the sofa.

"How are your babies, Anne?" Carter smiled as the clerk smiled back at him. Prescott was now frozen uncomfortably in his chair as his command of the situation gradually evaporated.

"Just fine, thanks. Bonnie turns two next week."

"Already? Seems like you just had your first a couple of months ago. Bonnie's the baby isn't she?"

"Yes. Brenda's four now."

"Time flies." Carter shook his head, smiling again.

She looked down at a phone on her desk as a red light on one of the office lines went dark.

"The judge can see you now. Go right on in."

Carter and Ramirez beat Prescott to the door and introduced him to the judge. Thomas Noble was on his second eight-year term as a United States magistrate judge, having been hired by the judges of the United States District Court some ten years earlier. Prior to taking his current post, he had served as an AUSA himself, and had worked a case or two brought in by a young detective named Dixon Carter.

"Good to see you again, DC, Juan." Noble shook hands with both Carter and Ramirez, temporarily ignoring the papers offered by Prescott. "How are things in Anacostia these days?"

"Busy as usual, Judge." Carter made sure he used the title whenever he addressed the chief magistrate, both to signal respect for the position, and because he was aware that Magistrate Noble had spent a good bit of the last ten years lobbying unsuccessfully to secure a district court appointment, that is, to become a "real federal judge." Since the District of Columbia—unlike any of the fifty states—had no senators, however, the good magistrate had found himself without any effective political sponsor, and the dreams he had once entertained of using the magistrate position as a stepping-stone to the higher bench were fading away.

"Aren't we all?" Noble scanned the complaint affidavit, then looked up at Prescott with a scowl. "One ounce of wet is now a *federal* case?"

"I had exactly the same reservations, Judge..." Prescott attempted to defend himself.

"We know it's a bit of a stretch, Your Honor," Carter interjected, darting a warning glance at Prescott, "but there's good reason to believe that this case may be related to a homicide—a murder of one of our informants."

"There's nothing in your affidavit about that."

"I know that, Judge. It's circumstantial at this point, and wouldn't have made any difference in your determination of probable cause for the PCP or the gun charge, but it *is* the investigative reason why we took this to Mr. Lassiter and asked him to process it federally."

"I see." The magistrate skimmed the affidavit again, shrugged his shoulders, and then signed the complaint. "There is probable cause, and there *are* violations of federal law, although I'm not sure it's the appropriate use of resources or an appropriate choice of forum." He looked up again at Prescott. "I'll call Bob Lassiter about this myself. You have your complaint, Mr. Prescott, and I know it probably wasn't your decision to bring it here, but you'd be well advised not to waste my time with a detention hearing on something this minor. Our holding facilities are full of much more deserving defendants."

"I had no intention of doing so, Judge," Prescott said, shaking his head as to indicate that he would never have contemplated such heresy. He did not notice the glances that immediately passed between Carter and Ramirez.

"Good. I'll see you in the courtroom shortly for the initial appearance. The marshals are done processing your defendant, and I am told that his retained counsel is present."

"If I might ask, Judge..." Carter did his best to speak matter-of-factly, hiding the surprise in his voice, "Who is Mr. Fellows paying to represent him?"

"I was surprised to see that he had retained an attorney, myself." Noble nodded. "I was prepared to appoint counsel, since the intake interview indicated the defendant had no financial resources. The young man must have a friend or family member with money, because a member of the bar entered his appearance a few minutes ago. I haven't actually seen the paperwork yet, so we'll find out together in the courtroom."

The magistrate's courtroom was a duplicate of those used by the district court judges, with several rows of pews, hewn from oak, facing the well of the courtroom. Two large counsel tables faced the elevated mahogany bench, from which the judge could look down upon the proceedings. Huge, New Deal era chandeliers lit the room.

"Wonder how much it costs the public to heat and cool these monsters," mused Ramirez. He and Carter had taken their customary places on the first of the pews in the spectator section, immediately behind the counsel table where Prescott was now seated.

"Just another monument to the federal judiciary," Carter responded. "You didn't really think a federal judge's ego would fit in a room without a forty-foot ceiling, did, you?" Carter nodded toward a very well dressed black gentleman in his late thirties, who was seated at the counsel table across from the one occupied by Prescott. "You know the mouthpiece?"

"I've seen him over in super court. Can't remember the name. Never had a case with him."

A side door opened into the well of the courtroom, and two deputy US marshals escorted Ronald Fellows to the table occupied by the defense counsel. Fellows was restrained by both handcuffs and leg irons, and was wearing a bright-orange prison jumpsuit. He shot a look of contempt in Carter's direction, an obvious repudiation of Carter's prophecy that only a public defender or appointed counsel would show up for the defense. Fellows and the attorney reviewed the complaint and affidavit for a moment, and the lawyer nodded to the courtroom clerk, who pressed a button at her desk.

"ALL RISE."

Another door opened into the courtroom, this time from a rear hallway that ran between the courtroom and the chambers of the chief magistrate. Noble, wearing his black robe of office, strode briskly to his bench and took his seat. He then looked up and instructed all others present to be seated.

"Counsel, please state your appearances."

"May it please the Court, Benjamin Prescott for the United States."

"Thank you, Mr. Prescott."

"Spencer Goode appearing for the defendant Ronald Fellows, who appears in person and in custody, Your Honor. I have reviewed the complaint and affidavit with my client, and we waive formal reading of the affidavit and the complaint."

"Thank you, Mr. Goode. That will save us some time."

"Mr. Fellows..." Noble looked at the defendant, who—on cue from his counsel—stood up when he was addressed. "You may remain seated for the balance of these proceedings." Fellows sat down again, scowling at his lawyer for the inconvenience.

"The purpose of this hearing is to advise you of the charges brought against you in a criminal complaint filed today by the United States. That complaint is in two counts. Count One charges a violation of Title 21, United States Code, Sections 841(a)(1) and 841(b)(1)(c), that is, an allegation that you did, on the date alleged, in the District of Columbia, knowingly and wrongfully possess, with the intent to distribute, some amount of a mixture and substance containing a detectable quantity of phencyclidine, or PCP. Count Two alleges a violation of Title 18, United States Code, Section 924c, and states that on the same date, in the District of Columbia, you did—in furtherance of the drug-trafficking offense alleged in Count One—carry a firearm.

"The maximum penalties you would face upon conviction of these offenses are as follows: For Count One, not more than twenty years imprisonment, a fine of not more than one-million dollars, a term of supervised release—following your release from prison—of not less than three years, and a statutory assessment of one hundred dollars. Count Two carries a minimum penalty of five years imprisonment, to run *consecutively.* That means in addition to any sentence of imprisonment adjudged for Count One. A fine of not more than two hundred fifty thousand dollars, a term of supervised release of three years, and a statutory, one-hundred dollar assessment."

"Do you understand the charges against you and the penalties which could result from those charges?"

"Yeah." Fellows took a discreet shot in the rib from his attorney, smirked, and then said, "Yes, Your Honor."

"Very well. The United States is not requesting detention in this matter; that is, they are not asking that you be held without bond. Accordingly, I am setting your bond at ten thousand dollars, on a promise that you will return to court as instructed for any future appearances. You will not be required to post any cash, but you could be ordered to forfeit that amount if you fail to appear for future court hearings, or if you refuse to abide the conditions of release which I am setting today. Do you understand that?"

"Yes, Your Honor."

"Very well. Those conditions are set forth in a written order which will be explained to you by your pre-trial services officer, a member of this court's probation office. Generally, you are to commit no other offenses of a local, state, or federal nature; you are not to consume any controlled substances or alcohol; you are required to seek employment, and to abide by all other conditions in my order. Failure to comply with those conditions may result in the revocation of your release status and the forfeiture of your bond."

"Unless either party has something else, I'll see you all back for the preliminary hearing on Thursday at 10:00 a.m. The defendant is released, and these proceedings are adjourned."

"ALL RISE."

Prescott took his time getting back to his office, pausing for a few minutes in the courthouse hallway to speak—and flirt—with an attractive young reporter for the *Post* whom he'd met at a party a week or so before, and who had seemed appropriately impressed by his status. The same matter that had previously seemed so minimal to the chief magistrate had suddenly become a very serious case, meriting considerable explanation to an inquiring mind.

Prescott took the elevator up to the fifth floor after parking the Mercedes, and as the doors opened on the floor, saw the doors closing on an elevator directly across the hallway, an elevator occupied by Detectives Carter and Ramirez, both of whom simply nodded at him. He was walking past Lassiter's office toward his own when he was summoned.

"Ben, in here. Now, please." Lassiter sounded anything but pleased.

"What's up?" Prescott didn't know exactly why he was about to be dressed down, but knew it was coming, and tried to appear as innocent and nonchalant as possible.

"Why didn't you move for detention at the initial appearance on Mr. Fellows?"

Prescott attempted to shrug off the inquiry, despite the piercing gaze in which Lassiter now had him locked.

"Judge Noble basically told me that he wouldn't rule in our favor, and that I'd be wasting time with the hearing. In addition, I didn't want to sacrifice my credibility with him for future—"

"You'd better be more concerned with your future credibility with me and within this office," Lassiter interjected. "I told you when I handed you the file to move for detention, and Dixon Carter told me that he repeated that request when he met with you before the hearing."

"Well, I thought that the judge's remarks to me after reading the complaint kind of changed the situation regarding your instructions, and as far as Detective Carter is concerned, I'm not aware that he ever graduated from law school."

Lassiter shot up from his chair, was at the door to the office in four quick strides, and slammed it hard. "Sit down, *Mister* Prescott."

The younger man sank slowly into one of the side chairs, surprised by the fury in his superior's voice.

"Since *you are* a graduate of a fine law, school, I'm *sure* you are familiar with all the parameters of the federal detention statute. What are the two grounds upon which we can ask for pre-trial incarceration?"

"W-well," Prescott began to stammer, but quickly caught himself. "If the defendant is likely to flee—and we had no evidence of that—he can be locked down, and…I think that's the main point."

"That's one of two grounds. The other inquiry happens to be whether the defendant is a danger to the community. What is the statutory presumption regarding that test? And don't try to bluff if you don't know the answer."

Prescott paused. "I guess I don't."

"It's very *apparent* that you don't. Even an ounce of PCP in a distribution charge carries a presumption—mandated by Congress—that detention is appropriate because that offense is a drug-trafficking crime carrying a maximum penalty of ten years or more. In this case it's twenty, and there's a consecutive five-year gun charge to boot. That presumption—and the balance of the statute—state that when we ask for detention at an initial appearance, and when we ask for a continuance of that hearing, the court is *required* to give us a delay in the hearing, not to exceed three days. During those three days, the defendant gets locked up. Even if we lose the hearing later, that's up to three days we get to try and get a handle on a situation like this. If we fail to ask for that hearing and that delay, *as you did today*, we waive our right to ever seek it again in this case, unless the defendant violates his bail conditions."

"Judge Noble said…"

"I don't give a *happy damn* what the head of our junior varsity judiciary whispered in your ear today, Mister." Lassiter's voice was not raised, but measured. "Dixon Carter may not be an attorney, but I guarantee that if I had asked him the same questions which I just asked you, the answers would have been correct. Hell, he could probably have quoted the statute to me, *verbatim*. More important, it is his professional opinion—*one which I value a helluva lot more than yours*—that this kid is likely to end up getting killed by whoever paid for that defense attorney, in order to keep him from flapping his gums about his dope supplier, who has already probably killed one of our informants."

"I didn't know..."

"And didn't bother to find out, or to listen, or to follow instructions. We have a separation of powers in this country. The courts have their job to do, and we have ours. Far too often, they get to tell us what to do and when, but the judges know that the line exists, and most stay on their side of it. I'm not about to start giving them the ground that we still own. The real bottom line here is that you didn't want to be barked at by a freaking magistrate judge who had no discretion to deny your request—*had you made it as instructed*—and your concern about your future credibility may well result in somebody *dying* in the next couple of days. That's what this job is about, Ben. *It is not about you.* The next time I tell you to do something, I expect it to be done, and the next time you feel yourself about to disagree with Dix Carter, you see me first before you do something as stupid as you did today. *Do you understand me?*"

"Yes."

"Shut the door behind you."

Prescott rose and walked out. Lassiter's eyes followed him, still burning. The door closed.

"Idiot," Lassiter said under his breath.

Spencer Goode, Esquire, dialed the number on his cell phone from memory as he pulled the Acura away from the courthouse.

"Yeah, mon."

"He'll be out in an hour. They didn't even try to keep him locked up. Probably think he's just a punk kid out selling wet, which is what they got him for—that and a gun."

"What kinda time is he lookin' at?"

"At least five years if convicted, and that's if the judge doesn't give him anything for the dope."

"Hmm. Okay. T'anks for handlin' dis, mon."

"You got what you paid for. See you soon."

Chapter Nine

"So how was the first day in felonies?" Lynn reached around his shoulders and kissed him on the cheek as he sat in the apartment's living room, reading over a stack of trial folders.

"Not too bad, actually—at least it's a major improvement over the misdemeanor bullpen."

"Good. Tell me about it."

"Well, for starters, we each actually have an office. There are four of us on each trial team—myself, Tim, a guy named Clark Becker, and Kathy Tapp…"

"Kathy?" She asked pointedly.

"Yes, Kathy." Trask chuckled. "She's actually quite cute—a little blonde, if you must know, and…"

"And what?" Lynn interrupted, feigning an icy tone.

"And we have a secretary?" Trask tried to continue the skit with a straight face, but lost the attempt and began to crack up.

"What does *she* look like?"

"Maybe you better read me my rights." Trask laughed. "Actually, Kathy is head over heels in love with a detective on the metropolitan police force. Why, I'm not sure, since no self-respecting prosecutor should be caught dead being romantically involved with an investigator."

"Keep it up, smart ass."

"Okay, our secretary looks like she's about fifty."

"Great!" Lynn heaved an exaggerated sigh of mock relief, and sat on the coffee table facing him. "What's the work like?"

"About the same drill as in misdemeanors, with all the stakes raised. More serious cases, of course, with fifteen scheduled for trial every week. The judge gave Tim and me a pass today, since it was our first day on her docket. She's already in trial on another matter through Thursday, so we can get used to the place until Friday. I have a good idea which one I'll have to try then." Trask held up the file he'd been reading, and arched his left eyebrow. "A burglary of an upscale, Georgetown fur coat boutique by a ruffian named Derrick Vest."

"Oooh, boutiques and ruffians always get my attention. What's your *judge* look like, since you said 'her docket'?"

"The Honorable Edie King is fortyish, smart as a whip, tough as nails, darker than any black woman I've ever seen, and married to a *retired* detective."

"What is it with all you legal types and us investigative types?"

"I guess we're all just cop groupies at heart..." Trask arched the eyebrow again, "Or maybe it's the other way around..."

"Guilty in this case." She bent over and kissed him again.

"Both of us," he smiled. "Has to be a conspiracy."

"But you like your judge?"

"Yes, I think Lassiter's still looking out for us. When we told folks that we were going to Judge King's trial docket, they asked us who we had bribed or had dirt on. I watched her do a probation revocation sentencing hearing today—some habitual car thief that another judge had put back on the street after his second conviction. He got caught trying to steal another car while serving his probation. The clown's lawyer starts the usual violin strings—broken home, bad neighborhood, disadvantaged youth—Judge King cuts him off at the knees.

"She says, 'I grew up in that neighborhood, Mr. Levine. It's not a bad neighborhood. It's got a few problems like your client, who just keep choosing to commit crimes.' Then she gave him sixteen years. Maxed him. He'll probably just serve five or six, of course, given the overcrowding in Lorton, but he got what he deserved today."

"I'm glad you drew a good one, babe. I know how hard it is for you to work around a bad judge."

"Yep, it's always the wild card in the deck when you're trying to put a trial together. If you have a judge who's even-handed and goes by the rulebook—the rules of evidence—you can plan the case fairly well. In Superior Court, the rules of evidence seem to be whatever the individual judge wants them to be. We're in a federal jurisdiction, but most of our local judges seem intent on seceding from anything related to the federal government, and refuse to use the federal rules. Judge King told us that she generally uses the federal rules, so it's good not to have to worry about that for a few months."

"How's the burglary case look?"

"Kind of tough, actually." Trask's voice dropped to a sober, thoughtful tone. "The guy has a record, but not an especially bad one. A shoplifting beef two years ago. I'm not sure if we'll be allowed to bring that up. Nobody saw the actual break-in at the furrier. A cinder block was thrown through the display window, and about seventeen grand worth of mink and chinchilla got hauled out. Five different police units rolled on the thing; it happened at two in the morning last Thanksgiving while nothing else was going on in Georgetown. The cops in one car see our defendant just walking up the street as they roll in to respond to the alarm, lights on and siren blaring. They detain him, backtrack toward the store from the spot where they found him, and find the coats stashed between two parked cars on the street."

"No other witnesses at all?"

"That's my other problem." Trask thumbed through the case jacket, stopping when he located the statement. "Mr. Howard Denton claims he saw someone run by him with his arms full of fur coats, and haul ass in the direction of where the coats were recovered. Mr. Denton, however, is one of the city's homeless, and is legally blind without his glasses. He was lying on a sewer grate, sleeping off a bottle of rotgut wine when he noticed the thief run by with the coats. Mr. Denton also says that the lower half of the crook's face was obscured by the bundle of coats as he ran by. The thief's clothes—as described by Mr. Denton—matched those worn by Mr. Vest, but aren't really that distinctive—blue jeans and a dark-colored hoodie."

"Will this homeless guy even show up to testify?"

"The cop I spoke to on the phone this afternoon was able to find him at a shelter and serve the subpoena. He said that the witness fee of $28.50 would keep Mr. Denton in wine and grub for at least a couple of days, and that he thought our star witness would certainly be in court on Wednesday."

She sat on his lap and kissed him on the forehead.

"If anybody can do this one, you can."

"Thanks, but place no bets. I plan on driving out there tomorrow to look over the scene. Want to do lunch in G-town?"

"Make it dinner. I already have a working lunch tomorrow. Can we do something French?"

"Of course."

"I meant dinner, you dirty old man."

"Damn. I suppose so. I've heard some good things about a place on M Street. It might even be better to see the area at night; it'll be close to the same lighting conditions that confronted our Mr. Denton."

"Great. It's a date." She grabbed her bag and headed for the door.

"You're leaving this early?" Trask had become accustomed to her staying at his place most evenings. He got up and followed her to the door.

"As long as I actually have a separate address, I feel compelled to clean the joint at least once a month, and to pay some bills. I'll see you tomorrow night… for the French *food*." She kissed him and headed for her car. Trask watched from the doorway until she started the engine and backed out. The safety monitoring wasn't lost on her.

"Thanks, and I love you, but I'm a big girl, and a trained killer," she admonished from the driver's window.

"I love you, too, but there are big boys out there who might not respect your training. Be careful."

She smiled and drove away.

———

"That was phenomenal!" Lynn gushed, holding his hand as they walked eastward on M Street toward Wisconsin Avenue.

"Glad you liked it, although I wish you liked the wine more. It really was a very good pinot."

"I'm sure it was, babe. I'm just a girly-wine drinker, though. Light and fruity whites, nothing dry at all. One glass of a red of any sort is about all I can do."

"Well, you're driving home then. I had four glasses to your one. I wasn't about to leave any of that bottle on the table. I'll just call it case research, since

I'm about in the same condition as Mr. Denton when he saw our defendant whiz past him."

They turned north on Wisconsin, walking up to the victimized establishment on the east side of the avenue. The broken plate-glass window had long since been replaced, as it had taken the usual months for the case to wind its way through the processing stops at Trask's place of employment. The file had crept through felony papering, screening by supervisors, the superior court grand jury, then to one Robert Lassiter, who had seen fit to send the puzzle to the desk now occupied by Trask. The sign above the storefront was rendered to attract clients of taste—and considerable financial means—into *Currier's Furriers.* Lynn rolled her eyes and pretended to stick her finger down her throat when she saw the marquee.

"How can anyone selling this stuff come up with something that corny?" She was gazing at a prominently displayed, full-length mink, which could be hers for a mere half-year's salary.

"The bigger question is how they could stay in business in a liberal arts college town like this without having animal rights types throwing red paint all over the place every other evening." Trask pointed toward two security cameras pointed down at them from the corners on the inside of the display windows. "Maybe those have some deterrent effect, after all."

"I'm sure the bucks coughed up by the senators' wives and other society matrons keep them afloat." Lynn was still shaking her head, looking at the mink. "For the record, I never want one of those."

"Rats. I'll return it tomorrow, then. You're getting very hard to shop for." Trask was still looking hard at the cameras. "I wonder if those were working on Thanksgiving morning. Let's step inside for a minute."

They were greeted stuffily by a woman in her late thirties who was fashionably rail-thin, and who had correctly guessed that they were not casually dressed trust fund babies or internet moguls there to make a major purchase. Lynn surmised that she was a failed runway model who had latched onto this career in some hope of remaining chic. After flashing his credentials, Trask asked for, and was introduced to the manager, who explained that the security cameras had been functioning on the night of the burglary, but that he had forgotten to rewind the videotape on the surveillance recorder. There was no film for evidence. This had all been explained to the detective in a previous interview, the gentleman said. He had received a trial subpoena to testify, and assured Trask that he would appear to establish the monetary worth of the stolen property, which he had itemized for the initial police report.

"It was worth a shot," Trask said, as they left the store and continued northward on Wisconsin.

"Didn't the detective who took the complaint mention the cameras in his report?" Lynn asked. "Seems pretty slipshod if he didn't."

"Not that I recall."

"If *you* don't recall, then it wasn't there. I remember going over my own reports with you before trial. You knew them as well as I did, sometimes better. I think you have an obscenely photographic memory," she paused, "which makes it a *pornographic* memory."

"Only where you're concerned," Trask laughed. "And I plan on loading up that database until it's full. We need to turn right here."

They headed eastward, stopping at a steaming sewer vent in the sidewalk on the south side of Oak Alley.

"This would have been Mr. Denton's bedroom during the early hours of Thanksgiving morning. A poor man's space heater on a cold night." Trask stopped to note the illumination provided by the security lights of a furniture store on the corner. "Enough light to see pretty well here, even after guzzling a bottle of fine French wine—or maybe two bottles of cheap hooch, given an alcoholic's tolerance for the stuff."

He paced a deliberate number of feet down the block, stopping to mentally note the location where the furs had been dumped along the curb, and then walked an additional distance to approximate the location of the arrest of Derrick Vest.

"I have the feeling I'm still overlooking something," he said, turning to take in the scene in each direction.

"A very smart young JAG once told me that when he felt that way, he needed to get his head out of the paper—off the report pages." Lynn was standing in front of him now. She reached up, took his face in her hands, and kissed him. "Remember the Henry case at Shaw?"

"Sure, the Airman who was selling dope for his father in Chicago. Why?"

"Remember how he was wiring money to his dad for the cocaine shipments?"

"Of course."

"I remember this bright young JAG gently reading a fairly senior OSI agent—one of my co-case agents—the riot act for only checking the Western Union office on base, when there were two other Western Union offices off-base, within a ten-minute drive. I remember that bright young JAG putting the OSI agent in a car, driving to one of those off-base offices with a photo of Airman Henry, and walking out with copies of about twenty money wires, all addressed to Henry's dear old dad."

Trask chuckled. "I'd forgotten about that."

"You shouldn't have. It was a helluva lesson for him. He'd gotten lazy, just for a moment, and you showed him up. So get your head out of those half-written police reports, and see what went down here."

Trask smiled at her, took her hand and walked back to the corner of Oak Alley and Wisconsin. They turned north again on Wisconsin, walking about half a block to the point where Prospect Street approached Wisconsin from the west, teeing into the avenue. Trask looked back southward toward the fur store. A smile crossed his face, and he hugged her shoulders with his right arm.

"Thanks for the jolt. I *was* getting paper-bound."

"What did you figure out?"

"I'm not sure, yet—need to check some things at the office tomorrow—but I think I do have another card or two to play now."

Trask had heard about the Friday Panels before, but nothing could have prepared him for the spectacle assembled in the rear of Judge King's courtroom. Called in on the previous Monday for a week of jury duty in the so-called Superior Court of the District of Columbia, the seventy-five citizens now sitting in what would later be the spectators' section were not readily subject to any description. They had, after all, been part of an initial call of about five hundred, but unlike their counterparts who had either been selected to serve in another case, or permanently excused for some emergency, these residents had been rejected in courtroom after courtroom, and then told to return to the main jury room for the next panel call. They were the worst of the worst, the dregs of the barrel, and any sentiment of dutiful public service which they might have initially felt had long since been eroded by the inconvenience of their week-long wait.

He looked at the jury list provided by the clerk of the court. The information for each prospective juror was limited to the area of the city in which the panelist resided, his or her occupation, age, and any spouse's occupation. Trask looked back and forth from the list to the rear of the courtroom, displaying as pleasant a demeanor as he could while assigning names to faces. He saw that the thirty-sixth juror in order was a nineteen-year-old young woman named Melissa Stark, who was *at least* eight-months pregnant, and who had chosen to wear to court a long, white T-shirt which boldly proclaimed to the world, "I Got Screwed." Beneath this message was a wide, black arrow pointing downward toward that part of Ms. Stark's anatomy where the proclaimed event had occurred.

Trask made a note to save a peremptory challenge, if he could, to spare Ms. Stark the trouble of serving on the jury. He reasoned that voir dire, the process of jury screening, was often an application of stereotypes, sometimes accurate, sometimes not, but that Ms. Stark's attire could very easily be a comment on her lack of respect for the judicial system. There were days when he probably shared her opinion, of course, but he could not take a chance that such an attitude might have arisen from a totally anti-law enforcement bias.

He thought to himself that anyone who still used the phrase *jury selection* had to be an idiot. Any of the prospective panelists who ended up being sworn in were often the unfortunate remnants after the worst of the lot had been eliminated, either through a challenge "for cause," based upon some bias or stated inability to follow the applicable law, or through a peremptory challenge, exercised by the attorneys in the case for virtually any reason whatsoever. Trask knew he would have to treasure and spend his peremptories wisely on this occasion. He—like the defense—had only ten.

Those precious ten disappeared in no time. Six prospective jurors hinted strongly that they would not trust the prosecution or believe a police officer under most circumstances, although they said they would be able to set aside such an opinion and be fair to both sides. Two others looked so incoherent as to be qualified for immediate commitment to a psych ward. One didn't know her own name, and another snarled at Trask like a rabid dog before he could be asked anything. The defense also exercised its ten peremptories rather quickly, and following the excusal of four other panel members for cause, Trask watched in horror as Melissa Stark was seated as the twelfth and final juror for the trial.

The proof in the prosecution's case went in very smoothly thanks to quick, accurate, and decisive rulings on some defense objections by Judge King. The high point had been the testimony of Howard Denton, who surprised everyone in the courtroom, including Trask, by making a persuasive, in-court identification of the defendant Derrick Vest, despite not having been able to do so when he was showed a photo spread by the police the day after the robbery. Mr. Denton had slowly explained that the photographs he had initially seen displayed the entire faces of six people. He didn't know the defendant's face, but he could recognize Derrick Vest's eyes.

Trask then had little choice but to ask why the eyes of the defendant were so remarkable, and his witness had then explained—after an objection by the defense had been overruled by Judge King—that he always studied a man's eyes very closely, because he had been kicked and beaten up dozens of time, being a homeless man and all, and Derrick Vest's eyes "looked angry." Besides, the fur coats Vest had been carrying had covered up only the bottom of his face.

The defense had then stressed—in a lengthy cross-examination of Mr. Denton—that he was elderly, intoxicated, living on the street, and blind as a bat. The attorney for Derrick Vest would have been well advised to have stopped at that point, but could not resist one additional question.

"Mr. Denton, with all due respect, being seventy-two years old, visually impaired, having downed two liters of wine, and waking up late that night, I just have to ask, how far can you actually see under those conditions?"

"I had my glasses on, sonny," came the answer, "and I can see to the moon, which is ninety-thousand miles away."

The outbreak of laughter from the jury box gave Trask some reason for hope. The jury had obviously enjoyed the fact that Howard Denton had handed a lawyer his head. The final exhibit Trask offered was a street map of the area, which was apparently not threatening enough to merit a defense objection.

When it came time for closing argument, Trask summarized the evidence as briefly as he could, being careful not to overstate the reliability of Mr. Denton, or to oversell his evidence. He admitted that it was in large part a circumstantial case, but one that still called for a logical conclusion of the guilt of Derrick Vest on both counts—one of the burglary of the store by breaking into and entering the display window, the second of the grand larceny of the furs.

The defense waded in with both barrels blazing, railing at how outrageous it was that the case should have ever been brought by the prosecution, and speculating that any number of miscreants in the vicinity could have committed the crime, then escaped into the darkness leaving "poor Derrick in the wrong place at the wrong time." It was the exact argument that Trask had hoped that he might hear.

"Rebuttal, Mr. Trask?" Judge King asked.

"Thank you, your honor." Trask walked confidently to the center of the courtroom, carrying an easel, and his final exhibit—the map. "We are apparently looking for a phantom—or phantoms—in the darkness, folks. Remember the testimony." He put the poster-sized blow-up of the street map on the easel.

"The store alarm goes off at 2:04 a.m. The police dispatch call goes out over the radio one minute later. All the officers say it was a quiet night in Georgetown that Thanksgiving morning. They all rolled on the call immediately—had nowhere else to go—and all got to the location of the store within two minutes. They're all on patrol, all driving, and Georgetown isn't that big an area. They get there fast.

"Officer Watkins rolls eastward on M Street, and turns north on Wisconsin to get to the store." Trask took a felt-tip marker from his pocket, wrote a *W* on the map, then drew an arrow representing what had been Watkins' direction of travel. "Officer Watkins saw no one on the street.

"Officer Nealis comes westward on M Street, and also turns north on Wisconsin." Another arrow was drawn on the map, marked with an *N*. "Officer Nealis saw nobody, either on M Street or on Wisconsin. We know that whoever broke in and took the coats probably wasn't driving, since they would have been insane to commit this robbery and throw the loot out of their car window." Trask noticed a couple of jurors giggling at the thought—a good sign.

"Officer Roberson drives in eastward on Prospect, then turns south on Wisconsin. Nobody on the street there, either." Another arrow, another letter. "Sergeant Moyers comes in westward on Oak Alley, passes the intersection of Congress Court, and sees one person—one person only—walking eastward on Oak Alley, and trying to appear nonchalant as four police cruisers come in with their lights and sirens cranked up.

"The defendant, ladies and gentlemen, wants you to believe that he's innocent, and that his being here today is only because of speculation by the officers that he was the burglar, the thief. In fact, it is *the defendant* who speculates that it could have been 'any miscreants in the vicinity' who committed this crime. But *the evidence* is that there were no other miscreants in the vicinity. In fact, other than Mr. Denton and the defendant, there were no other *people* in the vicinity.

"The only miscreant who *was* there was Derrick Vest, the defendant, and between Mr. Vest and the store that's been robbed, the police find the coats stashed along the curb. Yes, Mr. Vest *was* in the wrong place at the wrong time *because he'd done the wrong thing.* If anyone else had been on the streets of Georgetown that morning, the officers—who just happened to converge on the site from every possible direction—would have seen them.

"Someone *was* there, of course, who saw something more. Mr. Denton, who admittedly is down on his luck, elderly, and homeless, but who can see to the moon...," Trask rubbed it in a bit, and saw the jurors grinning as he did so. "Mr. Denton saw something about five feet away. He saw the angry eyes of Derrick Vest as Mr. Vest ran by him, carrying the load of furs, which he had to stash when he saw the police cruisers approaching. Mr. Vest, ladies and gentlemen, is guilty."

Trask tried to lower the expectations of the arresting officers as they congratulated him on his presentation of the case, and waited on the jury to return with their verdict. He reminded them that it was still a thin prosecution, through no fault of their own. They hadn't selected a homeless, nearly blind drunk as their star witness; they took their witness as they found him. Still, old Mr. Denton had done pretty well on the stand, and things might go well. It was all now in the hands of a Friday jury. The jury was back in thirty-five minutes.

"Ladies and Gentlemen, I have reviewed your verdict form, and see that you have reached a unanimous verdict on each of the two counts," Judge King announced. "I'll ask the defendant and his counsel to rise." She nodded back toward the jury as Vest and his lawyer stood. The judge then returned her gaze to the jury box. "Would your foreperson please stand and read your verdicts?"

Trask's heart sank as Melissa Stark rose, and the bailiff returned the verdict form to her.

"We, the jury, unanimously find the defendant, Derrick Vest, *not guilty* of the crime of burglary in the first degree."

Yeah, yeah, Trask thought. *Nice set-up punch. Now hit me with your right.*

Vest and his lawyer were smiling, and the attorney was slapping his client on the back.

"Settle down gentlemen." Judge King admonished. She fixed her gaze squarely upon Trask, and he thought he saw a smile in her eyes. "How does the jury find on count two, Ms. Stark?"

"We the jury, unanimously find the defendant, Derrick Vest, *guilty* of the crime of larceny in the first degree."

Trask exhaled hard, then turned and saw that it was now four police officers who were backslapping in the rear of the courtroom.

"You gentlemen also need to control yourselves," Judge King warned, though not quite as sternly as before. "The jury is excused. Thank you for your service here today, folks. Mr. Vest, step back please." Two bailiffs cuffed the defendant and led him across the courtroom to a detention cell. "Sentencing will be set following the completion of a pre-sentence report. We're adjourned." The judge struck her gavel on the bench, and nodded with approval to Trask as she left the courtroom.

Trask hung around the courthouse lobby for a few minutes, as was his practice following a jury trial. It was never a bad idea to see if any jurors wished to talk with him about the case. It didn't take long for Melissa Stark to emerge from a hallway. She crossed the floor and shook his hand.

"Thanks for the hard work, Mr. Trask. I know you're wondering about the first count. We just had some folks who weren't willing to convict on that one because no one saw him throw the concrete block through the window. Since Mr. Denton saw him with the furs, we had an easier time on the second count."

"I figured that might be the reason," Trask lied, his brain almost short-circuiting as it tried to make sense of the verdict. "Good luck with your baby."

"Thank you very much. He might be born tonight, after all of this stress today."

Trask laughed. "It's a boy, then?"

"Yes. I'm going to have my hands full."

"You'll make it." Trask smiled, much more confident of that assertion than he would have been earlier.

Chapter Ten

Detective Dixon Carter watched intently as the assistant medical examiner carefully finished cutting the duct tape away from the head of the body in the morgue. Carter shook his head and walked out of the autopsy room, taking a final glimpse back at the partially decayed face of Ronald Fellows. Willie Sivella met him at the door.

"Where'd you find him?" Sivella could see that this killing bothered Carter a lot more than the usual murder.

"In another damn dumpster, this time in the park by the river." Carter referred to the park that ran along the eastern bank of the Anacostia. "Wrapped exactly like Junebug, with the duct tape covering his whole freakin' head. He was just eighteen, boss."

"Any leads at all from the crime scene?"

"Nothing physical. The only thing we got was an approximate date and time of death. The medical examiner's best guess is that he was killed sometime late Monday night or early Tuesday morning."

"The same night he was released on the complaint."

"Yeah. That worthless Prescott could have at least kept him alive a day or two longer by asking for detention…"

"Not your fault, Dix. You did your job. I already talked to Lassiter, and he's as pissed about it as you are. You need to focus now on the follow-up. Who found the kid in the dumpster?"

"A guy coaching a little league team that was practicing down there. He went over to the dumpster to toss something, and recognized the smell, said he knew the odor from his tour in the first Gulf War. He saw the long shape in the trash bags and cut a hole in one, saw the body, then called it in."

"Where's Ramirez?"

"We saw the kid leave the courthouse Monday. He got into a Capital City Cab. I wrote down the cab number. Juan's having the cab dispatch check the log to see where our young Mr. Fellows went after they let him out. It may mean something, may not, but I thought we'd borrow the van and set up on the place, wherever it is."

"Sure. Take it, as long as it's in town. If the cabbie took him out of the District, we'll have to clear it with their department. We can't be playing in somebody else's back yard without permission."

"Got it. Can we burn some overtime on it tonight?"

"Long as you can stay awake. Be careful."

Ramirez knocked on the office door, then opened it without waiting for permission to enter.

"A Caribbean restaurant on Fourteenth Northeast—The Caribe. Cab log says he went straight there after court, and the dispatcher said the cabbie had to wait for the fare while the kid went into the joint to get it."

"Good luck." Sivella flipped a set of keys to Carter as he stood up and followed Ramirez out of the office.

The 7D surveillance van was a marvel of technology and police deception, and one of the few pieces of equipment in Willie Sivella's fleet that was always ready, thanks to the personal intervention of the district's commander, who kept the keys in his desk to keep the asset from being used for anything other than essential, and selective, police work. The exterior had been intentionally "stressed" to convince any would-be car thieves that the van would not be worth their time. There were sections which had been spray painted over sloppily applied primer, there were strategically permitted areas of rust along the edges, and the tires had been similarly selected to have just enough tread to be functional, so that they would not be separate theft targets. It was still occasionally necessary for a shabbily dressed detective to emerge from the interior to chase away some tamperer in order to prevent the vehicle from ending up on blocks along a curb, but the thing looked bad enough on the whole to blend in with the other indigenous vehicles of southeast DC, and had not yet been burned as a police vehicle by overuse.

The inside—to the rear of the shabby curtains drawn closed behind the driver's and shotgun seats—was a different story. There was a computer station and digital communications center, a small refrigerator, and two comfortable captain's chairs. There were also one-way windows which appeared from the outside to have been blacked out, but through which the officers pulling surveillance duty could aim binoculars or a digital movie camera with infrared capability.

Dixon Carter sat in one of the captain's chairs, periodically peeking through the curtains toward the front of The Caribe, and—with the aid of a penlight—staring at photos of the discarded body of Ronald Fellows. The crime scene techs had photographed the dumpster when they arrived on the scene in Anacostia Park. Ramirez was watching the rear of the restaurant and had parked the van across the street from the entry to the alley that ran the length of the rear of the property. They'd been on the scene for more than two hours. It was approaching 9:00 p.m., and Ramirez was starting to wonder whether it had been a waste of time.

"Dinner crowd's thinning out. You ever eat here?"

"No. Why?"

"I just thought that being a cultured, adventurous dude-about-town, you'd have sampled some of (some of) this island food with Melody."

"Not yet," Carter said. "I prefer my chicken fried, not jerked. Did you get a title profile on this place?"

Ramirez reached for a folder and handed it forward, still looking through the window at the alley. "It's incorporated. Corporate president is some guy named Reid. No priors. You'll want to look at the name of the attorney for the corporation."

"Our friend Spencer Goode." Carter reached over and slapped his partner on the back. "I think we're in the right place."

"Maybe. I'm not seeing much sitting here on my ass all night. Want to go in?"

"No. If Mr. Goode's hanging out here tonight, he might recognize us from the hearing."

Carter handed the folder back to Ramirez. "Got any plans for the rest of the weekend?"

"Just Mass Sunday morning."

"You should try my church," Carter said. "Music's better. No Gregorian chants."

"Naah. I prefer my confessions to be private, not wailing on the front steps of the altar while all them sisters are carryin' on."

"The only time you've been to my church was at my wedding. We don't throw ourselves on the floor and all that crap. When we want to confess something, we talk directly to the man upstairs. We don't need to use a child molester as an intermediary."

"You're goin' to hell."

"Maybe. If I do, I'll meet several popes there."

"*What!?* Like who?"

"Several of them. Roderigo Borgia, for example."

"Never heard of him."

"That's because yours is the only church whose leader uses an alias."

"You're goin' to hell."

"Pope Alexander VI. Fathered Lucrezia Borgia and her brother Cesare with a mistress, partied a lot, and he and his rotten bastard kids poisoned and stabbed half of Italy."

"Baptist propaganda."

"History, you papist lackey. You'd know all this if your church allowed you to read for yourselves. Maybe you could buy a dispensation or something and they'd let you check a book out of the library."

"You're goin' to hell. Doesn't Notre Dame play Maryland this year? I hope they kick your butts."

"Oh, yeah. Like Ramirez is a good Irish name. Your dogma even tells you which football team you have to follow. The Terps are gonna roll those little nun-school boys up like a bad rug. I believe you better fear the turtle, baby."

"I believe in the one true church, asshole, the one founded around 33 AD, and not some new splinter sect. What do you believe in?"

"I believe *The Da Vinci Code* is historically accurate."

"You're goin' to hell. Wait a minute…" Ramirez nodded toward the alley. A panel truck had turned in behind the restaurant, stopping with its rear gate facing the surveillance van. "What's wrong with this picture?"

"Let me see, *Kingston Distributing Company, Fine Food and Beverages, Brooklyn, New York*." Carter read the sign on the lift gate just before it was rolled up by the driver, who began to unload small cases out of the rear of the truck. "I don't know what's wrong with this picture. What're you thinking?"

"That it's a helluva drive for a beer route. Know any other local restaurants supplied with beer directly from New York City?"

"No. What kind of beer is it?"

"That Jamaican stuff. Red Stripe. He's got about twelve cases out of the truck. Cans."

"Red Stripe in cans? I've only seen it in the brown bottles around here. I saw it in cans when Mel and I took that trip to London last year, but I…hold it." Carter flipped through the photos showing the body of Ronald Fellows in the Anacostia Park dumpster. "Look at this one."

"What, the body?"

"No! There to the right, about a foot from the head."

Ramirez took the 8 x 12 print and examined it. The photograph showed the body, wrapped in two large trash bags, sealed at the center with a roll of duct tape, and lying among the refuse of several picnics. Several inches to the right of the bag that contained the head and shoulders of Ronald Fellows was an empty beer can. A Red Stripe beer can.

"When does waste management pick up in Anacostia Park?"

"I don't know." Ramirez was already scrambling through the curtains into the driver's seat of the van. "Maybe we can beat 'em there if they haven't emptied that one yet."

The van raced south on Fourteenth Street, turned southeast on Pennsylvania Avenue, crossed the Anacostia River on the Sousa Bridge, and sped into Anacostia Park, screeching to a stop near a dumpster by the park's field house. They were both out of their seats and trotting from the van toward the receptacle when they slowed, seeing it was empty.

"Son of a bitch." Ramirez grabbed the back of his neck with his right hand. "Maybe…do you think…?"

"Nah. Not one lousy beer can. By now, even if we already knew the trash truck route—and we don't—odds are it's already dumped at one of the waste transfer stations, maybe Fort Totten, and we'd never find a single beer can—

probably already compressed and contaminated—in acres of rotten garbage. Any DNA or prints which might have been on it..." Carter shook his head. "Shit."

"He won that thing, Bill." Lassiter said, looking up from the stack of felony jackets that had come through papering the night before. "That case was barking at me when it hit my desk. So much for my intent to administer a dose of humility before he gets up here."

"Yeah, my jaw hit the floor, too." Patrick nodded. "A homeless drunk who makes an ID off half of a face, and then he draws a Friday jury call on top of that. I'd have run away from that one myself."

"Edie King called me after the verdict came in. She said she couldn't wait to see him in federal court."

"How's that? She gonna be in the peanut gallery?"

"Nope." Lassiter flipped a copy of an email to the front of the desk. "She's been nominated by the president to the district court bench."

"Well, hallelujah! There must actually be some modicum of adult supervision at the White House. A good jurist who'll sail through the confirmation hearings because..."

"Because she's competent as hell, and because she also checks off favorably on two big diversity squares?"

"You said it. I didn't."

"If you had, it would have been accurate, unfortunately. The end result, anyway, is we get an excellent new judge—for life."

"Yeah. Article III—your favorite part of the Constitution."

"Bullshit. When somebody builds me a time machine, I'm taking two trips back in time. One to find the inventor of the necktie and strangle him with one. The other one...I'm going to grab the founding fathers and drag them up here to watch Jarvis Peters try to preside over a criminal trial." Lassiter referenced the ninety-one-year-old senior judge of the district court who refused to retire, despite advancing senility. "The Marshals found him wandering the halls last week, and had to lead him by the hand back to his chambers. He was lost in his own courthouse. We had a guilty plea set in front of him on Tuesday, and Judge Peters tried to sentence the defendant before the plea went in."

"You heard that Tim Wisniewski didn't fare so well."

"Yeah—I gave him that overflow case from homicide—thought it was a slam dunk. Guy comes home from work and his lover throws boiling lye in his face, stabs him twenty-seven times in the back, castrates him, then burns the body. Then she gets acquitted because she says she was an abused, common-law spouse."

"Jury nullification. They believed her *and* ignored the court's instructions on the law. She had an opportunity to retreat, to cool off, and to report the abuse, if it happened. She took the law into her own hands, and the jury refused to take it into theirs as instructed. Welcome to superior court."

"Well, at any rate it throws off my plan to promote Tim as early as I'd planned. He'll have to build a positive track record of some sort—not a long one, but *something* positive—before I can leapfrog him over some of the others down there."

"Agreed."

"He'll survive this. I heard from some of my spies that he was making jokes about himself, saying that if only the body had been decapitated, then he'd have had enough proof to win the case."

Patrick laughed. "Sick, but funny. You moving Jeff up already?"

"Not quite. Assign this dope case to him. It smells bad, like the last one, but for different reasons. I want to see what he does with it. J. T. Burns represents the defendant."

"You settin' Jeff up?" Patrick knew from personal experience, having lost to him twice, that James Thomas Burns was perhaps the best defense attorney in the District. Burns had an even better reputation with judges and prosecutors than he did with the clients he represented, chiefly because he was ethical. He was well prepared and a straight shooter. Many of the prosecutors themselves said that he'd be their first choice if they ever ended up on the wrong side of the courtroom as a defendant.

"Not exactly." Lassiter allowed a wry smile to break over his face. "I just have a feeling about this one."

"What do you have so far?" Willie Sivella stood behind Carter as he worked his laptop in the bullpen at 7D.

"Not much, Cap. Red Stripe Beer had one prior run-in with Customs back in 1989; somebody found a load of grass in their shipping containers going into Miami. Nothing that could be directly blamed on Red Stripe, though. Might have been independent smugglers just abusing the brand to get the weed ashore."

"Yeah. Jamaica's always been a smugglers hotbed—all the way back to the days of the pirates."

"Pirates, huh? Did you know any of 'em?"

"Screw you," Sivella said, playfully slapping the top of Carter's head. "I haven't been around that long. I was here for the Jamaican posse wars in the eighties, though. What about the distributor?"

"All I could find out is that it's another Jamaican operation. I called a friend in New York with ATF. He said that half of the Jamaicans in the country now live in Brooklyn. Couldn't find any dirt, other than the fact that the owner appears to be a reformed gang banger from someplace in Kingston called Tivoli."

"Tivoli Gardens. Bad neighborhood in Kingston. That means Shower Posse."

"Excuse me?"

"Shower Posse, Dix. A hyper-violent and very well organized street gang that sells tons of crack. Real bunch of badass cutthroats. They'd rather just shoot a cop or go down firing than think of doing time. I was a detective in this district myself in the posse days. Got joined at the hip with a Park Police sergeant who knew more about the Jakes than anybody. You may have heard of him, Pat McNellis. The Shower thugs had virtually taken over Anacostia. Pat took a two-by-four in the face hitting a door on a crack house one night. Knocked all his front teeth out. He never had much use for the posses after that, specially the Shower types. Where's your restaurant owner from—the guy at The Caribe?"

"Don't know yet. Juan phoned in what he had to Immigration and Customs Enforcement. They were going to pull the guy's file." Carter shouted so as to be heard over the walls of his cubicle. "Hey, bean-breath, you hear from ICE yet?"

"Major Sivella, the senior detective to whom you have assigned me has been belittling my heritage and my faith." Ramirez appeared in the cubicle doorway, wearing his best oppressed face.

"That's okay." Sivella patted the shorter man on the back. "He's from another downtrodden minority group, which means he gets away with it unless it's sexual. It isn't sexual is it?"

"I do have a substantial man-crush on my little Latin love puppet," Carter quipped.

"With respect, sir…" Ramirez bowed slightly toward Sivella. "Fuck you both."

"What did ICE have to say about the restaurant guy?" Sivella asked.

"Demetrius Reid, came in from Jamaica on a work visa in the late 80s…"

"With a load of Red Stripe Beer?" Carter mused.

"Nope. Cruise ship into Miami."

"Same port, anyway," Carter observed.

"*Who* obtained and is trying to read this vital information to our commander?" Ramirez pretended to be highly offended.

"I'm sorry, honey, please continue."

"No priors…" Ramirez ignored his partner. "He bought the restaurant a few years back after working there. Resident alien status. Has not applied for citizenship yet."

"That could be a tell." Sivella said. "Many of the legitimate Jamaicans who take up permanent status here *do* try for naturalization. The dope slingers used to talk about *going foreign*, making their drug fortune here or in some other country—sometimes Europe—and then taking their money home with them to live like minor nobles in a country where nobody else has much. You guys may be on to something bigger than a couple of homicides."

"Any suggestions?" Carter asked.

"We may want to go federal on this. I'll talk to Lassiter about it."

Chapter Eleven

Spencer Good, Esquire, sat in front of the same video poker machine at Harrah's in Atlantic City, waiting to be paid by a floor manager for another progressive jackpot. Instead of the self-satisfaction he usually felt at such times, however, he felt himself breaking out in a cold sweat of fear. On his lap was an open Saturday edition of the *Washington Post,* which he'd picked up on the way out of town after beginning his usual drive to New York. He was looking at the front page of the metro section, below the fold, and was re-reading a single-column, four-inch story about the cops finding a body in Anacostia Park the day before. The story sent chills through his viscera.

He had me give the kid the address of the restaurant, he thought to himself. *He never would have had the kid go to his legitimate place of business—unless, of course—he knew the kid would never be able to speak about it to anyone, and he made sure of that. SHIT! I never signed on for this. This isn't business, it's a goddamn MURDER, and I set the kid up for him. That's why he was so adamant about winning the bail hearing. If the kid's locked up, he might say something to somebody.*

The floor manager returned with a slot attendant; they were both beaming and congratulating him for his win of $1,355. He thanked them—for what he had no idea—he'd won the damned money. He tipped the slot gal twenty bucks, again wondering why, and picked up the paper.

Maybe the Jamaican hadn't done it. Bullshit. Of course he did it. Nothing else made sense. Hell, nothing makes sense at all anymore. I'm now a co-conspirator, an aider and abettor to murder, in the eyes of the law. Only the law doesn't know. The law thinks I'm one of their own, an officer of the court. I wouldn't be a suspect unless the Jamaican himself ratted me out, and he's no rat. Hell, he's the rat killer.

He put another twenty in the machine.

I'll be okay. Maybe I could go to Canada or something, just keep his stupid aluminum case with the two hundred grand and keep going. It would last me a while. No, that's not enough. I'd burn through it in no time and be out of work. The exchange rate sucks now, and I can't practice law in Toronto with a DC bar card. That son of a bitch would find me, too, wouldn't stop looking for me until he did. Him or one of his damned posse bruthas. They'd break every bone I had, then wrap MY head with that stinking tape. I'll ride this out. Hell, I'LL be the one representing him on this. He couldn't even try to strike a deal without going through me. I'd know, and they'd never offer him anything if they pegged him for the murder. I'll be okay. I'll be okay.

The sweat beaded on his forehead anyway. He needed something to take his mind off it. He looked around the casino floor and saw a Megabucks slot machine with a sign advertising a progressive jackpot of over ten million. He'd usually avoided the one-armed bandits—the odds sucked—and he prided himself on getting the best odds. It was why he was a VP player instead of a stupid slot cranker. He had control over his game, didn't rely on some dumb random-number generator chip to determine his fate without any input from him whatsoever. Still, he thought, I'll be playing with their money, and I could run with that much, take no chances. He sat down, put a hundred in it, and waited for the three right symbols to line up.

The first hundred was gone in ten minutes. With the second, he actually played for half an hour, and on three pulls, two of the three jackpot symbols lined up, but a blank popped up in the third row. He told himself he was close, and it took three hundred more to convince him that he'd been played. *No matter, I'll make it back.* He returned to the quarter-machine row, but forty dollars returned nothing, and he figured the row had gone cold. The jackpot was low again anyway, thanks to his hitting it earlier. He headed for a row of dollar-level video poker machines. Five hundred dollars later, he was back at even for the night, and was as pissed at himself as he was at the Jamaican for getting him into this whole mess.

He didn't feel like staying the night, as was now his usual custom. He left the casino floor for the parking garage, noticing for the first time the hollow look in the eyes of some senior citizens as they passed him on their way to lose their social security checks. *Addicts.* He opened the door to the Acura, and headed north toward New York and the Kingston Distributing Company.

Trask sat behind his desk, looking over three new case jackets, each bearing the cover letter reflecting that these matters had now been assigned to him. He looked up as Tim Wisniewski walked through the doorway and lowered his tall frame into a side chair.

"Anything challenging?"

"Who knows? With the juries in this town I'm not sure anymore." Trask did his best to balm the sting he was sure Tim still felt after the loss in his homicide trial.

"I appreciate the thought, but I'm over it. Maybe somebody told the jury I used to be a cop."

"That's a hell of an indictment of you, isn't it?"

"Lay of the land. So when are you moving up to the federal side?"

"I have no idea. You know something I don't?"

"Nope. Just thought after that miracle you worked with the homeless-guy witness, you'd be on your way."

"Apparently not for a while." Trask pointed to the newly assigned case files. "New matters, fresh from the desk of one Robert Lassiter, and now assigned to yours truly. This guy's represented by J. T. Burns himself. "

"Aaah. The boss wants to see how you do against stiffer competition. What's in the file?"

"Strange one. Patrol officer working traffic in 7D pulls a car over for speeding. The passenger—a college kid—gets out and starts to run, freezes when the cop draws down on him. Cop does a sweep of the car for weapons, finds a kilo of cocaine in a backpack under the front passenger seat where Joe College had been sitting. Nothing else in the pack. No ID, nothing. Cop writes the driver for speeding, but since the driver denies any knowledge of the dope, and says he picked the other guy up hitchhiking, the officer only arrests the passenger for possession with intent to distribute. I was wondering why both of them weren't charged—either by the cop or by our guy in papering."

"Who did the papering?"

"Ben Prescott. I don't know him, do you?"

"Yale guy. Word is he's more impressed with himself than he should be. I've only met him once. He didn't do so well down here.

"Where is he now?" Trask asked.

"Federal floor. I hear his daddy's well connected."

"That's the way of the world. Anyway, I don't see any rap sheets in the file, on either the defendant or the driver. Think I'll have somebody run 'em. Something doesn't smell right about this one."

"Good luck." Wisniewski stood up. "Guess I'll go see what new treats Mr. L has in mind for me now. Probably a couple of parking violations."

Trask laughed as Wisniewski shuffled, shoulders slumped, back toward his own office.

He picked up a leather binder in which he'd stored business cards he thought might be worth keeping and found one he'd received from Detective Dixon Carter. A cell phone number had been handwritten on the back.

"Carter."

"Dix? Jeff Trask."

"How goes it, Counselor? I hear you really wowed 'em last week in that Georgetown burglary case."

"Thanks. Better lucky than good."

"That's not what I hear. Judge King's husband and I go way back. He told me the judge was pretty impressed with you."

"I'll take all the friends I can find around here. That's why I'm calling you."

"Happy to help if I can. What's up?"

"You know a traffic cop in your district named Merkelson?"

"Yeah. Let's see, how do I put this diplomatically... hmmm...he's a moron. That's why he's spent fifteen years working traffic."

"I see." Trask summarized the story of the traffic stop and ensuing arrest.

"Give me the names. Both of them." Carter said. "I'll get you an NCIC in a few minutes. Assuming what went into our friendly National Crime Information Center in this case isn't the proverbial garbage-in, I'll be able to give you something more than the garbage-out."

"Thanks." Trask said. "I appreciate it."

"No sweat. Back with you in about ten."

Carter was true to his word.

"As I was saying, Merkelson's an idiot. The driver has a sheet as long as my leg, and a lot of it's dope-related. Six drug arrests, two convictions, one a felony for coke distribution. The college kid's clean as a whistle. Never been cited for anything, as far as I can tell. Where's he going to school?"

"Maryland. He's a junior."

"That just proves his innocence."

"Right. I forgot you were a tortoise-thing."

"*Terrapin*, sir. *Terrapin*."

"Thanks for the help, Mr. Terrapin."

"Anytime."

Trask had just put the telephone handset back in its cradle when the phone rang.

"Jeff Trask."

"Mr. Trask, my name is J. T. Burns."

"Yes, sir. I've heard of you."

"Nothing good, I presume," Burns chuckled.

"Quite the contrary. What can I do for you?" Trask decided to play dumb, at least initially.

"I represent a young man named Dennis Hightower, who was recently arrested for possession of cocaine. I was told you'd been assigned the matter."

"Just got it. Haven't really had time to put flesh on the bones yet."

"Maybe I can help with that. I know it's a bit unusual, but I'd like my client to speak to you about this."

"That *is* unusual," Trask confessed. "Can't say that's happened to me before, at least in a case this serious, but I'd be happy to speak with him."

"We're downstairs now, if you have a moment."

"I'll be right down."

Trask took a minute to compose his thoughts, feeling a bit off-balance. He was sure Burns had intended that to be the case, calling from within the building. He made a quick phone call to Detective Greenwell, the felony section's assigned investigator, explained what he'd learned from Carter, and asked Greenwell to meet him to witness the statement. They took the elevator down to the first floor, where he saw Burns and a younger black man waiting by the security checkpoint. He shook hands with both, and escorted them to an interview room on the side of the lobby.

"Have a seat, gentlemen." Trask motioned to a small sofa, taking the single chair himself. He noticed that J. T. Burns was as distinguished in appearance as he was by reputation. A tall, slender, black man with flecks of gray throughout his close-cropped hair, he wore a three-piece, gray suit, and wore it well.

"Tell him your story, son." Burns was direct.

"Mr. Trask, I was working at one of my jobs in Prince George's County," Hightower began, referring to the suburban Maryland County directly to the south and east of the District of Columbia.

"*One* of your jobs?" Trask asked.

"Yes sir. I wait tables in a restaurant in Temple Hills. My other job is here in the District—for the library. My folks can't afford all my tuition, so I do what I can to help out."

"Okay."

"I usually take the bus in from the restaurant to the library on Fridays, but we got slammed at the restaurant around lunchtime Friday, and I missed the bus, so I decided to try and thumb it in."

"I saw in the police report that the driver said he picked you up hitchhiking." Trask glanced from the nervous young man to his counsel, who was nodding in agreement.

"I have a copy of the report." Burns said.

"Anyway, when the officer pulled in behind us, the guy that picked me up told me to run, because he was going to shoot it out with the cops."

"No gun was found in the car," Trask noted.

"Maybe not, but that's what he said," Hightower continued. "I took about five steps, and the officer was pointing his gun at *me*, so I froze. Mr. Trask, I think that guy wanted me to run to take some heat off him. That wasn't my dope under that seat. I had no idea it was there. I never would have gotten in that car if I even suspected such a thing. I've worked too hard to..."

"Just keep working hard, then. Would you be willing to testify against the driver?"

It was now Burns who was a bit off-balance.

"Are you willing to dismiss just on his word, Mr. Trask?" The older man asked.

"Call me Jeff, Mr. Burns. Of course not. We usually hear this kind of story for the first time in court, where I never believe it, but I've had a little time to look into this case." Trask shot a glance at Greenwell, who nodded in agreement. "I believe your client. I'll need to clear this with my supervisors, but I don't think there will be a problem with a dismissal."

"I'd be happy to testify, Mr. Trask. That dude tried to ruin me."

"I'll be in touch very soon," Trask rose and shook hands again with his visitors. As they headed for the lobby exit to the street, he went to the elevator, and the fifth floor. He found Lassiter in his office, speaking with Bill Patrick.

"Come in, Jeff," Lassiter motioned to the unoccupied chair in front of his desk.

"Great result in that Georgetown case, Jeff." Patrick rose, shaking hands with Trask as he approached the desk.

"Thanks. I just got one that I don't think I could win, or should even try to." Trask explained his last hour's experience with the Hightower file.

"Fine," Lassiter said. "File a motion to dismiss it, and send the file back to me. We'll go to our federal grand jury to indict the driver, given his prior felony. Your Mr. Hightower can testify for us in the grand jury."

"Thanks." Trask rose and headed for the door. "I'll let you get back to your other business."

"Not a problem," Lassiter said. "But one more thing, Jeff. What you just did—clearing an innocent defendant—is even more important than convicting the guilty ones. I expect that you'll remember this one until the end of your career with as much satisfaction as any of your cases."

Trask smiled. "It does feel good." He left the office.

Lassiter waited until he heard Trask's footsteps get some distance away.

"Move him up, Bill. I just talked to our friends in 7D about those two homicides again—the duct-tape jobs. Willie is convinced they're drug-related, and that the posses may be trying to get back into town. I know he's ready, now."

"Because of a dismissal? If I'd only known in my early days..."

"Of course not." Lassiter shot him The Look. "Because I can trust him to do the right thing, and not just to put another notch on his gun. And move Prescott over to appellate for a ninety-day stint. They need some help over there, and maybe he can learn something."

As the freighter, an aging tub of Panamanian registry, slowly worked its way into the port of Jacksonville, a young man with coal-black skin and dreadlocks anxiously surveyed the docks. He had been fortunate enough to outrun his pursuers in Panama, more fortunate still to find an old barge like this that needed an extra deckhand, and supremely fortunate because that same ship was headed to the states. Still, he had to be careful now to avoid the customs and immigration agents, and—he hoped—lucky enough again to find the right man to listen to him. If he failed to do so, they would send him back, and that would mean his death.

Chapter Twelve

Barry Doroz, acting supervisor of the violent crimes and narcotics unit of the Washington field office of the Federal Bureau of Investigation, hardly had the appearance of the stereotypical FBI agent. He was swarthy, about five nine, and of very mixed heritage—a combination of Armenian, Lebanese, Cherokee, and Italian ancestors, all of whom had been hell-bent to marry outside their respective communities. His apparently indeterminate ethnicity had given him a unique, chameleon-like ability to assume several undercover roles. With the appropriate language training, he had passed for a Colombian drug dealer, an Egyptian merchant, and an Iraqi.

He had performed superbly in every assignment, thanks to his appearance, an incredibly quick mind, and a ready smile beaming from a salt-and-pepper goatee that accented an impish but disarming sense of humor. People liked him, and he used this to his advantage, whether dealing with the bad guys or the various egos who were supposed to be on his side. Unlike many of the blow-dried Ken dolls who seemed to have jumped off some FBI recruiting poster, he knew how to work with local and other federal law enforcement agencies without playing the J. Edgar Hoover "I'm here to take over" card. This meant that more information flowed into his case files from the bottom up, and as a result he had become a living legend within the bureau. He had been responsible for several major investigative successes while out in the field, helping to solve the Oklahoma City bombing case while in the Kansas City Division, going undercover in South America to neutralize a cocaine-smuggling conspiracy operating on three continents, and thwarting more than one terrorist threat on American soil—threats which had never seen and would never see any press coverage.

The bureau's hierarchy would have forced him to rise higher within the organization if they had been able to persuade him to make the climb, but he had no desire to be a SAC (a Special Agent in Charge), an ASAC (Assistant Special Agent in Charge) or even a squad supervisor. It was only when the assigned supervisor was absent that he even consented to warm the chair for a while. He loved working criminal cases and had even successfully resisted his superiors' efforts to transfer him into the specialty *du jour*, prolonged anti-terrorism work. He knew it was important, and had done it when necessary, but he preferred putting the cuffs on the thugs and pushers who chronically inflicted misery on the American populace.

He looked out into his squad area and took inventory of his current human assets. Seven able-bodied agents—down from the seventy-five who had been assigned to such duties prior to 9/11—a squad investigative analyst, and a secretary. He smiled to himself when he thought about Bonnie, the secretary. She was even older than he was. Bonnie was a product of the central Virginia hills with the manner and vocabulary of a southern truck-stop waitress, but she loved her boys, as she called the agents on the squad, and kept the place afloat. He watched as she greeted a young man who had just entered the squad area, dressed in a business suit and carrying what appeared to be a brand new briefcase. The visitor looked to Doroz to be about fourteen years old, if judged only by his face, but was about six two, and probably weighed 210 pounds. The fellow had his back to Doroz's office as he was introducing himself to Bonnie, while Doroz leaned out his doorway.

"Well aren't you the freshest little bowl of puddin'?" Bonnie asked, looking up from her typewriter.

"I...uh...thanks, I guess," the young man stammered, blushing a bright red. "My name is Michael Crawford. I'm the new first-office agent, and I was told to report here to Mr. Doroz."

"Right here, Mr. Crawford." Doroz shook the new man's hand as he emerged from the office. "We've been expecting you. Let me introduce you to the squad." He turned the young man around to face the other agents who were peering up from their low-walled cubicles to get a look at the new guy.

"Gentlemen, your attention, please." Doroz announced. "This is the new agent on the squad. His name is..." He paused as a sardonic thought crossed his mind and an evil grin crossed his face. "Puddin'."

The roar of laughter from the squad area drowned out the "Oh, no," groaned by Crawford, and the, "Bear, you are sooo bad," offered apologetically by Bonnie, who realized that she had just branded the new agent, probably for the rest of his career. Individual introductions were then made, with every one of the older agents immediately forgetting the new man's name, but vowing to themselves to never address him by anything other than Puddin'.

"Make yourself at home." Doroz was still chuckling as he slapped Crawford on the back. "Then come see me. I think we may have already found you some crime to fight. You're coming with me to a meeting in half an hour."

"You've heard of the OCDETF program?" Lassiter asked as Trask sank into the passenger side seat of Lassiter's car.

"Sure. Organized Crime Drug Enforcement Task Force?"

"Correct. Some bureaucrat's acronym for the program that lets us bring state and local cops on board and pay them to work with federal agencies. Up to now, I'd guess that most of your cases have been investigated by a single agency?"

"For the most part. Sometimes on the military side, I'd get a mix of OSI and some civilian police force. Since I've been downstairs, it's been all local police."

"Exactly. Welcome to the world of intramural investigative squabbling and turf wars. On this floor, we deal with the FBI, DEA, ATF, ICE, Secret Service, Capitol Police, Park Police, our own Metropolitan Police Force, investigative arms of the cabinet secretaries such as HUD and the State Department, and every other mother's son who wants Congress to give them more money. Are you familiar with our deconfliction desk?"

"Not yet."

"At the end of the hall there's an office bearing that title. It's staffed full-time by one of our secretaries. She registers targets and addresses. As an investigator identifies someone he thinks is a worthwhile investigative target, he registers them with that office. That way, we minimize—but never eliminate—fights over who is investigating whom. She also registers addresses for the same reason, so that DEA can't say that they didn't know an FBI target lived in a certain house, or vice-versa. She also has to check off on any proposed search warrant in the District, even before the investigator takes it to an attorney. That way, we don't have two different tactical squads hitting the same address on the same night, and the good guys don't shoot each other in the dark."

"Good grief."

"A lot of bad grief, actually. Before we established that desk, it almost happened on more than one occasion. And that's the easy part. With OCDETF proposals, it takes on a whole new level. We add another tier of the federal budget to the mix, in the form of OCDETF program funds, money that lets one of the federal agencies deputize state and/or local cops, do bigger cases, make bigger headlines, and thereby lobby for a bigger chunk of the allocated federal investigative budget for the next fiscal year. That's where the real competition and back-stabbing can come into play, especially between FBI and DEA."

"I thought we were supposed to be on the same side."

"That's part of your new job description on the federal level—to make sure that everybody *is*. It's much easier said than done."

"Any suggestions?"

"Plenty. The first thing to do, of course, is to get a good scouting report on your investigative roster. I think I've given you a good one for your first investigation. You remember that autopsy that you rode to with me?"

"Sure. Junebug Wilson. Captain Willie and The Twins."

"Right. There's been another duct-tape suffocation homicide. Probably related. The 7D guys did some street surveillance, and they think that both murders are tied to a restaurant run by some Jamaicans in Northeast. They saw a beer truck dropping off cases in the back of the place. Nothing unusual about that, except the truck was from Brooklyn. Willie thinks it may be dropping off some dope, too, but we don't know that yet. We don't even know for sure that the restaurant owner has anything to do with either death. We could have some nut-job serial killer out on a spree, or it may be tied to an interstate drug ring, in which case an OCDETF proposal may need to be written and approved. In cases like this one, where the local cops have gotten the thing going and have some sweat equity in the case, I like to ask *them* which group of their federal comrades they prefer to join. That's if—as in this case—the local guys know what the hell they're doing, and Willie, Carter and Ramirez do."

"Who are our federal guys on this one?"

"Certainly not DEA. Willie hates 'em. His police district has had some real battles with the local Drug Enforcement Field Office. The last time they tried to work together, Dix and Juan had an undercover buy-bust set up on a big-time heroin dealer. The DEA boys rolled in before the buy went down and arrested the target on their own smaller case just so they could take all the credit. They wasted months of time and effort by 7D, and their arrest resulted in a much lower-level prosecution and a lot less jail time for the bad guy. The Twins won't work a DEA case at all after that fracas."

"We have met the enemy and he is us. Who'd they pick instead of DEA?"

"Barry Doroz from FBI. Bear to those of us who know him. Best agent I've ever worked with. That's why the meeting's here today."

"You lost me there," Trask said.

"You have to play the turf game, and recognize how important it is to these guys. Again, this one started as a 7D case. I have the initial sit-down in Willie's office, to reinforce that notion, even if a federal agency is jumping on board. Bear doesn't wear his FBI badge on his sleeve with cops, and they trust him, but it's part of the game. Ultimately, everybody knows that Bear will actually be running the show, especially where the out-of-the-District investigation is concerned. The actual meeting place doesn't matter as much with these guys. They've worked well as a team before, but we keep the system in place none the less."

"Thanks for easing me in on a good note."

"Don't thank me yet. Assuming that you plant the investigative flags on the target and the restaurant, and nobody else squawks about it, you'll still have to verify that it's a drug case, otherwise we'll send it back downstairs to the homicide guys in superior court. If a good amount of dope does show up, then you'll have to fend off all the other sharks who'll suddenly appear to say it was their case all along."

"We should just merge all these investigative agencies."

"Think about what you're suggesting. When has Congress or the executive branch done anything that makes that much sense? One political party thinks it's anathema to have anything with *Federal* in its title—especially if you're talking about a national police force—even if one already exists in a fragmented condition. The other party has a powerful lobby made up of criminal defense attorneys and ACLU types, some of whom have no real interest in seeing a significant upgrade in the efficiency of federal law enforcement. When the White House convinces them that something *should* be done—like merging the Customs Service and Immigration after 9/11—that gets screwed up, too. Some maniac decided that to make those agencies like each other—and they never had before—the supervisory levels should be layered, so that a former Customs agent was always working for a former Immigration guy, and the Immigration guy was always working for a Customs boss. Now neither function is working as well as it used to, everybody hates their bosses, and their bosses hate *their* bosses. The only benefit I've seen is that the old Customs guys enjoy having the additional authority to arrest illegal immigrants just for being here."

"Great." Trask shook his head. "I had no idea..."

"Nobody could imagine how screwed up it can be without seeing it first-hand. DEA hates the FBI, and hates CIA more. ATF has an inferiority complex, and thereby blunders into operations like the WACO compound disaster trying to get publicity, instead of taking the head of the snake off when he's alone on one his morning jogs. The Customs guys used to know their stuff, but now they have more hats to wear. The Immigration guys were more administrators than cops and still just warehouse people instead of building criminal cases. And some of the federal agents who don't know how to really run a case *do* know how to pull rank on an experienced local cop. Don't get me wrong—there are some great people in every one of those agencies, heroes who keep us safe despite the obstacles their own bosses keep putting in front of them. You just have to take the time to find them. When you do, some amazing things can happen."

"I'll keep my eyes open."

"Good. Here are *our* heroes now." Lassiter nodded as he pulled up in front of the seventh district station, where Willie Sivella and The Twins were standing outside the front door.

"I know where your office is, Willie," Lassiter laughed as he shook Sivella's hand. "Didn't really need an escort, but thanks anyway."

"It's not for you, you old warhorse." Sivella retorted. "We know how important it is for us to be assigned a rising star like Mr. Trask, here, and thought we'd give *him* the tour." He shook Trask's hand, and bowed slightly. "Actually, no tour for anybody. We just got back from lunch, and you pulled up before we could get inside. Bear should be here any minute—said he was bringing a new guy with him to help out, too."

They walked through the entry room past the customer service counter, where a clerk and a desk sergeant nodded at them from behind bulletproof glass. They paused at a set of double doors at the far end of the lobby where a buzzer sounded, signaling that they were free to enter. Inside the doors, they turned to wait for an elevator, and got out on the third floor. Sivella's office was at the end of the hall.

"How are things, Willie?" Lassiter sank into one of several chairs around a coffee table in the front area of the room. It was the typical district commander's office in some ways, with souvenirs, photographs of police academy classes, and framed newspaper stories of significant cases hanging on the walls. It was atypical in that the commander's desk itself was piled high with investigation folders. Sivella was a working boss, and he saw that Trask had noticed the piles of paperwork.

"A clean desk is a sign of fear," he said, nodding in Trask's direction. He then turned back to Lassiter. "Same old 7D. The hellholes just shift around from time to time. At the moment, it's Ainger Place, Evans Road. Yuma Street as usual."

"Are you gentlemen starting without us?" Barry Doroz stood in the doorway, a taller, very young-looking man at his side.

"Come on in, Bear." Sivella and the others stood for the introductions to be made. Trask got the feeling that he was being scanned by an X-ray as he shook hands with Doroz.

"He's a good one, Bear." Dixon Carter said, vouching for him. "Bob pulled him all the way up from the misdemeanor shop in about three days."

"More like three weeks," Lassiter corrected the exaggeration. "But I have a lot of confidence in him. Teach him well, and don't be surprised if he teaches you guys a thing or two. Who's *your* apprentice, Barry?"

"Very Special Agent Michael Crawford, newly minted by the Academy..." Doroz paused and turned to the new man, as if to cue him. Crawford rolled his eyes skyward.

"But they call me...Puddin'."

"Gaawd," howled Ramirez. "Did you tag him with that, Bear?"

"I believe that Bonnie made the nomination. I just seconded it." Doroz grinned. He was glad to see that the younger agent had a sense of humor.

"Let's get down to business, guys," Sivella said.

They all took seats around the coffee table. Dixon Carter summarized the murders of Junebug Wilson and Ronald Fellows, and also recounted the surveillance of The Caribe restaurant.

"You were here during our first set of posse wars in the mid-eighties, Bear," Sivella said. "We had Shower and Spangler troops shooting up Anacostia left and right. Coke and crack was everywhere, we had TEC-9 automatic pistols going off every five minutes, and they didn't care who got in the crossfire. One of the Maryland counties—PG, I think—took six bodies out of a house after one posse hit, and four of the vics were women. They tore the town up for years, and I don't want to see them gaining another foothold here."

"I know some real good ATF guys working the Jamaican task force in Brooklyn," Doroz offered. "I'll give 'em a call later today. I haven't been to this restaurant yet. I'd like to drive by and get a look at it."

"Why don't you guys take the van?" Sivella was flipping the keys again, this time to Ramirez. "There's plenty of room in the back."

"I'd like to see it, too." Trask volunteered, wondering if he should have checked with Lassiter first.

"Good." Lassiter stood. "I've got some other fish to fry." He patted Trask on the back. "They can drop you back at the office afterward."

"Show 'em Ainger on the way out," Carter instructed Ramirez from one of the captain's chairs in the back of the van. "Our Caucasian friends here will never see it any other way."

"Sure." Ramirez pulled the van out of the rear of the station, where it had been locked in a covered garage, headed north on Alabama, and then turned left, heading northwest on Ainger Place before turning left again, and driving southwest on Langston Place.

"Fairly tame looking here early in the afternoon..." Carter began to narrate, "But...SHIT! Pull it over, Juan! Rape in progress!"

Trask could hardly believe his eyes or ears. As Ramirez screeched the van to a halt along the right curb, the sliding door along the side of the vehicle flew open, and the massive figure of Dixon Carter flew through the opening. Over the big man's right shoulder, Trask could make out two young hoods who had already ripped the blouse off a screaming young woman, whom they had pushed to the concrete in an alley between two buildings.

Doroz was out of the door immediately behind Carter, Ramirez a step or two behind them, having had to stop the van and run around the front of the vehicle. Trask instinctively jumped out behind Doroz, and noted that the rookie agent Crawford was flying past him on the left. Everybody else had a gun drawn and was yelling at the perps to freeze, and Trask suddenly realized how unarmed and untrained he was for such an incident. Then he heard the gunfire, and flopped down prone on the sidewalk, feeling his suit pants rip on something.

Dixon Carter was down, and Ramirez had jumped in front of his partner, pointing his weapon, screaming obscenities at the bad guys and shielding Carter's body with his own. Crawford was already bent over Carter, doing something to the downed man's leg. Doroz was running straight at the thug who was firing at them and also holding the half-nude, screaming woman in front of him while shooting over her shoulder with his right hand. Trask jumped up and quickly scanned his eyes left and right to the front, looking for the other rapist. *I know I saw two of them.* He spotted the second man behind a stack of cartons along the right side of the alley wall, just as Doroz fired a single shot, which slammed into the other gunman's shoulder, forcing him to drop both the gun and the woman.

Trask saw with horror that the second man—with a gun of his own—now had a bead drawn on Doroz's back. He felt a large rock in his right hand that had come from somewhere, and as he fired the rock hard at the thug's face, he heard himself yell, "BEAR!" His shout was just enough to cause the second goon to pause before shooting, a microsecond that allowed the rock to slam into the left side of the gunman's head. The impact caused the shot from his weapon to pull left and down, and the round hit nothing but concrete. The shot fired by Doroz in return did not miss.

Sirens were blaring from every possible direction. There were uniformed cops on the scene, and aside from a couple of officers who were not-so-gently "treating" the live shooter for his wounds, and one who was covering the dead one with a sheet of plastic, there were EMTs working feverishly over Dixon

Carter. Trask saw a lot of blood on the ground where Carter lay. Ramirez was kneeling down over his partner's face, alternatively pleading softly with the big man to hang on, and then turning and screaming condemnations of every sort at the surviving rapist. As the EMTs got Carter into a waiting ambulance with Ramirez at his side, Trask heard someone speaking to him.

"Femoral artery. He lost a lot of blood." Barry Doroz was looking at Trask's ripped pant leg, which Trask now noticed for the first time was also soaked in blood. "You OK?"

"I think so." Trask opened the tear in his pants to see a bleeding but superficial gash in his calf. "Just a cut."

"Come on with me. We'll get up to MedStar, check on Dix, and get you sewn up. You may need a tetanus shot, too. By the way, I owe you. Thanks."

The ER doctor had just finished the stitches when Trask looked up to see that Doroz had returned to check on him.

"How's Dix doing?"

"He'll be fine." The weight of concern had lifted from the agent's face. "The docs said he lost enough blood to send him into shock, but thanks to my new guy's tourniquet at the scene and the stuff they got into him in the ambulance, he held on long enough to get here and get filled up again. His wife was here by the time they took him into the operating room, and he was conscious enough to look up and say, 'Johnson's OK, honey.' Willie Sivella's in there now chewing his ass out for burning the surveillance van. Told him he had three days off; then he has to repaint it."

"Great." Trask said. "How's Juan?"

"I think he's more shaken up than his shot-up partner. He was outside, bawling."

"And how're you doing?"

"I'm OK for now. It'll hit me harder later. Part of the job. Third time for me, but it always sucks. Anyway, the *right* people—including the girl those two grabbed—are all OK. Can I do anything else for you?"

"If it's not an imposition, I could use a ride to my car."

"Imposition?" It was Doroz who was chuckling now. "I'd have a forty-caliber vent in my back right now if not for you. I think I can get us a ride. So, were you a pitcher?"

"Nope." Trask, shook his head. "Other end of the battery. Nine years in the tools of ignorance. I just got lucky with the accuracy for once."

"I think," said Doroz, "that we both did."

The young man with the dreadlocks thanked the trucker for the ride and climbed down to the shoulder from the cab. He was tired and hungry after hitchhiking from the port, but he felt compelled to get out and walk for a while. He needed to think, and he knew he did not want to go farther south, not to Miami where the truck was heading. He walked a little way before noticing an exit sign for Patrick Air Force Base. He paused, and then walked up the exit ramp, leaving the highway.

Chapter Thirteen

"How's the leg, hero?"

Lynn wrapped her arms around Trask over the back of the couch where he'd sprawled out to read the Department of Justice's manual on electronic surveillance.

"Not bad at all. Just a little cut that bled like hell. I need to go back to Penney's and see if they still have some suit pants to match the coat."

"We need to talk about this." She walked around and sat beside him on the couch. "Do you realize how stupid you were out there?"

"I knew this was coming," he said, "And yes, I'm quite aware of both how dumb and lucky I was. It just seemed like the right thing to do at the time."

"Well, it wasn't, even though it worked out for the best. Those other guys are trained for that sort of thing, Jeff. So am I, for that matter, but you aren't, and you weren't armed or wearing any body armor. You could be in the goddamn morgue right now, and I'd be a wreck for the rest of my life. I didn't wait this long to lose you this fast. Let the cops do the cop stuff next time, please. Promise me that."

"Point well taken." He kissed her on the forehead. "I promise that the next time I'm out there in the badlands, I'll be wearing Kevlar from head to foot, and I'll take my slingshot."

"It's not funny." She didn't even smile.

"I know that, babe." Trask sat up and took her hand in his. "I don't expect anything like that to ever happen again. DC just happened to see what was going down with those thugs and that girl, and we had to get involved. If there had been time to have a marked unit roll on the call, we'd have *all* stayed in the van." He paused for a moment. "You know that I can't promise I'll never get hurt in this job, and *you* couldn't promise *me* that, either. Hell, what am I going to go through if they put you on another one of those undercover assignments?"

"I'm trained for it, I'm careful, and I know what I'm doing."

"Dixon Carter was trained for what he did, too, and he's the one that took a slug in the thigh. I was carefully and skillfully diving into some concrete, and just caught a leg on something."

She punched him in the arm. "And who trained you to take on a gun with a rock?"

"I forget, but you can see how effective that training *was.*"

She shook her head, realized the futility of her lecture, and then kissed him on the cheek. "Just remember that I love you, and that you have to come home every night. And be more careful, dammit."

"Yes, ma'am. I got it."

"What's that you're reading, anyway?"

"Nice, safe lawyer stuff. The departmental manual on wiretaps and bugs. I'll be listening from a secure location while our target talks himself to death, or at least into a jail cell. No guns, no rocks, no evil snags lurking to rip my skin or wardrobe."

"Good. What kind of case is it?"

"The duct tape murders. Carter and Ramirez think they *may* be related to some drug conspiracy which, *if* it exists, *may* be connected to a Jamaican restaurant. Whoever is responsible for the murders isn't any dummy, though, and I can't see how we're going to get anywhere without a tap or somebody on the inside. I'm trying to figure out how to go up on the restaurant owner's phone. Problem is, we don't even know which phone he's using, and if we did, we'd still have to get firm evidence of some crime-related calls before we could tap it."

"Why not just run an undercover in on the restaurant?"

"We've done a little preliminary work on that. We tried to send a young officer in there this morning supposedly looking for work, but the manager he spoke with—some guy from the islands by his accent—said they weren't hiring at the moment. When he came back, the cop said everybody from the cook to the busboys had an accent. I don't happen to have a Jamaican undercover asset at my disposal at the moment, or I'd send one in. We're kind of stymied for now.

The FBI guy is working on the other end of it, looking at the beer distributor up in New York."

"Is that the guy who shot the rapists?"

"Yep. Barry Doroz."

"I'd like to meet him, and thank him for saving your ass, since your famous rock didn't take out the shooter."

"It got his attention for the rest of his life, short as it was. I'll call you next time we decide to eat at the FOP. You can join us."

"How's Carter doing?"

"He's on bed rest tomorrow. He said he'd be limping back to his desk day after tomorrow."

"He's a lucky guy."

"We all were. I know that. Doroz had a brand-new baby federale with him who had his belt cinched up on DC's thigh right after he got hit." Trask thought for a moment about telling her the tale of "Puddin," but decided that Mike Crawford had earned the right to his own name, at least for the time being. "It's a good group. We'll make the case one way or another."

Robert Lassiter turned the key, opening the door to his dark brownstone, a couple of blocks from Capitol Hill. He tossed his keys and the mail from the box outside onto a hall table. There was no need to look at the mail. It was all bills, as usual. He forced himself to go through the ritual of paying them twice a month, and it wasn't time yet, so the stack kept growing. He hung his tweed jacket on a coat tree by the table, and walked into the kitchen, where he found one frozen dinner left in the fridge.

Turkey again. Why do I buy so many of these damn things? It's because they keep putting that stinking broccoli in with everything else that I'd eat otherwise. I'll have to stop by a grocery tomorrow, or maybe I'll just eat at FOP again. Maybe I'll forward my mail to FOP and sleep there, too.

He heated the dinner in the microwave, grabbed a can of Diet Coke from the fridge, and ate in front of the new, high-definition TV that he'd splurged on the month before, surfing through every history and news channel he could find without seeing anything that really grabbed his interest. He finally settled on watching *The Longest Day* for the fourteenth time. *When we knew how to fight a war,* he said to himself. He thought of 1969, and The Point.

He remembered getting off the bus from the airport. He'd walked out with his luggage into the mass of upperclassmen, being directed with all the other new cadets through the processing lines. A buzz haircut first, then the uniform lines, new underwear, socks, the gray tunics, pants and shirts, the scarves, overcoats, hats, shoes, combat boots, fatigues. So much gray. The long, gray line. The hazing they called training and the training that he thought at the time was hazing. He recalled the pride in his father's eyes when the appointment to the Academy came through, and the pain in those same eyes when he'd told him that he wanted to leave the place. His dad had not understood. His father's war had been the one the country had fought to win. The country had actually *declared* war, fought it with commitment, fought to win unconditional victories.

His own war—or at least the one he thought would be his own—had been 'Nam. He studied with the others, learning the military history, tactics, strategy, and engineering from the Greeks and Romans through the D-Day invasion. They'd taken ground then and held it, never giving back a foot without the enemy paying dearly for every inch. The cadets had compared it all to 'Nam, and knew while they studied it that Robert McNamara and his whiz kids were doing everything wrong.

The soldiers were paid to fight the war, except they weren't given a war to fight. It was instead a "police action," like Korea, with no declaration of national will or commitment to back it up, and with not enough boots on the ground to keep the acreage bought with so much dearly spent blood. They'd lose fifty men by day to take a hill, then retreat and give it back to the NVA or the Viet Cong the next night, then lose fifty more men the next day taking the same hill back again, only to retreat once more when darkness fell. As the thing had dragged on, he'd watch the papers and bulletin boards to see the names of those who had graduated the year before as they came back in body bags, young lieutenants who served proudly and died in a war that the politicians kept screwing up.

The country lost so *much* faith in the thing that the draft was converted to a lottery. *A damned Powerball drawing for the privilege of serving the nation. What a message.* He remembered sitting in the theater at West Point when the balls had been drawn. The going wisdom was that if your birth date number was 200 or lower, you'd be in a rice paddy in six months; 300 or higher, and you could buy the drinks at somebody else's going-away-to-die party. He'd told himself that he'd tempt fate and leave if his own number had been 250 or higher. The ball drawn for his birthday had been number twelve. And so he stayed, preparing himself for the fate suffered by so many others he had known. At least this way he could have some control of a small part of the situation. Better to command your own platoon than to die as a corporal in one led by some other guy. He stayed for himself, and for the father who didn't understand why he didn't want to stay.

He had not stayed for her—the girl he thought was *the one*. He closed his eyes and allowed himself to see her face again. He had planned to marry her, had discussed all his feelings with her, had told her he wanted to leave the place. Then the phone call had come. "My dad says that if you quit, I can't see you again." *And what did you say to that?* "I can't go against my father's wishes. I love you, but he's my father." *She made her choice. She chose her path. I stayed, but not for her.*

He tried to pretend that it didn't matter when he went home on summer leave, but it did matter. He tried to explain to her that he wasn't a coward, wasn't a quitter, he could simply see what was coming because he had studied the history of such things. He just didn't want to throw his life—their life—away on something the nation no longer believed in and was therefore destined to lose.

They started shutting the war down with "Vietnamization"—turning the fight over to the South Vietnamese—about the time he graduated in 1973. He started his training in the air cavalry, but a shoulder injury diverted him into law school and the JAG Corps instead. By the time he was out of school, Saigon had fallen.

He'd married on the rebound, too afraid of the loneliness to come home to an empty apartment every night. They'd tried to make it work for years, but he finally admitted his mistake to himself, and to his wife, and they had gone their separate ways.

Then came the dreams. He saw her face just as it had been in high school, except that this time it was from a hospital bed, and she was holding her chest, calling for him. Then there was the phone call from his sister, the little girl who had taken piano lessons from her before their dates.

She died on the operating table, a tumor wrapped around her heart. He wiped away the tears hat came every time he thought of it. *The war killed parts of me, and I never even saw the stinking place.*

McNamara, Rumsfeld, the current idiots in place—the same mistakes time and time again. No declaration of war. Not enough boots on the ground. Take the turf and then give it back. Then take it back again. Can we just once elect a historian rather than a goddamn business major? These are not just dollars we're spending. We're spending people. Good people dying for nothing.

He went back to the fridge and filled a tumbler with ice, then poured the Crown Royal over it and sank back into the chair in front of the television. One of the American generals had been shot, but the sergeants had taken over, and they finally had the troops moving off the beach and out of the crossfire. He was asleep ten minutes later.

Chapter Fourteen

Trask looked at his watch and shook his head with disapproval. It was almost lunchtime and he hadn't gotten a damn thing done. He was now the office curiosity piece, with everyone looking at him as if he were either some new super hero or just nuts. The phone calls that had destroyed his morning schedule had been running about fifty-fifty. He was sure for the moment that neither spin on the story was accurate, even though a similar debate was raging between the *Post* and the *Times,* copies of which had been presented to him by his secretary.

The former had a short article on the Ainger Place incident buried on the third page of the Metro section, but also ran an editorial which was very critical of the United States Attorney allowing his assistants to go on shooting patrols with the city's police, since that meant that the prosecutors might get too close to the officers on the street, and they could not then be counted on to be neutral and sensible buffers against police excesses. The editorial strongly suggested that such an excess might have occurred in this case, in which two teenagers had been shot, one fatally. There was no mention that these misguided children had been fired upon only after trying to rape another citizen and wounding a police officer.

The *Times,* by contrast, had gotten most of the facts right, and had sung the praises of Special Agent Doroz and himself, although Trask was certain that his little rock toss had not been made from as far away as the reporter had asserted. *I haven't been contacted by any ball clubs offering me a contract, anyway.* He looked at his watch again. The one call he had welcomed had been from Tim, who had asked if he wanted to grab a burger at noon.

He left for the elevator at ten before twelve, ignoring the phone, which was ringing again as he left his office. He waited for five minutes or so in the lobby before Wisniewski walked out of the elevator.

"I'm supposed to be down here waiting for you, hero. Haven't you read the story of Truman and MacArthur?"

"Knock it off. I don't want to hear that word again for a long time. Doesn't fit. Not me. Carter took the slug."

"I'm proud of you, anyway. I saw that arm in the outfield when we played softball last summer. I bet you knocked that asshole silly."

"I think the agent's .45 had a slightly bigger impact. Let's go eat."

They had gone half a block when they stopped in their tracks. Three superior court felony assistants were hurrying back toward the office, and Trask saw that one of them was wearing a suit covered with a foul-smelling brown stain.

"Shit, Brent, what happened to you?" Wisniewski asked.

"Shit is exactly correct," Brent Posner said. "They brought my defendant up from lockup for trial and didn't check his jumpsuit. He'd taken a dump downstairs and stuffed it all in his pockets. When the jury came in, he stood up and started slinging it everywhere. He got the jury, me, the judge..."

"Which judge?" asked Trask.

"Benton Pike. This was going to be his first case back on the felony side."

"Maybe it'll be his last." Wisniewski tried hard not to laugh, but lost the battle. "I'm sorry, man, if it was anybody other than Pike..."

"Yeah, maybe I'll think it's funny too, after I shower and burn these clothes," Posner said. "They're probably going to have to remodel that whole courtroom. It's everywhere."

Trask and Wisniewski expressed their condolences and moved on.

"I think," Wisniewski said, "that you may have just been bumped from the front page of the office rumor mill."

"If so, I'm grateful. Too bad it had to happen to Brent. I've got about forty bad puns running through my head now, but I'll spare you."

"I'm sure others will take up the cause. 'A shitty thing happened on my way to the forum' beats out your being a rock star."

"That's terrible."

"Sorry. Best I could do on short notice."

"When are you going to give me some sane company upstairs?"

"Lassiter told me that all I have to do is convince a couple of juries of my courtroom stature—in other words, win a couple of trials—and all will be forgiven and forgotten."

"Good. Hurry up, dammit, I could use some help up there already."

"I'm not riding with you on your surveillance trips."

"Bite me."

He had just gotten back from lunch when the phone rang again.

"Trask," he answered impatiently.

"What's with the attitude?" Lynn's voice was on the other end.

"Sorry. It's been a rather unusual morning."

"Anything wrong?"

"Have you seen the *Post?*"

"Of course. I liked the *Times* better."

"I don't think our United States Attorney subscribes to the *Times*. Anyway, Lassiter had to spend half the morning in Eastman's office covering my supposedly heroic backside, then I had to spend some time in Lassiter's office, and whenever I was back here the phone wouldn't stop ringing."

"Are you in trouble?"

"I don't think so. Lassiter said he cooled Eastman off."

"Good. Do you still need a Jamaican informant?"

"Sure," Trask said, laughing. "Why? Got one in your pocket?"

"I might," she said, coyly.

"This is not the time to toy with your friendly neighborhood rock chucker."

"OK, here's the deal. DEA was apparently working this guy as a source in Panama against some Jamaican posse types. I think our guy told me they were Spanglers. According to the informant, they got all of the information out of him they wanted, used him to do a couple of undercover deals, and then just cut him loose—put him back on the streets down there with no cover or backup or anything. He figured he'd be dead in a day or two if he hung around, so he signed onto a freighter and jumped ship in Jacksonville, hitchhiked south to

Melbourne, and walked right up to the gate at Patrick. Asked some security police gate guard for asylum. The cop called the OSI detachment; they interviewed him, and then called me. I told 'em that—assuming the guy's legit—I knew someone who might be interested in employing him for a while. What do you think?"

"I can see it now. Rock-throwing AUSA smuggles illegal immigrant into capital city..."

"I was just trying to help."

"And you may have. What's this guy's name?"

"Desmond Osbourne."

"Get me whatever other bio data you can, please. Date of birth. Where he's from in Jamaica. I'm going to give your phone number to Barry Doroz. He's done some out-of-country stuff before. If we can actually do this he'll know how. I'll need to clear it with Lassiter, too."

"Get back to me soon. We can put this guy up for a night or so, but we have a budget, too."

"Thanks, babe. See you at home."

"So how'd it go with the boss?" William Patrick lowered his large frame into the chair facing Lassiter's desk.

"What was Bill Murray's line in *Ghostbusters*? 'I've been slimed?' I was allowed to skillfully trap myself."

"Uh-oh. How so?"

"I was explaining to Mr. Eastman that our young Mr. Trask had done a heroic, if foolhardy thing, and that as a result one rapist is in the morgue and the other's in the Lorton Hospital. I explained that but for Mr. Trask, Barry Doroz might be in the morgue instead, and that I had personally blessed what I thought—what *everyone* thought—was going to be a nice, safe ride-along in a surveillance van to check out a target premises. It seems, however, that Ross had spent most of *his* morning answering questions from the *Post*, as well as a couple more questions from some deputy assistant attorney general at Main Justice, who appears to have agreed with that editorial."

"Was Ross pissed?"

"Actually, I don't think so, but I think he wanted me to *believe* that he was. He kept talking about how sound judgment needed to be the cornerstone of a federal prosecutor's mental makeup, and said that this incident certainly calls that into question. Once I saw that I wasn't going to talk him out of that notion, I had to just say that I thought every other decision we'd seen out of Trask justified giving him a second chance. Once I put *that* on the table, he smiled, nodded, and I was then reminded that one Benjamin Prescott might be similarly deserving of a second chance."

"Oh, boy."

"Yep. The only way I was able to keep our good kid on the floor was to grant the other kid a reprieve from appellate. Prescott's moving back in tomorrow."

"What're you going to do with him?"

"Keep him in a second-chair status until he proves to us that we can trust him to do the right thing. Have him work for Steve Dominguez in the dope section, and pass along those instructions, please. No solo trials and no lead attorney status until I say so. He always works under supervision."

"What about duty-phone calls, papering, that sort of thing? Those involve judgment calls, too. A detective or agent bumps into something at 3:00 a.m. Do we want him answering the duty phone?"

"Not really, but let him pull his weight, or try to, anyway. Let's not punish the rest of the staff by rewarding him and excusing him from the painful parts of the job."

"I thought you *enjoyed* the midnight phone calls."

"Sometimes I still do."

"Yeah, it's not like you keep regular hours." Patrick paused. "Are you getting any sleep, Bob?"

"Enough."

"Bullshit."

"I'm glad to see my credibility is still unassailable with you."

"You need a life outside this job. When's the last time you had a date?"

"Can't say that I remember. Not that it's any of your business."

"I'll make it my business if I choose to."

"What exactly does that mean?"

"It means, old friend, that Ross Eastman may not be the only one around here who knows you well enough to trap you. When I do it, though, it'll be for your own damn good, and you may even enjoy it."

"I don't do blind dates anymore, Bill."

"Fine. I guarantee that whoever we pick out for you will at least have retained the power of sight. Are there any other specifications I need to plug into the computer?"

Lassiter thought for a moment. He could be firm and nasty enough to avoid the subject for good, but the thought of offending Patrick was unattractive, and the possibility of some quality female companionship was attractive, especially if the date was, too.

"No judges."

"*No judges?*" Patrick roared with laughter. "Why would you think I would ever have crossed that bridge?"

"Just making sure."

"Hell, Bob. I know better than to set you up with somebody that might even *think* they outranked you. Of course, if you'd network the barest bit, you could be on the bench yourself by now. What have you got against dating judges, or better yet, being one?"

"Not interested in either. Let me ask you something. When you were eight, or ten, or twelve, and you and the other kids were choosing sides for football or baseball, did you ever tell them that you'd prefer not to play, but would gladly serve as the referee?"

"Can't say that I did."

"I didn't either. Never will. I don't know where we came up with this idea that wearing a goddamn robe was the pinnacle of our profession. I also don't understand why we have to pay them more than *we* make, for what it's worth. I know some of the big civil firm partners make a gazillion dollars, but what about the men and women in this office who work their butts off all their lives to keep the people safe in their beds at night? Since when does the umpire make more than the star center fielder?"

"The credit belongs to the man who is actually in the arena."

"Yes. Teddy Roosevelt." Lassiter said. "You're better read than you look."

"It allows me to occasionally confound you."

"Well, as usual, you've brightened my day a bit."

"Part of my job description. Keep cranky, hermetic supervisor from going over the edge into self-inflicted lunacy."

Lassiter laughed. "You do a fine job of it, too. They just ought to pay you more for it."

"As I remind anyone who asks why I don't join one of those big civil firms, or go over to the dark side. But where else am I going to make this kind of money saying nasty things about people I don't like? I'm not getting rich, Bob, but I'm happy and comfortable."

"And for that..." Lassiter nodded, "I envy you."

"Am I interrupting?" Trask stood in the doorway, wondering whether his status in his present position was being reevaluated.

"Not at all, Jeff, come in." Patrick stood up to take his leave.

"Sit back down, Bill." Lassiter motioned for Trask to take the other side chair. "I may need a second opinion from now on where this assistant is concerned." He saw that the jab had put Trask off balance. "Just kidding, Jeff. What's up?"

Trask described the phone call from Lynn.

"I talked to Barry Doroz, and he called a guy he knows in ICE. The immigration guy says he'll grease it so we can parole this Jamaican into the country on a temporary S-Visa?"

"Sure," Lassiter nodded. "We all joke that the *S* stands for snitch. We do it occasionally when an illegal immigrant has rendered services to the realm, and when the individual isn't otherwise a menace to society. Who's checking him out?"

"Barry and the immigration guy. The Jamaican kid's from Negril—on the west coast of the island. It's unlikely he'd be recognized by anyone from Kingston. No record that we know of."

"Those being the crucial words at the moment," cautioned Lassiter. "You're in no hot water with us right now, but I can't say the boss would kiss you if this went wrong. Make sure this kid is who we think he is, then go ahead and plug him in. You might also want to do a memorandum of understanding with someone other than your girlfriend at Air Force OSI so that they—or she—won't get stuck holding the bag if this goes south on us. I'll send you a go-by in an email. We'll have to assume responsibility, and I'll get ICE and the department to sign off on it, too."

"Thanks." Trask paused for a moment. "I know you probably had to stick your neck out for me once today already. I didn't mean for you to have to do it again so soon."

"I'm not doing it *for you*." Lassiter corrected. "I'm doing it because you did—and are again doing—the right thing. Good luck."

"Thanks again," said Trask as he rose and headed for the door.

"You're right." Patrick said when Trask had left the room. "Good kid. And you see that his actually having a girlfriend was very helpful here. Now, blonde, brunette, or redhead?"

"Don't you have some real work to do?"

"I'm on it!" Patrick headed for the door.

The two years Demetrius Reid spent in Ocho Rios were certainly the most peaceful of the Jamaican's young life. His work in the kitchen of a resort overlooking Turtle Beach actually excited him at first. His skills with the entrees he had learned at his mother's shoulder in Kingston were soon noticed, and he was given a free hand to experiment with the native fruits and more expensive preparations that his late family could never have afforded on a regular basis. He worked with ackee and star fruit, sour sop, and stinkin' toe. There were mangos, limes, guavas, yams, and papayas to choose from, and he created special dishes and sauces that became mainstays on the resort's menu.

On his days off he hiked the river valleys, earning extra money as a tour guide, escorting the guests from the cruise ships to the base of Dunn's River Falls, where they marveled at the water's six hundred foot plunge on the final leg of its flow to the sea. He marveled in turn at the wealth of the tourists, with their five hundred dollar cameras and hundred-dollar sunglasses. They tipped him generously, and he accepted the money gratefully at first. The routine of his employment soon bored him, however, and he began to view the tips as handouts from *bakras,* or slave masters. While he ate better and slept more safely than he ever had in his life, he felt himself becoming soft and complacent.

The news from the states began to reach him, and he listened intently as returning Shower brothers told him of the posse operations underway in New York, Miami, Washington, Kansas City, and Dallas. The demand by the American public for cocaine had transformed the posses into money-making machines for the political bosses in Kingston, with the usual cash crop of high-grade sinsemilla marijuana forced aside by the white powder which could be easily transformed into the more addictive crack. Cocaine was easier to smuggle and much more profitable. It didn't carry a heavy smell like *ganja,* and went for as much as twenty-five grand per kilogram—a little over two pounds—for the pure product, whereas the saturated pot market only paid $1,000 a pound for the best weed. The money was making the posses rich.

The thought of easier money appealed to him. He signed on with one of the cruise ships as a galley chef, and worked one passage only—from Ocho Rios to Miami—before disappearing into the arms of the Shower posse's agents in South Florida. He was welcomed by some of the old Tivoli gang, and soon began cooking again. This time, however, he was cooking powder cocaine into crack.

The Shower posse had some fifty crack houses in Miami alone and was raking in more than nine million dollars per month from the addicts of the city. The cash flow also required the establishment of money houses, where the profits were stored and counted. There were even immigration houses, where the new arrivals from Kingston were processed and given the most basic instructions before being assigned to other commands.

This lucrative business was hardly risk free, however. The heavy foot traffic to and from the crack-house doors did not go unnoticed by the police, who set up surveillance teams and cameras, then swarmed in with search warrants after using informants to make undercover buys from the posse's salesmen. While he was out one afternoon buying supplies, a Metro Dade task force hit the house where he'd been staying, arresting six of the nine house residents and killing one young soldier who had tried to prevent their entry with gunfire from his TEC-9. All the others were jailed, and he never saw any of them again. He and the one other survivor were simply told to report to another house in the city.

The bosses were taken completely by surprise when he refused, and instead demanded his own house.

He reminded them that he was the ranking member left from his unit, he knew how to cook the coke, he could control any new recruits they might want to assign to him, and he had learned from the mistakes of his predecessors. Whether it was his confidence, or the glare from the eyes of the young giant as he expressed it, the posse elders acquiesced.

It did not take long for him to locate another three-bedroom bungalow in southern Miami, or to secure a six-month lease in the name of a cooperative local female who had been all too willing to sign the papers for five hundred dollars. The other survivor from the raided house followed him, one new teenager from the island showed up, and he surprised his bosses by telling them that he now had all the help he needed. They asked him about house security, but he said he would handle it his way. He called his two subordinates into the living area of his new command post and announced the new rules for their operation.

They were to shed the dreadlocks they had worn into the country. The island hairstyle marked them to the police. They would instead wear the style of the neighborhoods where they lived and worked. The newest posse arrival had the bad judgment to question this at first, but a slap of a massive hand sent him sprawling across the room. When the boy recovered from the blow, Reid calculated—correctly—that there would be no further resistance.

His second order was that the house was to be used for eating and sleeping only, and that their sales operations were to be conducted in other parts of the neighborhood in order to eliminate the telltale flow of customers to and from their door. The actual sales were to be conducted in the local custom—they would recruit local juveniles to do the hand-to-hand transactions and to act as lookouts for the police. He had observed the local competition, and had been impressed at how some of the small-scale dealers had apparently been able to operate for years without being arrested.

The American police, he explained, were different from the constabulary forces back in Kingston. While it had not been unusual for the posses in Jamaica to engage in—and occasionally win—pitched battles with the police, the American law enforcement agencies were better equipped, better trained, better organized, and *generally* not subject to corruption.

They would take satisfaction from the money they made, but they would not flash it. A low profile was required to avoid attention from the cops and to keep them from becoming a prime raid target for the Spangler cells in the area. Finally, he noted the smiles of his charges when he emphasized that their share of the profits was only going to be split three ways, instead of eight or ten. Even the new arrival's ego seemed to be healing at the promise of the extra pay.

His system worked well for more than a year, and he lined his pockets well before paying the required tribute and costs to the posse bosses. Those same bosses did not, however, share his operational views regarding low profiles, and the wars he had known in Kingston began to erupt up and down the eastern seaboard. When the Spanglers—now out of power in Jamaica and hungry for their piece of the cocaine trade—arrived to organize in the United States, automatic weapons began to chatter up and down Highway 1 in south Florida.

The police, almost always operating in a reactive mode, were complacent at first. As long as "those damned Jakes" were merely "whacking themselves," the local cops were content just to close one posse murder as a former suspect's body was found, and to open a new case with the new victim. The numbers of homicides generated by the posse wars grew too steadily, however. Nearly a thousand died during the mid-1980s, and Miami saw victims piling up in its morgues.

Two killings then changed the climate.

The first was the execution of a Jamaican female, the sister of a low-level Shower boss who had commissioned her to manage one of the money houses. When the posse command determined that she had "messed up" the money, she was shot several times as she answered the door to the house. The shooting received more than the normal hue and cry in the press when it was determined, first, that the dead Jamaican was a female and, second, that she had been eight months pregnant at the time of her death, and that one of the bullets which passed through her body had also passed through the baby.

The final straw came when he and several members of another Shower house were en route to hit a Spangler enclave. One passenger in a vehicle carrying Spangler troops had recognized the Shower team on a public street as they were passing, and the two gangs exchanged fire from their cars. Although only one Shower member was nicked in the crossfire, a stray bullet fired from the

Shower car flew past the Spanglers and killed a six-year-old boy who was walking out the door of an ice-cream parlor.

The people of Miami had finally had enough. Reid was ordered out of Miami by the Shower dons just in time to avoid being swept up by a wave of federal agents who descended upon South Florida with directions to take out the posses. He was directed to Washington, DC.

The federal law enforcement emphasis was like nothing he had ever seen before. The FBI and ATF agents in Washington and New York actually talked to each other, and even went so far as to catalogue posse members by photographs, collecting every arrest photo from every local agency and compiling volume after volume of intelligence and profiles. When more and more of his posse's cells were completely wiped out by federally coordinated sweeps, he again did the smart thing, temporarily separating himself from his posse acquaintances and becoming a law-abiding cook in The Caribe restaurant.

Desmond Osbourne's eyes were wide as quarters as he was led onto the Patrick Air Force Base tarmac by a special agent of the Air Force OSI. The OSI man spoke for a moment to an Air Force captain in a flight suit, who nodded and then motioned Osbourne up the steps and directed him into a very nicely padded seat inside a C-20B, the military twin of a Gulfstream Aerospace business jet used to ferry VIP's to important meetings.

"Make yourself comfortable, sir. I'm the co-pilot. Can I get you anything to drink? Maybe a soda?"

Osbourne asked for a Coke, which was promptly delivered.

"Buckle up," the captain instructed him. "We'll be at Andrews in no time."

When he landed at Andrews Air Force Base in a Maryland suburb of Washington, DC, Osbourne was met at the bottom of the plane's stairway by an FBI agent and a short, Hispanic, police detective.

"Welcome to Washington, Mr. Osbourne," said Barry Doroz, chuckling as he saw that his new asset was wearing beach shorts, sandals, and a t-shirt, and that he was carrying no luggage whatsoever. "It looks like we need to take you shopping."

Chapter Fifteen

Demetrius Reid walked out of his office in the rear of The Caribe and into the kitchen area. He was generally satisfied with the hum of the operation. Cooks he had personally trained were getting the luncheon crowd fed in an efficient manner without any sacrifice in the quality of the dishes, and the busboys were keeping up with the flow of traffic in and out of the restaurant. He walked into the dining room and exchanged pleasantries with a few of his regulars, happy to play the role of the successful restaurateur. He stopped at the checkout counter and removed some of the large bills from the cash register, noting that it had already been another good business day.

He stepped back to let his counter girl do her job, and thanked several customers for coming as they paid their bills and left. While doing so, he kept his eyes on his newest employee, a busboy named Desmond from Negril. He was always happy to hire those from the home island, as long as he could trust them. They did not have to participate in his other business. He had established a wall between the two ventures that only three could cross—himself, his attorney Spencer Goode, and his restaurant manager, Donald McFarlane. McFarlane was another product of the Tivoli Gardens; Reid had known him for years. Like Reid, McFarlane had been savvy enough to avoid a criminal conviction, despite having served his time in the posse conflicts. No one else at The Caribe knew of their other business.

McFarlane saw his employer watching the new boy from across the dining room, and walked over to join Reid behind the counter.

"He seems to be doin' the job well."

"Yah, mon." Reid agreed. "A good hire so far. Ya say he just walked in off the street?"

"He did. Said he hitched up from Florida, and was headin' for New York when he heard about our place here from a local who dropped him off on the beltway."

"Did ya put him up in the house?"

"Yah." McFarlane answered. "I figured you'd want to keep an eye on him at first."

"Good." Reid slapped him on the shoulder. "Which room did ya put him in?"

"Number eight."

"Good. I'll be out for a bit."

Reid walked through the dining area and the kitchen, and then out the rear of the restaurant into the alley. He turned north and walked about a block and a half before entering a large boarding house on the east side of Fourteenth Street, NE. There were twelve units in the three-story building Reid had purchased with profits from both of his businesses. It gave him a place to put his new people in the restaurant. He needed such a place. His employee turnover was always high as his workers succeeded in achieving permanent resident status, took better jobs, got married, or simply went home to the island. Having access to their rooms also provided the opportunity to make sure that no one was working against him, either for the police or an old rival from the posse wars, and he made a little more profit by charging them a nominal amount for rent.

He took the stairs two at a time to the second floor, reached into his pocket, and took out a key ring as he reached the door bearing a metal 8. The master key opened the door, and he stepped inside. Reid saw that his new employee had not added any furniture. There was the metal-frame bed in the center of what had been arranged as a studio apartment, a small dresser against one wall, an even smaller desk next to the dresser, and the kitchenette in the back corner.

He opened the desk, carefully removing the few items he found, and replacing them in the same locations. The dresser drawers contained only some underwear and socks. He opened the refrigerator, saw a few cans of soda and little else, and then turned his attention to the closet, finding what appeared to be a couple of new pairs of inexpensive jeans, some T-shirts, and a worn-looking windbreaker.

No phones, no pagers, no notebooks. Desmond Osbourne appeared to be who he said he was, another poor boy from a poor homeland trying to make a go of it, and probably hoping to send some money home to this mama. Reid locked the door to the apartment and walked back toward The Caribe.

"Could you see which room he was in?" Carter asked Ramirez, who was closer to the window in the sliding door of the newly and badly painted surveillance van.

"He was checking our boy out, all right." Ramirez pointed out the window where he had seen Reid. "That's number eight on the right. Second floor, next to the fire escape."

"If he set it up like we told him, we shouldn't have any problems." Doroz took his turn at the window. "We got him some cheap jeans, some shirts, and a beat-up jacket from a thrift store. He's not supposed to even have our phone numbers in there."

"How does he contact us then?" Carter asked. "I seemed to have missed the meetings for some reason." He shifted in the swivel chair to rest his left leg on one of the front seats, sticking it through the curtain that separated the front of the van from the rear.

"How's that thing coming?" Doroz nodded at the leg.

"Feels like I bruised it all the way down to the toes. The doc said all the blood that didn't spurt out of me ran down the inside of the leg. Would have been worse if Puddin' here hadn't belted it up."

Crawford acknowledged the nod with one of his own from the rear of the van.

"Our man Desmond has a couple of business cards with phone numbers in a false sole in his new tennis shoes," Doroz said. "He was instructed not to call us unless it was an absolute emergency, and then to go to a pay phone away from the restaurant. We've got a regular meeting time and place set up with him on his day off at The Mall at Prince Georges in Hyattsville. He can hop on the Metro green line and make it out there pretty easily."

"What's his day off?" Carter continued to fidget with his leg, trying to find a comfortable position.

"Saturday, oddly enough," Doroz responded. "Most of the restaurant's business is during the week; it's heaviest during the lunch hour.

"Any other marching orders?"

"We told him to just be aware of regular activity that didn't appear to be normal restaurant stuff. Back door visitors, unusual supplies. We didn't tell him about the beer truck from Brooklyn. That'll be one of our checkpoints to see if he's being level with us."

"He didn't require much in the way of a cover story," Ramirez said. "He's from the west side of the island, so any Kingston posse members have probably never seen him before, unless they were hooked up with the Spangler group in Panama, and ICE says our Mr. Reid here is from a neighborhood that was run by the Shower Posse—arch enemies of the Spanglers. The kid's an orphan, but we told him to tell anyone that asked that his uncle had given him two hundred bucks and a ticket to Florida on a freighter. That's about the amount we spent on his new wardrobe."

"He's lucky it's summer," noted Carter. "If this takes a while, he's going to need a coat."

"He's more than willing to ride this for a few months," Doroz said. "He thought his days were numbered after DEA cut ties with him in Panama. They ran some operation with the national police, picked up most of a Spangler cell dealing cocaine in Panama City. They didn't get all of 'em, though, and the ones still on the street had figured this kid for the snitch. His DEA handlers told him that he was worrying about nothing, gave him a couple of bucks and wished him good luck. He said that a friend of his got whacked just before he jumped on that freighter."

"Their loss, our gain," Carter said. "What is it with DEA, Bear?"

"I don't know. I've never really had a problem dealing with their worker bees. The trouble seems to start with their promotion system. It's all supposed to be purely objective—all stat-based. Some ambitious types want their promotions, and they pile up stats in a couple of ways. Muscle in on as many local street-corner busts as possible. That way, you can rack up numbers of defendants and weight just by adopting some local cop's work and taking it to federal court. Or wait until somebody builds a real good, large-scale case with lots of targets and drug amounts, and just steal the investigation. Either way, you have to have those numbers to go from a GS-13 to 14, 14 to 15, and so on.

"The other thing I've seen is supervisors who come back stateside after working out of country. Colombia, Peru, Panama. They get used to operating in an environment where it's pretty much anything goes, and then they're back here with our prosecutors and the court system telling 'em what they can and can't do. Some don't make the adjustment very well. At any rate, if we have to write an OCDETF operation on this, I don't plan on mentioning that we're using one of their former sources. They'll scream like stuck pigs."

"Let 'em scream," snorted Ramirez. "They horned in on one of our reverse stings a while back, and didn't even have the sense to realize that if they'd waited another hour, they'd have had more defendants and more weight to throw on their silly report cards."

"Let's just let it be our secret as long as possible," cautioned Doroz. "If they find out about this kid, they might screw up both the investigation and his chances of getting permanent immigration status. If he goes back to Jamaica, he's a dead duck. Even in Negril."

Spencer Goode, Esquire, walked toward his lucky video poker machine in the twenty-five cent section at Harrah's in Atlantic City. He could already feel a slight elevation in his own metabolism, the result of the increase in adrenaline, which had kicked in when he walked into the place. A cocktail waitress recognized him and smiled pleasantly as she said, "Welcome back." He smiled and nodded in return, only to lose the smile as he turned the corner into his row and saw that his seat and machine were occupied by the same dour old hag who had been so jealous of his first jackpot. He knew she saw him approaching, but she didn't even look up. Instead, she kept her face and leathery hands glued to the machine, playing slowly, methodically. *Not a problem. I meant to play the dollar machines anyway. I brought a little extra play money. She can keep the quarter jackpot tonight. I'll go find a real one.*

He found a double-double bonus machine with a progressive jackpot of over $6,300, and saw that only one of the seats in the bank of ten machines was occupied. He took a seat at the end of the row, read the pay table, and was mildly disappointed to see that it was only an eight-five machine, paying eight times the bet for a full house, five times for a flush. He knew that this meant lower odds on the paybacks, but reasoned that the progressive—fifty per cent higher than the normal royal flush payout of $4,000—justified the risk. He opened his wallet, pulled out one of the five hundred-dollar bills he had allocated for the night, slipped it into the waiting slot, and pressed the max-play deal button.

He worked the initial hundred up to $180 on straights, three-of-a-kinds, and flushes before the machine took it all back. Not swayed, he put the second hundred in, and five hands later hit four threes for a $400 win. He saw that, in addition to the profit he'd made, he was also racking up a considerable number of player's club points on his club card, which he could redeem for meals, or even his room if he collected a few more. He cashed out the ticket for the $400, promising himself that the ticket would not go back into the machine. It was money he would keep after he played the rest of his stake. *Even if I don't hit anything else, I'll only be down a hundred this way.*

The third hundred was gone so fast he barely remembered it, and the biggest hand he'd hit on it had only been a pair of jacks. He pulled his card out of the machine and moved one seat to his left. He managed to hit four sevens for $250, and telling himself it was an omen of good luck, kept playing. The entire amount was gone twenty-seven minutes later. He moved another seat to his left, and put in the fourth bill, looking up at the sign over the bank, which indicated that the progressive jackpot was now up to $6,410. He got thirty minutes of play out of the machine before the last five-dollar bet disappeared. *I'll move back to the end machine. I won on that one.*

He didn't win on his final hundred, but he did note that on six occasions, he had finished the hand with four of the five cards required for a royal flush. *This thing's going to hit. I've been so close. I can feel it!* He took the four-hundred-dollar cash ticket out of his wallet, and put it into the slot. An hour later, it was gone as well. *Damn. I didn't bring any more cash to play on. I've got my credit card, but I need it for expenses on the road and in New York, and I don't know what my pin number is for cash advances—never wanted to know. Never needed it. I can beat this thing if I play just a little longer. Not ready to quit yet. Persistence is the key.*

He pulled his players card out of the machine and walked briskly through the casino floor to the parking garage, pulling the metal briefcase out of the rear of the Acura. He looked around to see if anyone was watching him, and—satisfied he was not being observed—opened the case. He removed a folded stack which he knew represented a thousand dollars, locked the case, and locked the Acura by pressing the button on the key fob. He headed back into the casino.

"Here he comes now," Ramirez noted, nodding toward the figures approaching their table. Doroz had gotten there early enough to get his pick of the tables in the place—an Outback Steak House located just outside the main entrance to the Mall at Prince Georges—and had grabbed one in the back of the restaurant, where he and Crawford had been joined by The Twins. "Looks like he brought a date."

"Gentlemen, this is Special Agent Lynn Preston of Air Force OSI," Trask announced as he reached the table. "She's the reason we have a meeting this evening."

"Barry Doroz. Nice to speak to you in person." Doroz smiled as he rose to shake her hand. "Quite a little shell you guys found on the Florida beach for us." He introduced the rest of the party to her.

"Very impressive, Jeff." Carter nodded toward Lynn. "And smart, too."

"Smart enough to get me to pay for a steak dinner at a business meeting," Trask remarked. "She cooks very well, but..."

"But I prefer not to," Lynn cut him off. "So don't get any fancy ideas about parties at our place."

"Duly noted," Carter laughed. "She's a cop."

"So where's your new resource?" Lynn noticed that there was still an empty chair at the table.

"Coming in now." Doroz stood and raised his hand, a gesture noticed by Desmond Osbourne, who walked over to the table. Doroz made his second round of introductions, making it a point to remind the new arrival that he would not be in the country but for the alertness and resourcefulness of the lady at the table and the prosecutor assigned to the case.

"I'm very grateful. I owe you my life." The young man's dark eyes moistened as he spoke.

"It's an opportunity for you to earn something very valuable," said Trask. "But we're asking you to do something very risky in return." He looked as sternly and seriously as he could at Osbourne. "We can't yet tell you everything about this investigation. We *can* tell you that you must follow the instructions given to you by the guys at this table. If you don't, no permanent immigration status. Understand?"

"Yes."

"Good." Doroz nodded. "Why don't we get some food, and then you can tell us what you've seen so far." He waived the waiter over.

After the orders had been placed, Osbourne summarized his first week inside The Caribe.

"I haven't really noticed that much unusual. Several of the employees are like me—from Jamaica—but most are from Kingston. Mistah Reid and Mistah McFarlane run the place. Reid is the boss, for sure. He works a lot with the cooks, and Mistah McFarlane does most of the business-type work—ya know—orderin' the food from the suppliers and payin' the bills and such."

"Have you seen any of the suppliers?" Doroz saw his chance to get in a question without emphasizing its relevance.

"A couple. A local company brings in most of the meat and veggies. Twice a week—Tuesdays and T'ursdays. A beer truck from New York came in yesterday, Friday."

"From New York?" asked Carter, feigning surprise.

"Yah. Brooklyn is what the sign said on the truck. Brought in some Red Stripe. I heard Mistah Reid tell a customer that he had to have some authentic island brew to go wit' the food."

"Did you notice how much they brought in?" Doroz asked.

"A whole lotta cases of the bottles. Some cases of cans, too."

"I've had Red Stripe before—never seen it in cans, though." Carter looked at Ramirez as if he were making a simple observation.

"I'm from Jamaica, and I never saw the cans before," Osbourne responded. "I asked Mistah McFarlane about that, and he said they got a lotta international folks who eat lunch in the place, and some of them are from Europe, and are used to the cans they get from England. He said it tastes a little different in the cans. But I know that some of the cans don't get sold to the lunch crowd."

"What do you mean?" Doroz asked.

"Well, I know that one guy—tall, thin, young guy—came to the back door, and asked for six-packs for somebody named Fats. Mistah McFarlane went into Mistah Reid's office and got two six-packs outta the office, instead of outta the kitchen cooler, where they keep most of the stuff. I didn't see the guy pay for the beer. He just drove off."

"What kind of car?" Ramirez was now in full debriefing mode.

"A little Honda. I remember the plates."

"Shoot." Ramirez had his pocket notebook out with a pen.

"DC plates. 'Taxation Without Representation.' What does dat mean?"

"It means," said Ramirez, giving his partner a poke in the ribs, "That some people in the District of Columbia have delusions of statehood in the future. Did you get the numbers?"

"Yah, mon. JB-0804. I remembered that because I was born on August the fourt'."

"Good job." Carter patted the young man on the shoulder. "Anything else?"

"The only t'ing besides that was last night, right after the dinner rush. A guy in a suit drove up to the back in an Acura SUV and went inta Mistah Reid's office for a little while—left wit' a metal case."

"What kind of metal case?" Ramirez was back on point.

"Yah know, like a briefcase, mon."

"Did you get his plate numbers, too?"

"No, mon. Sorry. I was real busy bussin' tables at the time."

"No matter, nice work," said Doroz. "We don't know if any of it means anything yet, but we'll check it out. Keep your eyes and ears open, and we'll meet back here next week." He looked up to see that the food was being delivered. "Enjoy your steak. And by the way, your S-Visa is being processed. We don't foresee any problems as long as you keep on course here."

"T'ank you all again very much," Osbourne said. He enjoyed his steak while the rest of the table settled into general conversation. When he'd finished the meal, he said his good-byes and left the restaurant. He walked across the parking lot toward the front entrance of the mall, thinking that he might spend a little of his first week's paycheck on a book. He held the door for a woman pushing a stroller, and as his eyes followed her to make sure she'd cleared the doorway, he stepped into the mall, bumping squarely into the chest of a larger figure. He looked up into the smiling face of Donald McFarlane.

Chapter Sixteen

"JB-0804 comes back to a Honda registered to a David Greene. Twenty-six. Lives about six blocks north of The Caribe in Northeast. U.S. citizen. No record." Ramirez handed the computer summary to Carter, who had his left leg elevated on his desk. "I ran Greene, too. Five eleven, 175 pounds on his driver's license update last year. Don't think anybody would call him fat."

"What's the address?" Carter dropped his leg to the floor and pulled up closer to his own computer terminal.

"1440 Monroe."

Carter entered the address. "No incidents, no arrests, no citizen complaints for that address."

"Any other residents listed there?" Doroz looked up from an immigration file on Demetrius Reid. He'd decided to spend the afternoon at 7D.

"There's a Roderick Greene, date of birth makes him mid-forties. Probably David's old man." Carter typed a few more entries. "Bingo. Six two, and—*good lord, seven hundred pounds?* He did time in Lorton on a local dope case. NCIC says he was sentenced to eight years but only served three. He was born in Kingston, Jamaica." Carter reached into his desk and pulled out a frayed schedule, then swiveled around in his chair and faced Doroz. "Curbside trash pick-up in that neighborhood is tomorrow."

Doroz dialed the FBI's Washington Field Office. "Bonnie? Page Puddin' for me, please." He waited a few seconds. "Ever ridden a trash truck before? I need you to get to work early in the morning. Wear something old and lousy. Your worst sneaks and jeans. See you about six."

"Beggin' your federal pardon, Bear," Ramirez was scowling. "Do you really think that kid can dress down enough to pass for a garbage man in that neighborhood? The shine on his bright young face might set off the lookout alarms for miles."

Doroz shrugged. "Good point. We'll see how he looks when he shows. If he looks too Ivy League, we'll put him in the collection car. I'll ride the truck with you, and we'll meet gimpy back here when we bring in the bags." He motioned to Carter, who had his leg back up on the desk.

"Yeah, he's milking it for all it's worth." Ramirez looked at his partner. "He'd stick out about as bad as Puddin' anyway, as big as he is. We'll just let him get his hands dirty."

"I shall be happy to glove up and assist in that process," Carter said, leaning back in his chair. "I'll also have the complete criminal history on one Roderick Greene by that time. I'm very pleased to be able to help you gentlemen in any way I can, despite the fact that my service-related disability temporarily prevents me from joining you in the field."

"If your hands still work, run Spencer Goode and see what kind of wheels he has registered." Ramirez got up from his desk. "I gotta take a leak."

Carter punched his keyboard a few times. "What a surprise, an Acura SUV."

"Sounds like we may be giving our special ops group some overtime." Doroz mused. "Very good surveillance bunch, Dix. We'll have to be careful, though. We get burned, and this lawyer will at least *try* to put us through the wringer for following him."

"I'm afraid that Juan and I would have to disqualify ourselves; as drivers, anyway. Goode's seen us in court."

"Understood." Doroz stood up. "I'll meet you here in the morning."

———

As the garbage truck slowly rolled past the 1400 block of Monroe, the two men riding the back worked efficiently, trotting behind the truck and grabbing the cans and bags from the curb, then slinging them into the bed just in front of the mechanical compactor. This procedure was repeated for each bag of trash in the block, with one exception. The four large plastic bags which had been placed at the curb in front of 1440 Monroe were tossed into the truck bed like all the rest, but were thrown behind the compactor blade, so that when the rest of the trash was pressed toward the front of the truck, the garbage from 1440 Monroe was left undisturbed toward the rear. As the truck turned the corner at the end of the block, it pulled into a commercial parking lot, where it stopped for a moment beside a gray sedan. One of the men on the back of the truck jumped down, and placed the bags from 1440 Monroe into the trunk of the waiting sedan.

"See you back at 7D," Doroz said as he shut the trunk and jumped back onto the rear of the garbage truck. "We've got to do another couple of blocks before we hand this fine job back over to the regulars."

"I'm going to hit a drive-through for some breakfast on the way back," Crawford said. "Can I get you guys anything?"

"We'll have whatever you're having," Ramirez shouted as the truck groaned away from the parking lot. "But you're buying if we're doing this."

"No problem." Crawford grinned as he climbed into the sedan's driver's seat. He had worn his worst clothes, and had fully expected to be one of the trash throwers himself, given his rookie status. Doroz had instead handed him the keys to the collection vehicle, saying that he looked like he had just climbed out of an Abercrombie & Fitch advertisement.

As he pulled the sedan back onto the cross street, he looked up to see the Honda leaving Monroe and approaching him at the intersection. The driver, a young black man in his mid-twenties, paid him no attention, but turned in front of him and headed south.

———

"I bought four of everything." Crawford placed a sausage and egg biscuit, order of hash browns, and a coffee in front of Carter, Ramirez, and Doroz, keeping one for himself as he joined them at the large table in the center of the detectives' squad room. "Hope everyone approves of the menu."

"The price is right, and I assume you haven't been picking up garbage with your hands like these other gentlemen." Carter opened the bag, and nodded approvingly. "This will do fine, thanks. I get 100 percent of my daily minimum requirement of grease and cholesterol, with a modicum of nutrition thrown in.

I suggest we tackle these smaller bags before we open those." He motioned toward the four large trash bags in the corner.

"Amen," Doroz agreed, opening his own breakfast.

"I'm afraid the details I got on the elder Mr. Greene are about as appetizing as that trash." Carter said, holding up a file. "He was sent to Lorton for a crack deal. Sentenced to eight years. When he went in he weighed a svelte three-twenty. Some genius in the system put him to work in the kitchen. Three years later, he'd doubled in size, and they medically paroled him for morbid obesity."

"You're shittin' me," growled Ramirez. "The SOB *ate his way out of jail?"*

"He's so perceptive," said Carter, looking at Doroz but tilting his head toward his partner. "That's why I keep him around. It seems that the District of Columbia's prison system was not equipped with a bed which could hold Mr. Greene, nor were they willing to provide a day nurse to hand bathe him in order to keep him from developing festering fistulas between his rolls of fat. He didn't fit in a regular tub, and couldn't make it to the showers."

"I'm gonna puke." Ramirez swelled his cheeks like a chipmunk.

"Save it for the trash pull." Carter countered. "We'll all probably feel that way when we see what the Greene family eats on a weekly basis." He rolled the wrappers and napkins from his breakfast up in the paper sack, and arched a perfect shot into a large can across the room. He picked up a pair of plastic gloves from his desk. "Let's do this outside, shall we?"

An hour later, the concrete patio outside the squad room was strewn with litter, and the four men were sweeping the stinking piles of chicken bones, pizza boxes, and potato chip wrappers back into the plastic bags.

"Dammit." Ramirez complained. "Get up before dawn, sling trash all morning, and these bastards haven't got the common decency to put a shred of evidence in their garbage. No plastic baggies. No kilo wrappers. No residue. No broken bongs or anything else that would get us in on a warrant. Zilch."

"Looks like a pretty dead end," Doroz agreed. "For a guy who worked in the kitchen, Fats sure doesn't cook much. Let's clean this place up."

"Before we do that, there's one more bag we ought to check."

The three older investigators looked up to see Crawford holding a kitchen-sized trash bag, which was evidently full.

"And where did this come from?" Doroz asked.

"After you guys left in the trash truck, I was pulling out of the lot where you gave me the other bags, and I saw the young Greene dude in the Honda pull out in front of me. He went straight to the Hardee's drive-through where I was headed. He orders at the window, gets a big bag of takeout, but then instead of just leaving, he parks for a minute, then circles back around to the back of the building and takes this out of the trunk, and throws it into the restaurant dumpster."

Doroz grabbed the sack and ripped the top open, looking inside.

"Gentlemen," he said. "I do believe that Special Agent Crawford here has made our morning a good one." He reached into the bag and pulled out an aluminum Red Stripe beer can. The can had been ripped open along the side, revealing a dividing plate about a third of the way up from the bottom of the can. Doroz wiped his gloved finger around the inside of the bottom half of the can and held it up for the others to see. It was coated with a dry, white residue. "Good work," he said, beaming at Crawford. "No, *great* work."

"How many of those are in there?" Ramirez took the bag from Doroz. "Looks like six. How much coke do you think they get into a six-pack?"

"No real way of telling at this point." Doroz answered. "Depends on whether they want the can weight to feel legitimate. If somebody picked one up to check it, odds are they'd want it to feel like a real beer with the correct ounce-weight. The divider separates the actual beer on the top from the cocaine on the bottom. There's no residue in the tops. Anyone checking the contents might pop the top on one, find there's beer inside it by tasting what comes out the top of the can, and think nothing of it."

They took the bag inside to the squad room and covered the conference table with a plastic sheet to preserve the evidence. They put the cans, a broken digital scale, and some empty sandwich bag cartons on one side, separating them from wads of paper towels and anything else in the bag that would not be logged into evidence.

"They're 484-milliliter cans, right?" Carter was working a calculator at his desk. "About sixteen fluid ounces. If you figure ten ounces of beer on top of six ounces of powder...six times twenty-eight grams in an ounce gives you 168 grams of dope in each can. Six times 168 is 1,008 grams. You have a kilogram in each six-pack, assuming you could pack six ounces of coke powder in the space allowed."

"I think there's ample room for that." Doroz agreed. "There's our math."

"And there's our crack in their wall," added Carter. "Fairly smart group. No evidence in the trash, no stream of dope customers to and from the house. At least none reported by the neighbors. Sophisticated smuggling operation, too. We might even have trouble getting some of our judges to issue a warrant for the house. I can hear Noble now: 'I have no probable cause to believe, Detective, that the garbage left at the drive-through was ever in the house—it came from the man's car, after all—and no one has told me anything to support an inference that these defendants were selling the drugs from their home.' We'd leave his chambers with our hands empty. What I think we have, for now, is some very valuable information, but I wouldn't want to rush this."

"I'm wondering where the canning operation is," mused Doroz. "I asked New York about that when you first mentioned cans of Red Stripe. Joe Picone—the ATF guy I talked to from Brooklyn—says that from what he can piece together, Kingston Distributing is strictly a warehousing and shipping operation. No cannery at the place in Brooklyn. They've gotta be getting the cans in from somewhere else. He was working last week on getting a surveillance camera set up on the back of the place to video their loading docks. Said he knew the owner of the warehouse across the street, and wouldn't have to stick it on a phone pole..."

"Good idea," Carter agreed. "As savvy as this crew seems to be, the first thing they'd look for would be a pole-cam, or anybody looking like a phone company employee installing extra equipment."

"Exactly," said Doroz. "Joe thought he could get a video camera put in the window of his friend's office on the second floor. He'll just transmit the feed to his office, and hook it up to a recorder. Our targets will never see a phone company truck or anybody climbing a pole. I told him to be on the lookout for anything we might be interested in on this end. I'll give him a call and tell him we're interested in who's making deliveries *to* the place, as well as where the beer's going once it leaves the warehouse. We'll get videos and still shots if he sees anything."

"They're not going to all this trouble to smuggle in one lousy kilo in one lousy six-pack," offered Ramirez. "We're looking at the tip of somebody's iceberg."

"Yep," nodded Doroz, "And I think I'm looking at writing that OCDETF proposal tomorrow. Dix, if you don't mind, you and Juan can brief Willie, and I'll call Lassiter. We'll have to jump through all the deconfliction hoops on the Greenes, Reid, McFarlane, Kingston Distributing. Hopefully we won't bump into somebody else's claim."

"Sounds like a plan," Carter nodded, then looked at Crawford. "Not that I'm complaining, given the way he helped keep me from bleeding out, but I just have one question, Bear. Why did your understudy here let us wade through all this other crap before bringing out his treasure trove?"

"I think..." Crawford responded, "that I just wanted to show you that the proof was in the Puddin'."

"*That was terrible!*" Ramirez yelled. He grabbed a handful of the non-evidentiary garbage that had been separated from the cans, and hurled it at the punster across the table. He then picked up one of the cans, turned it over, and rubbed his finger along the bottom rim. "We're not looking for a canning operation, Bear."

"How's that?"

"Take a look at this. The can was probably just full of beer at one time, when it left wherever it was when they originally canned the stuff..."

"That would be jolly old England." Carter was back on his computer, working the internet. "Only place they brew it and put it in cans instead of bottles, as far as I can tell."

"England, then. They cut the bottom off, drain some of the beer out, wedge this dividing plate in—it has a soft plastic rim around the edge. That seals the beer in the top half, and then they solder the bottom back on." He flipped the can to Doroz. "Run your finger around the bottom there. You can feel a slight soldering ridge."

"Yep. We're not looking for a canning operation after all. If the beer's coming in clean from England, the factory there isn't involved in any smuggling. They're packing the dope in the cans here—probably at the Kingston

Distributing Company. That still means that somebody's getting the dope to Brooklyn, so the camera's still a good idea."

"This isn't their first can scam." Carter turned his computer monitor so that Doroz could see it. "Chicago case from 2004. DEA worked it. Jamaicans smuggling coke into the country from Panama in baby formula cans. They actually rented babies and had female couriers traveling with them so that no one would suspect anything. The different twist here is that their current use of the beer cans is all *in-country*. Either the coke's already here, or it's crossing the borders in some other fashion."

Doroz pulled out his cell phone. "Joe? Barry Doroz in DC." He summarized their discovery and theory, then held his phone down for a second. "Joe's in his buddy's office now, looking at the joint." He put the phone back to his ear. "We agree the camera's a good idea. Let's let it run a couple of weeks, and see if any pattern shows up. Great. Thanks for the help. Later."

As Special Agent Joseph Picone folded his cell phone and put it back into his pocket, he noticed an eighteen-wheeler pull into the lot and up to the rear loading docks of the Kingston Distributing Company. The driver of the semi jumped down from the cab, and seemed to be very angry about something. Bending over to look at the tires on the front of the unmarked trailer, he gestured wildly at them as another man emerged on the loading dock. Picone watched as the second man went back inside, and then emerged from a ground-level door pushing a large hydraulic jack. *Dude's really pissed about that flat.* He pulled a small notebook from the vest pocket of his jacket, noting that the trailer bore Ontario plates, and that it was Thursday, August 7, at 4:17 p.m.

On Saturday, August 9, Barry Doroz sat looking at his watch in a rear table of the steakhouse near the entrance of the Mall at Prince Georges. Desmond Osbourne had been due at 6:30 p.m., and it was now 7:45. Doroz waited until eight before he left the restaurant.

Chapter Seventeen

Demetrius Reid drove the Ford Explorer slowly down Rhode Island Avenue NE. The vehicle was a "rental," street terminology not for a vehicle from Hertz or Avis, but for transportation acquired in exchange for a rock of crack. The party from whom he had rented the SUV had already rented it from another addict, and so it was virtually untraceable.

He was in the right lane, and was barely moving down the avenue, with the front passenger window about halfway down so that he could communicate with the hookers walking "the track." He recognized one from two previous liaisons, but when she asked him if he wanted a date, he declined, and kept rolling. Those encounters had merely been a pair of amusing and defensive red herrings. If any cop asked her about him, she would say he had been a routine trick—a quick roll in a car for forty bucks. Nothing kinky, nothing threatening. The word would then spread among the girls that he wasn't a high-risk john. He did what he was supposed to do and paid what he was supposed to pay.

He saw her about thirty yards ahead, and was glad to see that no other vehicles had pulled in front of him. Unlike most of the few white girls that dared to walk the track, she was neither overweight nor rail-thin like the crack or meth addicts. He figured she was new to the game and probably new to town. He pulled to the curb beside her and lowered the passenger window even more. She walked over immediately, her high heels accenting every strut on the sidewalk.

"Hey, baby. Did you need some company this evening?"

"I wasn't even t'inking about it until ah saw your fine self walkin' down the street." He smiled as broadly as he could.

"Oh, I love your accent. Where you from, baby?"

"Trinidad," he lied, correctly calculating that she'd have no basis for comparison.

"So what did you have in mind, tonight?"

"How much for the whole night?"

"Ooh, that would mean an all-night special rate for you, baby…"

"How about five hundred?" He cut her off, not wanting to prolong either the negotiations or his exposure on the street.

"Five hundred?" She giggled and almost swallowed the gum she'd been smacking. "Baby, you just bought yourself a whole night of fun." She climbed into the passenger seat. "So you gotta room near here, or what?"

"No, a house. I t'ink we'll be much more comfortable there than in some cheap motel room, if that's OK wit' you."

"It's your money." She shrugged her shoulders and giggled. "Long as I get back here tomorrow."

"Of course."

He drove northwest on Rhode Island Avenue until he was out of the District, and turned left onto Jefferson once he reached the suburbs in Hyattsville, Maryland. He pulled into the driveway of an ordinary-looking split-foyer, and reached up to the visor, activating a clip-on garage-door opener. It was almost midnight and no one had seen him even enter the block, but he did not want any neighbor's eyes watching him escort the girl to the front door. The garage door slid back on its track, and he drove the Explorer in, parking beside the Cavalier. He pushed the button on the garage door remote once more, closing it behind them. When it had stopped, he got out and walked to her side, opening the car door for her.

"It's always nice to meet a gentleman," she cooed. "How do we get inside?"

"Right through that door." He smiled, motioning to some steps to the left of the garage.

They entered through the kitchen, and he led her to a seat on the sofa in his living room, facing a large plasma-screen television. Her drink of choice was whisky, which surprised him, but he had a bottle of Seagram's on hand. Half an hour and two stiff drinks later, she was ready, and he led her up the stairs to the bedroom. He pulled the condom on while she undressed. He was pleased with her body's appearance, and as whores went, her personality and manners were better than most. He used her twice before he excused himself, saying that he needed to use the bathroom. When he returned, he was carrying the trash bags and the duct tape. She was small, and her struggles ended quickly, but not before he watched the life drain from her eyes. He had missed that. It had been too long.

He dressed and carried the bundle down to the garage, where he loaded the body into the rear of the Explorer. He then walked over to the far wall of the garage, on the other side of the Cavalier, where he retrieved an identically wrapped bundle, and placed it beside the other body. He covered the corpses with an old blanket, and backed the Explorer out of the driveway.

Doroz followed the girl to a corner table, and sat down to review the menu of fare offered by The Caribe. He ordered the jerk chicken. As he waited for the food, he scanned the dining room, watching the employees of the restaurant as they hustled in and out of the kitchen. The boy bussing the tables was not the one he was looking for. His meal was delivered about ten minutes later, and he was pleasantly surprised with the quality of the food. He was about to leave when he was approached by a large black man who greeted him with a smile.

"And how was your lunch today, sir?"

"It was very, very good," Doroz answered.

"That is what we always like to hear," Donald McFarlane said, continuing to beam his smile. "Can we get you anyt'ing else today?"

"No thanks. I had more than enough. Very nice place. First time I've been in."

"Well, I hope that it will not be the last."

"Oh I'm sure it won't be." Doroz returned the smile as McFarlane moved onto another table. He looked down at the check, which had been left by his server, and began calculating the tip.

"Excuse me sir, I t'ink yah might have dropped this."

Doroz looked up into the face of Desmond Osbourne. The young man was holding out a piece of torn notebook paper that he seemed to have retrieved from under the table. He stood beside a cart carrying a large plastic bin full of dirty plates and silverware.

"Why, yes I did. Thank you very much." Doroz nodded and accepted the paper, placing it into a pocket of his trousers. He immediately rose and left the table to pay his bill, stopping again to shake hands with McFarlane and congratulate him on the quality of the meal. He left the restaurant and walked to his car, starting the engine and looking around carefully before looking down to read the note, which was written in pencil. *Sorry I missed the meeting. McFarlane followed me to the mall. He was there the week before, but I don't think he saw you, just me. Everything's OK. I'll call you later.*

Special Agent Joe Picone waited for the call to go through as he held the binoculars up to his eyes with his other hand.

"Hello. Bon jour."

"English, please." He hated to say it because he loved hearing the French of the secretary at the Royal Canadian Mounted Police, but he wouldn't have understood a word other than the ones she had already spoken.

"Of course. RCMP. May I help you?"

"Yes, thanks. This is Special Agent Picone, ATF in New York. Who's in charge up there today?"

"Just a minute, sir. I'll connect you."

"Thanks again." He propped the cell phone up on his left shoulder, the side of his better ear, and switched the binoculars to his left hand as he wrote down the license plate on his notebook with his right. He put the binoculars down as the voice came up on the other end of the call.

"This is Inspector Prefontaine."

"Joe Picone here, Inspector. I'm with ATF in Brooklyn, New York. I'm doing some surveillance on a suspected cocaine smuggling operation here in Brooklyn, and I keep seeing vehicles with Canadian plates—mostly from Quebec—showing up at this location. I was wondering what it would take for you folks up there to help us out with some plates."

"Happy to help, Joe." The Inspector's English was flawless, but still carried enough of an accent to let Picone know that French was the Mountie's first language. "I just need to verify who you are. You said you were working out of the Brooklyn office?"

"That's right."

"I'll call them, verify that you are with ATF, and I'll call you right back. Give me your cell phone, and your fax number at the office."

Picone provided the requested information and put his cell phone down to wait for the return call. He saw through the binoculars that the sedan had pulled away from the back of Kingston Distributing, and was leaving the parking lot. He tried to get a decent view of the driver's face, but the angle was wrong. He double-checked the license plate against the number on his notebook, and put down the binoculars to answer the call.

"Picone."

"Joe? Claude Prefontaine here."

"Thanks for the call-back, Inspector."

"Call me Claude, please. What was the number that you needed help with?"

Picone gave him the plate numbers from the sedan, and as a long shot, read off the plate information from two other vehicles that he had seen on the tapes from the camera in the office during the past two days.

"Joe, I assume that you are not carrying your office fax machine with you at the moment?"

"That would be an accurate assumption."

"It's about eleven thirty now," Prefontaine said. "Check your fax about two-thirty this afternoon. I should have some information for you by then."

"Great, Claude, thanks for the help."

"Happy to oblige. Call me after you get the fax. I'll make sure you have everything you need."

At 2:15 p.m., Picone checked the fax machine in his squad room. The cover sheet indicated that he was receiving an incoming fax from the Quebec Provincial Headquarters of the Royal Canadian Mounted Police, and that the fax would total forty-five pages. He started scanning the materials as they came through the machine's printer. From the three tag numbers he had given to Prefontaine, the RCMP had collected and forwarded the registration for each vehicle, a summary of the purchase information for each vehicle, the name and criminal record—if any—for each person currently associated with each vehicle, the residence of each person so identified, a photograph of each person so identified, their immigration status, any telephone numbers associated with such persons, and a copy of the last month's cell phone call records for any cellular telephone associated with those persons. When the fax had finally stopped printing—a process that required Picone to reacquaint himself with the paper-reloading procedure for the machine—he picked up his cell.

"Hello. Bonjour."

"Inspector Prefontaine, please." He was tempted to say something to make her repeat the greeting, but did not. "Joe Picone calling."

"Hello, Joe. Did you get everything you needed?"

"Christ, Claude, I got more than a judge would have given me with a court order. How did you do that?"

"Oh, we of the RCMP are quasi-judicial officers of a sort. For drug cases, we carry something called a 'writ of assistance.' If we find it necessary, we can use it much as you Yanks use your warrants. We just carry our own writs in our tunics, and execute them whenever and however we see fit. As long as we don't abuse them, there's no problem, and it makes our job much simpler."

"Yeah, I should think so. Can you get me one of those things?"

There was a hearty laugh on the other end of the line. "Sure, come on up. We have some great food up here, you know. I might even know a judge who would give you one, but I doubt your courts would find them very amusing."

"Probably not."

"As a slightly younger nation, we watched your system evolve, and learned from your mistakes. We just made some minor adjustments, and I think their success is reflected in our lower crime rates."

"You don't have to sell me. Anyway, thanks for all the help."

"Certainly. Feel free to call again. Let me know what you turn up down there. I'll do the same, and we'll start keeping an eye on these people. Coke smuggling, you say?"

"Yep. And let me know if you notice any Red Stripe Beer cans showing up."

"Red Stripe in cans? I think not. I've seen it in London, but not here. Our environmental types shoved a law through a while back taxing the hell out of any aluminum cans coming into the country. Added about ten percent to the cost of the imports. Made it pretty cost-prohibitive. I'll watch for them, though."

"Thanks again."

Spencer Goode, Esquire, sipped his coffee as he flipped his copy of the *Post* over while he scanned the front page of the metro section. His eyes caught the single-column story on the right side just below the fold. *Metro Police Find Two More Duct Tape Victims.* The story summarized the grisly overnight find of the bodies of two suspected prostitutes in Rock Creek Park. The bodies had simply been dumped by the side of the road in the park. Each had been wrapped in trash bags, and had been nude except for the duct tape that bound their hands and feet and encased their heads. He felt the cold sweat returning to his forehead. He took a napkin from the cradle on his table, mopped his brow with it, and then shook his head. *Copycats. Had to be. He's just not that stupid. Those hookers had no connection to our business. I'm OK. I'm not involved. I'm OK. I'm OK.*

He locked the front door and got into the Acura parked in the driveway. As he headed for his office, he failed to notice the gray sedan that pulled out a block behind him.

Chapter Eighteen

Trask waited for his cue. The United States Attorney's conference room was hardly full, but he knew that the small audience—Eastman, Lassiter, Patrick, and Barry Doroz—were about to judge his ability to actually handle the challenge Lassiter had given him. He also knew that it was Ross Eastman who would decide his professional fate with all the icy objectivity that politics could introduce into the process.

The discovery of the two dead hookers had changed the equation. The press was now involved, and when the press was involved, the politicians swarmed to the spotlight like moths. The mayor was already demanding action to catch the "serial killer" and to end his spree. The mayor really didn't matter that much, except that he fed the press, and the press then grew hungrier. The mayor had no authority over the U.S. attorney, but when the mayor went to the press, his friends in Congress listened, and stepped in to ask their own questions in their own televised sound bites. There would be calls from congressmen, which the U.S. attorney could not ignore. It was now Trask's job to convince Eastman that the case would be satisfactorily resolved, and that such resolution would satisfy more than the mere demands of justice.

Trask felt that he was up to the challenge. He had been called upon in the past to brief general officers who—like Eastman—were always worried about the superiors who were looking over their shoulders. It had been easier, of course, when the party being briefed cared more about simply doing the right thing. Still, he had managed to carry the day on those prior occasions by structuring his presentations in such a way that his audience came away convinced that the right thing to do was also the best thing for the career of the officer making the decision.

"So, Jeff, what have you got so far?" Eastman's familiarity was designed as much to disarm as to encourage.

"Mr. Eastman, what we have uncovered to date is, at the minimum, a large-scale cocaine distribution conspiracy, international in scope, which is very probably also engaged in murder in order to conceal the activities and identities of the conspirators. We also, in my opinion, have a psychopathic serial killer operating within a high level of that conspiracy."

"Couldn't the Rock Creek Park murders be the work of a copycat?" Eastman held up an old copy of the *Post* reporting the Ronald Fellows murder. "The duct tape business has been in the papers."

"It's always possible, but not likely in this case." Trask was careful not to dismiss the question out of hand. "Although the press latched onto the fact that the murders of both Fellows and Wilson were the result of duct tape suffocation, it was neither mentioned to nor reported by the press that each of the four victims so far was found packaged inside identically sealed pairs of trash bags. We've also spoken to the best crime scene investigator in the police department, Frank Wilkes, and it's his opinion that all of the victims were killed by the same individual. He says everything about the bindings around the feet and hands, as well as the wrapping around the head of each victim, is identical."

"I see." Eastman was already making mental notes about his responses to the coming inquiries from both the press and from the Hill. He could not deny that the problem was as severe as it obviously was. To do so would be politically fatal when the truth was discovered later. "So where are we in identifying and arresting this maniac?"

"We have an OCDETF approved, as Mr. Lassiter has told you," Trask responded. "We have the two detectives from the police department—Carter and Ramirez—federally deputized -"

"Detective Carter was the officer wounded in your little rock-throwing incident, wasn't he?"

"And I was the officer who wasn't wounded or killed in that rescue of a rape victim, thanks to Mr. Trask," Doroz interjected. "That rape victim may very well have been killed but for the actions of everyone in that van, Ross." Doroz could play the first-name game, and Eastman was aware that the FBI agent had friends of his own. "This young man saved my bacon that afternoon. I know you may not be convinced that he should have been there, but I'm sure as hell glad that he was."

"Water under the bridge." Eastman waved off the issue. He'd been trumped, at least for the moment. "Please continue, Jeff."

"Yes, sir. Agent Doroz hooked us up with ATF in Brooklyn, and they've had a camera up on the loading docks at Kingston Distributing, which we know from our own local surveillance to be the probable source of the cans of beer used to bring the cocaine into The Caribe. ATF has also been in touch with the Mounties in Montreal, after seeing several vehicles with Quebec plates at the loading docks. The plates come back to some Jamaican nationals in Montreal. The significant thing about that is that these Jamaicans all come from the Tivoli Gardens section of Kingston, which indicates that they may all have Shower Posse connections. You were involved with the posse wars here when you were a line assistant, I believe." Trask framed his remarks as a reminder, not a suck-up, but knew that the historical reference would have both effects.

"You're correct. Nasty bunch, as I recall."

"Yes, Sir. It's also the same neighborhood that both the owner and manager of The Caribe came from, according to the immigration guys."

"So who's the killer?"

"We're not sure yet. It could be Demetrius Reid, the owner, or his manager, Donald McFarlane. My money's on Reid. He's smart and seems to be a real control freak."

Lassiter had to suppress a smile. The kid's good. No better way to keep Eastman from acting like a control freak than to call the murderer one.

"Why do you say that he's smart?"

Trask summarized the events leading to the discovery of the Red Stripe cans with the hidden compartments. "Whoever is running the show is careful enough to instruct his street-level dealers not to put anything in their own garbage. We also got a monthly cell phone statement from the trash bag that the cans were found in. No connection was found in the call record to any number associated with either Reid, McFarlane, or to the restaurant itself. A couple of department store pay-as-you-go cell phones, and that's it. We may never know who was on the other end of those calls, and they could be tossing and replacing the cell phones on a weekly basis. They may be avoiding phones altogether."

"That's unfortunate. I've always found electronic surveillance to be essential in cases like this."

"And we expect that it will be very important in this case," Trask responded, picking up the chance to bow to the wisdom of his superior. "We just think that we'll find probable cause for a bug in the restaurant office faster than we'll get PC for any phones."

"Good idea," Eastman said.

"We also have an undercover asset in place in the restaurant," Trask continued. "He's also from Jamaica, and is giving us some very valuable information. He's the one who led us to Roderick and David Greene. Mr. Doroz here and some of his friends at ICE put him in place."

Doroz nodded slightly as if to acknowledge the credit, noting that Trask had entirely avoided the story of how his girlfriend had set in motion the process of smuggling a discarded DEA asset into the country.

"Nice work, Barry," Eastman said, nodding in Doroz' direction.

"Our concern now," Trask said, "Is maximizing our continuing investigation of the entire conspiracy while minimizing—and hopefully eliminating—the body count of our duct-tape artist, whoever that might be."

"And how do you propose doing that?" Eastman leaned forward on his desk.

"I asked Agent Doroz to contact his profile experts in the bureau," Trask answered. "We're walking an admittedly fine line here. They agree with Frank Wilkes that this guy is challenging us to stop him, and that there will probably be more killings just to jerk our chains. On the other hand, any attempts to focus on him right now might actually prod him to kill again in an attempt to raise our bet, which at this point is nothing but a bluff. We're not at a point where we can grab anybody at the restaurant. The only guy we could get an arrest warrant on now is probably David Greene, and we have nothing pointing to him as the killer. The profilers think that the safer course for now is to give the killer the impression that we're stumped—let him laugh at us and just get comfortable for a while, basking in his own superiority." Trask turned toward Doroz. "Am I stating that correctly?"

"Exactly," Doroz said.

Eastman leaned back from the table. "So my position with anyone who may inquire is what?"

"To state that we are working the case with our best assets, and that we have several leads." Lassiter took the lead. "It's true, because we are and we do, but it will sound so generic and canned that our killer won't think we have anything. In the meantime, Barry's surveillance guys from the Special Operations Division are helping to keep eyes on our principle targets." Lassiter omitted the fact that one party under surveillance was an attorney.

"If they see anything dangerous happening, they can move in, and I promise that Jeff won't be sitting in a surveillance van with a stack of rocks."

Trask was glad to see that some of the laughter that followed came from Eastman.

"Sounds like a plan for now, guys." Eastman rose, offering his hand toward Trask. "Very impressive effort, Jeff. It would certainly appear that you have a handle on it for now. Thanks for the update."

Eastman shook hands with Patrick and Doroz. "Always good to see you, Barry, Bill. I'd like to speak with you for a moment, Bob." He waited until the others had left the room.

"Very impressive young man, your Trask."

"Thanks. Now you could see why I was so anxious to move him up."

"Of course. That being said, Bob, I want you to take the lead on this. If the press or some Congressman starts trying to pin me on this thing, I can't be in the position of saying that I've assigned my newest federal prosecutor to the most important case in the District. I don't give a damn if he does all the heavy lifting—it looks like he could handle it—but I want you looking over his shoulder to make sure. If I can tell somebody that my Criminal Division chief is personally supervising the investigation, it will look like we're taking this case seriously. Understand?"

"Yes. My name will be the lead on all the pleadings, and I'll keep a hand in it. Jeff won't have a problem with that."

"He certainly shouldn't."

"And he won't. We're all on the same page, I think, Ross. Thanks for the audience."

"My door is always open."

And your butt is always covered, thought Lassiter as he left the room. He headed back to his office, and found Patrick, Doroz, and Trask waiting for him.

"So you're the lead counsel, and Jeff stays on it?" asked Patrick.

"Funny how that works." Lassiter chuckled.

"I think," said Patrick, shaking his head, "That you should be shot."

"It's nice to pull the strings on the string puller once in a while," Lassiter said. "I owed him one after that Prescott second-chance thing."

Special Agent Michael Crawford stared hard at the images on his computer screen as they ran through the latest DVD that had been forwarded to him by Joe Picone. He watched as the sedan with the Quebec plates came and went, and saw the light in the video fade as night set on another day in the rear of the Kingston Distributing Company. He was about to switch the computer off, as night was also about to set in Washington, but he noticed the lights of another vehicle turn toward the loading dock in the back of the warehouse. He hit the pause button on the machine and enlarged the image, which centered on an Acura SUV. He squinted, and enlarged the image again before writing the plate numbers down on a note pad. *DC plates?!* He then switched to a local information database, and entered the plates. *Holy shit!* He picked up the telephone and punched in the number of Barry Doroz' cell phone.

"Bear? It's Mike. Want to take a stab and guess whose Acura was at Kingston Distributing on Saturday?"

Chapter Nineteen

"The last time we were out here was the first time we ever heard of the Kingston Distributing Company." Carter was sprawled out in the rear of the surveillance van, speaking to Doroz as Ramirez peered through the window toward the back of The Caribe. "We saw a Red Stripe beer can next to the head of the body of the Fellows kid in a photo of the dumpster. Raced like hell to get there, but the trash trucks beat us to it. The can probably wouldn't have told us anything, anyway."

"Not as careful as these assholes seem to be," agreed Ramirez. "The bodies of both of those hookers gave up nothing. Frank Wilkes said there'd been sexual activity, but a condom was used, so no DNA there. Our man had taken the time to wash the bodies down before he bagged 'em. He even cut the fingernails off and scraped and washed underneath 'em in case they'd scratched him during the sex or any struggle. Frank said he got nothing, other than the method evidence. Same wrap jobs as before. Helluva way to die; especially for a scared little girl, hooker or not."

"Well, one thing's for sure," Doroz mused. "When we catch this guy, premeditation's more than established. May well be a federal death penalty case."

"*In this town?* No way." Ramirez shook his head. "My man Dix's homies think that every execution is racially motivated—just another way to keep the black man down. The jury would never vote for it."

"He's probably right," Carter said, "even though some of our victims are also black. It would take a very compelling presentation to get a death vote."

"What was the story on the last two victims?" asked Doroz. "Have they been ID'd yet?"

"Yeah, thanks to a friend of ours in vice—Gordy Hamilton. He said the older gal was a veteran—probably been working K and Fourteenth since the Carter administration when there was a hooker down there on every parking meter. Jeannette Barnes. The other vic was only twenty, fairly new to town, and working the track on Rhode Island Avenue. A runaway from someplace in Kentucky. Darla Miller. Hammer had arrested 'em both before in some vice ops. None of the hookers that knew 'em had anything to offer. They're all scared shitless now, though."

"Maybe they'll stay home for a while."

"Oh sure, Bear. We'll let Hammer give you a complimentary vice tour some time. Only thing that keeps the hookers off the street is a jail cell. They're all hooked on something themselves; gotta support their habits as well as their pimps." Ramirez sat back away from the window to ease the tension on his back muscles. "No visitors yet. Didn't our guy inside say that the pickup is usually on Friday nights?"

"Yep, but he said that he heard Reid tell McFarlane that the bill would need to be paid on Thursday this week, which is why we're here. He thought that meant the bag man might show tonight."

"Well he's late, and I passed up a chance to see a good soccer exhibition to sit on my ass in here. The Brazilian national team's in town for a good will tour."

"Soccer," sneered Carter. "The last Communist conspiracy."

"What the hell are you talking about now?" Ramirez turned away from the window to face his partner. "It's only the world's most popular sport."

"I seem to have read," Carter said, putting on his best professorial airs, "that the first recorded references to soccer come from Japan, about 1004 BC, and records currently kept in the Munich Ethnological Society in Germany refer to matches played between Japan and China in 50 BC. The records of the early Olympics in Rome—that's in Italy, Juan—also refer to games with twenty-seven players on each side. It is significant that these purported records of antiquity have only referred to, or surfaced in, countries with ties to the World War II Axis Powers, or world communism."

"You see what I have to put up with?" Ramirez asked Doroz, who was starting to grin.

"When the Norman French carried this corrupt game with them to England in 1066," Carter continued, "proper Britons attempted for centuries to prevent the spread of its mind-numbing torture. King Edward issued the first proclamation banning the 'sport' in the early 1300s. The ban appears to have been based in large measure on the prophetic warnings of the King's physician, one Sir Ronald Tewkesbury, who predicted that prolonged involvement in soccer, with its headers, would almost certainly result in misshapen skulls, damage to the brain, elongation of the neck, and atrophy of the upper limbs, the usage of which is unnaturally forbidden by the rules of the game. You can see what it did, for example, to Mick Jagger, Keith Richard, and His Royal Highness Prince Charles."

Doroz was now laughing, while Ramirez sat shaking his head in disbelief.

"Similar proclamations banning this alleged sport were later issued by Kings Henry IV and Henry VIII, appropriately labeling the game 'vulgar and indecent,' and stating that players were to be jailed for at least a week, to be followed by church penance. Despite the best efforts of sane men, however, the sport of hooligans has persisted, kept alive by those hell-bent on the destruction of Western civilization. In Europe, as well as in Asia, the game resulted in the gradual, near-total elimination of any hand-eye coordination and upper body strength."

"You are *so* full of it." Ramirez countered. Doroz was almost doubled over.

"The evidence is clear, amigo. You need only compare American baseball velocity and accuracy with the ridiculous bowling technique employed by cricket 'bowlers,' who haven't got enough arm to get their balls to the wickets in the air. The successful intervention of the American armed forces in both world wars is due, in my humble opinion, to their superior employment of hand grenades. You'll note that both the German and Japanese forces were so abysmal at grasping and throwing their own devices that their governments eventually had to put handles on *their* grenades." Carter was now so pleased with himself that he almost lost his poker face.

"In this country," he continued, suppressing a laugh, "this heresy has been adopted by lazy parents who found the game to be good for tiring out unruly children. Socialists have also adopted the game as part of their 'don't keep score' campaign for young children, depriving America's youth of the thrill of victory and the lessons to be learned from defeat. The game's almost total lack of scoring makes it ideal for such propaganda, as seen in the asinine and near-orgasmic displays by players, sportscasters, and spectators who actually witness a soccer goal. In its modern version, the proponents of this satanic ritual have even hidden the play clock from view, an attempt to perpetuate a myth that this is a timeless sport. We'd best come to our senses quickly. Time is running out."

Ramirez was laughing now. "You made all that shit up!"

"I did not," Carter responded with mock indignation. "Well, only that part about Doctor Tewkesbury."

"I think," said Ramirez to Doroz, "that my partner is finally feeling better." He laughed again. "Welcome back, DC." He turned back to the window. "You almost made me miss our target, though. Silver Acura MDX in the alley."

Doroz picked up a radio. "Papa Bear to all units. Goldilocks is in the house. Get ready to hit the road."

Lassiter laughed at himself. He was a good fifteen minutes early, preferring to seize the ground and establish his defenses as he had been trained to do at the Point; only this wasn't supposed to be a fight, but his first date in months. Patrick had told him where they'd be dining—an upscale, continental-style place on Wisconsin Avenue NW in Georgetown—and had given him the appointed time. He had not told him her name, where she worked, or what she looked like. His old friend had probably and correctly figured that any information would start him on a covert intelligence mission, and that anything at all negative might have resulted in his cancellation. He had already downed his first drink at the bar—a bourbon on the rocks—and was motioning to the bartender for a refill when they came up behind him.

"I promise you that you don't need two shots of courage just to have dinner with me."

He turned on the stool to face Patrick, his wife Danielle, and a stunning brunette who was holding out her hand to him.

"Angela Trotter, Bob Lassiter." Patrick made the introductions.

"Very nice to meet you, Angela. I'm sure Bill will back me up when I say that the two shots have absolutely nothing to do with you," Lassiter said as he affectionately hugged Danielle. "Do I have Mr. or Mrs. Patrick to thank for this pleasure?"

"This one's all on Bill," Danielle said. "My past attempts were all failures."

"Not your fault, Danni." Lassiter patted her on the shoulder. "You gave it your best."

"I know that; that's why this is Bill's doing. I've about given up on you."

"Angela is the new ASAC at the DEA field office, Bob." Patrick explained. "I met her last week when I covered one of the task force meetings for you. We figured we'd give this a shot since you're both in the same business."

The waiter stuck his head into the bar and informed them that their table was ready. Lassiter followed her into the dining room, succumbing to the temptation to look over the very attractive shape in front of him. He pulled her chair back and helped seat her at the table, then sat down on her left side.

"I hope you'll take no offense from my saying that you are certainly the most attractive assistant special agent in charge that DEA has ever presented to the District," he said.

"Of course not, as long as you soon realize that I'm also the most competent."

"Fair enough. I'll fill those blocks out on your report card in due time, and with an open mind, unclouded by your appearance."

"Fair enough," she said. "And when and how should I fill out your report card?"

He laughed. "Whenever you feel the time is right, and that you have sufficient information for your evaluation." He shot a look at Bill Patrick, who was grinning from ear to ear.

"I didn't think this was possible," Danielle remarked, shaking her head. "We've tried this with him before," she said to Angela, touching her hand, "and he's usually answering a fake beeper call five minutes into the dinner. For better or worse, you seem to have struck the right chord."

"I've been in a state of near terminal depression," explained Lassiter, "because Bill found and tied Danni down before I could get to her."

"Ooooh, pleease," Mrs. Patrick corrected, rolling her eyes. "You're a morose hermit who's married to your work."

"More true than I usually like to admit," nodded Lassiter. "But I get the feeling that Ms. Trotter might understand and appreciate that dedication."

"I think I might," she smiled. She was now patting *his* hand.

"A match made in both heaven and hell, then," said Bill Patrick. "It's only a first encounter, but I'll drink to it. Especially since Bob has a head start on me."

———

Spencer Goode, Esquire, put the final hundred from the thousand dollars that was his pay for the trip north into the dollar-denomination, double-double bonus, video poker machine. His luck had been horrendous all night, both on the quarter machines where he started, and then on the higher-denomination machines he had switched to in an effort to recover his losses. He had actually been up earlier in the evening after hitting four aces with a three for five hundred, but that small jackpot had occurred within his first ten minutes of play, and Mr. Goode was now what the pros called an action junkie, one to whom the play was more important than the return, and who was virtually incapable of walking out of the casino with an early win in his pockets. The five hundred and his original thousand-dollar stake had now all been consumed by the well-disguised computers in front of him.

When the last hand was played, and he found himself with nothing, he also found himself returning to the rear of the Acura. He looked around the parking garage and, seeing no one, lifted the rear door and pulled the aluminum briefcase out from under the cargo cover. He turned the key in the lock and pulled out one of the folded bundles of bills, telling himself that this was the last time he'd ever take such a risk. *I'll bring more of my own on the next trip. What the hell, I made it back last time and I'll do it again. I can feel my luck starting to change.* He closed and locked the Acura, and headed back toward the casino floor.

"Did you get that?" asked Carter.

"Just like I worked at Olan Mills." Ramirez checked the images on the digital camera's monitor. "See, here he comes to the car, he opens the door, pulls out a case with about five of my annual salaries in it, grabs a wad—probably a thousand-dollar dope bundle—and heads back in. One of Barry's guys has been on him inside all night, and says he's already dropped over a grand. Wonder what our men Reid and McFarlane would do if they knew their bag boy was using the dope payment case for his gambling stake?"

"More important," mused Carter, "What would Mr. *Goode* do or say if he found that someone might *tell them* about it? Would he trade some time off a sentence for his life?"

"It's sure worth exploring when we get back to town, assuming that whatever's left in that case goes where we think it's going." Ramirez put the camera down and shoved the memory card into an input slot of one of the van's computers. "Even better in an eight-by-ten glossy, don't you think?" He swiveled the computer's monitor screen so that it faced Carter. "Grab a coke out of the cooler and throw it over, please."

"The SOB just hit a royal flush for five-thousand bucks." The voice came over the radio in the rear of the van. "He's headed back your way."

"We're on it," responded Carter. Ramirez shoved the memory card back into the camera, and recorded Goode's movements as he re-opened the Acura and the briefcase and replaced a stack of bills that had been folded in half and bound with a small rubber band.

"He actually thinks he's had a good night," Ramirez observed.

———

Lassiter offered to take her home, and she had accepted, thanking Bill and Danni Patrick for the introduction and a wonderful dinner. He hadn't felt himself flying so high in years, and had to keep checking the schoolboy impulse to babble. She asked him in, and he felt his senses flood when she turned and kissed him. He tried to keep everything going in a slow and controlled manner, but the moment overcame both of them, and they settled for a rug on her living room floor instead of the bedroom.

"So, should we just be ashamed of ourselves?" She asked, lifting her head from his bare chest.

"Probably, but I won't tell if you won't."

"That's a deal."

He stroked her hair and kissed her again. "I forgot to ask you at dinner—seemed to have my mind on something else—where did DEA have you before bringing you to DC?"

She kissed him back. "Panama."

Chapter Twenty

"Well, it's about time," Trask said, as he stood in the doorway, arms folded, watching Tim Wisniewski unpacking his boxes. He was moving into the empty office between Trask's and Prescott's.

"Yeah, Lassiter said you were hopelessly lost up here without me, and that you needed some adult supervision to keep you out of trouble. He also said he wants me to assist in some kind of international, super-secret Ocelot or something."

"OCDETF, you idiot," Trask laughed. "Organized Crime Drug Enforcement Task Force. That's what we big, federal-side narcs do up here."

"Well why don't you fill me in while I'm unpacking?"

Trask outlined the investigation of The Caribe to date, and then told him about the more recent homicides of the two hookers found in Rock Creek Park. He saw that Tim had stopped his unpacking for the moment, and was staring at him, hands on hips and mouth wide open.

"So now, let me get this straight. Right after you get your ass in hot water with the front office for helping to whack a rapist, you and Lynn smuggle in a discarded DEA source from Central America, plug him into a target commercial establishment, and now you're up to four on your body count?"

"Not exactly. The former DEA source smuggled himself in. We just relocated him without telling his former handlers, and the body count in the drug case is only two; we just have reason to believe that one of our targets is also killing hookers, and that *that* body count—which is apparently not part of the drug case—is also two."

"Assuming they weren't smothered in duct tape for drinking from some weird cans of beer."

"More or less."

"Lassiter was right, hot shot. You need a baby sitter."

"I'm happy he selected one that I knew already."

"I'm not sure I am."

"Oh, come on, this'll be fun when we sort it all out. Besides, there's more."

Wisniewski put down the box he had just picked up, and sat on the edge of his new desk. "Go on."

"Barry Doroz, The Twins, and the Special Ops—meaning surveillance team—guys from the bureau tailed The Caribe's bag man after he left The Caribe on Thursday. They had to use about six different cars to keep from getting spotted. Followed him to a casino in Atlantic City, then all the way up to Brooklyn, where he drove up to the back of the Kingston Distributing Company. We have good reason, including some great photographs, to believe that he was making the payment for one of the coke shipments."

"That's great. Why not just grab this dude and try to spin him?"

"It's an attorney, Spencer Goode. He's on the restaurant's corporate papers."

Wisniewski turned and started carefully putting things *back into* a box.

"Give it a rest. You *know* you're gonna love this one," Trask laughed.

"I know I'm gonna need a year's supply of Rolaids. I thought a scorned lover with a pot full of lye and a sharp knife was complicated."

"No lye here, just duct tape. You want to get some lunch?"

"I suppose, as long as we're not eating anything from the West Indies."

"Not today. We'll grab our usual burger and then I'll show you our other office."

"What?"

"The bureau took some of the OCDETF funds and rented some commercial offices about a block away. Doroz and The Twins and the rest of the task force have moved in there for the time being. Helps to create an atmosphere of teamwork and cooperation. All the cops and agents assigned to the task force are working solely on this case, for now. We'll be spending a lot of time down there."

"Lead, on, sahib."

As Trask turned to leave, he almost bumped into Benjamin Prescott, who was now standing in the doorway.

"Oh, sorry, Ben, have you met the new guy on the floor, Tim Wisniewski?"

"I've heard the name, but have not had the pleasure." Prescott smiled weakly and held out his hand toward Wisniewski for a similarly weak handshake. "Welcome."

"We were about to get some lunch," Trask said. "Care to join us?"

"Can't today, too busy. But thanks for the invitation. Some other time."

"Nice meeting you, Ben," said Wisniewski as he and Trask headed down the hall toward the elevators.

Prescott nodded, and watched until he was certain that they were leaving the building. He closed his door, sat down behind his desk, and reached for a small, softbound directory which had been part of his own stack of welcoming materials from Lassiter. He looked at the cover, which bore the legend, "Telephone listings for Law Enforcement Agencies in the District of Columbia." He found the entry he was looking for, and dialed the number.

"Drug Enforcement Administration," said the secretary's voice on the other end.

David Greene turned the Honda north on Fourteenth Street, NW , cranking the thump up on the radio to the point where he could hear nothing else. He was trying to drive his father's nagging out of his mind. *Fat old fool, can't even get out of bed any more. Just barks orders at me all damn day. I do the work and take the risks and he keeps 80 percent of the money. Pick up the shit at the restaurant. Cook it up. Make the deliveries. Dump the trash. Collect the green. I get 20 percent, while he lies there and gets fatter every damn hour. Has to have a nurse come in and bathe his fat ass. Shit.*

He crossed Otis Street, still headed north. Despite his mood, he was still trying to be careful, looking out for cops, staying under the limit. Even though the kilo of crack was safely stashed in the hidden compartment under the dash—a drawer on the passenger's side that could only be opened by an electronic switch hidden in the console—he knew not to risk a traffic stop. If the cops found the stuff in his car, he was looking at a minimum of ten years, and probably more. His father had drilled that into him time and again.

Him and his buddies from the island. Have to do everything their way, no changes. Don't use the phones, everything face-to-face. Nothing on paper, everything by cash. Watch your deposits.

Don't drive a car worth having. Paranoid old fools. We been rollin' just fine now for damn near four years, and the stupid cops ain't caught onto shit. I could be drivin' somethin' really nice right now, get some chrome spinner rims...

He did a slow roll through the stop sign at Michigan Avenue in order to merge with the traffic heading north and west toward the city limits, where Michigan turned into Queens Chapel Road as it wound through Prince Georges County on the way to Hyattsville. *Think I'll keep 50 percent today. We'll make a cool four large off this bird of crack. What's he gonna do about it, anyway? Try to roll his fat ass outta bed and chase me? I'll just... What the fuck?*

The police cruiser had been following him for two blocks, lights on, and had activated its siren full volume. It had wailed for almost twenty seconds before a break in the gangsta rap on Greene's radio allowed the siren to pierce the passenger compartment of the Honda. Green pulled over.

Do like dad said—he does know this shit. Be calm, polite, apologize, don't give him no reason to search the car. If he asks for permission, give it to him. That's what the drawer's for. They won't find shit unless they bring a dog up. Don't give 'em any reason.

"What's the problem, officer?"

"You rolled through a stop sign back there, sir."

"I'm sorry about that. My old car here has trouble getting into the traffic flow unless I fudge a little. I'll watch it next time."

"I appreciate that, sir. I'll still need to check your license and registration. If you haven't had any trouble before, I might let you go with a warning on this one."

"Great. I don't have any tickets." Greene retrieved the registration from the glove box and removed his license from his wallet.

"Thanks, Mr. Greene. I'll check a couple of things and be right back with you."

"OK."

The officer returned to his car, and entered the Honda's license plate into the computer. The screen changed, and he saw the alert notice that came up with the usual registration data.

"Dispatch, unit 520."

"Five-twenty."

"I have a Honda stopped on Michigan registered to a David Greene, who is the operator. System has an alert filed by a Detective Carter. Can you patch me through?"

What the fuck is taking him so long?

Greene's calm facade was starting to crack, and the sweat that was now covering his forehead was more than should have been generated by the heat outside. He checked his rearview mirror, and could see that the cop was on the radio with somebody.

Stay cool, ain't nuthin' to worry about yet.

He checked his watch, and checked it again ten minutes later. The cop was still in the car, still on the radio. He saw the second police car pull in behind the first one. The second cop opened the back door to his cruiser.

Shit! Motherfucker! Shit!

The second officer walked the large German shepherd around the outside of the Honda. The dog appeared agitated, and when it got to the passenger-side door, began frantically pawing at the seam between the door and the front fender. The first cop was back at his window now.

"Mr. Greene, I'm sorry to inconvenience you, but our canine unit here is a trained drug dog, and he's alerted on your vehicle for some reason. Do you have any drugs in the car?"

"No, sir." The sweat was dripping off the end of his nose now.

"Is something wrong, Mr. Greene?"

"No...no, sir. It's just warm out today."

"Would you mind if we had a look in your car, Mr. Greene?"

"No, officer."

"Step outside please."

The first cop escorted him back to stand beside the first cruiser, while the one with the dog opened the passenger door and let the dog inside. It almost tore the drawer out of the underside of the dash. The dog's handler groped around the dash, then opened the console, and began fumbling inside it. The switch to the drawer tripped, and the brick, wrapped in plastic tape, fell onto the floor beside the passenger seat.

"Put your hands on the hood of the car, Mr. Greene."

"Barry Doroz, Tim Wisniewski." Trask made the introductions as they stood beside Doroz' cubicle in the newly rented task force space. "I was hoping to introduce him to the rest of the guys today." Trask looked around, noting that Doroz and Crawford were the only ones in the room. "The Twins around?"

"Not right now. Dix got a call from a traffic unit up in 5D. They stopped our David Greene for something, and the patrol officer saw our code on the computer. Dix called a canine unit out, and it alerted. We got a whole kilo of coke. Dix and Ramirez are on their way up there to see if they can convince Mr. Greene of the error of his ways."

"Excellent!" Trask looked around the squad area. "I see the file cabinets came in."

"Yep. Computers are up, too. We're set here. Just need to start collecting some more evidence. Joe Picone's coming down tomorrow from Brooklyn. We plan to start our brainstorming session about ten in the morning."

"Great. Let me know if Dix and Juan need anything from me today."

"Sure will." Doroz shook hands again with Tim. "Welcome to the funny farm. It's probably going to get nuts around here pretty soon."

"So I've heard," Wisniewski said.

Carter sat across the table from David Greene in the interrogation room at 5D.

"Do you understand your rights?"

"Yeah."

"Do you wish to waive those rights and talk with me for a few minutes?"

"Yeah. Why not? Let's see how it goes for a while."

Carter could see that he was not dealing with another Ronald Fellows. This kid was already halfway there; ready to break, nervous as hell. He wondered how much he could say without spelling everything out, how many of his cards he would have to play before this young pup would realize that he wasn't bluffing. He decided that a few cards on the table were worth the risk.

"I'd like to start by telling you a story. It's about a young man much like yourself. A young man named Ronald. Did you know him?

"Wh…who? Ronald? Ronald who?"

"That's not important. You may very well not have known Ronald, but I'd bet you know some people who did know Ronald."

"Like who?"

"Let me get back to Ronald's story. We think Ronald was moving some dope for some folks here in town. We arrested Ronald, and tried to talk to him. Like yourself, Ronald was looking at some very serious time. *Federal* time. Do you know what that means?"

"Yeah. Longer stretch. No parole."

"Exactly. I knew you weren't stupid. You don't want to do a lot of federal time, do you?"

"Nope." Greene shook his hand while answering, and Carter saw that he had his first concession from his subject. The dam was ready to break.

"Ronald didn't let us help him. He didn't want to talk to us. We told him—like we told you—about all his rights, but he wasn't as smart as you. He didn't want to talk with us at all. You're doing the smart thing, feeling us out, trying to see how much we really know…" He could see that the twist was confusing Greene, who looked very puzzled, very off-balance now.

"That's the smart way to do this, and I don't blame you at all for doing it. It's what I'd do in your shoes. Anyway, Ronald wasn't that smart. He lawyered up right off the bat, without trying to figure out what we knew. You need something to drink?"

"I could use a Coke."

"No problem at all." Carter went to the door and spoke to a uniformed officer, who returned quickly with the soda. He handed it to Greene, noting that the young man was relaxing a bit more, although still somewhat confused, still off-balance. *Perfect.*

"Getting back to Ronald. He believed the guys he worked for. He figured they'd do what they'd promised to do if he ever got in trouble—you know, get him a lawyer, back him up and help him beat the rap. Only he didn't really know those guys. They were bad guys, from down south. I mean *way* down south. He didn't know the lengths these guys would go to in order to protect their own asses. *They* knew that if Ronald cracked and talked to us they'd be screwed, too. What we could have told Ronald—if he had really let us talk with him—was that he had three choices. He could help us out, and not do a whole lot of time. He could try and beat the charges in court, and see how that went, but the odds were that he'd lose at trial and be gone for ten to twenty years, a very long time." Carter paused as if he had completed his current train of thought. He waited.

"You said he had three choices."

"You're absolutely right." Carter reached down and opened a nylon briefcase. He retrieved a photograph, and placed it in front of Greene. "This was his third choice, actually the choice of his employers, who didn't want to risk Ronald changing his mind and talking to us."

Greene stared hard at the photograph of the body of Ronald Fellows on the medical examiner's autopsy table, the head encased in duct tape and the body contorted backwards with the hands and feet pulled together by more tape. He looked back up at Carter, the tears merging with the fear in his eyes.

"Believe me when I tell you something, son." Carter lowered his voice to a near whisper. "I do not want to see you like this."

"I think I need to talk with my dad."

"We need to talk with him, too." The statement had the intended effect.

"Why?"

"You know why, don't you?" Carter stared hard into the younger man's eyes. Greene lowered his gaze to the table. "There's something called a conflict of interest in cases like this," Carter continued. "It means that while it may be in your own very best interest to talk to us, because it keeps you out of jail and alive, others might think it would be better if you ended up like Ronald. I'm sure that your dad wouldn't want that, but some of his friends might, and we think that Ronald was working for some of your dad's friends."

"My dad's sick."

"Your dad ate his way out of jail after going down himself on a dope count, David. A local charge. This is federal. There's another side to this conflict of interest I was talking about. That is, the same attorney can't represent everybody that's involved in this thing. The reason for that is that he might really be working for the big guy that's paying him—trying to keep you from helping yourself in order to protect the guy or guys at the top."

It was time to play the ace.

"So let's just say, hypothetically, that the big guy would want to hire a lawyer for you, just like he said he would if you ever got into trouble, just like you are now. Let's just say—I'll pick a name out of the air, one of the local criminal defense attorneys—let's just say he hired Spencer Goode to represent you…"

He paused only for a microsecond, but it was enough to read the surprise in Greene's eyes.

"If Mr. Goode was actually working for somebody else, that would be something that you should be concerned about. Do you have a family attorney, someone you plan to hire?"

"No…not really."

"Just remember, whoever represents you needs to have *your* interests at heart. That's going to be important for you *and* your father. One wrong step, one bit of misplaced trust, and both of you could end up like Ronald."

"My dad won't believe that."

"I know," said Carter. "Your dad's like me, isn't he? Old school. Trusts his friends? Set in his ways?"

It was another chance to strike a responsive chord, get another nod in agreement.

"Yeah."

"Those friends could kill both of you. You saw the picture. I'm not kidding."

"I'll think about it."

"You'll probably only have about three days to make up your mind. If you get bond, and hit the street after making the wrong move, we could find *you* in a dumpster. They'll take you down to federal court now. You'll get an initial appearance on a criminal complaint. We'll ask for a continuance on your detention hearing to give you those three days. I hope you make the right choice."

Greene simply hung his head and nodded. Carter left the interrogation room. He had set the hook, and it was all he could do for the moment. Ramirez left the side room where he had been watching through the one-way mirror, and met him outside.

"I think you've got this one, Dix."

Trask and Wisniewski waited at the counsel table for the Chief Magistrate Judge to make his entrance. David Greene sat alone at the other counsel table, because he was not yet represented by counsel. Carter and Ramirez watched from the front row of the gallery. They all rose when commanded to do so by the courtroom clerk, and Judge Noble read the charges and statutory penalties to the new defendant. He also explained that the government was seeking that the defendant be held without bail, and that a hearing on the matter would be held in three days. He was about to question Greene about his ability to pay for a lawyer, when a voice from the rear of the courtroom interrupted the proceedings.

"Excuse me, your honor, but that won't be necessary."

"Oh?" Noble asked.

"Yes, your honor." The attorney carried his briefcase through the swinging door that separated the spectator section from the well of the courtroom. "Spencer Goode appearing for the defendant, Your Honor. I've been retained by Mr. Greene's family."

Greene turned in his chair and glanced at Carter. There was surprise and fear in the young man's face.

Chapter Twenty-One

"Hell, Bob, I'm sorry. I really had no idea." Patrick shook his head.

"I'm sure you didn't. Not your fault. I had no idea either, and didn't think to ask her until we were—how shall I say—otherwise involved."

"Uh-oh. I mean I'm glad that you..."

"No, you were right the first time. Uh-oh. I had no business getting that involved without knowing exactly what—and whom—I was getting involved with."

"Does it have to be a problem?"

"Let's work through this, shall we? On the professional side, I certainly don't have to tell her up front that the source she kicked to the curb in Panama is now working as the prime undercover asset in an OCDETF operation on which I'm listed as lead counsel. The problem, professionally, arises only when and if she finds out about that. At that point, it's not a problem for me, *professionally,* because I have no reason to believe that DEA as an institution still had their flag planted on our source. It may be a problem for *them,* because they'll feel like we should have told them, but most of the equities are on our side in that argument. The *real* problem is that it's not just a professional situation anymore, because I allowed myself, quite *unprofessionally,* to mix the professional with the personal *in the most personal way possible.*"

"Even if it was just a one-night stand?"

"I don't think either one of us felt that way. She's left three calls on my answering machine this morning already."

"Uh-oh."

"Yeah. You said that already. I'd really like to see her again, but I'd have to tell her about this at some point, the sooner the better. She will feel, perhaps correctly, that I've at least lied to her by omission, and there goes what's left of any relationship."

"Can you talk it out now? Prevent the problem from getting worse?"

"I don't think so." The statement came not from Lassiter, but from Trask, who was again standing in the doorway of Lassiter's office. "Sorry to interrupt, and I didn't mean to eavesdrop, but I just got a call from Barry Doroz at the new Task Force office. Somebody flashed some badges at the security guard late last night, and emptied all our file cabinets. There's not a report left in the place."

"*What?!*" Lassiter was on his feet. "Do we have a leak? Who grabs a room full of files?"

"Yes, we have a leak, but I don't think it's anybody on the task force. The security guard said the badges were DEA, and the team that cleaned us out was led by a female agent. They told him they were part of the task force, and they were just taking the records for copying."

Lassiter sat down and buried his head in his hands for a moment. "This is my fault, Jeff. If you gentlemen will excuse me, I have some phone calls to make."

"Sure," said Trask, "but I have to dump a couple of other things on you before I head home. One, I feel like hell—some kind of stomach flu, I think. More important, we grabbed David Greene yesterday with a whole kilo of crack. We have a complaint on him that I filed this morning, and he's on a three-day detention hold. That's the good news. The bad news is that Spencer Goode showed up to represent him at his initial appearance before Judge Noble."

"OK. Go home, lie down, get better. We'll get with Tim and get a full update, and I'll try and dig myself out of this fine little mess, see what I can do about Mr. Greene..." He paused and shook his head. "And get your files back."

Trask nodded and headed back toward his office to get his car keys. Patrick rose, apologized again, and headed for the door, which Lassiter asked him to close on his way out.

The first call he made was to Ross Eastman, explaining in full detail the events which had led up to the apparent seizure of FBI files by another agency, and his own personal involvement with the agent who had apparently ordered the intramural raid. Although he had been as contrite as possible, his *mea culpa* had not been necessary.

"Frankly, Bob, I don't see that you're in any way at fault in this. DEA had already de-certified your asset as a source?"

"Yes. We even called their field office here about that, although we pretended to be inquiring because he'd supposedly been spotted in Florida. The desk guy we spoke to said he was out of their system, and that they had no interest in him anymore."

"No problem then. It's outrageous that she had the gall to pull this stunt, and I'm going to call the director at DEA."

"Can you do me one favor, Ross?"

"What is it?"

"Let me talk to her first. In light of the situation, I'd like a chance to resolve it at a lower level, maybe save some face for everybody concerned."

"OK, but I'm not sure she deserves the courtesy. Keep me posted. I want to know what you hear immediately. If it isn't satisfactory, I won't be talking to just an ASAC."

"I understand." He sat back for a moment and stared at the ceiling before picking up the phone.

"Are you calling in a personal or professional capacity?" Her tone was icy.

"Both, if you can believe that. I would say that I owed you an apology, except for the fact that I had no idea that you were ever in Panama before the other night. That being said, I think that if you are the party who is currently holding our OCDETF files, you'd be very wise to return them before my very irate U.S. attorney gets your director on the phone. I don't want to see you get hurt, either personally or professionally."

"Don't you worry about the personal side of it, Mr. Lassiter," she said coldly. "I'm a big girl, and it was just something between two mutually attracted adults. Nothing really special. I just can't believe that you wouldn't take the time to check your new source with the agency—make that the *agent*—who'd already worked him before signing him up again, or that you'd set this operation up with the bureau when we're supposed to be the primary drug investigation agency, especially after 9/11."

He paused and took a deep breath. "As to your first issue, Ms. Trotter—the first *professional issue*—we did check with your agency, and got an all-clear. The deconfliction check is documented. As to your second issue—again a *professional* one—this is a case in which I allowed the local police, who had done a great deal of the early work, to tell me which federal agency they would prefer to have join them. They opted for the FBI, based upon their prior positive experiences with the agent who is now in charge of the case. That agent, Ms. Trotter, is not you, and you no longer have a dog in this fight."

He paused, but there was only silence on the other end of the line.

"Regarding the personal issues," he continued in a softer tone, "I had a wonderful time the other evening, and had intended to call you again, hoping for and expecting to have another wonderful time. Whether that is a possibility is entirely up to you. Returning to the professional situation, should I tell my boss that we will be getting our files back immediately, or do you want him to get involved in this?"

"We consider your office's handling of this matter to demonstrate a security risk and an incompetent investigatory approach. We'll hold onto these files for now. Make your call, if you like. The *professional* one." She slammed the phone down in its cradle.

Lassiter turned and looked out the window.

No more damned blind dates. Ever. I don't care who sets 'em up. I'm too old for this. He picked up the phone and dialed a four-digit extension.

"Ross, you'd better call the director."

"No luck, I take it, with the face-saving approach?"

"No. Her heels are dug in pretty deep, I'm afraid."

"Sorry to hear that, for her sake."

"Me, too. Can you try and keep the consequences for her to a minimum?"

"Not sure that I can, or that I want to, but I'll think about it."

"All I can ask. Thanks." He hung up, and stared out the window.

Who the hell told her about the source?

"Tim? Dixon Carter. I tried to get Jeff and the secretary said he went home."

"Yep," said Wisniewski, "he looked pretty green around the gills. What's up?"

"I just got a call from the Marshal's Service. They have David Greene at the federal courthouse. He said he wants to talk to us."

"Doesn't he have counsel? That Goode character?"

"On paper, yes, but the marshals said that he told them not to call Mr. Goode, and that he didn't want him as his lawyer. I think he'll waive counsel, and since he's initiating the contact with us, can't we talk to him? Isn't that what the Supremes said in *Edwards v. Arizona?*"

"That's what they said. Tell you what, I'll type out something for him to sign, acknowledging that he initiated the new contact, wanted to waive counsel, and does not want to be represented by Spencer Goode. I'll see you in the marshal's interview room in about thirty minutes."

He slid the keyboard forward, reviewed and printed the waiver he'd drafted, and headed for the courthouse.

"I thought about what you said." Greene looked up at Carter after signing the waiver and handing it to Wisniewski. "If I help you, can you go easy on my dad, too?"

"We'll try to, but it's up to him," Wisniewski said, reaching into his briefcase for another letter. "He's got to make a separate peace with us, but with you already on board, it should be easier for him to make that decision." He slid the other paper across toward Greene.

"This is what we call a *Kastigar* letter. It's named after a Supreme Court case. It says that as long as you cooperate completely, and haven't done anything violent, anything you tell us today can't be used against you. It's off the table. Right now, all we have on you is the kilo we found in your car. That's what you get sentenced for as long as you cooperate. Anything else—again, as long as it's not a murder or something violent—is off the record. You can't be charged with it. Just the stuff we already know goes on your ledger."

"It's the smart thing to do," added Ramirez. "You limit your exposure, and with cooperation, the judge is very likely to cut you an even bigger break at sentencing."

Greene looked at the table and sighed, then looked back up and shrugged.

"Let's do it." He signed the paper, and slid it back to Wisniewski.

The debriefing lasted ninety minutes before they returned the prisoner to his cell. They were leaving the marshal's area when the door opened, and Spencer Goode, Esquire, nearly bumped into Carter.

"Gentlemen," Goode said formally. "I'm here to speak with Mr. Greene."

"We just spoke to him, Counselor," Ramirez shot back. "He said he no longer wants you to represent him."

"Wh...what did he tell you?" Goode stammered. Carter noticed that beads of sweat had started to form on the attorney's forehead.

"Enough." Carter edged past Goode, who stood frozen in the doorway. "Excuse us please, Counselor." They headed for the elevator. Goode was still frozen in place. When they reached the street level of the courthouse, Ramirez cracked up.

"*Counselor,*" he said, mocking Carter's last word and tone of voice. "That dude thinks David Greene just ratted him out big time. Greene didn't even mention his name."

"I never said he did," Carter replied. "Mr. Goode sure as hell looked like he was worried about it, though."

They left the courthouse and started back up the street toward the U.S. attorney's office.

"Any bets on his next stop?" Ramirez asked.

"I'd say he's probably hungry for some Caribbean food," Wisniewski ventured.

"A safe bet," Carter said. "We now have McFarlane good for about fifty keys of coke over the past couple of years, and we know from our man Osbourne that some of that came out of Reid's office, but this guy says he never, ever, dealt with Reid himself, and he doesn't know squat about Junebug or the Fellows kid getting snuffed out."

"It's something to work with for starters," noted Wisniewski. "If nothing else, it'll heat 'em up at The Caribe. Maybe somebody will do something stupid under pressure."

They reached the triple-nickel, and The Twins headed for the car as Wisniewski went inside and walked to the elevator. When he reached his office, he picked up the phone.

"Hello?" Trask answered.

"How you feeling, ace?"

"Like something ate me instead of the other way around. Most of it's gone now, though; a little from both ends."

"Yuck. Too much information. Listen. While you were in your little room there, I was in another one, with your man David Greene. He reached out for us and then gave us about two years of history on The Caribe and Donald McFarlane. He had next to nothing on anyone else."

"Nothing on Reid or Goode?"

"Nothing. Nada. Zip. If he's in the game, Reid seems to have really insulated himself. One step at a time, I guess. We did bump into Spencer Goode as we were leaving. Dix told him we'd been talking to his client and Goode looked like he'd seen a ghost."

"Are we good on Greene's having initiated the contact?" Trask asked.

"Yep. I had him sign an acknowledgment of the contact initiation, counsel waiver, and a Kastigar. I think we're fine on that under *Edwards v. Arizona.*"

"I hope so," said Trask. "Sounds like it."

"Get some rest. Just wanted to give you an update."

"I will. Thanks, Tim." Trask hung up.

Benjamin Prescott left the hallway, where he'd been standing between the door to his own office and the open door to Wisniewski's. He entered his own office and closed the door. He sat behind his desk and took out the office employee guide, a handy pamphlet designed to help the attorneys and staff get to know and interact with their co-workers. He turned to the page bearing the letter *W* at the top, then picked up the telephone.

"Santa Fe Information? Thank you. Do you have a listing for the New Mexico Bar Association?"

"Why didn't ya get 'im out like ya did the Fellows kid?" Reid demanded. "Then he wouldn't be runnin' his mouth!"

"I couldn't do anything about that," Goode explained. "Once the prosecutor asks for a detention hearing, it's virtually automatic that they get one—*and* a delay to prepare for the hearing. It's the law." He looked uneasily at Reid, who seemed to be staring through him, not believing a word he was saying.

"Who is this guy, Demetrius, and what does he know? *Who* does he know about?"

"His father is from Tivoli, like me, mon. He's one of our street guys—does kilos—one or two a week. I've told them to be careful. No phones, no trash, make sure not to sell to anyone but da regular customers. He only deals wit' Donald here. Never me. Maybe I need to tell Donald to head home for a while. What you think, mon?"

"Couldn't hurt." Goode stood up and paced across Reid's office. "You're sure he knows nothing about you…or me?"

"Nuttin', mon." Reid sat back in his chair and smiled. "If da cops ask me, I've had dis rogue manager selling shit behind mah back. I had no idea this was happenin'. I run an honest place here, doin' good business. Try to do an island mon a favor 'cause he's from home, and he stabs me in the back. Donald will be back in Jamaica tomorrow and they won't be able to touch him. I know Roderick—the daddy—will never talk to the cops."

"They may know about the Red Stripe cans now."

"They only have his word. All the cans in the cooler are full of beer, mon. They can pour 'em all out if they get a warrant, and they'll just owe me for a lot of beer. We'll just take delivery of nuttin' but beer for a month or two. No problem. He can talk about cans, but if dey don't have any, no problem. I know da boy's daddy is not so stupid as to leave 'em in the trash." He slid the metal briefcase across the desk toward Goode. "Go ahead and make the payment for the last load, and tell da boys in Brooklyn we're too hot for a while."

"Your girlfriend is being transferred," Eastman said, "along with the DEA field office special agent in charge. They've been fired from their current posts, but not from the agency. They're still agents, but no longer supervisors. A big demotion for both. The director was very apologetic. He guaranteed no interference in your investigation, and even promised some manpower. He said he had an experienced agent to send over to your task force who has no axe to grind."

"Thanks for the help," Lassiter said. "When are we getting the files back?"

"I was assured that they'd be back in place by the time I called you. Since I've now called you, I suggest that you verify that they're where they're supposed to be."

"I'll do that." Lassiter paused for a moment. "Ross, I can assure you that this will not happen again."

"I hope not. Hopefully, the rest of your case goes smoothly now."

Chapter Twenty-Two

He waited up the block from 1440 Monroe, biding his time until he finally saw the nurse come out of the house, get into her car and drive away. He left his own vehicle—another loaner—parked where it was and walked at a leisurely pace until he reached the front door. It was locked, but that was no obstacle to him, as one of the first new skills he had acquired within the posse was the use of the picks. The door surrendered in about ten seconds, and he was inside.

He walked confidently toward the bedroom where he knew he would find the first loose end. He hated *all* loose ends as a rule; all the careless or stupid people who simply did not deserve to exist in his world. They were all part of a problem, and there was only one solution to that problem.

He opened the door, and saw Roderick Greene lying under the sheet. The huge man was naked, having just received his bi-weekly sponge bath. He could see that the morbid obesity was consuming his friend. The tubes for the dialysis machine extended out from under the machine on the far side of the bed. An oxygen canister was there also, although it was not in use as he made his entrance.

"How did yah..." Greene realized the inherent stupidity in his question, and did not bother to finish it. He had seen Demetrius Reid pick hundreds of locks back on the island, most to gain entry into an enemy posse barracks in the middle of the night before the slaughters could start. He thought his visitor might have the same goal in mind on this occasion, and his eyes were already full of fear. He knew he could not flee. He could barely move anything anymore—just his arms and the mouth that he used to consume his meals.

"Don't sweat it, mon." Reid flashed his widest grin. "I knew ya couldn't get up to answer da door so ah let mahself in—the old way."

He put the paper sack he'd carried into the house down beside the bed, and pulled up a chair.

"Looks like yah've hit the bottom, mon. Kidney machines, air in a tank. How can yah supervise your part of our t'ing when yah can't even move?"

"David does it for me, D. Ah've taught him everyt'ing. No problems."

"Oh, you're wrong about that." Reid stood up, and shook his massive head from side to side. "Lots of problems, mon. He got real careless-like—got stopped in the car wit' a whole key—the cops found the dope, and when I send the lawyer over for him, he tells mah lawyer that he doesn't want him around—that he'll get another lawyer. But yah knows all that, 'cause he called yah. Still, yah didn't call *me* did yah? I t'ink, mon, that you may have raised a snitch."

Greene was now in complete panic. He knew he had no chance of reaching the loaded pistol in the nightstand. He couldn't have beaten Reid to the gun on his best days, and those were long behind him. His only chance was to play the loyal posse soldier.

"In that case, D, if yah are certain that he's turned, then he's no longer mah son. I will not have a snitch as mah son. I raised him better than that."

"I know yah tried to do that—to raise him right." Reid put a massive hand up as if to reassure him. "And yah followed the rules, right? No trash out front, no phone calls, no flashy stuff?"

""Yah, mon, ah mean, *no,* mon—none of that stuff. We been doin' it right, D."

"I wish that I could be sure of that. I wish I could be real sure that yah would not go and pick family over the posse. Family is a hard thing to give up. I know that."

"Yah don't have to doubt me, D. We go back a long way, now."

"Yah, mon, a real long way. All the way back to the Gardens. A long way, mon."

"So yah know I'd never break on the posse, D. Never."

Reid's eyes grew cold. He reached down for the sack by the bed and pulled out two gloves, and the roll of duct tape.

"Yeah, Rod, ah know yah never will."

The fat man's eyes were now wide with terror. Greene tried to will his right hand over to the nightstand's drawer to reach for the gun, but the sudden pain in his chest forced him to grab at his upper torso instead. Reid watched him gasp, then saw the bed start to shake with the flailing, massive folds of fat lying on top of it. He bent over Greene's head, and waited until the eyes stared blankly at the ceiling.

"T'anks for savin' me the trouble, mon."

He placed the roll of duct tape on the dead man's bare chest. "We go back a long way."

"I screwed up, didn't I?" Wisniewski leaned forward in the chair, his arms resting on his thighs.

"I'm afraid so." Lassiter nodded. "How badly you screwed up is now a matter between you and your friendly neighborhood bar association. From this..." he handed the fax back over to Wisniewski, "I'd say they aren't very happy, or flexible. I'll be happy to back you up on the circumstances, and on the basis for your action, namely that Goode's attempted representation was not genuine, but a severe conflict of interest. Your bar is pretty pissed that you made that call all by yourself. You did get the Hyde Amendment training when you first came on board, right?"

"Yep. It's just hard for me to think that I might be violating a so-called canon of ethics when I'm following an edict of the Supreme Court."

"It's hard for all of us—and ridiculous." Lassiter stood up, his hands in his pockets, and paced behind his desk. "If anyone at the department had possessed the smallest set of cojones when that silly-ass law was proposed, we could have simply called their bluff. We could have called all the state bars and told them we were about to abolish the departmental requirement that each AUSA had to be a member of good standing in a state bar in order to keep his or her appointment. Just establish a federal prosecution bar with our own canons, enforce them strictly, and deprive the precious bar associations of their so-called *discipline* and a few dues dollars at the same time. Unfortunately, the Republican anti-federalists in Congress were so hacked off about one of their own getting charged in a federal case, they linked up with the ACLU types on the other side of the aisle, and the Hyde-McDade thing is what we got."

"Who was McDade?"

"A Republican congressman from Pennsylvania. He got indicted for racketeering in the mid-nineties, and was acquitted at trial. As a payback, the GOP Congress decided to require that every AUSA had to comply with each set of bar association rules in every state that was affected by a case in which that assistant was involved, plus the rules of their own bar, whether or not that state was affected. So if you're investigating a case that involves the District, Maryland, and Virginia, you have to figure out which of those state bars has the most restrictive rules, and comply with those, unless your home bar—in your case, New Mexico—is even more restrictive. Then you have to comply with those, even if you're not a member of the bars of DC, Maryland, or Virginia, and even if what you did has the express blessing of the Supreme Court of the United States.

"Under most of the bar rules out there today, Gotti would never have been convicted, because that bug in his social club would have been considered an unauthorized contact with a represented party." Lassiter pointed to the fax. "At least, that's the learned opinion of the New Mexico bar. Once Goode entered his appearance in court, you were required to go through him before speaking with Greene under their Bar Rule 16-402. The first thing Goode probably did was to phone your bar and file the complaint. The bar won't admit that, of course; they're protecting the whistle-blower."

"What about help from the main department?"

"Don't get your hopes up. We—a few of us in the department—tried to fight this thing when it first came out. We pointed out that it was nothing less than a total capitulation of the supremacy clause, and that when the Supremes had said we'd done nothing wrong, it was insane to let the state bars—where we're outnumbered by defense counsel twenty-to-one—have the power to veto those decisions. Ross Eastman was at Main Justice at the time in one of the congressional liaison offices, and he fought hard against the bill. But it passed, and here we are. Here *you* are, and since you didn't obtain supervisory clearance first before talking with Greene, I doubt they'll even file a brief on your behalf."

"You're sure it wouldn't do any good to ask? Even the AG?"

Lassiter sat down in the chair next to him.

"I don't think I'm being cynical here. Just realistic. It may be better to just do a *mea culpa* with your bar, save the money and time you'd spend on hearings, and hope they don't whack you too hard. It's probably a cheaper and faster way to the same result. That's just my opinion, though. Feel free to shop it around with some others. I'll call Eastman and let him know about this."

Wisniewski nodded and left.

Lassiter picked up the phone. "Ross, sorry to have to say this, but we have another problem with our favorite case." He summarized the facts as he had heard them from Wisniewski, and the New Mexico Bar's fax notice of the complaint.

"This thing just blisters my backside, he said. "Tim's a good kid, didn't do anything wrong, and now he stands to get suspended or maybe even lose his license, when the evidence we got at the debriefing won't even get suppressed."

"I tried to fight it when I was at DOJ."

"I know you did, Ross. That's why we all think of you as more than just a mere United States Attorney."

"Thanks, I think. Tim didn't clear it with you at all?"

"I'm afraid not. Just took the time to read the controlling Supreme Court decision, and forgot to see whether his state bar had vetoed it. I'm half-tempted to say that he *did* check with me."

"No, and consider that an order. I don't need you putting your own ticket on the line on this. I'll make some calls and see if we can generate any support for him at all at the department. In the meantime, he'll have to get off this case."

"I understand. He won't like it, but he just got on board. We can shift him to something else until the New Mexico Bar thing runs its course."

"Good. I'll see what I can do."

"How's the gut?" Lynn leaned over the couch where Trask was sprawled and kissed him.

"Still watching the Hitler channel?"

"That's the *History* channel, as you well know. It's just that Adolf seems to have a starring role in quite a few episodes. It's better than watching the soaps or the forty-three different Judge Whoever shows. The gut's better, too. Finally got some soup to stay down."

"Good. Feel up to some chicken and rice for dinner?"

"Sure." His tone was still a bit flat, and she noticed the concern on his face.

"What's up?"

"Lassiter called. Tim's off the case, and may get suspended by his state bar. It probably wouldn't have happened if I'd been at work instead of home sick."

"Now explain that to me." She sat down beside him on the couch.

He outlined the events leading to the fax received by Wisniewski.

"And what in the world is wrong with that?" she asked. "They teach us that it's kosher to do that in our legal block at the OSI academy."

"According to the Supremes, it is. According to the State Bar of New Mexico, it's not, even if it's otherwise authorized by law and even if the defendant initiates the contact."

"That sucks."

"It sucks dead rats. So anyway, Tim's off the case and may get suspended, or even disbarred."

"Why would you being there have made a difference?"

"Because my state bar is a little more rational. The defense attorneys and state supreme court haven't been chewing peyote, as they apparently have on the outskirts of Santa Fe. If I'd done exactly the same thing, my bar association would have ruled it to be entirely proper, since the defendant called us and signed the waiver. Especially since it was the defendant's opinion—as well as ours—that Goode has a severe conflict of interest here."

"I thought the law was the law."

"It is—or should be—as far as the evidence goes. Even though Tim may have violated his state bar rule, the federal case law says no problem, and the evidence—Greene's statement—was properly obtained and shouldn't be subject to a motion for suppression."

"I think Shakespeare was right. The first thing we do is kill all the lawyers. Present company excepted, of course."

"They haven't all gone to the pipe yet. There are some really good defense bar members in town who are completely above-board, and who aren't in favor of completely castrating law enforcement. The system couldn't work without them."

"You aren't thinking of crossing over to the dark side, are you?"

"No," he chuckled. "But I do have some names in mind if I ever lose it and strangle somebody myself."

"Really, like who, for instance?"

"Oh, J. T. Burns, for one. He's the guy who brought in that kid we cleared in the traffic stop. Reasonable, no nonsense, no games, knows his stuff, and juries love him."

"I'll file that away for when you start abusing me and I have to shoot you."

He laughed out loud. "I know better than to try that. I've seen your targets from the OSI range. You're a better shot than I ever was."

"Don't forget that, mister." She leaned over and kissed him.

"On a lighter, or actually, a much heavier note..." he began. "Barry Doroz called, too. The mailman tried to deliver a package to Roderick Greene this afternoon—David Greene's seven hundred pound Jamaican father. The front door was wide open, and he could hear a machine, so he walked in and called out—found Roderick dead in bed with a dialysis box running. Willie Sivella's girlfriend Kathy did the autopsy. Said it was a heart attack."

"Nothing surprising about a guy that fat stroking out."

"No, but they found a brand new roll of duct tape lying on his chest."

"Anything other than hunches to tie these duct tape things to that restaurant yet?"

"Everything's still circumstantial. We were able to eliminate one guy for this one, however. Your man Desmond Osbourne called Barry last night and said that the manager at The Caribe—Donald McFarlane, Greene's hand-to-hand supplier—left the country yesterday for Jamaica."

"He could have put the tape on the fat guy before he left, couldn't he?"

"Not likely. Kathy put the time of death on Roderick as sometime this morning, hours after McFarlane skipped out on us. So now I'm pissed about Tim's trouble, I'm pissed that we didn't put the *habeas grabbus* on McFarlane with an arrest warrant, and Kathy's pissed at Cap'n Willie for sticking her with a corpse the size of a Buick. They had to knock the picture window out of the front of the house and take the body out on two four-by-eight pieces of plywood. It took eight guys to get him loaded onto a flatbed for the trip to the ME's office. He wouldn't fit in an ambulance or a hearse."

She kissed him again. "Sorry you had a bad day. I'll let you get back to your war while I get dinner started."

Chapter Twenty-Three

"Glad you're feeling better, Jeff," Doroz said. They were in the new space, and the inventory of the files had gone smoothly. Everything had been returned. Lassiter was there, too, as the purpose of the meeting was to clear the air and get past the problems of the last week.

"I'd like to introduce the new member of the task force, Craig Cornell of DEA." Doroz still had the floor, and gestured toward a stocky and powerful-looking man with a bushy red beard who looked like he'd just climbed off a Harley. "Craig has a world of experience in dope investigations, and comes to us from Minneapolis, where he most recently posed as a member of a biker gang. I've worked with Craig before, and can vouch for him completely. I also told him he didn't have to shave as long as he was here."

"I'm happy to be here," Cornell said. "And I'd like to apologize on behalf of my agency for the recent stupidity. I'm here to help with the solution, not cause more problems."

"To summarize for Craig, Bob, and everybody else, here's what we have so far," Doroz said. "We have five dead, counting Junebug, the Fellows kid, two hookers, and Roderick Greene. We have a six-pack of Red Stripe cans with coke residue, and one kilo of powder from David Greene's car. Speaking of David Greene, he's now clammed up, thanks to his father's death. Dix and I went to talk to him in the lockup yesterday after the autopsy results were in, and told him about the duct tape on his Dad's chest. He blames himself for that, and he's afraid for his own life. He told us that if we called him into the grand jury, he'd imitate a deaf-mute. We now have a DEA field office with an *acting* SAC and ASAC..."

"For which *I* apologize, at least in part," Lassiter interjected.

"Geez, Bob, you must be a *really* bad lay," Ramirez quipped. The room exploded in a combination of howls from the cops. Lassiter appeared to be disarmed, for once, as he blushed and laughed with them.

"*Anyway,*" Doroz returned to his summary, "We are also down a prosecutor now, thanks to somebody ratting out Tim Wisniewski to his bar association for following the guidelines set by the Supreme Court, and Donald McFarlane has left the country. Those are most of our problems. On the positive side, we have some good video from the camera in New York showing our favorite defense counsel's car in the back of the Kingston Distributing Company, and we have our man in place at The Caribe. What we do *not* have, gentlemen—correct me if I'm wrong—is enough evidence of any sort to put so much as a traffic ticket on Demetrius Reid."

"I'm afraid I agree with that assessment," Lassiter said. "Jeff?"

"I can't disagree with it," Trask answered.

"After the thing with Roderick Greene surfaced, I spoke with our best profiler at headquarters," Doroz continued. "He said he'd never seen anything like this before. In his experience, most serial killers who leave calling cards are actually inviting a sordid game of Catch Me if You Can. They leave a real clue here or there, even if it's some kind of misdirection. They try to show that they're smarter than we are—dare us to catch and stop them. That's why we often see them writing us—or the media—letters, and they may even attempt to get some relationship established with one of us to personalize what they see as the game.

"This guy—our killer—is not doing any of those things. In our profiler's opinion, he's just spitting in our faces. He's doing nothing at all to give us a clue—misdirection or otherwise—and believes we're really helpless to stop him. It's not that he wants a game. He believes he's at war with us, and has nothing but hatred for us and his victims. That's why he's chosen to kill them in one of the most torturous ways possible, both mentally and physically, and that's why he wants us to know he's doing it—to intimidate us, his enemies."

"Reminds me of some of the things I heard from the POWs after they came back from 'Nam," Lassiter said. "Some of the things the guards did at the Hanoi Hilton had nothing to do with getting information out of our guys. They just wanted them to suffer, and in some cases, die."

"Exactly," Doroz nodded. "What we have, guys, is a sociopathic sadist. Our profiler also said that I should warn everyone here to be extremely careful. This guy's hatred for informants and cops means he may very well want to go down fighting and to take some of us with him."

"Let's not give him that opportunity," Carter spoke in a somber tone. "He's a problem, but he's not worth anyone in this room going down. Let's be smart, and as careful as our target has been."

"If I might throw something out here," Trask offered, "We also need to start planning to rebut an insanity defense, assuming that we're able to take this guy alive and try him."

"Agreed," Lassiter said, "As well as a capital prosecution. We already have the required aggravation factors in evidence to justify a death-penalty case, even if we don't have proof of the identity of the killer. And a capital prosecution would mean that the defense would automatically consider an insanity defense, even if we didn't already have five murders so sadistic that a layman juror would already be thinking that the killer's nuts."

"So this asshole might skate because he just likes to kill. What a system." Ramirez was walking around the room shaking his head.

"Not necessarily. On the sanity issue, we probably already have a good head start." Trask was up now, addressing the group. "A guy who's legally insane could not ordinarily function properly with the management of an ongoing business. Barry, the next time you talk to Osbourne, tell him to start making mental notes of all the tasks he sees Reid doing well around the restaurant. Somebody who's hearing voices and suffering from delusions couldn't be consistently effective in that position. More often than not, it's the everyday observations of a defendant's friends and co-workers that destroy any defense efforts to portray him as a non-functioning loon. I'd also love to get inside the guy's crib at some point. If he's living in a dope-financed palace that's well organized and clean—instead of some pit that's wallpapered with photos of Jodie Foster—you get the point. Let's look for some probable cause to get into the residence."

"Jeff has a lot of experience with sanity cases," Lassiter said. "Follow his lead on that issue, guys. On the capital front, like I said, once we have the killer, we're more than halfway home. We've got plenty of evidence of premeditation. Our biggest challenge is going to be tying the killings to the drug business in order to get federal jurisdiction. If we can do that, it's probably one big conspiracy charge with the related killings going into evidence as part of the conspiracy. The hookers may only make it into the sentencing case. Without the linkage to the drug conspiracy, we're doing five separate murder trials in superior court, and depending on which judge we draw, the jury may not get to hear half the story. Most of the superior court judges won't let proof of one murder in to show proof of another one."

"In the meantime," Doroz concluded, "Let's keep the surveillance up. No bad guy is perfect in the commission of his crimes. We want to be there with our eyes and ears open when he slips up."

Reid studied the young man across the desk as he listened intently to his employer. "Like I told yah, Donald had to go home for a while to take care of some family t'ings. He did a lot around here, a lot of t'ings that I'm gonna have to take over now and do mahself."

"I know, Mistah Reid." Osbourne nodded, keeping his eyes on the big man's face.

"Now, I can't go promotin' yah from a busboy to a manager here in the restaurant; that would not be fair to some of the people who have been workin' here a lot longer time. What I did want yah to know, is that I've been watchin' yah, and yah work hard, and yah do a good job. So, even if I can't give yah a big promotion here in the restaurant, I do have some t'ings goin' on outside where yah could make a little extra money, if yah can do exactly as I tell yah. Yah understand what I'm talkin' about?"

"Yah, I think so, Mistah Reid."

Reid leaned forward. "And what *is* it that yah think I'm talkin' about?"

Osbourne paused, knowing that his life depended upon his next words. If he was too specific in his answer, Reid would wonder how he knew so much, why he had even been interested enough to notice certain things. If he mentioned the Red Stripe shipments, or even the more obvious things like the back door visits by David Greene and some others, he would appear to have already put his nose where it did not belong.

"Yah know, Mistah Reid," he said with his biggest smile, like it was the national joke of Jamaica, "Some *island* business. Like back home."

Reid liked the answer, and laughed. "Yah, mon, some *island* business. Yah ever do any island business before?"

"Oh a little here and there." Osbourne hung his head and kept grinning, looking up at Reid like his hand had just been caught in a cookie jar. "Some of the ganja, when I could get it."

Reid was pleased. One of the rules he had always set for himself, even in the posse houses in Miami, was to insulate himself from the buyers. Maintain plausible deniability, and stay at least one level above and away from the actual deals on the street. Now, with McFarlane back in Jamaica and the Greenes both out of commission, he needed someone else to trust with McFarlane's former role—the beer deliveries and distribution, especially the cases of Red Stripe. He'd already told New York that he would have to take a week or two off because things were really hot, but once he felt like it was safe to do so, he fully intended to resume operations.

He liked Desmond Osbourne. The boy wasn't as hard and seasoned as a posse brother from Kingston would have been. But he was the obvious choice above the girls who waited tables or ran the cash register, and Reid had been forced to come down hard on one or two of the boys who worked in The Caribe for not being circumspect enough about their own preference for marijuana. He had not seen such carelessness from Osbourne. The boy also reminded him of his little brother; he even had the same name.

"Good. Good. I haven't really got anyt'ing goin' on for the time bein', but when it picks back up again, I'll have some extra work for yah to do. Some extra money, too. I just have to be sure that I can trust yah completely, understand? "

"I do, Mistah Reid, and yah can."

"I hope so. Yah know that I was born and raised in Tivoli, don't yah? "

"Yes, Mistah Reid. I heard that."

"And yah know what that means, don't yah?"

"I do, Mistah Reid. Yah came up in the Shower Posse."

"Good. Then I don't have to tell yah what would happen if I found out that I couldn't trust yah."

"No, Mistah Reid. I figured yah was checkin' me out anyway when Mistah McFarlane followed me to the mall."

Reid laughed again. There was more to the boy than he had initially figured. "And yah were right. I can't be too careful here, yah know. The world is full of snitches and cops, and I had to be sure yah were who yah said yah were."

When Osbourne telephoned Doroz three hours later, Doroz immediately called Lassiter.

Trask had told her to dress nicely for the evening, and he wasn't disappointed when he picked her up at her apartment. She had on one of those little black dresses which, when properly filled, were absolutely guaranteed to turn heads. He had not told her where they were going, but she was pleased when they returned to the French restaurant in Georgetown. After another very good meal he escorted her back to the car. He surprised her once again when he turned west instead of back toward their apartments, and pulled into the entrance to the Kennedy Center.

"What is this?" she asked.

"Something you'll like, I hope."

"I love the company, and I trust his judgment."

They sat through the first half of a world music concert by Andreas Vollenweider, then he walked her out to the facade overlooking the Potomac.

"It's really pretty out here, isn't it?" she asked, looking at the lights of Arlington across the river.

"I hope you'll find that this is pretty, too." He reached around her and held out a small jeweler's box. She looked at him with tears welling in her eyes.

"I'm afraid to open it," she said, with a slight quiver in her voice.

"You shouldn't be."

She lifted the top and saw the ring, then smiled up at him.

"Lynn would you do me the honor of becoming Mrs.…"

"Yes, yes, yes, and yes!"

She jumped into his arms and kissed him hard, then pulled back, still holding him. "What the hell took you so long?"

He smiled down at her. "I had to make sure it wouldn't screw up our tax brackets."

"Oh…you!" She laughed, then kissed him again.

"We need to get back in for the second half of the show."

"No, we don't," she said. "I really liked it, but we what we *need* to do is go home. I've got an overwhelming urge to jump your bones."

Chapter Twenty-Four

It had been a month since the last delivery. Reid's direct customers were clamoring for their product, and *their* customers, the users on the street, were getting desperate. Reid knew that he had to be patient, to be absolutely certain that the tails he'd seen in his rearview mirror over the past weeks had actually dropped off from boredom and the futility of following him to and from the restaurant. He had been relieved to see that no police had approached him at The Caribe to ask him about McFarlane. Maybe the Greene kid actually kept his mouth shut after all. The wait was necessary to cool things down, but he could not wait too long; if he did not resume operations soon, his customers—and *their* customers—would move on permanently to other sources of supply. At the consumption point, the business was, after all, one of addiction, and strung-out addicts did stupid things. Now that the cops had calmed down, it was time to cool his customers down.

He picked up a throwaway cell phone he'd purchased at a department store, loaded with just ten hours of call time. He would not use the phone often enough or long enough for it to become the subject of any electronic surveillance by law enforcement. He dialed the number in Brooklyn from memory and requested the usual number of cases for the usual price. If the cops or the feds were listening to the call on the Brooklyn end, all they would hear was a restaurant owner placing a routine order in the normal course of business. The second call he placed was to the law offices of Spencer Goode, Esquire. The last call was to one of his street dealers, telling him to get ready to do some business, and also making another request for a vehicle—another crack rental.

———

Trask was back in the surveillance van with Doroz and The Twins. His own coast had cleared enough to make it safe for him to risk another "forward legal observer" ride. Besides, there had been precious little progress made in the last three weeks on the operational side of the case, and there was no point in rereading the case file for the fourth time.

David Greene had been indicted on a single count of possession of cocaine base with intent to distribute. There was nothing to be gained by throwing a conspiracy charge at him when they had no firm proof of the identities of his co-conspirators, other than Donald McFarlane, who was in Jamaica, and Roderick Greene, who was probably in a place even worse than Kingston. Better just to lock Mr. Greene down on the possession count, then load him back into the main indictment when the rest of the dominoes started to fall. There was always the chance that he'd come to his senses and resume his cooperation when the main threats against him were locked up in separate facilities.

They'd gotten the call from Osbourne saying that business was set to resume, and so they were back across the street from the entrance to the alley behind The Caribe.

"He said the Kingston truck came in last night." Ramirez was watching the window. "So if our friend Goode shows up today, we're back in the game."

"I hope so." Trask leaned back in one of the captain's chairs, sipping on a diet soda. "I'm getting tired of waiting for these guys."

"That's what he's probably been counting on," said Carter. "The smart ones know how to wait you out. We used to have an old heroin dealer in 5D who managed to stay out of the joint his whole life. He just had the instinct. We'd get close to him; he'd close down shop and not move a gram for months at a time. When we got tired of waiting and things cooled off, he'd start up slowly, selling a little stuff, and if nothing happened to any of his people, he'd be rolling full speed in a month or so. If the heat came back on him, he'd stop again. Never did catch him at it, but we knew he was doing it. Finally arrested his stupid kids after he retired and turned the family drug trade over to them. They didn't have their daddy's patience or smarts. Rolled flashy in big SUV's with spinner rims. Stuck out like sore thumbs."

"So you ready to head east with us tonight, Jeff?" Doroz asked.

"Yep. Lynn gave me a pass to get some work done."

"And how's re-married life treatin' ya?" asked Ramirez.

"Can't complain. Think I got this one right."

"You must have." Ramirez pointed at him. "Look at that smile on his face."

"You didn't invite us to the ceremony," Carter tried his best to look disappointed.

"We didn't invite anybody," Trask responded, "just went to the courthouse in Upper Marlboro and did the civil thing in front of some schmaltzy justice of the peace. Lynn didn't want to give me time to change my mind, and didn't want to waste money on a big production."

"Smart girl—and a keeper." Carter said. "If it weren't for her lining up our source there..." he pointed toward the restaurant, "we'd be high and dry right now."

"So how long you gonna play in our little pond here before you move on to bigger and better things?" Ramirez asked.

"Don't sweat that," Trask assured him. "This is the job I always wanted."

"I just thought you might want to do the judge thing—you know—be the next Oliver Wendell Holmes or something." Ramirez returned his eyes to the window.

"I'm not a big fan of Mr. Justice Holmes," Trask said. "I think he helped pave the way for a lot of the mayhem we're suffering through today."

Ramirez turned back toward him. "Really? The great dissenter, wasn't he? I thought he was some kind of genius."

"The reason he was 'the great dissenter' is that nobody else agreed with him, usually for good reason. He was appointed to the Supreme Court by Teddy Roosevelt—one of my favorites—but the president later said that the appointment of Holmes was his greatest mistake in office. Teddy said, 'Out of a banana I could form a firmer backbone.' Justice Holmes was also dumb enough to get shot three times in the same war...the Civil War, of course. Never learned to keep his head down."

Trask stopped for a moment, seeing that Ramirez was staring at him with his mouth open, while Carter and Doroz were trying very hard not to laugh.

"His view of the law is best expressed in his quotation: 'The life of the law has not been logic; it has been experience.' He wrote hundreds of illogical opinions, most in the minority. That's why they called him the Great Dissenter. He resigned from the Court at age ninety at the request of the other Justices, who by that time were probably glad to see him go. That is my viewpoint, although it is probably in the minority."

"Sorry I asked," said Ramirez, wide-eyed. He looked at Carter, who by now was in full belly laugh. "I thought *you* were full of academic crap."

Carter caught his breath. "Glad to see there's someone on board who can keep you in your place if I get laid up again."

"No way," said Ramirez. "I'm *used* to all your shit, and it's *shorter*."

"Just trying to show that I stayed awake during my Constitutional Law class," Trask said. "My professor, by the way, would have disagreed with everything I just said, but he was another nut."

"How did you ever graduate?" Doroz asked.

"Blind grading. They never knew whose paper they were marking up. A fact for which I shall be eternally grateful." Trask paused. "I thought I heard a car door out there, Juan."

"You certainly did." Ramirez turned to the window and refocused. "Silver Acura, and Counselor Goode going in the back door. Hot damn, this is gonna be fun!"

His first hour at Harrah's quarter machines had been a break-even effort, but he had thoroughly enjoyed it, since he had gotten used to playing every weekend, and the weeks off had left the neurons in his brain begging for a fix. The only thing that bothered Spencer Goode was the nagging feeling that he was being watched. He turned and scanned the casino floor, nodding to the waitress who walked by and smiled at him. He didn't see any faces that looked out of place. *Probably just tuning in on the guys in security.* He looked up at one of the dark globes in the ceiling, the windows for the cameras that were always monitored by the casino security staff. He nodded at it, too.

Time to make some real money. He got up and headed toward the dollar machines. *Hell, if I hit on these again, I might even visit the high-limit area tonight and see what I can do on a five-dollar machine.*

He turned the corner of an aisle into the row of machines, looking at the pay tables to see how high the jackpot had risen. He was about to pull a chair out and sit down at one when a very large hand reached out and held the chair in place. He turned, indignantly.

"I was here first."

"And so you were, Mr. Goode. Several times over the past few months." Dixon Carter had on the blank stare. It was effective when dealing with suspects who thought they were so much more intelligent than he was.

"What is the meaning of...?"

"The meaning of this, Counselor," Trask spoke up as Goode turned the other way to see that the prosecutor and Juan Ramirez had come up behind him, "is that we'd like to have a word or two with you in private."

"Am I...under arrest?" The hesitation in his voice strongly implied that he thought he could be.

"Not yet," Trask said. "We do think, however, that you'll find what we have to say—and show you—interesting." He motioned toward the door off the casino floor that led to the hotel. Goode followed Ramirez, who was leading the way.

They took the elevator to the eighth floor, and walked down the hall to a small suite. The bedroom door was closed. In the sitting area, Trask motioned him into a chair facing a coffee table, then took a seat across from him. Trask nodded to Carter, who handed him a manila envelope.

How very staged, Goode said to himself. *Who do these guys think they're dealing with? Some dropout off the street?*

"Are you going to read me my rights now?" he asked sarcastically.

"As you know, this is a non-custodial setting, Mr. Goode. We're not required to read you your rights. You are not under arrest..." Trask's tone was flat and angry, but controlled. "But just to make sure, I don't think that would be a bad idea. Juan, would you do the honors, please?"

Ramirez pulled the card from his wallet, and told Goode what he already knew about his rights.

"What the hell is this about?" Goode demanded.

"I saw tonight that you are a poker player of sorts, Mr. Goode," Trask observed. "I'd like to change the game just a bit, if I might, since I seem to be the one holding the cards at the moment."

He reached into the envelope and pulled out two, eight-by-ten glossy prints.

"Let's play a game of stud, shall we? Two cards up to start."

He laid the first photo out, facing Goode.

"This was taken by a well-informed special agent of the Bureau of Alcohol, Tobacco, and Firearms in Brooklyn, New York. His name is Joe Picone. Joe?"

Picone emerged on cue from the bedroom. "Glad to finally meet you, Mr. Goode," he said. He did not offer his hand. "I feel like I know you already, in some ways. You'll recognize the scene in the photograph from one of your several visits to the rear of the Kingston Distributing Company in Brooklyn. That's your car in the photograph, the silver Acura. The same one parked tonight in the casino parking garage. The same one that you presently intend to drive to Brooklyn and to that same loading dock. That's you standing beside your car, and the gentlemen you're speaking to in the photograph is Winston McFarlane. Winston is from Jamaica. Kingston, to be exact; the Tivoli Gardens neighborhood to be even more precise. He is, as you know, the older brother of Donald McFarlane, who was until recently the manager of The Caribe restaurant in Washington. Both of the brothers McFarlane are known to the Jamaican authorities as members of the Shower Posse."

"All I know is that they're beer distributors, and that I have an interest in that restaurant," Goode snorted. "If you'd bother to check…"

"The articles of incorporation for The Caribe?" interrupted Trask. "Oh, we have, Mr. Goode. We know that you're listed as counsel for the corporation, and that Demetrius Reid, another gentleman of Jamaican and Tivoli Gardens descent—another Shower Posse bigwig—is the owner of the restaurant and the president of the corporation. Nice try, but I think the next card calls that bluff."

Trask turned over the second photograph so that it also faced Goode.

"I'm proud to say that I took that shot, counsel," Ramirez said. "You can recognize the parking garage outside the casino here, and your Acura. That's you at the rear of the Acura. You are opening a locked aluminum briefcase."

Goode felt himself getting very sick. *If Reid sees this, I'm a dead man. Even if he sees it in jail. They'll give it to him in discovery. They'll have to.*

"The third card we'll turn over," said Trask, "is an enhanced close-up of the last shot. It shows the contents of the briefcase, and your hand reaching into that briefcase and removing one of Demetrius Reid's precious bundles of money for what was probably a very unauthorized use—video poker. You were lucky enough that evening to be able to replace it later."

The sweat was back on Goode's forehead. He was sitting motionless, looking at his shoes. *If I cooperate, I can ask for witness protection.*

"The next card that I think we'll show you this evening," Trask continued, "again comes courtesy of Special Agent Picone." Trask put another photo in front of Goode.

"That one," Picone said, "shows you handing a metal briefcase—very probably the one from the last photograph—to Winston McFarlane in the rear of the Kingston Distributing Company."

Goode barely looked at the picture, just glancing up, nodding, and then returning his gaze to the floor. *They know it all, now. All of it.*

"The *final* card in this particular hand," said Trask, more quietly and more slowly than before, "comes from the Seventh District Station of the Metropolitan Police Department. The commanding officer of that district is Major William Sivella. Those who know him call him Willie."

As Trask placed the photo in front of Goode, Sivella emerged from the bedroom.

"Those are Red Stripe Beer cans, Counselor. You know that they came from the Kingston Distributing Company, and that they are somewhat unusual, in that they contained much more than beer, at least in the bottom half of each can. Had you been able to continue in your representation of David Greene, you would have ultimately received these photographs in the course of discovery while you were getting that case ready for trial."

The steak he'd had for dinner suddenly left Spencer Goode's digestive tract, and spilled all over his four-hundred-dollar shoes.

"Pretty weak stomach for a high roller, don't ya think?" Ramirez couldn't help himself, and earned a quick warning glance from Trask. This was not the time to kick the wounded foe; they wanted him to recognize their leverage, but also to think of them as his way out of the mess, to begin the catharsis.

"What do you want?" Goode asked.

"We want the keys to your vehicle for starters," Trask said, "and the briefcase. Those now belong to the United States, and are subject to forfeiture as property used to facilitate drug trafficking. We'll drive those back to Washington tonight. You'll ride with us back to the United States Attorney's office, where you'll meet my boss, Bob Lassiter. We have a few hours of questions for you. Would you like something to drink to get that taste out of your mouth?"

Doroz watched from inside the van as they walked back out toward the Acura, and could tell by Goode's posture that he was beaten. Doroz had told the cops to play this one out; they'd earned it. His time with Goode would come with Lassiter and the all-nighter they were about to pull. He picked up the radio.

"Looks like it went well on this end, Puddin' ole pal. How's *your* target?"

"We haven't been able to find Reid all night, Bear. His car's still at the restaurant, and so are we. Nobody saw him leave, and we sent a guy inside. Haven't seen him in there, either. He hasn't been around all day."

"Well, it's not like we have enough to pull him in yet. But that may change shortly. Keep your eyes open for him."

"Will do."

From beside his crack rental in a corner of the casino parking lot, Demetrius Reid watched his attorney walk to a car in the company of The Twins, and felt his blood starting to boil.

Chapter Twenty-Five

"So let me make sure that I've got this." Lassiter sat at the head of the conference table. Doroz was to his right and a very dispirited and soon-to-be-disbarred Spencer Goode sat on his left. Trask, The Twins, Picone, and Sivella made up the rest of the party at the table.

"You've made at least ten trips to Brooklyn for Reid, carrying two hundred thousand dollars per trip. That amount represents Reid's cost for twelve kilos per delivery. So we have a total of 120 kilos that you were directly involved with. You always paid Winston McFarlane. The Red Stripe Cans were altered by McFarlane's operation there at Kingston Distributing in Brooklyn. The coke was smuggled in from Canada. Do I have that right, so far, Mister Goode?"

"Yes." Goode was looking at his shoes again.

"Fine. Now let's direct our attention to a more serious matter. What can you tell me about the death of Junebug Wilson?"

"Who?"

"They called him Junebug." Carter leaned forward in his chair, fixing an unforgiving gaze on Goode. "His real name was James. He was one of our informants. We found him in a dumpster at the end of one of the buildings in the Miller Gardens project off Wheeler Road."

"I never heard of him." There was no defiance left in Goode's voice now. The matter-of-fact denial rang true, given the fact that he had already admitted so much.

"Let me ask you this, then." Trask spoke up. "Are you aware of any connection at all between Reid and the Miller Gardens complex?"

"Just that I had to meet him there once to get the briefcase—the money. He said he had to scrape together the last of the money before one of the trips I made for him to New York."

"Can you tell us where it was in Miller Gardens that you met him?" Trask asked. "Which apartment?"

Goode thought for a moment. "I remember it was on the second floor, at the end of the hall, to the right as you're facing the front building, the one that faces Wheeler Road. I don't remember the number or anything like that. I was only there once."

Carter now glanced toward Sivella, who returned a knowing nod. They would be asking the complex manager for his consent to search the apartment before the night was over.

"And despite meeting Reid there, you never heard of Junebug, or James Wilson?" Lassiter asked.

"Never."

"Did you ever hear Reid discussing anyone who he thought might be an informant for the police in the Anacostia area?" Lassiter pressed the point.

"He never mentioned anything like that to me."

"Let's talk about your former client then," said Carter. "Young Mr. Fellows."

Goode's head hung even lower. "I had no idea he was going to do that."

"Who is 'he' and what are you talking about, Mr. Goode?" snapped Lassiter. "You know how this works, Counselor. We have to have information in order to characterize this effort on your part as cooperation. It's not a goddamn dental exam, so don't make us pull teeth!"

"Sorry. Reid sent me down to represent the kid, and probably wanted to make sure that he didn't say anything, but Reid never gave me those specific instructions. He just told me, 'Make sure he makes bail, and have him come see me.' That's the last time I saw Ronald—after I put him in the cab and told him to go to the restaurant. I had no idea he was going to be killed."

"Of course not," Ramirez shot back. "You're just a victim of circumstances, hauling two hundred Gs a week, and you're not at all plugged into the violent stuff."

"I really had no idea, Detective. I tried to confront Demetrius about it. Nobody deserves to die like that. I went to the office and asked what happened.

Reid told me he never saw the kid after he left the restaurant. He said he just wanted to give Ronald some money to make sure he didn't say anything. I didn't believe him, of course."

"But you kept working for him anyway, didn't you? You didn't come forward even after you found out that your little drug-trafficking arrangement had turned into at least one murder?" Lassiter's tone was now completely accusatory, and full of scorn.

"I was afraid for my own life." Goode's chin was so low that it was almost in his lap. He looked up at Lassiter with tears in his eyes.

"It had gotten out of control. I thought of packing up to run, but they'd have found me, and I'd be a dead man. I've had nightmares for weeks now—waking up sweating, feeling like I'm suffocating. Every time I think of duct tape I feel this tightness in my throat."

"I'll convey your concerns to all the families of the dead—the ones you could have saved by coming forward earlier." Lassiter was beyond the purpose of interrogation now, and felt nothing but contempt for the man sitting next to him. "Did you know Roderick Greene? David's father?"

"I just spoke to him on the phone after his son was arrested. Never saw him in person. From what I understood—from Reid, sorry..." he looked up at Lassiter, remembering that he was supposed to be providing the details as he went along. "From what Reid told me, the guy had gotten so fat, he could barely get out of bed to go to the john." He paused for a moment, then looked back up at Lassiter. "Reid was furious when he found out that David wasn't going to make bail. He didn't believe me when I tried to tell him about the detention hearing procedures. I really thought he might kill *me* that night."

"Ever been to Reid's house?" asked Trask. "Where is it?"

"Yeah, couple of times." Goode nodded. "Nice place. Up in Hyattsville. Doesn't look that special from the street. You only get an idea of his money when you get inside the place. Everything's top-shelf. TV, stereo, furniture. Real high dollar stuff. He had to have bought it with dope money; he couldn't have afforded it with what he made from The Caribe."

"Ever do any dope business there with Reid?" Trask followed up.

"Not really. Not me anyway. I do remember him mentioning that he was taking one of the special six-packs home with him on one occasion. He said he had an out-of-town buyer coming in who didn't know the town, and he was going to meet him someplace outside the beltway; another restaurant someplace."

Trask nodded, and made some notes on the pad in front of him. "How long ago was that?"

"Four or five weeks ago." Goode looked up at Lassiter again. "How much time am I looking at?"

"You know that it's up to the judge, and not us. You say you're not directly connected to the murders, and if that's true, then you benefit by comparison to Reid, especially if you help us take him down. We'll tell the judge the good and the bad. The scales are in his hands."

"What will you recommend?"

Lassiter leaned forward, and stared at Goode. "I'd like to recommend that you be shot at dawn, especially since you had the nerve to report a supposed bar violation regarding Tim Wisniewski after the Greene boy saw the light and didn't want you on his case any longer. All the while you were helping to move more than a hundred keys of coke. I'll be happy to make that report to *your* bar."

"I never made a complaint on Mr. Wisniewski. I have no idea which bars he belongs to, or where he's from." Goode hung his head again. "I'm not *that* big a hypocrite."

Lassiter looked at Trask, puzzled for a moment.

"I guess we're done for the evening."

"I could stand to use the bathroom," Goode said.

"I'll take him." Ramirez was on his feet, tired of sitting.

Lassiter waited until they were out of the room.

"Barry, can we put him in a hotel room for tonight and tomorrow? The local lockup may not be ready for a full suicide watch, particularly on a weekend, and with no notice."

"Sure," Doroz said "I'll get some case funds committed from the OCDETF guys. It shouldn't be a problem. We'll watch him in shifts. My concern is that we still don't have Reid spotted. Crawford and Craig Cornell—the new guy from DEA—have been working with our surveillance squad, trying to find him all night. His car's still at The Caribe, but he's not there. We ran a computer search for his house, and found it in Hyattsville, but there's no sign of him there either. Hope he hasn't already skipped town."

Lassiter shook his head in agreement, then looked at his watch and whistled.

"It's almost three a.m. We'll find him tomorrow." He looked at the tired faces around him, and gave a very approving glance to Trask. "You guys did some great work on this today—yesterday, I mean. Everybody go home and get some sleep. Willie, can one of your guys take Goode by his house to get some clothes and stuff?"

"No sweat."

"I'll get a suite rented someplace, and pull somebody out who's rested to take the first shift with him tonight," Doroz said.

"Good." Lassiter looked at his note pad. "Joe, I'm assuming that with this information, you can write a search warrant affidavit in your district for Kingston Distributing, and pick up our friend Winston McFarlane?"

"We'll have it on Monday," Picone assured him.

"Great. We should have our search and arrest warrants done here on Monday, too. Any line on where the coke's being stored north of the border?"

"I've been feeding information to an RCMP inspector up there, but asked him not to move on it until we were ready to roll down here. He has several addresses he's been looking at. The most promising is a boarding house in Montreal."

"Good. Nice of you to come down for our little party. Thanks for all the help."

"Wouldn't have missed it. If you guys will excuse me, I do need some sleep. I have a flight to catch at ten." Picone shook hands and made his exit as Ramirez returned with Goode in tow.

"Where do you live, Mr. Goode?" Sivella asked.

"I have a town home just off Capitol Hill."

"Juan, you and Dix can drive the counselor here over to pick up a change of clothes. I'll make sure a marked unit meets you there for backup. Barry will radio you to let you know which hotel to go to."

———

The marked unit and two uniforms were parked in front when Ramirez pulled up in front of the brownstone. Goode unlocked the door. It opened into a foyer. On the right side stood a flight of stairs that led up to the bedroom. Ramirez led the way up the stairs with Goode behind, but stopped when he noticed the frown on his partner's face. Carter had paused at the bottom of the staircase.

"Hell, Dix, I got this. Stay off the stairs."

"Okay," Carter said. "I'll go release the guys out front."

"Better yet, release yourself and go home. Get off your leg. We can ride to the hotel in the marked unit, then they can drop me off at 7D." Ramirez tossed him the keys to the Buick.

Carter nodded. "I'll let 'em know you'll be out in a couple of minutes. I'll see you tomorrow." He headed out the front door, spoke to the uniforms, then climbed into the Buick.

Ramirez watched as Goode gathered some jeans and a sweater, underwear and toiletries.

"You'll only need a couple of changes. They'll give you something to wear on Monday."

"Yeah," Goode said flatly. "I know." He packed the clothes into a small roll-aboard case. "I guess I'm ready."

Goode headed down the stairs toward the door, with Ramirez behind him. He reached the bottom of the stairs, passed the doorway to the darkened sitting room on his left, and started across the floor of the foyer when he heard a thud and an exhalation of breath behind him. He wheeled around to see Ramirez falling to the floor. The last sight he saw before losing consciousness was the large gloved fist as it smashed into his face.

Ramirez awoke in total darkness and with his head throbbing terribly. As his mind began to clear, he realized that he was bound—hogtied—and that something was covering his mouth. *Duct tape!* He heard moaning, and for a moment wondered if he was making the sounds himself. He realized that there was someone lying next to him, making the pitiful sounds. The other man was facing him, but with his knees at Ramirez' head. He also had a sensation of motion.

It's Goode. He's here, too. We're in a car trunk. He began to try to see if he could loosen his bonds, only to realize that his hands were also tightly wrapped. *More tape. It's Reid. He's got us. Oh God, no! Please, NO!*

He felt the car make a couple of turns, and then they were moving again. He tried to time the distance by counting in his head, reasoning that he needed to have some idea of where they might be if he was able, somehow, to break free. He had to fight to concentrate over the sounds of what he now realized to be Spencer Goode's hysterical, muffled crying. After what he estimated to be about two minutes since the last turn, he felt the vehicle leave the paved surface, heard the crunch of gravel and felt the tires slip in and out of the ruts. The car finally stopped. The trunk opened, and he saw Reid smiling down at them.

"It is a fine night for a funeral, don't yah think, Mistah Cop? That's what this is, yah know. A double ceremony."

The big man's hands reached down and lifted him out of the vehicle. Reid carried him by the back of his pants, and put him down on his right side. Ramirez could smell and feel moist grass on his face. The moonlight was just bright enough to let him see a row of trees about twenty yards away.

Windbreak. We're on a farm, or at least what used to be a farm.

Reid dropped Goode about five feet away from him, with the terrified man's eyes staring at him. He could see that Goode had been similarly bound, and that a strip of duct tape was wrapped across his mouth. Goode's cries made him think of the sounds a frightened rabbit made when caught: high-pitched, panic-driven squeals. The lawyer writhed on the ground in futility, straining against the tape, and continually shaking his head from side to side, as if the mere act of denying it all would make the terrible reality go away.

Reid was back with a small Coleman lantern, which he placed on the ground between them. He sat just in back of the lantern , watching their faces as he spoke.

He wants to see our fear. He's enjoying it, feeding on it. Goode's certainly not disappointing him.

"Yah see now, what mah dilemma is, gentlemen. Which do I hate more? Snitches or cops? Cops killed mah daddy. A snitch led 'em to him. One of yah gets to watch while the first one dies. I can see from the face of mah friend, Mistah Goode, here, that he's all ready to go. Look at his face, Mistah Cop. The face of a snitch. A face full of fear. I t'ink that watching him go first will make yah realize what's coming when it's your turn."

The pathetic squeals grew louder and the head thrashing more violent. Reid watched the show with satisfaction for a moment, then held the roll of duct tape in front of Goode's face. More cries, more thrashing. Reid laughed as he pointed toward Goode's crotch.

"Yah see, Mistah Cop? Usually they wait 'til I wrap the nose shut before they piss all over themselves." He pulled an end of the tape away from the roll and affixed it to the left side of Goode's head, then pulled it across the terrified man's nose as he pulled Goode's head off the ground. The circular motions continued three times until Reid stopped the tape just under Goode's eyes.

"Watch this now, Mistah Cop. Watch the eyes. I always do. They will almost bug out of his head, and then they just kind of go flat."

Ramirez closed his own eyes to avoid the sight, and drew a slap from Reid for doing so.

"I told yah to watch!" he screamed.

Or what, asshole, you'll kill me?

He looked at Goode's face as the last signs of life drained from the man's terrified eyes.

If that's what you want from me, you won't get it.

He took in as deep a breath as he could through his nose, and looked calmly up into Reid's eyes. He raised his eyebrows and tilted his head back for an instant, as if he wanted to speak. Reid bought it.

"Yah want to talk to me, do yah now?" Reid laughed heartily. "Or maybe yah want to scream out for help?" More laughter. "It won't do yah no good to do that—nobody around to hear yah."

Ramirez told his eyes to laugh back at Reid. He tried to force a smile through the tape.

"Why not? Why not then? It might just be wort' mah time to hear yah!"

The massive hand reached out to the edge of the tape on the left side of Ramirez's face, and pulled the tape down toward the ground, peeling the skin from his lips as the tape came away from his mouth.

NOW! Ramirez shoved his head forward, mouth open, and brought his teeth down onto the massive wrist, biting as deeply as he could and clenching his teeth hard around the flesh.

"Fuckin' Cop!"

Reid pulled his hand back, yelping in pain. He kicked Ramirez hard in the stomach.

Keep them clenched, don't spit.

The massive hand returned with the roll of tape, and Ramirez felt a drop of blood land on his cheek as the wrapping started. The hands re-covered his mouth, and Ramirez pushed the wad of flesh and blood as far to the front as he could with his tongue.

Get it on the tape! Find this Dix! Frank will know what to do. Keep the teeth together! His head was roughly lifted, and he felt the tape squeezing across the bridge of his nose. He looked up at Reid, and felt the horrible pain starting as his lungs burned and the blood vessels in his eyes began to swell.

Hail Mary, full of grace, the Lord is with thee. . . THIS HURTS. . . blessed art thou among women, and blessed is the fruit of thy womb, Jesus. OH GOD! Holy Mary, Mother of God, pray for us sinners, now and at the hour of our death—MY DEATH.

OH GOD, this HURTS!! DON'T LET THE BASTARD SEE THE FEAR!!! JESUS. . .

Reid's sneer disappeared as he saw the smile return to Ramirez' eyes, just before they faded into death. He kicked the corpse and spat on it, then wrapped his bloody wrist with more of the tape before he picked up the shovel.

Chapter Twenty-Six

"So where are we?" Eastman asked from the head of the mahogany table in his personal conference room. "It looks like we had a bad weekend all around."

"A catastrophic weekend, especially for one which started with so much promise." Lassiter was crushed. "The police department has very probably lost one of its finest detectives, and we lost a critical witness in the case, one we'd spent a month preparing to take down."

He choked back the emotion in his voice, then continued.

"The uniformed officers waited outside Goode's house for about fifteen minutes after Dix Carter left, Ross. When they went in to check on Juan and Goode, all they found was Ramirez' badge and gun on the hallway floor. The cops called Willie Sivella, and the whole police department tossed the place inside out. No prints. No clues. Just the badge, his gun, and another brand new roll of that damn tape. We have to assume that they're both gone. Ramirez would certainly have gotten word to us by now if that wasn't the case." His voice was starting to shake again. "Jeff has a *little* positive news."

"Not nearly enough to offset the bad," Trask began, "We were able to persuade Magistrate Judge Noble to sign off on an arrest warrant for Reid, and a Maryland judge issued a separate warrant for a search of his residence in Hyattsville. Our guy inside the restaurant corroborated enough of what Goode told us before he disappeared to supply probable cause for the warrants. He'd seen Reid carrying some of the Red Stripe six-packs out to his car, which backed Goode's statement that Reid had told him he was taking some of the coke home."

"What did we find in his house?" Eastman asked.

"Pretty much just what Goode said we'd see. The FBI did the search there. Real high-dollar assets—electronics and furniture, and a floor safe which had been cleaned out. The place looked pretty inconspicuous from the street, but once inside, Taj Mahal. No cocaine or residue, however, and only a single roll of duct tape, brand new. I haven't had a chance to look over the video from the search team yet to see if there's anything else."

"Do you have an asset forfeiture team evaluating things?"

"Yes, sir. FBI should have an estimate of value for us in a day or two. Through our ATF guy in Brooklyn, we were also able to get a search warrant for Kingston Distributing. We got lucky there. Donald McFarlane—the former manager at The Caribe—apparently couldn't stand to stay in his homeland. He was there with his brother Winston and a few other Shower Posse soldiers. ATF found the machine shop where they were doctoring the Red Stripe cans. They also seized about forty kilos of cocaine and about half a million in cash."

"Will we be getting Donald McFarlane back for a case here?" Eastman directed the question to Lassiter.

"They've got the venue over the big dope haul and the cash, Ross. We've got nothing linking him to the murders here. Not yet anyway. I've talked to our guys in Brooklyn. The Eastern District of New York will just be charging the defendants there with possession with intent to distribute for now. That will let us keep our conspiracy options open—no double jeopardy issues. If we're able to tie Donald McFarlane to something more than the dope, we'll be free to proceed."

"Lucky we're not dealing with the prima donnas in Manhattan," noted Eastman. The Southern District of New York had a reputation for demanding complete control over any case connected with their jurisdiction, and for not playing well with others. "Can I tell the press that their arrests were based in some part on information developed here?"

"I'm sure your counterpart in Brooklyn would have no problem with that," Lassiter said. "You could probably talk him into a joint press conference." The statement was not intended as a challenge to Eastman, but there was an uncomfortable silence for a moment.

"I don't feel the need to grab attention for this tragedy, Bob. I'll wait until we have the bastard that did this until I'm able to congratulate everyone involved for his arrest."

"Sorry—didn't mean it to come off that way."

"Not a problem. I know you were close to the detective. How's his partner doing?"

"Not good. They had to sedate him last night to let him sleep. He blames himself for leaving Goode's house. He's off the case, of course. Too close to it."

"Very unfortunate. Did Ramirez have a family?"

"Just the one he worked with every day," Lassiter answered.

"I'll send a note to his partner then." Eastman jotted a note on his legal pad. "You said you might need my personal assistance on something?"

"I'm not sure," Lassiter said, regaining some control. "Ross, we know we've had at least two leaks, if not three. The first is someone calling my date from DEA about our source in the restaurant. We have no idea who did that, but we know it wasn't passed along to Reid, or our guy on the inside would be dead or missing like Goode and Ramirez. Instead, we've pulled him out—he's safe—and we're processing a parole visa through ICE so that he can stay in the country. Then someone called the New Mexico Bar about Tim Wisniewski. We thought Goode had done that himself, but he strongly denied it, and I believed him. The third thing that concerns me is how Reid knew that we'd put the grab on his man Goode."

"When you pulled Goode out, did that make him late for his delivery to Brooklyn?"

"Not according to what he told us Saturday," Lassiter answered. "That's why we spent the whole night debriefing him. His usual routine was to gamble all night in Atlantic City, then go on up to Brooklyn on Sunday—usually getting there in the late afternoon. He missed all the weekday traffic that way. Whoever grabbed him—probably Reid himself—did it early Sunday morning."

"I see."

"Jeff had an idea that might have some merit, if you'd consider it. Since you have a good relationship with the director at DEA, could you see if he can lean on Ms. Trotter to see who called her about our guy in the restaurant?"

"I'd be happy to." Eastman wrote another note on his pad. "But I agree with you. We may be talking about multiple problems here; otherwise, your source would be dead. At any rate, we'll see where it takes us."

"Thanks."

"Any leads at all on Ramirez and Goode?"

"Nothing yet." Trask filled the gap after it became evident that Lassiter was not going to. "The police have checked every dumpster, staging area, and landfill three times. Nothing. They also did a thorough search of the parks, since those are the two methods of body disposal we've seen previously. Nothing at all. I'm not sure we'll find them in town."

"Why do you say that?" Eastman inquired.

"Just a hunch, I guess, but with the other victims, the bodies themselves were a message to us, kind of an expression of contempt, according to the FBI profiler Barry Doroz called in. Even when he put them in a dumpster, it was pretty certain they'd be found. Reid was saying that the victims themselves were trash. That was the case with the first two, anyway. The hookers were just dumped by the side of the road in Rock Creek Park. No real effort to conceal them, either. It was if he was saying that a streetwalker deserves to end up on a street. If this guy wanted us to find the bodies, we probably would have found them by now. We also know that Juan Ramirez would not have voluntarily given up his badge and his weapon. Reid probably intended *those* to be the message in this case. He's eliminated another witness against him, plus a detective, and he's telling us that he's done so. He's also disappeared himself."

"Do we have all the appropriate lookouts set up for him?"

"Yes, sir." Trask said. "Border patrol, FBI, the works. We've even got a call out to America's Most Wanted. We're watching all the airports, and our DEA guy has his photograph and description out to the interdiction teams that work the airlines."

"Wasn't the dope coming across from Canada?"

"ATF also alerted the RCMP," Lassiter said. "The inspector in Montreal who was originally on the case has been transferred, but the Mounties hit the addresses that ATF had helped them identify. They found some empty kilo wrappers in a boarding house, and a garage in the back where it appears they'd been stuffing cocaine into truck tires for the trip south. Someone, probably associated with the Kingston Distributing defendants, had tipped them off, though. They all left in a hurry. The Mounties are still looking for them."

"All right," Eastman made a few more notes on his pad. "That gives me something to work with, to feed the media hounds for now." He looked up at them. "Despite our best efforts, we can't win 'em all. You've both done some very good work on this case, and I want you to know that I know that. Keep plugging, and let's get this guy." He nodded toward Trask this time. "I'll call the director at DEA."

"Hello, Sam. Mind If I have a look in apartment 25? Nobody in that unit now, is there?"

"No, Cap'n. Been empty a while now." The Miller Gardens manager knew Sivella all too well from official visits over the past two years. "I'll get the key."

"Thanks. This is Frank Wilkes, Sam, one of our crime scene guys. We just want to look around a little. It shouldn't take too long."

"Take your time, Cap. They keepin' you busy?" The old gentleman shuffled up the stairs to the second floor as Sivella and Wilkes followed, being careful not to rush their host.

"Far too busy, I'm afraid, Sam. You know Juan Ramirez and Dixon Carter, they call them The Twins?"

"Yes. Good policemen, like you. Juan and DC are always good to folks, unless they have a reason not to be." They reached the apartment door, and he opened it for them. "This about that fellow Junebug they found in the dumpster a couple months back?"

"Nothing gets by you, does it Sam?"

"Not much that happens in my building, anyway."

"You remember the guy who was in and out of this unit?"

"Only saw him once or twice. He wasn't the one that rented the place. He sent some lawyer fella to do that."

"Is that the lawyer?" Sivella handed him a photo of Spencer Goode.

"Yep. That's him."

"What did the other guy look like?"

"Big dude. Talked kinda funny. Sounded like one of them reggae singers when he talked."

"Do you see him here?" Sivella handed him a photo spread—six mug shots on a single sheet of paper—three above three. Reid's Maryland driver's license photo was on the bottom in the center, number five.

"Can't say for sure. Number five kinda looks like him, though."

Sivella made a note on the back of the sheet. "When did the last lease run out for this one, Sam?"

"First of the month. Haven't had anybody even want to look at it since then. Nobody wanted it for a good while before the lawyer. Damn dumpster cover down below's been gone for over a year now, and it stinks the place up. I keep calling the city about it, but don't nobody do nothin.' It's a waste of a good apartment. One across the way in the other building's been empty, too. Same reason."

Sivella headed for the window overlooking the gap between the two buildings. He braced himself to raise it, half expecting the usual glue job of multiple coats of paint. He was surprised when it opened easily. He stuck his head out, and looked down, seeing the open dumpster directly below, then almost gagged from the smell, and closed the window again.

"I see what you mean, Sam." He glanced at Wilkes, who was eyeing the carpet in the front room. He pointed to the rug. "Was this here during the last lease, Sam?"

"It wasn't here *before* the last lease. That big dude brought it in and left it. That and the furniture."

"Do you mind if I take a sample from the rug?" asked Wilkes.

"Take the whole thing if you want it."

Wilkes rolled the area rug up, and tied it with a length of cord he produced from a nylon brief case that he'd carried in. He started looking around the rest of the apartment.

"Have much of a rat problem in here this year, Sam?" Sivella asked.

"No more than usual. Once in a while I see one. You know I try to keep my people safe in here, Cap. I put out bait in the empty places. Just put some more in here last week." He led them to the hall closet, and pointed out the blue corrugated cylinder on the floor. "I usually pick 'em up if I get a tenant in. Specially one with kids. Don't want the kids playin' with those."

Wilkes picked up the poison and dropped it in an evidence bag. They had what they needed.

"Thanks a lot, Sam. You're always a big help."

"No problem Cap'n. I hope you find the guy that did Junebug."

"We will, Sam."

They drove not to the 7D station, but to 300 Indiana, NW , otherwise known as the headquarters of the Metropolitan Police Department, and still otherwise known as the Daly Building, named after a sergeant who'd been killed there by an armed assailant during the nineties. Wilkes cut off a small scrap of the rug, leaving the rest in the car trunk. They entered the building, and headed for the crime lab.

Sivella watched as Wilkes prepared a microscope slide, using a strand he'd pulled from the carpet scrap. The technician then retrieved another slide from an evidence cabinet. He lined the two slides up, side-by-side, on a microscope, and peered at them for a moment through the device.

"I think we have a match," he said, looking up at Sivella. "I won't be able to say so for sure until I do some more work, but the color and texture look the same. Same core width, too. I'll firm up the ID tomorrow, get some good cross-section matches side-by-side, and shoot some slides for court."

"If it's good enough for you, it's good enough for me. Thanks for the help, Frank."

"Any time, Willie. This one's for Juan. Get that guy."

Chapter Twenty-Seven

Trask looked around the task force space, now the command post for the search. The faces were somber now, and had a look of fierce determination. The transformation the unit underwent after losing one of its own was severe. The humor that usually pervaded the investigative team—a defense mechanism against the perversions of that fraction of mankind that forms law enforcement's workload—disappeared and would be restored only by the apprehension of the party responsible for the loss. Lassiter was there, as were Sivella, Doroz, Crawford, Frank Wilkes, Craig Cornell, and Dixon Carter—back on his feet, but involved now only in an advisory capacity.

"I don't think he had a chance to put them in one of the rivers," Sivella said, looking at the map of metropolitan Washington, DC, that was spread out over the conference table. "If we were dealing with the run-of-the-mill thug, it would be my first thought, but I don't think he had a chance to do that. He couldn't take the time to stop on one of the bridges to dump two bodies. They're too well lit and heavily traveled, even late at night. Besides, we had the town swarming with every badge we could put on the street within ten minutes of the call from the uniforms at Goode's house."

"I made sure we had people along the water in the riverside park areas, too. The Park Police guys were great, and had their choppers in the air quick." Sivella looked at Trask. "I agree with you, Jeff. Juan's badge and gun are all he wants us to find, and the odds are that he hauled the bodies off to bury someplace where he thinks we won't find them."

"The question then, guys," interjected Doroz, "is where the hell do we start looking? Logic says he'd look for a fairly remote area, but most of the metro is pretty heavily developed. On the other hand, he may have put them in some old lady's back yard, just to throw us another curve ball."

"If he had time to plan this out, like everything else he's done, I'd agree with your curveball theory." Dixon Carter had the floor whenever he wanted it. His was the heaviest loss, a partner of several years. His twin. "I don't think he did. Somehow, he got wind that Goode was changing sides, and he acted to eliminate that problem as quickly as he could. I suggest that we center our search area on the places he was most familiar with. It would only be natural for him to fall back on those areas he knew best. Let's start our sweeps from the restaurant, and his house. Concentrate on the areas where those search grids would overlap."

"Good idea, Dix." Sivella nodded. "But that still leaves a helluva lot of ground to cover, and a lot of it is outside DC. We've got to get the Maryland guys involved right away."

"I talked to their state police this morning," Doroz said. "They'll give us whatever we need in terms of manpower."

"There's something else they can give us." All the heads in the room turned toward Frank Wilkes. "They have some new airborne equipment on their choppers. Very helpful for forensic archaeology. One of their birds now has GPR capability." He saw the looks of minor annoyance.

"Ground Penetrating Radar. It has the capability, when properly calibrated and interpreted, to show anomalies—areas where the normal soil patterns and structure have been disturbed. It uses electromagnetic pulses, kind of like underwater sonar, to profile the earth's subsurface. Penetrates two to five meters in good conditions. Military uses it to find buried mines. I suggest we overfly your search areas to try and identify any potential burial sites."

Dixon Carter walked over to where the thin man with the glasses was sitting, and gave him a hug. "Frank, you're a strange, scary, and very valuable guy, and I love you." Some smiles—and moist eyes—appeared around the table.

"Get 'em in the air, and let's see what they can do," Sivella said. "Barry?"

"I'm on it. I also know some local cadaver dog handlers we can line up to check any sites we identify."

"I've got one suggestion, too," said Trask.

"What are you thinking, Jeff?" Doroz asked.

"We know that Reid was having our guy Osbourne followed for a while, doing his own counter-surveillance, if you will. I don't suspect anybody in this room of leaking anything, intentionally or otherwise. What if Reid was tailing Spencer Goode?"

"We didn't see him while we were up on Goode," Doroz responded.

"But if I'm not mistaken, we didn't see him *at all* Saturday, even though your surveillance squad was trying to find him. Didn't you say his own car was parked at the restaurant the whole time, Mike?"

"Correct. Craig and I got damned tired of looking at it," Crawford said.

"Which means he was using another set of wheels all day. That's how he got to Goode's house, and that's what he used to take Juan and Goode away from the house, right?"

"Where are you going with this, Jeff?" asked Lassiter.

"If there's no leak, then the only explanation is that Reid himself saw something that night which burned Goode as a snitch. If we had a true leak inside this room, then, as we discussed earlier, Osbourne would be dead or missing, too. I think we need all the surveillance tapes from Harrah's on Saturday. They have those camera globes set up all through the casino—to watch for people cheating their machines and dealers at the tables—and even in the parking garage for normal security."

"Good idea, I think." Everyone turned again toward Frank Wilkes, who appeared to have gotten a bit more assertive after Carter's bear hug.

"Then I'm on that, too," Doroz said. "I'll call their chief of security for the tapes—the same guy that gave us the suite Saturday night."

"If everybody now has something to do," Sivella said, "then get the hell out of here and do it."

Lassiter got out of the elevator on the fifth floor of 555 Fourth Street, NW , and headed for his office. He was passing his secretary's desk.

"Mr. Eastman wants to see you, ASAP."

Instead of unlocking his door, he returned the keys to his pocket, and walked the hallway to the corner office occupied by the United States Attorney.

The secretary nodded and waved him inside. Eastman was behind his desk, and was obviously doing a slow burn. When he saw Lassiter, he pushed the intercom button.

"Gerri, please have Mr. Prescott come see us, immediately."

"Yes, sir."

"How's the search going, Bob?"

"We've got some ideas working. What's up with Prescott?"

"You'll see. I'm too furious to go through this more than once."

The intercom buzzed. "Mr. Prescott is here, Mr. Eastman."

"Send him in."

Benjamin Prescott entered the room, attempting to maintain his patrician air despite his distinct feeling that something was about to go very wrong.

"Yes, Ross?"

"That's *Mister Eastman,* to you from now on, *Mister Prescott.* I want to know where you get off thinking that it's your job to pass judgment on the morality of what other attorneys in this office do in the process of their own investigations!"

"I'm sorry. I should have told you earlier, but as I read the canons of ethics, when I see another attorney violating those canons, I am legally and ethically bound to report those violations."

Eastman's forehead creased and he leaned forward in his chair.

"What the hell are you talking about?"

"Well, of course, I…uh…thought you were asking about Timothy Wisneiwski's unauthorized contact with that represented defendant."

"*You called the New Mexico bar on Wisniewski, too?*" Eastman was standing now, as was Lassiter.

"What do you mean, 'too,' Ross?" Lassiter asked.

"This sanctimonious little snake is the one who called Angela Trotter about your source in the restaurant. At least that's what she told the director at DEA." Eastman turned back toward Prescott.

"Clean out your office. I want your letter of resignation on my desk in ten minutes. It is only a matter of courtesy to your father, a man who *earned* everything he has today—except a low quality son like you—that I'm giving you the option of resigning. If I do not have that letter in ten minutes, you will be fired.

Get out." He remained standing until Prescott had left the room, then sat back in his chair, shaking his head.

"I've got more bad news, I'm afraid, Bob. Another letter of resignation." He handed the paper to Lassiter.

"Wisniewski?"

"I'm afraid so. The New Mexico Bar accepted his statement, and was going to put him on probation, but they hit him with the costs of the matter, about five-grand in their esteemed estimation, and were going to publicly sanction him with a letter of censure. He decided instead to tell them to go play with themselves."

"What's he going to do? He just bought a house up near Georgetown."

"He told me," said Eastman, smiling a bit, "that he's joining the Metropolitan Police Department, where he can make more money—with overtime—and where he only has to worry about the bad guys in front of him."

In a Chicago motel, Reid stared at his watch. He was waiting until 3:00 a.m., the time he'd chosen to take the car, the time he'd decided that the world would be the most asleep. His mind kept repeating the analysis. The people in Brooklyn had all been arrested, no doubt because of what that weakling turncoat Goode had told the cops. He was also concerned that the crack rental he was driving could be hot by now, because the real owner might well have come out of his or her own haze and reported it as stolen. It had, after all, been three days since he had left Washington.

He reasoned that he would be better off taking another vehicle. He could be at or near the border by the time the real owner woke up and reported the theft. He had already removed anything that could tie him to the crack rental, had wiped it down to eliminate prints, and had his clothes and the money from the floor safe in his house ready to transfer to the new car. He had also walked the row of vehicles parked in front of the various rooms, and had located the one left unlocked by its careless—or road weary—owner. The minute hand finally moved into place at the top of the dial, and he made his move, walking quickly but quietly in front of the darkened windows to the gray Accord. He opened the driver's door, tossed his bag onto the passenger side floor, and reached under the dash for the wires.

As he neared the outskirts of the town, he was pleased to see that the owner had filled the tank before stopping for the night; otherwise, he would have had to hot wire the car again after stopping for gas. He saw the sign indicating that Detroit was 240 miles away, and calculated that he had both the time and the fuel to make it across into Canada.

At 4:48 a.m., however, Billy Creighton, the legal owner of the gray Accord, awoke with a horrid case of diarrhea, the result of an undercooked burger he'd gulped down at about 9:33 p.m. The fast food cook who had been in the process of cleaning his grill hadn't felt like cooking it much when Billy pulled into the drive-through at 9:26 p.m., four whole minutes before closing time. When he finally emerged from the motel bathroom at 5:17 a.m., he took a weary peek out the front window. At 5:19 a.m., Billy got his brother Frank, a Chicago cop, out of bed, and reported the theft of the Accord. Frank called it in five minutes later.

As Reid pressed on toward Detroit, he planned ahead. Those posse members who had escaped the dragnet in Brooklyn had gotten the word to the people in Montreal, who had been able to get out before the cops hit the house there. He had phoned them, had learned of the arrests in Brooklyn, and had been forced to change his plans to cross into Canada from New York. He headed west instead, and the rest of the posse cell agreed to meet him at the house in Windsor. He had enough money in the bag—about $350,000—to last a while before heading south again, and that, plus the sum in the Cayman Banks, would make him one of the new kings of Kingston.

When Reid crossed the bridge from Detroit to Windsor, Ontario, he had no idea that a very diligent officer of the Royal Canadian Mounted Police, being rather bored with checking the border traffic that morning, had been checking his notices between inspections of the cars headed southeast into Canada from Detroit. There was a fresh bulletin from Chicago concerning a stolen gray Honda Accord, and there was also a recent alert posted personally by the new inspector in the district—one Claude Prefontaine, recently promoted from the Montreal office—to be on the lookout for a Jamaican male of average height but thick and heavy frame by the name of Demetrius Reid. The bulletin bore a large likeness of Reid, taken from his Maryland Driver's license photograph, which had been forwarded to Prefontaine by Special Agent Joe Picone of the Brooklyn office of the ATF.

As Reid pulled up to the Mountie's gate, the officer recognized, but did not reveal, that the Accord was, in fact, the stolen vehicle from Chicago. After all, it still had plates registered to Billy Creighton. The Mountie also thought he recognized the face of the driver, and after re-checking the bulletin, he was convinced of it, even though the driver had a passport in the name of William Coleridge. And so it was that minutes later, Demetrius Reid, aka William Coleridge, found himself face-to-face with several firearms and a smiling RCMP Inspector Claude Prefontaine, who took some sort of writ from the inside pocket of his jacket, and politely informed Reid that the Queen and the Prime Minister did not wish him in Canada.

An hour after that, a very pleased Special Agent Joe Picone of the ATF was on his way to meet a very pleased Special Agent Barry Doroz of the FBI in Detroit, Michigan.

In Washington, DC, a very pleased assistant U.S. attorney named Trask was showing a group of investigators a freeze-frame of a Harrah's security camera video, showing Demetrius Reid watching from behind a pillar as agents led Spencer Goode to a car in the Atlantic City Harrah's parking garage.

Chapter Twenty-Eight

"It's been six days now." Sivella paced around the task force office while Wilkes stared at the strange graphics displayed on the computer monitor in front of him. "Are we missing anything from your GPR info, Frank?"

"I'm afraid not, sir. Not that I can tell, anyway."

"It was a good idea, Frank, but after almost a week and turning over half the eastern side of the metro, all we have is some compost pits and a couple of newly buried family pets. What do we do next? Anybody have any ideas?"

"You said *half* the eastern side of the metro, Cap." Dixon Carter was staring at a large map of the District of Columbia and the surrounding counties of Maryland and Virginia which had been affixed to the wall with some push pins. "We assumed Reid would be working from either the restaurant or his home in Hyattsville, up here at about two o'clock." He pointed to the upper-right quarter of the map. "This area is much more highly developed than this area down here, about five thirty off the beltway." The large index finger dropped to the suburbs of southern Maryland, toward Forest Heights and Oxon Hill. "And we know that Reid had a base of operations in our neighborhood. Southeast in 7D. He had to be familiar with these areas too, out Highway 5 toward Camp Springs, and down Indian Head Highway. There's still a lot of undeveloped farmland down there. Can we get the Maryland guys in the air to do some surveys down there?"

"Sure," said Doroz. "It's worth a shot, and I can't think of anything else to do. I'll line 'em up."

"We could add something else to the mix this time," mused Wilkes. "In addition to the GPR, we could also put some thermal imaging equipment on board the aircraft."

"For buried bodies, Frank?" Sivella raised an eyebrow. "I know we've used that stuff from our own choppers during night chases, where we're talking about some perp who's all heated up from running his ass off, trying to get away from ground units or chase dogs. Will bodies show up on that equipment after being dead a week?" He realized what he'd said, and turned toward Carter. "Sorry, Dix."

"It's okay, boss. Juan's gone. I know that. I feel it."

"It depends on how deep the bodies are buried," Wilkes continued. "Decomposition..."

"*Christ*, Frank!"

"It really is okay, Cap." Carter assured him. "Let him finish. The sooner we can find them, the sooner we can put this on Reid."

"Sorry, Dix," Frank said. "As I was saying, rates of decomposition are affected by a number of factors. Outside temperature, the depth of burial, humidity, rainfall totals, the type of soil at the burial site. Deeper burials—four feet or more—inhibit the decomposition process because they limit the air, insects, and potential carnivores which can get to the body. All you have in such cases is essentially decomposition from the inside out. But we're dealing with a clandestine gravesite here, not a by-the-code funeral home operation. Odds are we're dealing with a shallow grave, and decomposing bodies do give off heat.

"My guess is that they're probably in a common grave; no reason for someone like Reid to give them the dignity of separate burials, and holes that deep are hard to dig. The weather's turning cooler now, and if we do both the GPR and thermal imaging, we might be able to overlay them—use a GPS coordinate to map the areas of disturbed earth, then see which of those anomalies are looking warmer than the surrounding landscape. That will give us a more select group of sites to check."

"Makes sense...I think." Sivella said. "Let's get on that. When's our defendant due back in town?"

"Trask told me that he has a removal hearing tomorrow in Detroit. Joe Picone stayed out there to testify in case Reid tries to fight it. All we have to establish is that Reid is actually Reid, and not that fake ID on his passport. We have his driver's license photo and prints, and we got his file from the immigration guys, so it shouldn't be a problem. Once the court rules, then it's up to the Marshals' Service and their con-air system to transport him back here."

———

J. T. Burns, the unofficial dean of the District of Columbia defense bar, and a distinguished professor at the Howard University School of Law, was in the process of closing his office for the day, when his secretary stuck her head in the door.

"Yes, Sue?"

"Judge Noble's on the phone, Mr. Burns. Sorry to disturb you—I know you were on your way out—but he said it was important."

"That's perfectly all right. When the federal court calls, I answer." He put his suit jacket across the back of the tall leather swivel chair and sat back down.

"Yes, Your Honor?"

"Sorry to call this late, J. T., but I guess you've heard by now that they caught this Reid guy trying to flee into Canada, and that he'll probably be back from Detroit in a week or two."

"I did. I saw the article in the *Post*. I've had a couple of cases involving Detective Ramirez, and I had met Spencer Goode before. I hope they turn up all right somewhere."

"We all do, but I'm told that's probably a pipe dream. Horrible thing. Anyway, I got a call from Bob Lassiter, and he tells me there are four other bodies in the case, and that the Department of Justice might certify this as a death-penalty case. He suggested the defendant would need a top-notch defense counsel, so naturally your name was at the top of my list. You are death-penalty certified, aren't you?"

"Yes, I am."

"I thought I recalled that you were. This is going to be an appointment, J. T. The FBI has seized all of Reid's cash as being the proceeds of drug trafficking, so he's probably got nothing left to pay you with. If you take the case, and want to contest that, we can shake it all out later, but for now, I'm looking for someone who's very competent and qualified to accept the matter on an appointment by the court. I can give you some time to think about it if…"

"No need, your honor. I'll be happy to do it."

"Excellent. If it is actually certified as a capital matter, I'll find someone else to assist you. If you have another attorney you'd like to work with, who would also be willing to work on an appointed basis…"

"We have some good young lawyers here in my firm, Judge. I'll find someone."

"Thanks again, J. T. Always a pleasure."

"And for me as well. One more thing, Judge."

"Yes?"

"You say that, not counting the detective and Mr. Goode—who have not yet been located—we have four other victims already?"

"That's what Lassiter told me, subject to some forensic verification. He says the *modus operandi* is such that the prosecution will probably be able to link the four. It's those duct tape murders."

"I thought it might be. We could well be asking for some funds for a mental evaluation."

"Not unexpected. We'll entertain your motions after you have a chance to meet your client."

"We've been at it for another two days now, Chief," Sivella said, cradling his cell phone as he drove back toward the District. "So far we've found two dead deer and a cow that a farmer buried. Yes, sir, we'll keep at it. We've still got another two sites we're checking this afternoon. The cadaver dogs have been a big help. Even with the GPS grids, some of these little plots of disturbed dirt are hard to find. We…hold on, Chief, I've got someone on the radio." He answered the radio call, then dug a deep rut through the grassy median of Maryland Route 5 as he swung his car in a U-turn and headed back toward the southeast. He picked up the phone again. "That was Frank Wilkes, Chief. He thinks we've found them. Some farm between Route 5 and Indian Head. Yes, sir. I'll keep you posted."

The unmistakable smell told him they were in the right place.

Trask fought back the tears. He wiped his eyes dry and moved around behind the CSI techs to the other side of the pit, hoping to gain some small relief from the stench of decaying flesh. It wasn't any better upwind of the dig, so he circled back, trying to get a better view.

The crime scene specialists worked somberly, methodically, speaking only when necessary. Trask watched closely as they brushed away the clay and dirt from the two corpses, and was grateful for their care and precision. He knew that every speck of evidence had to be preserved, every clue maintained, all to confirm what they already knew.

The bodies were visible now. The feet were tied together, the hands taped behind each back, with skeletal digits showing where the flesh had fallen away from the fingers. The dig team was working around the heads, buried at the deeper end of the shallow trench. Trask saw one of the CSIs take a brush and gently flick the dirt from one body's partially buried head—a head that had been wrapped from neck to crown in gray duct tape.

He turned and walked into the trees to retch.

He recovered after the spasms ended and walked back toward the road, nodding to Doroz and Sivella as he passed them. He heard Sivella barking instructions into his cell phone.

"Tell those idiots from Channel 16 to get that goddamn chopper higher in the air or out of here entirely! The prop wash is starting to get heavy down here, and if they screw up this crime scene I swear to God almighty that I'm going to have some of these fine Maryland troopers shoot 'em out of the sky. I think we have a stinger missile around here somewhere, don't we?"

Trask passed the shallow grave and headed back toward the road, the same road that he'd used in the past to cut down to the Indian Head when the traffic on Route 5 was just too heavy. He walked toward the large, dark figure who was leaning against the green Buick, crying like a baby.

"We found him, Dix. We found him, and we can take him home now."

Chapter Twenty-Nine

Trask looked out the window and saw the sun shining off the aluminum spires of the Academy chapel as the jet started to climb over the continental divide between Colorado Springs and Denver. The last time he'd seen the chapel was the day he graduated, a short while before taking the walk across the stage in the stadium to accept the diploma, dressed in the white parade trousers and dark blue jacket with the two rows of buttons, and the hat that he would throw away into the sky after the ceremony. The sky was now the same bright blue, but instead of a June morning, it was January, with the sun beating down through the clear mountain air onto the snow, making the row of shiny spires even brighter. He smiled to himself.

Back in the mountains. Finally.

He turned and looked at Lynn. She had pulled the armrest back between the seats, had her left arm wrapped around his right, and was now sound asleep with her head resting on his shoulder.

Lassiter had asked him to go to the autopsies. After some negotiations between Eastman and the U.S. Attorney for the District of Maryland, it had been decided that the DC office would handle the entire matter, at least for the time being. It was, after all, the District's police officer who had been killed in the course of a District investigation.

Trask had been glad to see that Frank Wilkes was there, double-checking everything with the medical examiner. The first examination had been performed on the body of Spencer Goode, and Trask had watched in horror as the tape was carefully peeled away from the face, revealing the death scream frozen on Goode's face as he fought futilely for a final breath. The jaws were wide open and thrust forward. The flesh was the consistency of soap.

"Adipocere," Wilkes had explained. "Some call it grave wax. Most of the soil in Maryland is what they refer to as sassafras—a good-draining loam. In PG County, where we found the grave, there's a lot higher clay content, and the old farm had a good bit of it. It helped seal the bodies and preserve them. The only part any air got to was the ends of the fingers. The rest of the flesh, as you can see, is still there; it was vacuum-packed in wet clay, about twenty inches down."

Trask had watched as Wilkes examined the duct tape from Goode's body, again looking for a fiber from a carpet or automobile that could tie the murder to a person or a place.

"I can't find anything," he had said. "The floors in Goode's house were hardwood, after all."

The autopsy of Juan Ramirez had been different. Trask had never seen Wilkes look so astounded, and the medical examiner had also gaped in astonishment.

"I can't believe it," the ME had exclaimed as the tape was unwound from around the jaws. "His teeth are clenched together, not open like the other one. Maybe the pain of the suffocation process..."

"No!" Wilkes had shouted, pointing to the bared teeth. "Look at this. Something is still between them. *He bit the guy!* And there, on the cheek. Blood? From where? There are no wounds on the body."

Wilkes had been careful to collect every scrap that he could. The tissue from the teeth. A separate scraping from the inside of the duct tape where it had covered Ramirez' mouth. The blood drop carefully scraped from where it had fallen on the cheek.

The blood evidence prompted Trask. "Frank, can you...?"

Wilkes had anticipated his question. "DNA? Very probably. We've had some luck getting useful samples from adipocere. The stuff in the teeth might be harder—probably mixed with Juan's saliva. We may have to try and separate the two mixed DNA profiles—you know, Juan's and the killer's. The flesh on the duct tape might be a bit better. It seems to have some hair mixed in with it—probably from an arm. Might be able to get some cleaner DNA from a root ball at the base of the hair. We can try the blood, too, and with PCR...you know, PCR?"

"Yes. You can grow enough DNA to test from a very small sample." Trask had done some DNA work in connection with other murder cases he'd worked in the past.

"Right. Polymerase Chain Reaction. Assuming we can isolate a good sample of the killer's DNA, however small, we amplify it with some special enzymes—clone it, if you will—until we have enough to compare with a sample from your subject."

It had then been Trask's great pleasure to tell Lassiter, and Dixon Carter, that Juan had probably taken a chunk out of his killer, and was pointing him out to them from the grave. That theory proved valid a month later, at Reid's initial appearance in court in DC. Magistrate Judge Noble granted their motion to force Reid to provide a DNA sample, and ordered the marshals in the courtroom to pull the sleeves up on the orange jumpsuit, revealing the large jagged scar on the defendant's right wrist.

The judge had also, however, granted J. T. Burns's motion for a full psychiatric examination, a process estimated to take two to three months. When Trask returned to the office after the initial hearing, Lassiter gave him some unusual instructions.

"Get out of here."

"What? I don't understand?"

"Take a vacation, Jeff. Get away from this joint for a while. You've worked your ass off, and you're starting to look like hell. Like me, for heaven's sake. Get away from this thing and come back rested. One of us will have to be fresh, and you're going to handle the insanity rebuttal. You need to take a break and come back with a clear head. We've got weeks now before that report comes back from the shrinks. Take that beautiful young bride of yours on a trip somewhere. If you don't have a honeymoon planned, do that."

"We haven't really talked about it yet."

Lassiter paused for a moment, and Trask saw the light bulb go on over his head. "Do you ski?"

"Some. I did go to college in Colorado, you know."

"So you keep reminding me. Do you *like* to ski?"

"Yeah. A lot. I just never had the time or money to get very good at it."

"Ever been to Utah?"

"No."

"Greatest snow on earth, or at least that's what it says on their license plates. I'm thinking you need some asset forfeiture training."

"Excuse me?

"The Department is holding an asset forfeiture conference at Snowbird in two weeks. You know, seize the proceeds of the criminal conduct and take it away from the bad guys. Like the stuff in Reid's house."

"I know what asset forf—"

"Tolerate three days of that boring..." Lassiter looked up, arching an eyebrow, "but *important* dogma, and you'll only have to pay for Lynn's plane ticket and then an extra three or four days of lodging and lift tickets. The office will pick up the tab for your flight. I've decided that you're going. I'd just buy you a damn trip myself, but that would violate some ethics rules. Can't be overly nice to your employees, you know."

The trip arrangements had gotten even nicer when the United States Air Force's Office of Special Investigations had decided that Lynn needed the same training, at the same time, at the same conference.

Trask looked back out the window as the plane soared over the peaks and snow of the Wasatch Range. The plane turned northward and went into a final circling approach over the Great Salt Lake before landing in Salt Lake City. After collecting their luggage, they picked up the all-wheel drive rental he had reserved. As they were leaving the parking garage across from the terminal, it started to snow.

"It's pretty here," she said, staring across the valley through the snow at the mountains.

"From what I saw on the web, even prettier when we get there."

They drove south from the airport, then curved eastward on I-215. Along the way, a stretch of orange cones forced them to merge right as a lane was closed for roadwork. Trask noticed that the traffic from the two merging lanes was flowing evenly, as the vehicles alternated to converge into the lane on the right.

That would never happen in DC. I'd have to ride the bumper of the car in front of me and force my way over, then ride the stripe on the right to keep some jerk from passing me and cutting in off the shoulder.

He took the exit onto Wasatch Boulevard and began driving south again along the East Bench—the part of the city where the more expensive homes overlooked the valley. Trask turned the SUV east into Little Cottonwood Canyon, and they began the curving climb up toward the ski resorts of Snowbird and Alta.

"Lassiter said that he loves this place. Apparently these are the hills that the locals like. Less crowded than the tourist resorts in Park City. Higher and more snow, too."

They completed an S-curve switchback, driving along the creek that ran along the bottom of the canyon, and laughed seeing that someone had wedged an old ski pole under the washed-out bottom of a huge boulder, making it appear that—but for the pole—the monstrous thing would roll onto the road. A half-mile up the canyon, they pulled over with several other cars to take a photograph of a moose cow grazing on the side of the canyon across the creek. As they resumed the climb, the plowed banks of snow on the sides of the road grew higher.

"The website for Alta said that they had over a hundred-inch base already," he said. "This is going to be great."

"It already is."

He pulled the car into the lot of the Cliff Lodge at Snowbird. They checked into a room on the seventh floor. It had a sliding door and a balcony facing the mountain. Two queen-size beds lined one wall, and light-oak dressers and an armoire with a TV faced the beds.

"Which bed do you want?" he asked, then ducked as a pillow sailed by his head.

"This one," she responded, "will be for laying out clothes. We'll sleep in the one closest to the shower here, away from the draft by the window."

He turned and looked at the shower. It was a large one, running parallel to the beds, and had its own window, which looked out over the room and toward the balcony and the mountain. Inside it, a curtain covered the window.

Interesting. Flash your roomie, or the mountain, or both. I'm sure the skiers can't see in. He looked out toward the ski run facing the lodge. Two skiers were working their way down the steep face, completing their last run of the day.

It's a black run, anyway. They wouldn't be trying to peek in from that slope.

He started to unpack the ski clothes, the business casual stuff for the conference, and the laptop with the single disk of casework that he had decided to carry along.

Classes Monday through Wednesday, then rent some gear. Wonder if my legs remember how to do this. It's been too long. Where did she go?

He looked up to see that the curtain in the shower window had been pulled back. The water was running, and she was standing there, looking at him.

God, she's gorgeous.

He was with her in seconds, and the open curtains to the balcony and the mountain and the skiers just stayed that way.

The conference was informative, but dry. By the second day he had the laptop on their table, pretending to pay attention to the lectures—as with any good conference, they gave you a big notebook with all the pertinent stuff in it—and kept reviewing the video of the search of Reid's house.

The interior looked good for the government's case. All the high-dollar furniture and electronics, everything neat and orderly; not what you'd expect to see from someone in the throes of a severe depression or psychosis.

"If you break that damned thing out in our room, I'll kill you," she whispered in his ear.

"I think I'm missing something. It's here, but I'm not seeing it." He smiled at her. "Don't worry. Outside this hall, you have my complete attention. Maybe I could take a video of you in that shower. It would sure keep me awake in here."

"Only if we move to a table in the back of the room, and you get one of those screen guards."

He paused the frame as the camera turned through Reid's living room, showing a built-in bookcase. He zoomed in, and started scanning the titles.

"What're you looking for there?"

"I'm not sure. Just one of those feelings."

Nothing registered, but he made a mental note to check on some of the titles when he got back to DC. The last lecture of the day concluded, and he folded the screen down and applauded politely, even though he hadn't heard a word the guy had said.

She was a better skier than she had told him, at least for an advanced beginner. The form wasn't perfect, but she controlled her speed well and was able to traverse even the steep, blue-marked slopes at Snowbird.

Intermediate, hell, he thought. *These things would be marked as blacks on some other hills.*

A snowboarder cut in front of him, and he had no choice but to go down. He finished the run called Lower Bassackwards in a fashion completely consistent with the name of the slope.

She hockey-stopped beside him, laughing. "Nice yard sale there, Jean-Claude." She handed him one pole. The other came a moment later, courtesy of a ski patrol member who zipped down the hill, also laughing.

"Let's try Alta after lunch," he said. "Not as steep, and no grungy mountain surfers. I need some more space until I get the hang of this again."

They shuttled to the Albion base at the top of the canyon, and dropped into the chair on the lift. The snow was starting to fall again as they rode up, and it was cold enough to leave the well-defined flakes on their sleeves and pant legs for long seconds before the radiating body heat melted them.

"They're just gorgeous," she said, pointing out one, then another. "I love it here. Clean, quiet, and so beautiful."

The slopes *were* wider and less crowded. They did a warm-up on a green slope, then rode back up and skied down to connect to the Sugarloaf lift, which took them to the top of the peak of the same name. They ran along a cat trail at the top, then found a good spot to drop in.

"You go first," he told her. "Go as far as you want, then take a break. I'll catch up with you. I feel that need for speed."

He watched her go until she was several hundred yards ahead. He jumped over the edge and flew down into the Devil's Elbow run, fighting to stay above the fronts of the skis.

Get centered, butt forward; stay out of the backseat; stack the bones!

He found his balance and his rhythm, and there it was again. He was flying.

"Should I be timing you or something?" she giggled as he pulled up beside her.

"No. No competition for me out here, even with myself. It's probably the only thing I ever do purely for fun. Besides, if I try to compete with the mountain, the mountain always wins. You have to take what it gives you, and just follow its lead." He looked back at the slope they'd just descended. "I like this one. Let's do it again."

The next day, it snowed thirty-seven inches. The road up the canyon was closed, and the blowing snow resulted in what the skiers called a whiteout—a zero-visibility condition that meant no skiing for them.

"Nuts," he said, staring out past the balcony at the blizzard. "I was just getting into it again. Oh well, I suppose my legs could use a rest."

"Let's just rest all day, then. Come back to bed."

———

J.T. Burns looked at his client across the stainless steel prison table.

"Anything you need?" Burns asked.

"Just the indictment and a couple a books from home," Reid said, handing him a scrap of paper. "Yah still have da keys, right?"

"Sure. The marshals are giving me access, for now. I'll pick them up for you tomorrow. They'll be transferring you up to Rochester for that evaluation in a couple of days. I'll make sure you can take the books with you."

———

Lassiter closed his office for the day, and walked across Judiciary Square to the friendly waiting arms of the Fraternal Order of Police. He ordered his dinner, and a couple of drinks turned into four, then five. At eleven thirty, he decided that driving might be a hazard for both other motorists and himself, not to mention his occupational status. He called a cab and, when he got home, fell into bed still dressed.

Chapter Thirty

Trask sprawled on his apartment couch as he studied the indictment of Demetrius M. Reid and nodded with approval and admiration as he reread the charging document drafted by Lassiter. The first count was a descriptive conspiracy, charging Reid and his co-conspirators—the McFarlane brothers, Roderick and David Greene, and others—with conspiring to distribute more than five kilograms of cocaine, an offense that carried a minimum sentence of ten years, with a maximum of life imprisonment. The conspiracy count also included a "manner and means" section, describing in some detail the general role each conspirator had played in the scheme. There was a list of specific "overt acts" which the various participants had committed in furtherance of the conspiracy. Counts two and three charged the murders of Junebug Wilson and Ronald Fellows as the murders of potential witnesses to the conspiracy, and—following departmental review and approval—each of these counts carried the maximum penalty of death.

The murders of Juan Ramirez and Goode were not charged as stand-alone counts, but as overt acts committed in furtherance of the conspiracy. If, for some reason, the federal prosecution in the District were to be unsuccessful, the Prince George's County district attorney could take his stab at Reid for these murders. There would be no double jeopardy violation, since the federal case was based upon the drug conspiracy, and the District of Columbia authorities did not have venue over these killings, which had occurred in Maryland. Lassiter had made sure that the murders were alleged as overt acts in order to keep some overly restrictive judge from refusing to hear the evidence on the grounds that they had not been charged, or that they were unrelated to the conspiracy.

There was no obvious connection to the conspiracy in the killings of the two prostitutes, so Lassiter had explained that they would save that evidence for the penalty phase of the capital trial, assuming that the jury returned a conviction on the other counts. That way, the jury, having already heard of four murders, and having convicted Reid of either or both of the Wilson and Fellows homicides, would get the additional evidentiary jolt when they learned that the body count was six instead of four, and that Reid had simply killed the women for pleasure and not for any other purpose. The evidence was simply not strong enough to prove that Reid had played any actual part in the death of Roderick Greene. As always, they had what they knew, but only charged what they could prove.

The indictment concluded with the forfeiture allegations, providing that upon Reid's conviction on the drug conspiracy, the restaurant, the house in Hyattsburg and its expensive contents, and the $350,000 seized from Reid at the Canadian border would all become the property of the United States government. These properties had either been used to facilitate—or represented the profits of—drug trafficking.

The document was signed by the lead attorney on the case, Robert Lassiter, and by the foreperson of the federal grand jury.

"Why isn't your name on that, too?" Lynn asked, looking over his shoulder.

"It wasn't required. No big deal. My name's all over everything else we filed, but Bob's the lead. Fine with me. He can handle all the noise with the press. You should have seen the courthouse yesterday at the pretrial conference. There must have been twenty satellite trucks parked on Pennsylvania Avenue. The marshals opened the back door for us so that we could sneak in through the judge's entrance without getting mobbed by people who wanted to stick microphones in our faces."

"Who's your judge?"

"Harry Browne, an old Carter appointee in senior status. We drew him off the wheel so nobody could say we went forum shopping. He could be a real problem. Very pro-defense on his evidentiary rulings, and a capital punishment abolitionist. He may not keep the case, though. His health isn't good, he's pushing eighty, and the word is that he's asked for it to be reassigned."

"How will that happen?"

"They'll probably go back to the wheel with it."

She studied his face. "How does Jeff Trask feel about the death penalty?"

He shrugged. "I'm not against it, especially where a brute like Reid is concerned. There've been others like him who, when there was no capital punishment, kept killing in jail—other inmates, guards—and laughed because they were already doing life, and we couldn't give them any more time. There's another side of me that says that if we truly locked him down like the animal he is—twenty-three hours a day in a solitary cell where he couldn't hurt anyone else—he'd actually hate that more. I do think we as a society need to keep the ultimate sanction option for cases like this one."

"What's the thick folder?" She pointed to the accordion-style binder in the center of the coffee table.

"My cross to bear for the trial. The sanity stuff. The initial opinion from the shrinks at Rochester—the Bureau of Prison docs—was that he was just antisocial, albeit with some paranoid traits. Then J. T. Burns had his own guy look at Reid, and—what a surprise—he's totally bonkers. A raving paranoid schizophrenic."

"Have you seen that diagnosis before?"

"Yep. Actually pretty common for serial killers. Their favorite flavor."

"How do you fight an expert testifying about that?"

"With facts. Sometimes the defense won't give the shrink everything, and you can attack their opinion because they don't know the whole story about their patient. If the expert is a paid charlatan—you know, a witness for hire—you can occasionally beat 'em up with that. Regardless, you have to study the diagnosis and the professional literature on the disease and be prepared to go toe-to-toe with them in their own field."

"And you have to compete with all their training and experience when you're on their turf?"

"Obviously, you can't do that across the breadth of the field. You *do* have to be prepared to go to battle on that *part* of their field represented by their diagnosis. You study the crimes, the defendant, and you get some help of your own."

"Who's that going to be?"

"Two very expensive hired guns from L.A. Dexter and Morris. One's a very experienced psychiatrist—medical doctor *and* a shrink. The other guy is a psychologist. Doesn't have an MD, but he's hell on wheels as far as the leading psycho tests are concerned. Lassiter says that the department has used them several times in the past. I shipped them every scrap of paper in the case, including the photographs and autopsy reports on all six victims, just to make sure the defense couldn't claim that *our* guys were working from a lack of factual knowledge of the case. Since Burns moved to have his own shrinks do an exam, he had to agree to have Reid submit to an exam by our guys. So I get to do my own homework, then bounce it off our guys to see if I'm on the right track. They'll help me prepare a cross of Burns' expert, then testify for us on rebuttal."

"Why is he going this way—you know, insanity?"

"Burns is screwed on the facts of the case, and he knows it. The carpet fibers from the apartment at Miller Gardens matched the ones on the inside of the duct tape from Junebug Wilson's head. Poor Juan Ramirez had the presence of mind to bite the hell out of Reid's arm before he died, and the DNA from the stuff in his teeth matched Reid. Then there are the cans we got with the coke residue, and all the surveillance stuff from Joe Picone in New York. Plus we have the story from Goode, and the testimony from David Greene, who's back on board now that Reid's locked up. He blames Reid for his father's heart attack, probably with good reason."

"Burns doesn't want to attack any of that?"

"He's good, Lynn. Picks the ground he has the best chance on, and digs in there. The bad defense lawyers are like poorly aimed shotguns. They attack every little thing you do, regardless of how credible it is, try to turn saints into liars, and object to every little thing, thereby emphasizing the importance of it in the minds of the jurors. Lassiter calls them springbutts because they jump out of their chairs every time someone says something about their client. Their cross-examination is usually just getting your witness to repeat everything he said on direct, so he gets to tell the same story twice. They usually alienate even the carpet in the courtroom by the end of the first day of trial."

He took a drink of the *pinot noir* she had placed on the end table beside him.

"Burns did file one set of motions trying to keep out what Spencer Goode told us, since he's obviously not going to be testifying."

"How *can* you introduce statements from a dead man?"

"Exactly the point. There's normally an almost absolute prohibition against it. Rank hearsay. Denies the defendant his right to cross-examine the witness. Violates the Confrontation Clause. All that's in Burns' motion. We responded that it should be admitted because Reid's the reason that the witness is unavailable to testify, and that barring the admission of the testimony would be letting Reid profit from his own misconduct. Reid *confronted* Goode when he killed him—so much for the Confrontation Clause."

"Has the judge ruled on that yet?"

"Nope. He's probably going to hand that hot potato to the new judge—whoever that will be—with the case file."

She leaned over and kissed him. "Don't stay up too late with this. You need some sleep."

———

Reid took the copy of the indictment that Burns had given him and folded it into thirds so that it fit neatly inside the business envelope that the guard had provided for him. He addressed and stamped it, and handed it out through the bars to the trustee who was collecting the prisoners' outgoing mail. The prison staff member who reviewed the contents the next day saw only an indictment—nothing of interest for further investigation. She sealed the envelope and tossed it into the mail bin to go out with the next pickup.

———

Lassiter stood in Trask's office doorway, holding two documents. Bill Patrick was behind him, completely unable to suppress what in most police circles would be described as a "shit-eating grin."

"Don't get up. I think you'll want to see these," Lassiter said as he crossed the room and tossed them onto the desk.

Trask opened the first folded document, and read it aloud.

"By order of the Honorable Harry D. Browne, Senior United States District Judge, and with the consent of the receiving judge, the matter of the *United*

States v. Demetrius M. Reid is hereby transferred for all purposes to the Honorable Edie L. King." He jumped out of his chair and pumped his fist. "Yes!"

"Look at the other one," Lassiter instructed.

Trask unfolded the other paper.

The Court, having considered the defendant's motion to suppress the statements of the late Spencer Goode, hereby adopts the proposed findings of fact and conclusions of law set forth in the response of the United States, and accordingly, defendant's motion is hereby DENIED. Signed, Edie L. King, United States District Judge.

"I think," said Lassiter, "that *my* portion of this trial suddenly got a lot easier. We did lose on one thing, however. She denied our motion to keep him shackled in the courtroom. Said it would prejudice the defense in the eyes of the jury. Oh, well. We expected that. We'll renew the motion at trial if he causes any commotion in the courtroom."

In a small house on the outskirts of Windsor, Ontario, a man with long dreadlocks opened the envelope. He took out a red marker and circled the name at the bottom of the indictment. His target would be someone named Lassiter.

Chapter Thirty-One

"We've got some help for you." David Dexter began, "but we have some unanswered questions, too." Trask and Lassiter exchanged glances across the conference table. "To begin with, there's no way this guy is clinically insane. You can't spend any time with him without getting the impression that he's *extremely* focused, and in my opinion, extremely dangerous. I've examined some real winners, and this Reid scares me to death. Not because he's crazy—he's certainly not—but because he *hates* with such an un-tempered ferocity. I had the distinct impression that he wanted to kill *me*, and *would have* if he thought he could do it without consequences."

"What about the defense diagnosis?" Trask asked. "The paranoid schizophrenia?"

"That gets back to what I was saying." Dexter paused. "What he tells us—about his delusions, about his motivations—is entirely consistent with that diagnosis. That's where our unanswered questions start. The problem with the defense diagnosis is that nothing else supports it. Not the guy's recent history, not the motive for the crimes, not the tests we've run, and certainly not his genuine demeanor."

"What do you mean by his *genuine* demeanor?" asked Lassiter.

"There's the way he acts when *we're* speaking with him, or administering a test," Paul Morris answered, "and then there's the way he acts when he doesn't realize we're watching him—when he's in the day room or the yard with the other detainees. Since those are moments when he's not aware that we're watching him, we tend to interpret those times as being more genuine than when he's on his guard with us."

"Describe the specifics for me, please." Trask was already writing.

"Certainly," Dexter said. "His demeanor when he knows we're watching him is very dull, blunted, flat. Something that would—like the reported delusions—be consistent with the defense diagnosis. On the other hand, when we look at the tapes of him with the other prisoners, he's almost strutting. Cocky, a big man in the yard, and there are lots of very big men in the yard. He doesn't take any crap from anyone, from what we've seen on the tapes. He even plays chess at night. Schizophrenics are generally not capable of playing chess."

"Delusions and a possibly faked demeanor, or as you guys say, affect," Trask noted. "What did the F scales say about him on the MMPI-2?"

"The what scales?" Lassiter asked. "Excuse me, gentlemen. I've been around since dirt was invented, but I've been lucky enough to avoid this type of defense until now."

"He's done this before." Morris smiled, pointing at Trask. "The MMPI-2 is the second version of the Minnesota Multiphasic Personality Inventory, the grand-daddy of psychological testing, both forensic and otherwise. It has some indices, or scales, built in to try and identify anyone who attempts to manipulate their answers in order to fake insanity or mental illness. The normal test scoring has F scales, which attempt to ID a subject who's trying to 'fake bad.' There's even been a recent attempt to further enhance the ability to ID a malingerer, and it's called the FBS, for fake-bad scale. I ran them all, and this guy's way up there on both, which you would expect for someone with such a strong antisocial personality. Most of the subjects with antisocial personality disorders score much higher than normal on all the F scales."

"That's good for us, then," Lassiter observed.

"To a point," Dexter responded. "As is the case with a lot of the literature in our profession, you can almost always find something to support the opposite conclusion. For example, it makes sense that someone with an antisocial personality would be uncooperative with us. A lot of the studies say that. We're the enemy, after all. He knows we're working for you guys, even though we *would* testify that he's insane if we thought he was. Anyway, you expect the antisocial to be uncooperative, but we see a lot of malingerers being *overly* cooperative, especially when it comes to describing their supposed symptoms. There are studies that logically come to that conclusion, and some empirical findings that go both ways. In a medico-legal setting like this when the guy's life is on the line, you'd expect him to throw those delusions right out on Front Street so that we'd diagnose a psychosis."

"He didn't do that?" Trask asked.

"Not at all. We had to work from the defense guy's notes to pull it out of him. He acted like he didn't want to talk about it—like he was ashamed of the supposed delusional thought processes."

"What do you think of the defense expert, this Doctor Grant?" Lassiter asked. "He's generally pretty well respected," answered Dexter. "Of course, he's making a pretty good living—as we are—testifying in courtrooms. He's on the defense side most of the time. Hates the death penalty. You'll have to be careful with him though; he's no dummy."

"Would he coach a defendant in order to earn an acquittal?" Trask asked.

"I don't really think so," Dexter said. "We've certainly run into some who have. The problem for those that do is that their subjects have a bad habit of ratting them out for it when they get convicted. The allegations turn up in the defendant's petitions attacking both the defense counsel and the mental health professional for ineffective assistance at trial. The bad guys lose at trial, then on appeal, then go after those who tried to help them. Another antisocial personality trait. Grant knows that if he gave this guy specific suggestions and the post-appeal petition was at all credible in claiming that he coached the guy to get him off, he'd lose his very substantial meal ticket."

"Sounds like—as usual—we need to stick with the facts," Trask said. "Let you guys fight it out with Doctor Grant."

"That would be the safer course for now," Morris agreed.

"One further question." Trask gathered a thought. "Is Grant honest enough to admit a mistake in his diagnosis if we found a smoking gun?"

"Interesting question," Dexter replied. "I can't imagine what you might find that would be so conclusive, but—assuming you did—I think he'd have to try and maintain his credibility for future employment."

"Thanks again for the help, guys," Lassiter stood, shaking the doctors' hands as they headed back to their hotel. He looked at Trask. "Do you have something?"

Trask shook his head from side to side. "At this point, just a hunch, boss. Remember what they said. The symptoms are too good. They think he's faking it, but aside from the elevated MMPI scales, which are subject to multiple interpretations, they've got nothing to prove that. They don't think Grant would coach him, but he's acting like he *has* been coached."

"Where does that leave us?"

Trask paused for a moment and looked at his notes. "Reid's no dummy. In a lot of ways—criminal ways, certainly—he's a self-made man. He trusts only himself. Hell, he kills those who are closest to him if he thinks for a minute that they might do him wrong." He looked at Lassiter. "I think," he said, "that Mr. Reid has been studying."

"Nice thought," Lassiter said. "As long as it doesn't turn into some obsession that you can't prove to the jury. Remember what I said about getting tunnel vision with your theory of the case. The evidence has to back you up."

"Understood." He picked up the remnants of the case file spread across the conference table, then paused and put the copy of the video disc into his briefcase. *I'll check this again tonight.*

In Windsor, the man with the dreadlocks was cutting them off. They would grow back. After a trip to a local barber, he emerged with a very conservative look. He appeared perfectly suited to his new role, that of an exchange student. The suitcase was packed with absolutely nothing suspicious. He'd have time to acquire what he needed for the job when he reached New York.

"How many times have you gone over that thing?" Lynn asked as she picked up the plates from their dinner. Trask was looking at the video of the search of Reid's house again, and had once more frozen the frame on the bookcase.

"At least one time fewer than was sufficient."

She walked between him and the laptop, bent over and kissed him on the forehead. "It's not healthy for you to have trial head two weeks before this thing starts. You get so focused on the case, I get the feeling that if I walked around the room naked right now, you wouldn't notice."

"Try it," he chuckled. "I'll call that bluff."

"What do you keep looking for?" She was sitting beside him now, staring at the screen.

"I don't know—a psychology textbook—something like that. I get the strong feeling Reid's been reading up on his defense. They give prisoners access to law books in the can, but usually not shrink manuals. I just don't see anything like that here. Of course, I don't know what all these titles are about."

"Write a list of the ones you don't know and Google 'em," she said.

"Good idea. Maybe I do have trial head already."

He zoomed in and scanned the first shelf, jotted down one title, found none on the second shelf worth noting, then scanned the third, and wrote down three. He launched a browser and ran a search on book number one. *Nothing there.* Book two. *Nope.* Book three. *Some Jamaican political propaganda.* Book four. *What the hell? Maybe?* He looked at his watch. *I have enough time.* He grabbed his keys and a jacket.

"Where are you going?"

"*We* are going back downtown—to the library." He kissed her hard. "You helped me find it. Maybe. Come on!"

They reached the Martin Luther King Memorial Library at 901 G Street, Northwest, the heart of the District of Columbia Public Library system, in forty minutes, thanks to the lack of rush hour traffic. Trask checked his watch.

"It's eight fifteen. We have forty-five minutes. I've got to check the inventory to see if they have something. You can help me out by finding the thickest book on the MMPI you can find."

"That shrink test?"

"Exactly. Look in the psychology section."

"Any particular title or author?"

"No. Just something authoritative, and *thick*."

"Got it. Thick." She scurried off toward the reference aisles.

He found the author listings on the computer. *They've got it!* He jotted the Dewey Decimal System number down on the palm of his hand. *960.0971 F214.* He found the aisle, found the book, pulled it from the shelf, and scanned the index. He found the page he was looking for and read it once, twice, three times.

You wanted a smoking gun? Bang! I've got you, Reid, you bastard, you cold-blooded, duct-taping bastard.

She found him at the desk, filling out the new library membership application. She was carrying two of the thickest books he'd seen since looking at a copy of Samuel Johnson's *Dictionary of the English Language.*

"I didn't know which one would be better..."

"They're both great—perfect! We'll take all three." He pushed them forward toward the librarian with the completed application.

They drove back toward Waldorf with Trask's new library card and the three books.

"How are you going to find the time to read all that with your other case prep?" she asked.

"Oh, I'm not going to read much of it, not the ones you got for me, anyway."

"Then why did I get them?"

"I'll let you know when I'm crossing Grant," he said. "You'll see then."

The man who had formerly worn the dreadlocks picked up the phone from his hotel room in Brooklyn. "Same order as the last time, mon," he said in the *patois* accent of his home country. "I'll be pickin' it up in two days."

Chapter Thirty-Two

On the morning that trial was to begin in the matter of the *United States v. Demetrius Reid,* Trask parked in his usual spot north of 555 Fourth Street NW. His normal walking route would have been straight down Fourth Street to the E. Barrett Prettyman federal courthouse, but he was early enough—and the streets were quiet enough—to allow for a slight detour.

He angled west and then south through the National Law Enforcement Officers Memorial, thinking of Juan Ramirez. He crossed through the heart of Judiciary Square, passed the statue of Lincoln, and then descended through John Marshal Park, the landscaped garden that separated the Superior Court from the Daly Building on the north and the Canadian Embassy from the federal courthouse farther south. On the west side of the federal courthouse, he passed the seated bronze statues playing chess on the terraced stone wall, and contemplated his own chess match to come. He was about to turn the corner to the front of the courthouse when he noticed the army of reporters and satellite trucks already gathering, hoping that an off-guard assistant prosecutor or witness would blunder into their ranks for an interview. He doubled back and walked behind the courthouse, where one of the U.S. marshals nodded in recognition and admitted him.

Lassiter had beaten him to the courtroom, despite what had probably been another late night with dinner and a drink or two at the FOP. His superior's eyes were tired, yet still sharp and alert.

I couldn't keep up that pace, even at my present age. I don't know how he does it.

"Ready to go?" Lassiter asked him.

"Ready as I'm going to be." Trask placed the case under his side of the table, grateful for the opportunity to put down the two large tomes—and the other book—which were inside.

Burns arrived a short time later with a very attractive young assistant. He introduced her as Julia Rogers, a member of his firm. *She'll have instant credibility with any men on the jury. Wonder what her participatory role will be in the case?* Trask noticed that there seemed to be a genuine respect between Burns and Lassiter. No tension, no wondering about any dirty tricks to come. Everything was out in the open. The chess match was about to start. *I feel more like a pawn than a bishop.*

The rear of the courtroom was starting to fill, too, mostly with a cadre of the media types from the front steps. *Sivella's in the front row. I knew he would be.* Trask nodded at the district commander, who gave him a confident smile in return. *No pressure here at all. I'm just trying a murderer who killed a cop and five others, and the lead trial attorney in the office in the nation's capital city wants me to take apart the expert witness who's been prepped by the best defense attorney in town.* He took a deep breath, which did not go unnoticed by his co-counsel.

"You'll be fine." Lassiter patted him on the shoulder. "Just like football. Once the first hit's behind you, you concentrate on the game. You ever play?"

"No varsity experience. Just the full-pads intramural game at the Academy. They had me trying to play outside linebacker at 145 pounds. I told them they should rename my position speed bump. Seems like I got run over every play."

Lassiter laughed. He seemed relaxed, in his element.

The side door opened and the marshals brought Reid in. It was the first time Trask had looked him in the eye. He returned the hard stare, and Reid broke the gaze first. *Round one to me, I think, or did he just start staring at Lassiter instead?*

Burns had brought Reid a suit to wear, and it fit as well as one could without custom tailoring. The shoulders were wider than any Trask had ever seen, and the suit jacket's sleeves were probably two inches too long, the natural consequence of fitting the big man's chest with an off-the-rack purchase. He was shackled with leg irons and a chain that ran from the leg restraints upward to a large pair of handcuffs. The deputy marshals escorted him to the chair between the two defense counsels.

Trask felt another pat on his shoulder and turned to see Barry Doroz. Doroz saw Sivella, and walked over to shake hands with him before returning to his seat beside Trask.

"How's the shrink-buster today?"

"I think I'll just be observing for a while. I don't expect to see the good Dr. Grant for a few days yet."

"Our docs ready to go?"

"Oh yeah. They're back in LA; we'll let' em know when to travel. We can't afford to put those guys up all week. Their bill's going to be close to six figures already."

"ALL RISE."

Judge King appeared behind the bench and instructed them to be seated.

"Good morning everyone. Mr. Burns, I understood that you wanted to be heard on something before we got started with our jury selection?"

Burns stood and walked to the podium in the center of the courtroom.

"Yes, your honor. Two matters, actually. The first is a request, pursuant to the court's earlier ruling, to remove the restraints on my client. I think that having the jury see him like this would be grossly unfair, and would communicate the court's opinion that he is a danger to them."

"Granted. Marshals, please remove the restraints." She took off her glasses and stared down at Reid from the bench. "I must tell you, Mr. Reid, that *any* action or statement on your part which makes me reconsider that decision will mean that those restraints will immediately go back on. Do we understand each other?"

"Yes." The deep voice responded.

No "Your Honor," or even "ma'am," Trask thought.

"What else did you have, Mr. Burns?"

"I have the copy of the court's ruling on my motion to bar any evidence of the statements allegedly given by Spencer Goode to the prosecution. I would ask the court to reconsider that ruling in light of the Supreme Court's decision in *Giles v. California*, which holds…"

"I know what the decision says, Mr. Burns. It says that Federal Rule of Evidence 804(b)(6) requires that before the government can invoke the doctrine of waiver by wrongdoing, they must establish that your client killed Mr. Goode *with the intent* of preventing him from testifying. I've read Mr. Trask's offer of proof and—if the government's evidence goes in as he has said it will—I think that such evidence would circumstantially satisfy the intent requirement. Your objection is overruled. If you think that there is still some deficiency in the government's case once they have presented it to me, you can raise the matter again before we hear about Mr. Goode's statements."

"I understand the court's ruling, Your Honor."

Polite, no-nonsense, no arguing with the bench. He won't be making any dumb mistakes. Hopefully, his shrink will.

The jury panel, one-hundred-and-twenty strong, was ushered in by the courtroom clerk, and Trask watched as Lassiter and Burns each masterfully managed the process, an even more daunting task than usual due to the need to "death qualify" the jury in the capital case. Each juror who was totally opposed to capital punishment was excused "for cause" by Judge King, since it would be the jury—not the judge—who decided the sentence to be imposed if a conviction was returned on any capital charge in the indictment. Burns objected to these decisions politely at the bench, protecting his record for appeal. None of the panel members said that they would *automatically* vote for death upon conviction; they too would have been dismissed. Most of the prospective jurors expressed enough reservations about capital punishment to be excused. The pool was finally reduced to a scant thirty-five.

Twelve for the jury, plus three alternates is fifteen; we get six peremptory challenges to the defense's ten. One more peremptory challenge for each side on the alternates. Anyway, fifteen plus sixteen plus two is thirty-three. If we lose three more, we'll have to call in another panel.

No more excusals were made. The jury was selected by noon on the second day. Five men, seven women in the main jury. One white, one Hispanic, ten black. Two black women and one black man as alternates.

The population of the District is accurately represented. Reid has no squawk about this jury on appeal. None that will stand up, anyway.

They broke for lunch.

When they returned, Lassiter gave his opening statement.

He's got them in the palm of his hand, mesmerized. A complete chronology of this whole thing from memory, with no notes.

The case was outlined as if it were a trailer for a mystery movie. The murder of Junebug Wilson. The body of Ronald Fellows found in a second dumpster. Cocaine trafficking tied to the restaurant. The Red Stripe cans and David and Roderick Greene. The surveillance of the Kingston Distributing Company in Brooklyn. The disappearance and discovery of the bodies of Goode and Ramirez.

The way he's describing everything—they can see it in their minds. Look at them—all on the edge of their seats. How is he doing this? A bare minimum of vocal tone variation. Hell, it's almost a monotone, but the pauses, the perfect word-smithing. He hasn't even mentioned Reid yet, but the jury wants him to—there it is.

"The common denominator in each one of these sadistic, brutal killings is the same criminal who masterminded the very clever distribution of the cocaine which flowed into our city on a beer truck from the Kingston Distributing Company. That same criminal mind served during this period as the hands-on, efficient owner of a popular and successful restaurant. That criminal mastermind, ladies and gentlemen, that brutal murderer, is Demetrius McEntyre Reid." Lassiter turned and walked back to his chair.

"Mastermind, clever, efficient, successful." He's attacking the insanity defense without even mentioning it. Not even dignifying it with a reference of what's to come. He didn't even tell them which verdict to return—didn't have to. It's their conclusion now—he didn't want to force feed them. They'll hold onto it longer and stronger because it's their own mental process—their own idea that Reid's as guilty as hell.

J. T. Burns followed with his own opening statement.

He's telling them that it's all true! A couple of them are disarmed by this. He only needs one or two. We have to have all twelve.

"Mr. Lassiter is a fine prosecutor..."

He's using the word to mean persecutor.

"And he is telling you exactly what happened. The problem that Mr. Lassiter has, ladies and gentlemen, is that he can recall and describe what happened to each victim, but he can't tell you *why* it all happened. He can't look into the tortured mind of Demetrius Reid and tell you why an otherwise intelligent and productive citizen would lose control from time to time and commit crimes that were so horrible, so abnormal, that they are almost beyond description."

Prey on the perception that if it's horrible—'abnormal,' it must be sick. Sick means insane.

"Fortunately, there are those who are highly trained, and who have decades of experience in doing just that. We will call such an expert in this matter, Dr. James Grant, a respected and recognized psychiatrist who will tell you that he's examined each and every aspect of this case and has examined Demetrius Reid at length. He will tell you that the *normal* Demetrius Reid could never—would never—have committed these crimes. He will tell you, and we submit that the evidence will show, that at the times these horrific crimes were committed, Demetrius Reid had no control over his own actions. He was, ladies and gentlemen, and he sadly remains, legally insane."

"Each and every aspect of this case." Trask jotted the phrase down, word for word. *I'll make him eat a little of that crow. Reid's got the act down. Vacant stare, no emotion. Doing the zombie thing at the table. What's his plan, six months in a mental hospital after the verdict, then an escape? Living the high life in the islands on money he's stashed for years in the Cayman Island Banks?*

"You may call your first witness, Mr. Lassiter." Judge King was her usual efficient self.

Four o'clock, and she still wants to get some testimony in today. No wasting the jury's time. If they're here, we're working. That'll be good for us.

"The United States calls Detective Dixon Carter."

Lassiter's direct examination guided Carter through the deaths of Wilson and Fellows, and then it was time for the overnight recess.

No cross yet. Good for us. That'll give the jury something to sleep on tonight. Dix is doing okay so far. We haven't gotten to Juan's death yet.

"Have dinner with me, Jeff. The usual spot." Lassiter made it sound as much like an instruction as a request.

"Sure. I'll see you there. I just have to call Lynn."

He was at his usual table at the FOP. Trask sat down and ordered a club sandwich.

"Nice first day, I think. I loved your opening statement."

"Thanks. I ought to know how by now, I guess. Let's talk about your cross of Grant."

"Okay."

You've got a copy of Irving Younger's *Ten Commandments of Cross-Examination*, I hope?" Lassiter referred to the famous law professor's summary of how not to get your head handed to you by an adverse witness.

"Of course."

"Go over them again. Let's add a couple of things to them. You've probably thought of some of this yourself, but just in case. Don't give Grant an opportunity to comment on the work of any of our docs. Not the Bureau of Prison guys, not Dexter and Morris. Burns will want to do that with Grant. Don't let him repeat it on cross. It's not a winner for us and you won't be able to control it. We go last, and we'll have Dexter and Morris talk about Grant's shortcomings."

"OK."

"Remember that you don't want to ask this guy anything—*that's anything*—that you can get into evidence in another way—a *safer* way."

"Understood."

"Establish the common ground first, in as friendly a fashion as possible. Move from the stuff you know he'll have to admit to the more testing questions, but if he's being reasonable and not combative, there's no need for you to suffer by comparison. Be reasonable yourself. If anyone's going to lose it in there, we want it to be Dr. Grant. Remember that you've got a very good cleanup squad coming in behind him in Dexter and Morris."

"Gotcha." Trask was smiling.

Lassiter sat back. "You knew all that anyway, didn't you?"

"I had some good training. I still appreciate the refresher course."

"Fine. Finish your sandwich and go home. Get some rest. This will be a long one."

"You need some sleep yourself."

"I'll get enough when it's over. Right now I need another drink"

The man who had formerly worn the dreadlocks sat in his car a block up the street from 555 Fourth Street and watched the exit from the United States Attorney's underground parking garage where the supervisors kept their cars. He looked at his watch and wondered to himself if this asshole Lassiter ever went home. At eleven thirty, he gave up for the night and went back to his hotel.

Chapter Thirty-Three

Carter was on the stand for another hour, finishing his testimony with a gut-wrenching and tearful summary of the night his partner and Spencer Goode disappeared. When it came time for cross, there were only a couple of perfunctory questions, and not by J. T. Burns himself, but by Julia Rogers.

The old fox. The unspoken message to the jury is that this stuff isn't really important. He's looking as bored as he can, except when he has to look sympathetic. He's already emphasizing Grant's testimony, before he even hits the stand.

Crawford was next, testifying about following David Greene through the fast food drive-thru and grabbing the Red Stripe Cans from the trash. Burns remained in his seat, and there was no cross-examination at all. A representative from the DC city government came in to authenticate the articles of incorporation for The Caribe, and Lassiter used the documents to point out that Reid was the corporate president and that Spencer Goode had been the legal agent. David Greene was next, and Lassiter made sure that he stood at an angle away from Reid, so that the young witness on the stand had no opportunity to either be intimidated by having to look in Reid's direction, or to show too much hatred for the man who had probably killed his father.

No cross-examination at all. Burns has some balls.

After lunch, Trask called Desmond Osbourne, who testified credibly about the various events he had observed during his stint as an employee of The Caribe. Along the way, Trask was careful to elicit any detail—including the conversation in Reid's office—that tended to show that Reid was the man in charge of the operation, the man *in control* of both the restaurant and himself. Ms. Rogers again took the cross, having Osbourne admit that he'd been employed "as a snitch" in Panama by another government agency, and that he hoped to remain in the country as a reward for his cooperation in the current prosecution.

Well done. She didn't take any risks—got what she could and then sat down.

Joe Picone testified for Lassiter, and introduced the surveillance videos of Goode's car and the trucks from Canada as they had rolled up to the loading docks in the back of the Kingston Distributing Company. He then told the jury about participating in the raid of the building, and explained the various photographs taken during the search of the place; the metal shop, the stash of Red Stripe cans, both modified and awaiting the process, the kilograms of cocaine and the half-million in currency. He also had the arrest photo of Donald McFarlane.

Again, no cross. The old master is sticking to his script. He wants the jury to think that none of this really matters.

Lassiter had Barry Doroz on the stand next, recounting the debriefing of Spencer Goode. Burns again went to the bench to object in a sidebar, but was overruled. Trask followed with the security video from Harrah's in Atlantic City, which showed Reid watching Goode as he left the casino with the investigators. He then called Craig Cornell, who had taken the search video of Reid's house. Trask played the disc—exhibit 107—in its entirety, letting the jury see the general order of the place, and the tangible benefits acquired in a well-concealed life of drug trafficking.

A little jealousy won't hurt us here. Juror number four is shaking her head in disbelief at the stuff in his living room. She'd love to have that leather sofa.

Lassiter then called the Miller Gardens manager. Yes, Reid had used the apartment, and Goode had rented it for him. He finished the day with Frank Wilkes. The carpet fibers in the Miller Gardens apartment matched those on the duct tape on Junebug's body. The wrapping from Wilson matched that on the head of Ronald Fellows exactly. It began the same way in each case, showing a change of angle in the wrapping just below the eyes, a process that would have allowed the killer to watch the eyes as the suffocation process took place.

Burns asked to approach the bench, and objected. "Calls for speculation."

Judge King overruled the objection. "A matter for argument, counsel. The prosecution may argue the inference, which they can fairly say is supported by the evidence. You may argue that it is not."

Wilkes was back on direct with Lassiter. He explained all the technology and effort that went into the discovery of the location of the bodies of Goode and Juan Ramirez. The duct tape on their heads was wrapped in the same manner as it had been with Wilson and Fellows.

Lassiter then slowed the examination down to emphasize the discovery of the flesh in Juan Ramirez' teeth. He had Wilkes explain the DNA process. The DNA matched Reid's sample. The last thing the jury saw for the day was Reid—acting on the order of Judge King, given at Lassiter's request—rolling up the sleeve of his shirt to expose the scar on his right wrist.

High theater. We couldn't have scripted it any better. Trask caught himself, and smiled. *Hell, he DID script it this way.*

They broke for the evening, with Lassiter informing the judge that he would have two more witnesses to call before the government rested its case.

He followed Lassiter out the rear of the courthouse and through the judges' parking lot before they headed for the FOP.

"You saw the defense's witness list?" Lassiter asked him.

"Yeah. Rather short. Grant's the only one on it."

"Pure genius. In his opening statement he props the expert up as the only thing the jury needs to hear, and then sticks to his script through the whole case. That takes discipline—and guts."

"Is it the right move?"

"It is if that's all you've got, and that's all he's got." Lassiter finished his second beer. "That and some particularly good cross of our guys, I'd expect. You have 'em ready for that?"

"We went over everything I could think of—any differentials that were inherent in the diagnosis, any cross-indications in the literature…"

"Don't do that."

"Don't do what?"

"Don't talk like a shrink. Especially in court. You'll lose the jury, and you don't have to buy into all that jargon. Speak English. All this psychobabble makes me sick."

They arrived at the FOP, and Lassiter ordered a double crown and water with his sandwich. He looked at the ceiling for a moment, then shook his head.

"Psychology—I'll give the psychiatrists a *little* more credit—psychology has got to be the only profession in the world that's more illusory than law. We both hide behind a bunch of supposedly specialized jargon in an effort to make what we do seem more technical, more mystical. At least *we* use some real Latin on occasion. These clowns just make up 'diseases' and slap some silly bullshit name on 'em, then they bill some idiot with too much cash on hand for another session of therapy. Take their Seasonal Affective Disorder—SAD for short—I'm momentarily depressed because it's winter and I haven't seen the sun for four days. That's a mental disease? A behavioral disorder? Take a damn vitamin C pill, or better yet…"

Lassiter waived the waitress over.

"Trish, I'll have another one, please." His eyes returned to Trask.

"Or better yet, get some vitamin C and combine it with something else that feels good."

He took a long sip, finishing off the first drink.

"See? At any rate, use plain English when you get that windbag on cross tomorrow. Don't let him hide behind the fakery. Use plain terminology with our guys, too. They'll seem more honest and genuine."

The drink arrived, and he took a large gulp.

"I guess some of 'em do some good therapeutic work. I've never questioned that. I just never thought they belonged in the courtroom. Offering expert testimony as if they could tell what somebody was thinking months before at a given moment in time. What a crock."

Lassiter downed the remainder of the drink.

"I'm going home and get some sleep while I can still drive."

"I've got a better idea," Trask said. "Let us drop you off at your place on our way out. Lynn just pulled up outside, anyway. We'll pick you up tomorrow morning."

"Why not?" Lassiter half-stumbled to the door as Trask followed him out.

The man from Windsor was again parked behind the U.S. attorney's office, waiting for the Toyota Camry to leave. He had seen it arrive that morning, and was ready. His weapon of choice was leaning on the passenger seat from the floorboard, covered for the moment by a blanket. He had always liked the NHM-91. A Norinco AK-47 manufactured in China, it had a twenty-inch barrel instead of the usual sixteen-inch AK barrel, which made it more accurate. With the correct modifications—which he had applied—it could be made to fire in a fully automatic mode, and like most AKs, the weapon was a bitch for the ballistics experts to try and match to a spent round. The rifling in the barrel simply didn't leave the groove markings that the western-made weapons did. An ejected cartridge could occasionally be matched to the weapon from the tool markings on the ejector mechanism, but he didn't plan on leaving the weapon around to be found.

The only problem with the gun was that he had to use the Chinese magazines, which were harder to find than the Russian and old East German mags. He had purchased three with the weapon, however, so he was ready.

At 12:15 a.m., there was still no sign of the Camry. He decided that he truly hated this target, and considered wounding the man several times before firing any fatal shot. He headed back to the hotel, cursing Robert Lassiter as if he were a demon from hell.

The next morning, Lassiter called Billy Creighton, who testified that his Honda Accord had been stolen from outside his motel room—he had no idea who had taken it—and that his distressed bowels had caused him to awaken at an ungodly hour and report the theft to his brother the cop.

No cross again. Of course. Why would you cross-examine on that?

The government's last witness was an honest-to-God Mountie.

He could have worn a coat and tie, but that Dudley Do-Right suit does look sharp. Inspector Prefontaine told the jury about the arrest of Reid at the border, and the return of the fleeing murderer to the custody of his American counterparts in Detroit.

No cross again. All his eggs in one basket, and I have to destroy that basket.

"Your Honor, the United States rests its case-in-chief," Lassiter announced.

Chapter Thirty-Four

"We call Doctor James Grant." J. T. Burns took almost ten seconds to rise from his chair, the first time he had stood since his opening statement, except for those occasions when the clerk announced, *All rise.*

Milk it, Counselor. Trask turned toward the courtroom door to see the distinguished doctor make his entrance. He was of average height and average build, yet there was nothing average about his appearance. He carried himself with the air of royalty, moving at a deliberate pace to indicate that he would now preside over the courtroom. His close-cut gray hair framed a tanned face with a salt-and-pepper Van Dyke.

My God! The guy looks just like Freud! I wonder if he has a monocle that he wears around the office.

The clerk administered the oath to Grant, and he moved with the same deliberation to the witness stand, and settled in.

He might as well have just ascended a throne.

"Would you state your name for us please, Doctor?" Burns was being oh-so deferential to his expert witness.

Good job, Burns ol' man. Grant's the star of the show now.

"I am James Remington Grant."

Remington. Was he born with that, or did he add it later?

"And how are you employed, Doctor Grant?"

"I am self-employed. I have my own psychiatric practice in New York City."

"Would you tell us about your education and professional qualifications, please?" Burns stepped back, as if allowing the lead in a play to take charge of the stage.

Here it comes. Trask had seen the defense expert's *curriculum vitae,* and the post-graduate work, internships, residencies, publications, board certifications, and teaching and speaking engagements were going to take a while.

Trask and Lassiter sat politely still and stone-faced during the half-hour recitation, conveying their own message to any observer that they were just not impressed.

"Thank you, Doctor. Your Honor, we offer Doctor Grant as an expert in the field of forensic psychiatry." Burns stopped just short of going too far with the celebration of Grant's majesty, cutting the matter short when he saw that a juror was finally starting to lose interest.

"No objection, Judge." Trask said. His tone bordered on the dismissive. This was not a big deal to the gentlemen representing the United States.

"Accepted." Judge King's tone almost mirrored Trask's.

She's helping us out a little. It's if she just admitted a parking garage receipt into evidence.

"Doctor Grant, at my request, did you recently take the opportunity to evaluate the gentleman at the table, Demetrius Reid?"

"Yes, sir, I did."

"And following your evaluation, what conclusion did you reach?"

"In my opinion, Mr. Reid is suffering from an extremely severe case of paranoid schizophrenia. His mental disease is such that he is clinically and—in my opinion—legally, insane."

"Could you please tell the ladies and gentlemen of the jury about the various test results, interviews, examinations, and observations which led you to form that conclusion?"

As Grant began his prepared remarks, Trask sat forward at his table, pulling toward him a blank pad of lined paper. He reached inside his suit jacket and took the pen from his shirt pocket, clicked it ready, and looked as if he was—at least for a moment—prepared to memorialize some of Grant's learned testimony. After a minute or so, however, his face indicated that he was listening to something no more substantive than a town crier announcing the hour of the day. He clicked the pen closed, and put it back on the pad without taking a note. Two jurors watching him concluded that the young attorney at the government's table had either heard this all before, or had not heard anything about which they should be concerned. The older prosecutor seemed to be similarly unimpressed, as he was politely fighting the urge to take a nap.

"Specifically, Doctor Grant, what did you learn from Demetrius about his background—his childhood and formative years—which may have played a role in the later development of this mental disease?"

Good job again, Mr. Burns. Keep using the disease *word; make the jury think it's something like the measles that just reached out and grabbed poor little Demetrius. Use his first name. Personalize and humanize this monster for the jury.*

"In my clinical interviews with Mr. Reid, he told me about growing up in an impoverished area of Kingston, Jamaica. His father was killed by the police there when he was very young, so he had no male role model in the home. The only way for him to survive was to become a member of the local street gang—I believe he referred to them as a posse—and this gang was in a state of constant conflict with another gang, which brutally murdered both his mother and his younger brother while he was still a young teenager. This was an emotional shock from which he, in my opinion, never recovered, and which set the stage for the later development of his mental disease."

Nice case prep again, thought Trask. *They've not only provided a supposedly relevant biography, a very sympathetic one, but they've probably told the life story of some juror's relative who grew up on the streets of DC.*

"Did you use any psychometric testing in your evaluation of Demetrius Reid?"

You are good, Mr. Burns. The Demetrius *alone was starting to sound too sympathetic. Now we're talking about the case history of a very interesting patient, are we? Right out of a psychiatric journal.*

"Yes. I administered the MMPI-2. That's the Minnesota Multiphasic Personality Inventory; the refined, second version of that test. It's the gold standard in psychometric testing."

Trask looked as Grant pulled a reference book out of his brief case. The book was not that impressive looking, appearing to be barely one hundred pages in length. Trask reached down into the captain's case he'd been lugging all week, and withdrew the two large volumes he'd checked out from the library. He placed them quietly on the table, where the embossed titles would be clearly visible to the jury. He turned slowly until he caught the eye of Mrs. Jeffrey Trask, who was sitting in one of the front pews. She smiled slightly and gave him a knowing nod. She understood now.

"And what role did the results of that test play in your diagnosis of Demetrius Reid's mental disease?"

"The test results, in my opinion, are fully supportive of my diagnosis. There are various scales within the test which are very helpful in measuring both the extent of a patient's paranoia and schizophrenia." Grant went on for another several minutes.

No discussion here of the F-scales. No surprise, there.

Burns prompted his witness through a detailed discussion of the various diagnostic indications generally recognized by the psychiatric community for paranoid schizophrenia, utilizing the *Diagnostic and Statistical Manual of Mental Disorders, Fourth Edition Revised,* or *DSM-IV-R.* He asked the Court to take judicial notice of the book as a learned treatise. This would allow portions of the book to be quoted *verbatim,* to be entered into evidence, if relevant, and to serve as a portion of the basis for the expert witness' opinion. Trask again voiced no objection, and Judge King again accepted the proffer in a completely matter-of-fact manner.

"And keeping those diagnostic criteria for paranoid schizophrenia in mind, Doctor Grant, were you able to use them in your evaluation of Demetrius Reid?"

"Certainly. May I have the slide I prepared shown on the display system?"

Julia Rogers' fingers made a few well-rehearsed clicks on a laptop keyboard, and an excerpt of *DSM-IV-R* appeared on the courtroom's electronic monitors; there was a small one on each counsel table, one at the judge's bench, one at the clerk's desk, and two large monitors were arranged so that the jurors could see one from either end of the jury box.

"As you can see, this is a section of *DSM-IV-R* describing the diagnostic criteria for the paranoid type of schizophrenia—diagnostic classification 295.30. If I may quote the relevant portions:

He's reaching for. . .nope. . .glasses, not a monocle.

"The essential feature of the paranoid type of schizophrenia is the presence of prominent delusions or auditory hallucinations. Delusions are typically persecutory or grandiose, or both. The delusions may be multiple but are usually organized around a coherent theme. Hallucinations are also typically related to the content of the delusional theme. The combination of persecutory and grandiose delusions with anger may predispose the individual to violence."

"Thank you, Doctor. Would you tell us about any delusions or hallucinations that you came across in your examination of Demetrius Reid?"

'Came across?' Better attack that one. Trask took the typed notes he had prepared and scribbled the words in the appropriate spot.

"Yes. His hallucinations and delusions started with a series of nightmares after the murders of his mother and brother. He told me that he would lie in bed, not knowing whether he was awake or asleep. He would hear voices calling him in the darkness. These voices called him a traitor and a coward. They screamed at him, telling him his brother was dying. He said that these voices frightened him terribly, that he felt his heart beating very rapidly, and that he thought he was going to die. He said that as a result of these nightmares, he lost his appetite for several months, although he eventually regained it."

Trask shot a look at Reid, and noted that three jurors were doing the same.

He hasn't missed many meals lately. The guy is huge. He could snap a neck with one arm. He just preferred to take his time when he killed.

"These nightmares eventually took the form of a woman who came to persecute him when he slept. She told him that she would drain the blood from his arteries. As a defense mechanism, he began to develop the grandiose delusion that he could not be harmed because God was with him. God told him to kill his enemies and promised that he would not be harmed. He admitted to me that he had killed several of the opposing gang members in Jamaica. He would get temporary peace from this, but at night, the nightmares and voices would come to him. He said that they still come to him."

"The nightmares have occurred recently?"

"Yes. He told me that whenever he tries to sleep, these evil people come into his room and try to kill him. He said that he knows he has to kill them all, to spare none of them, or the attacks will continue."

"And what, in your opinion, is the relationship between those delusions and the homicides charged in this case?"

"It is my conclusion that because of the delusions, he thought his victims were members of this rival gang, or the corrupt police force that killed his father, and that he could not conform his conduct to legal societal standards at those times. He really believed that he had to kill out of a sense of preservation."

"And what about the manner of the homicides, Doctor Grant?"

"In my opinion, the use of the duct tape was a symbolic attempt to silence the voices that Mr. Reid believed he heard every night when they came to persecute him."

NICE TOUCH, J.T. Tie the murder weapon itself into your theory of the case. Was that your idea, or was it really the Doc's?

"Thank you, Doctor." Burns walked back to his seat before turning to face the Judge. "Nothing further, Your Honor."

"We'll recess for an hour. Lunch break." Judge King announced. "I'll see everyone back here at one."

"That was quite an earful." Lassiter observed. "Three hours of it." They had returned to the office suite retained by the U.S. attorney in the courthouse for use during trials. "Any surprises?"

"None that weren't favorable." Trask pulled out the third book and began moving several Post-it notes that marked the pages of passages he thought might be useful. There were four remaining when he finished and handed the book to Lassiter.

"What the hell is this?"

"That smoking gun you told me to find. Check the marked pages."

Lassiter scanned one of the book-marked pages, then the next, and the next before looking up at Trask.

"Are you kidding me?"

"I couldn't believe it myself."

Lassiter picked up the phone.

"Who are you calling?"

Lassiter waived off the question.

"Bill? Get your ample behind over here by one o'clock for Jeff's cross. No I can't tell you why. If I did, we'd be selling tickets." He hung up. "You're saving that for last, I hope."

"Yep. We actually have a few more rounds to fire before those."

Chapter Thirty-Five

They returned to the courtroom as the marshals were leading Reid back out from the lockup. Doroz watched the big man's eyes while the restraints were being removed, and noticed that he seemed to be surprised—and annoyed—to see that Lassiter was present.

"I don't think he's a member of your fan club, Bob."

"I'm not voting for him, either." Lassiter barely looked up from some notes. "Wait 'til he sees what Jeff's about to do to his shrink."

"All rise."

Judge King settled herself on the bench. "Doctor Grant, will you please return to the stand? Mr. Lassiter, you may cross."

Lassiter rose. "Your honor, Mr. Trask will be conducting the cross-examination."

"Very well. Mr. Trask?"

Doroz noticed the confusion turn to an angry stare on the face of Demetrius Reid.

"Good afternoon, sir. My name is Jeffrey Trask."

"Good afternoon, Mr. Trask."

"Doctor Grant, who first contacted you about examining the defendant?" *No Demetrius' here. He's the murderer. Not an errant schoolboy.*

"Mr. Burns."

"And didn't Mr. Burns tell you at that time that the defendant was facing trial for a series of murders?"

"Yes, he did."

"And he also told you, did he not, that the defendant was potentially facing the death penalty if convicted?"

"That's correct."

"Your first interview, with the defendant, Doctor, was not until nearly five months after the last of the murders, is that correct?"

"I believe that's correct."

"And how much time—in total—have you spent with the defendant?"

"Counting the periods of psychometric testing. I'd say it would be about twelve hours."

"Have you spoken with any friends of the defendant?"

"No."

"Have you spoken with any of the coworkers of the defendant?"

"I have not."

"Did you speak to any of the investigators or other witnesses in the case?"

"I read their reports. Mr. Burns provided those to me."

Oh no, you don't.

"That was not my question, sir. I asked whether you had actually spoken to them."

Our docs will say they did. We made sure that they did.

"No. I concentrated on speaking to Mr. Reid."

"What you are saying then, Doctor, is that your diagnosis is based solely upon your interviews and testing of Mr. Reid?"

"Not entirely, I told you that I read the case file provided to me by Mr. Burns."

"This isn't your first time testifying in court, Doctor. Didn't you say on direct examination that you have testified hundreds of times before?"

"Yes, that's correct."

"That being the case, you are certainly aware, are you not, that police officers writing reports about events or crime scenes are concentrating on those events or crime scenes, and that they have no reason to include observations about a subject's state of mind when his sanity has not yet been called into question?" *Bad question, too long.* Trask thought. *He's going to play with this one.*

"I would certainly think an experienced officer who saw someone behaving erratically would be expected to put that relevant detail in his report."

I knew that was coming. Get back on your skis, dummy. Stack the bones.

"Just the same, sir, you did not bother to ask to speak to them to see whether they did observe such behavior?"

Fair recovery.

"I did not."

Don't ask him why. He'll smack you again. Move on.

"You testified that you *came across* delusions and hallucinations. The manner in which you *came across* those symptoms is that the defendant himself told you about them, correct?"

"He did. They were also indicated in the MMPI."

"Don't you mean in the *defendant's responses* to the MMPI?"

"Yes."

"You *administered,* as you put it, the MMPI-2?"

"That is true."

"And when you say you *administered* this test, what actually occurred is that you gave him a book with a lot of questions in it, and had him sit down and take the test, much like a student in school would take a multiple choice test, isn't that true?"

"The MMPI is a paper test, yes. A very comprehensive one designed to determine the personality of the subject and some of his thought processes."

"But it's a big quiz, isn't it doctor? It's not an MRI or an X-ray, is it?"

"Of course not. I don't understand your point."

He's right. Get to the point.

"You're a psychiatrist, Doctor. You have medical training in addition to psychiatric training, correct?"

"Yes."

"My point, sir, is that an X-ray can give you a completely objective indication—at least in most cases—of whether a patient has a broken arm, correct?"

"That's certainly true."

"And an MRI can give you an objective answer as to whether a patient has certain kinds of knee injuries?"

"Yes."

"And certain blood tests can determine certain kinds of infections?"

"Of course."

"In fact, there are NO tests which can objectively prove the existence of paranoid schizophrenia, are there, Doctor? You can't look at a person's mind with an X-ray or an MRI or a blood test and determine whether they have this condition which you have diagnosed as a *mental disease*, can you?"

"Of course not. Those tests don't look for that condition."

"Would you at least agree with me that it is naturally difficult to make a retrospective diagnosis—to look into the past, if you will—and to tell what exactly was going on in that person's mind at that past moment in time?"

"Yes. I would agree with that."

"Let's look at your testimony regarding the MMPI-2, the test that you *did* give the defendant. You have testified that the results for the scales measuring paranoia and schizophrenia were elevated."

"They were."

"And what is the book that you have on the stand there which you referred to during your testimony?"

"It's an interpretive manual for the MMPI-2."

"It is actually what is commonly referred to as an MMPI 'cookbook,' isn't it Doctor Grant?"

"I don't call it that."

He's bristling a little now, a bit off balance. Good.

"But others in your profession do, don't they?"

"Yes, it has been called a cookbook."

He realized he was losing his composure. He's trying to regain it.

"With your many years in the field, Doctor, you're certainly aware of some of the more comprehensive treatises on the MMPI, like this manual by the inventors of the original test?"

Trask held up the first of the two enormous volumes on his table.

"Yes, of course I'm familiar with that manual."

"And a similar manual on the MMPI-2?" Trask held up the other tome.

"Of course."

"So you are certainly aware of the discussions in these manuals regarding the F and FB scales?"

Grant hesitated for just a second. "Of course."

"What are the F scale and FB scales used for, Doctor?"

"They are designed to try and determine whether a subject may be trying to manipulate the MMPI."

"The letters *FB* stand for *faking bad*?"

"Yes."

"And when you say *manipulate,* one of the motives a test subject might have in attempting to manipulate the results could be the escaping of conviction for a capital murder charge?"

"Yes."

"And it is also the case, isn't it Doctor Grant, that the F and FB scales in both your MMPI-2 and the one taken by Mr. Reid during his evaluation in the Bureau of Prisons were very high?"

"They were elevated, but one should expect some elevation of those scales when the subject is a paranoid schizophrenic."

Don't give him another opening. You've made your points. Reid may be faking it, and your books are bigger. Move on.

"Let's get back to your *DSM-IV* for a moment. How does a so-called mental disease find its way into that book, Doctor Grant?"

Grant was off-balance again, but only for a moment.

"Well, this is a compendium of a hundred years of diagnostic psychiatry. The best minds in the field share their thoughts on the various diseases and diagnostic criteria, and—"

"And they get together and vote every once in a while on whether the disease exists and what criteria to assign to it?"

"That's a very simplistic way of putting it, but I suppose it is correct in the sense that there are committees which work for years on each edition of the manual."

"And do they change their minds from time to time on whether or not a mental disease even exists?"

Let's see if he walks into it.

"I don't think that happens very often."

"Isn't it true that homosexuality, for example, has been considered a mental disorder in the past, but now it's not?"

"That is true." Grant gave an audible sigh.

Exhaling, trying to collect himself again. Push a little more.

"Not very consistent, is it, Doctor? Nobody ever voted a broken arm out of existence, did they?"

Burns was on his feet, objecting to the questions as being argumentative.

"Sustained," said Judge King.

"I'd actually like to answer that," said Grant.

Burns was sitting down, looking very concerned.

"I'll rephrase it then," Trask said. "The criteria in this manual are not necessarily very consistent, are they?"

Go with me, Doc. Just a little further.

"I think that, compared with many other mental diseases, the recognized criteria for paranoid schizophrenia have been generally consistent for a number of years. Certainly since *DSM-III*..."

Yes!

"Since *DSM* what, Doctor?"

"Since the third version of the manual, except for the recent narrowing of the scope of the term *psychosis* as it is used in schizophrenia, the criteria have been generally consistent."

"Let's look at *DSM-IV* one more time, Doctor Grant. You previously showed us a slide for the paranoid type of schizophrenia, correct?"

"Yes."

"Here's the previous page, dealing with the diagnostic criteria for schizophrenia."

Trask displayed a slide of his own.

"Do you recognize that page, Doctor?"

"Yes."

"And what is the fourth listed characteristic symptom of schizophrenia?"

"Grossly disorganized or catatonic behavior."

"You haven't seen any catatonic behavior in the defendant, have you? He's not lying around in a stupor?"

"No."

"Would it surprise you, Doctor, to know that the defendant was efficiently running an ongoing business involved in customer service, and that his home was kept in an immaculate condition?"

"No, because in the paranoid type of schizophrenia, that symptom—catatonic behavior—is not prominent."

He got you again; get back in control.

"What does the term *premorbid personality* mean?"

"That is the personality we would typically expect to see prior to the development of the mental disease."

"And what, Doctor, is the typical premorbid personality for a paranoid schizophrenic?"

"Someone in the premorbid stages of the disease could be expected to be suspicious, introverted, withdrawn."

"You would agree that the outgoing manager of a booming restaurant would not fit that profile?"

"The exception is often the rule in schizophrenia."

Good. The jury didn't like that answer. He's quibbling now.

Trask pulled the next to last volume out of his case.

"What is this book, Doctor Grant?"

"That's *DSM-III*."

"And *DSM-III* provides, does it not, that the diagnosis of paranoid schizophrenia should not be made without six months of inpatient observation, correct."

"It did. *DSM-IV* doesn't have that language."

"Let's look at *DSM IV*, then."

Trask handed a copy of *DSM-IV* to Grant.

"Would you please read criterion C on page 312 under the diagnostic criteria for schizophrenia?"

"Certainly. 'Duration: Continuous signs of the disturbance persist for at least six months.' It doesn't say that this must be observed in an inpatient setting."

"Nevertheless, your total time with the defendant was twelve hours?"

"Yes, during which he related to me a history which included the last six months."

"And you took his word for that?"

"I did."

"Back to *DSM-III* for a moment. Would you turn to page 340, please?"

Grant fumbled with the book for a moment, then looked up.

"What is the page you are looking at, Doctor?"

"This is an appendix used to make a differential diagnosis; it contains charts regarding various psychotic diseases and disorders."

"It's a diagram, isn't it?" Trask asked, hitting a button on his own computer to display the chart on the screen. "Kind of a troubleshooting chart for brains, like one of those diagrams you might get in the back of a stereo manual?"

"That is again a simplistic characterization."

"Let's go through the diagram anyway. You noted delusions and hallucinations in your interviews of the defendant?"

"I did."

"That would take you to the next factor, which is whether or not there was any kind of an organic problem. There was not, was there?"

"No."

"And since there was not, the next question is whether the symptoms were under voluntary control?"

"That's correct."

"And if, Doctor, we can *hypothetically* assume that the defendant had control over his symptoms, the next inquiry is whether or not there is a recognizable goal in displaying those symptoms?"

"Correct," said Grant, looking at the diagram.

"Would you consider the fact that the defendant is facing trial for multiple murders and severe punishment—possibly even execution—to be such a goal?"

"I would."

"And what is the diagnosis that the chart suggests for such a case?"

"Malingering," answered Grant. "That means faking it. But that's not appropriate here. Your hypothetical asked me to assume that Mr. Reid had control over his symptoms. I do not believe that to be the case."

He wants me to ask him why. That's not where we're going.

"Let me ask you another hypothetical then, Doctor. What facts would you have to see in order to believe that the defendant's symptoms *were* faked?"

The question caught Grant flat-footed. It was the ultimate issue in the case, stated in the opposite. Instead of, "Why do you think the defendant is insane," he had been asked what it would take to convince him that Reid was *sane*. He had to answer it fairly, to preserve any appearance of professionalism and objectivity.

"I would have to know," Grant said slowly, "that the symptoms he related to me were not real. That they had not occurred as he described them."

"Fair enough, Doctor."

Trask went to the case and pulled out the last volume. The book was much smaller than the others, and had brown paper taped over the cover.

"May we approach, Your Honor?" Trask asked.

"Yes."

Trask and Burns went to the bench, where Trask showed the cover discreetly to the judge and to Burns. He then held up a still photograph so that each—but not Grant—could see it.

"This is a still shot from exhibit 107, which has already been admitted into evidence, Judge. I intend to use this volume in the cross of Doctor Grant; specifically the four pages which are marked with the Post-it notes."

The Judge skimmed the pages, and nodded. "I'll permit it."

Burns objected weakly.

"I'm sorry, Mr. Burns," she said, almost gently. "Overruled."

"Are you familiar with Frantz Fanon, Doctor Grant?" Trask asked.

"I can't say that I am."

"I'd like to show you a book he wrote, *Wretched of the Earth*. It appears to be the work of a psychiatrist working with the Algerian revolutionaries in their fight for independence against the French following World War II. The second part of the book contains several case studies."

"Okay."

"Let's first display page 202 on the monitors. Would you read the highlighted language please?"

The doctor obliged: "'It was during the night he suffered the attack. For three hours he heard all kinds of insults, voices crying in his head and in the darkness: 'Traitor…coward…all your brothers are dying…'"

"Thank you. Page 197—the highlighted language please?"

"'He has lost his appetite and his sleep is disturbed by nightmares.'"

"Page 192, please."

"'Several times in the course of our conversations the patient mentioned a woman who would come and persecute him when night fell... The patient talked of his blood being spilled, his arteries drained, and an abnormal heartbeat.'"

"And finally, Doctor, the symptoms of homicidal impulses in a patient recorded on page 191."

"As soon as I try to get some sleep, they come into my room. But now I know what they're up to. Everyone wants to kill me. But I'll fight back. I'll kill them all. Every one of them."

The courtroom was buzzing now. Judge King cracked her gavel down hard and asked for order.

"Doctor Grant, what effect does that information have on your diagnosis?"

"Actually, none, Mr. Trask. The fact that almost perfect symptoms of the disease have previously been diagnosed in other patients merely verifies what I was saying—there are consistent themes in the diagnosis of this disease over the years, and you've shown me nothing to indicate that Mr. Reid ever saw that book before."

Trask nodded. He walked to the display system.

"Your Honor, I am replaying a portion of an exhibit previously admitted into evidence. Exhibit number 107. This is the video of the search of the defendant's residence in Hyattsville, Maryland. I am freezing the frame as the camera shows the defendant's bookcase in the rear of the living room. I am now zooming in on the lower shelf of the bookcase."

Trask left the podium and walked over to the witness stand. He looked at Grant with a challenging stare.

"Doctor, would you please read for the jury the title and author of the book in the center of the screen?"

"*Wretched of the Earth*. Frantz Fanon."

"I ask you again, Doctor. What effect does *this* have on your diagnosis?"

Grant swallowed, and looked apologetically toward Burns.

"It would change it completely."

The commotion to his rear caused Trask to whirl around, just in time to see the large mahogany defense table tossed into the air as if it were a foldaway card table. It blocked the marshals in the rear of the room from the man in their custody, who was now running full speed at the assistant U.S. attorney who had just destroyed the defense's theory of the case.

Trask would have turned and run, but he found himself trapped between the oncoming Reid and the judge's bench, a mahogany wall about five feet high. There was no time to climb over it. He saw Reid's right shoulder twitch and the huge fist draw back as Reid closed on him. He ducked instinctively, and shot his right foot out toward Reid's left knee. Reid flew over him, trying to take the weight off his shattered kneecap as he barreled headlong toward Trask and the bench. The punch he had aimed downward at Trask's ducking head also missed, and with his arms down, Reid had nothing to use to shield his head from the impact with the edge of the bench, which caught him under the bridge of the nose. The force generated by the big man's speed against the unyielding mahogany drove the cartilage in Reid's nose back and into his brain.

Burns had climbed up off the floor and was demanding a mistrial. Trask was trying to climb out from under the huge form of Demetrius Reid, which had lapsed into involuntary spasms. Three of the jurors were screaming.

Doroz arrived and helped pull Trask free. The FBI agent checked Reid for a pulse before looking up at the judge, who was standing in the elevated bench, looking down at the floor beneath her. Doroz shook his head from side to side.

"I'm afraid that it will not be necessary for me to rule on your motion, Mr. Burns. The jury is excused. Marshals, please clear the courtroom."

Chapter Thirty-Six

They had gathered back in the retained space. Lynn was there, asking him if he was all right.

"I think so," Trask said. "I may have cracked my left wrist when he came down on top of me."

Dixon Carter walked in and slapped him on the shoulder before nodding and walking out without saying a word.

Lassiter and Patrick were standing across the office, speaking with Eastman. The U.S. Attorney came over to him and shook his hand.

"I was there for your cross, Jeff. Brilliant. Outstanding work. I'm sorry the defendant deprived us of the conviction, which was a lock after you got through with Doctor Grant."

"I would have certainly preferred that," Trask said, rubbing his wrist.

"One of these days, you'll have to resolve these things in a more conventional fashion," Eastman said. "Otherwise we'll have to mark you down on that case resolution block on your report card." He was smiling as he said it. "You did the office proud today. Reid took himself out. Not your fault."

Eastman stepped back over to where Patrick and Lassiter were standing.

"Bob, you and I need to go out front for a minute or two. The hounds of the press require a feeding." He turned back to Trask. "I'd ask you to come, too, but it might make more sense for you to go have that wrist examined."

"Yes, sir. Thanks. I'll pass this time."

"I'll go get the car," Lynn said. "I just have to check my gun back out from the lobby downstairs. The marshals made me lock it up before I went up to the courtroom this morning."

"Yeah," said Trask. "Everybody has to do that. It prevents unnecessary violence in our courtrooms." He called her back as she started for the door. "I'll sneak around and meet you at the bottom of the park on the west side. Better yet, I'll walk you out that way and hide in the park while Ross talks to the media."

The man from Windsor gave up on the morning commute options at 9:30 a.m. As far as he could tell, the Camry had neither left the U.S. attorney's office parking garage the night before, nor had it arrived that morning. He wondered if his target just lived in the place. He knew the trial was well underway from the news reports in the papers and on the radio, so he decided to return to his hotel. The target would be in the courtroom until at least 5:00 p.m.

He had already been paid by the head of the Posse. He'd confirmed the deposit in his account with the bank on Grand Cayman. To fail to execute the contract would be to put one on his own head.

The difficulty now lay in the nature of the second option. The first would have been much simpler, if only the damned target had ever shown up. The cars entering the underground garage from the Third Street entrance had to slow dramatically for the security gate to be lifted, and a shot from up the block would have been unobstructed. His exit after the kill would also have been much simpler. There was no abundance of witnesses, no constant law enforcement presence to worry about. It would have been just a shoot-and-scoot, the target leaning against his steering wheel with a couple of rounds through his head.

He had already scouted the second option, which was much more technical. The rear of the courthouse did not offer level ground or clear lines of sight from Third Street, and there was nowhere to park. There were security officers who frequently checked on the cars parked in the rear at intervals that were anything but regular. There were also prison vans that came into the rear area to pick up and discharge prisoners. These could serve as a block, screening his target from his line of sight.

There were more viable options regarding the front entrance to the courthouse. He had seen the row of media vans parked in front of the building, outside the concrete cones put in place for protection of the building following the events of September 11, 2001. If his target was to be on those elevated steps at a time certain, he could actually use the vans as cover by firing between them. He had already mapped the route. West on Constitution, a right turn on the drive that ran in front of the courthouse, a quick shot—to the torso instead of the head because of the distance. The high velocity round would explode the fluids in the chest cavity. Then it would be west on the courthouse drive until it dropped south onto Pennsylvania. Northwest on Pennsylvania, north on Seventh, and he'd be back in the bowels of the city traffic, out of the first car and into the second in no time. He would not head for 395—it was the obvious escape route and they would expect him to go there.

It was just a matter of slowly driving along the row of media trucks and locating the point at which the gap between the trucks would provide the right angle for the shot. The problem was that he had no idea if or when the target would actually be at this location. He put the street map out on his desk for the hundredth time, wondering where, how and when the target would return to his office from the courthouse at the end of the trial day.

A news bulletin on the television interrupted his thoughts. The television reporter was standing in front of the courthouse.

"A dramatic conclusion in the trial of alleged serial killer Demetrius Reid, who died today after charging a prosecutor in a courtroom scuffle. We expect a news conference to be held here by the United States Attorney and his trial team in about twenty minutes. We'll cover that live. Back to you, Jim."

He was out of the hotel room before the station returned its viewers to their regularly scheduled program.

Eastman stood at the lectern that had been set up on the front steps of the United States Courthouse, facing the row of satellite vans lined up along Pennsylvania Avenue. Lassiter stood beside him.

"I'm okay if you want to wait for a second." Trask squeezed her left hand with his right. "This one still works, and I've got my shades on."

She smiled and kissed him on the cheek. The reporters all had their attention focused on the speakers on the courthouse steps, so she pulled him closer to the curb where they had a better view.

"We are of course saddened by the way this case concluded," Eastman said. "In a way, society and our city were deprived of our day in court by the attack and accidental death of the defendant Demetrius Reid. Nevertheless, I am confident in the accuracy of my conclusion when I say that Reid's conviction on all charges would have certainly resulted from this prosecution, had the matter gone to the jury. I am very proud of the professional and expert manner in which this trial was conducted by our trial team, Bob Lassiter and Jeff Trask. Mr. Trask required some medical attention, and cannot be here. Bob Lassiter, the lead counsel, is here if anyone has any questions. Bob?"

Lassiter was stepping toward the lectern when the shot rang out. He felt a sharp pain in his chest, but it was gone almost immediately. The faces above him faded, and *she* was there instead, holding him again. She kissed him, and said that all was forgiven now. Those standing over him saw him smile and take a long last breath.

The man from Windsor pulled the rifle back from the car window, where he had rested the weapon as he aimed it between the vans. He gunned the car forward, and then saw the two figures which had stepped out into the lane about twenty yards in front of him. They both fired at the same time, and the rounds from the 9 mm Glock and the .45 caliber Smith and Wesson crashed through the windshield, arriving at his forehead only microseconds apart. The car drifted slowly and harmlessly to the right, coming to rest against another of the satellite vans.

"Let's go check on Bob," Lynn Trask said as she and Officer Timothy Wisniewski lowered their weapons.

Epilogue

They stood in the darkness as the pipes played. Trask held Lynn's hand, and looked about the crowd. Dixon Carter was there, of course, as was Willie Sivella. Barry Doroz and Mike Crawford stood next to them. Craig Cornell was off to one side, standing next to Frank Wilkes. Tim Wisniewski was in his dress uniform on the other side of Lynn.

"A good turnout," she observed. "There are probably a thousand people here."

The National Law Enforcement Officers memorial glowed as the crowd—mostly wearing police uniforms—illuminated the scene in candlelight.

"We are proud to dedicate this ceremony to the memories of all those who fell in the line of duty this past year," said the speaker, "and to honor tonight two of this city's finest who paid the ultimate sacrifice on our behalf. Detective Juan Ramirez of the Metropolitan Police Department, and—for the first time by special vote of the board of directors—tonight we add and honor the name of the first prosecuting attorney to our memorial, Robert Lassiter of the Office of the United States Attorney for the District of Columbia."

Acknowledgments

I am deeply indebted to the editors, official and otherwise, whose painfully constructive criticism shaped and polished the manuscript. These include my sister Jamie, Ann LaFarge, and the fine folks of CreateSpace's Team I. My thanks also go to my review team, Michael Wims, Alain Balmanno, David Simon, Carol Dean Yeatman, Carolyn Cross, Tania Santander and Mary Jo Hardy, who provided chapter by chapter feedback both for the final manuscript and as the book evolved.

The book would never have been completed without the assistance, support and encouragement of my loving wife, Lea.

CPSIA information can be obtained at www.ICGtesting.com
Printed in the USA
LVOW04s0803200315

431250LV00024BA/767/P